SIX IDIOTS WITNESS A MURDER

Rob Hickman

Disclaimer

This is a work of fiction.

While all of the locations are real, the characters and incidents are fictional and any similarity to real people or situations is purely coincidental.

Although the part about the car purchase is based on a real event. As are quite a few other things, including Colin's car purchase and the rather unfortunate incident with the IT director, his laptop and the cleaner.

PART ONE

Chapter 1

Brighton, UK

Oh crap. Morning already.

Tom jolted up in bed at the sound of the alarm on his phone and rubbed his eyes. What time was it? More to the point, what day was it? Last night had been a late one where the beer had been flowing more freely than it should have done, although it probably didn't matter too much because it was Sunday morning. Wasn't it?

Tom was about to turn back over in bed but suddenly realised last night was Sunday which meant today was more than likely to be Monday. He looked at his phone and saw that it was just before 8 am, the time he would normally be getting into his car and beginning his regular 30-minute commute to work – or the Silo of Sadness as he and most of the other employees called it.

Suddenly Tom was in a panic and shot out of bed to begin his morning routine. Luckily, he had an ensuite bathroom and was able to stumble the eight steps from his bed to the shower in just a few seconds, although it still felt like it should be Sunday. Why wasn't it Sunday? After being on annual leave for ten days that included the Easter bank holidays, Tom had got his days mixed up and was now in a mild and slightly hungover panic as he stumbled into the bathroom. He showered, shaved and got dressed before grabbing his phone, running downstairs, picking up his laptop, wallet and keys from the table by the front door and heading out to his car.

The drive into Brighton took about 20 minutes and then he had a ten-minute walk from the parking space in the city centre that he rented from a rich person with a big driveway and no car of their own. It was a sensible and cost-effective arrangement and meant he didn't have to use public transport. Tom liked people – but not first thing in the morning before he'd had his first coffee.

It was 9:13 am when he arrived at work and tried to sit at his desk without too many people noticing. As with most things Tom tried, it didn't go well and his manager was waiting for him.

"Good morning, Tom," said Katrina, an accomplished young woman in her early 30s, just a couple of years older than him.

"Morning, boss," replied Tom with as much nonchalance as he could muster, which was not very much. "How's everything going?"

"We've had a good morning so far. Which you might have been able to participate in had you been here on time."

"Yeah, sorry about that, Katrina," said Tom.

"Don't worry – but try to make the time up," said Katrina.

"I will," Tom promised, settling into his seat.

His immediate focus was on remembering his password, logging into the main system and reading the 287 emails that had no doubt arrived during his time off – most of which he'd assume were about things that had subsequently been resolved so he could probably delete them. At some point, one of them was bound to come back and bite him but he could always ask the sender to resend it. That's what everyone else did.

As the Project Manager on the company's largest current IT project, Tom seemed to receive certain privileges that the other, lowlier (in his opinion) employees did not enjoy. Either that or his line manager found him incredibly charming, realised he was a misunderstood genius and gave him special treatment to ensure he stayed loyal to the company and wouldn't take his considerable talents to one of their competitors. That was probably the more likely explanation he thought as his screen flickered into life.

"How was your week off?" asked Sue, one of his colleagues on the team who also had the misfortune to sit directly opposite him.

"Not bad, thanks. A few too many late nights though," Tom replied, noticing that Sue's halitosis still hadn't cleared up.

He'd noticed it on the day he'd joined the company just over four years ago and, if anything, it had got worse since then. Either that or someone was gradually moving their desks closer together each night after work as a prank so he could smell her breath more easily. It was probably his friend Martin. That was just the type of thing he'd think of doing – if he was bright enough.

Tom went to make a coffee – the first of many if every other day was an indicator. Like so many people in offices around the world, Tom relied on coffee to help him get through the day. It disagreed with his digestive system, but he still needed at least eight cups to retain his focus while sitting at a desk all day. Sometimes he'd be offered an extra cup by the HR department if the manager called him up to respond to an accusation of inappropriate behaviour in the workplace. This happened quite often and, as he got back to his desk and looked at his online calendar, he saw an invite from HR for this morning. That was good news as the coffee was so much better up there than it was down in the IT department where he worked.

Most of his colleagues would be mortified to be summoned to HR more than once or twice in their entire careers but Tom saw it differently. Not only did he have his own seat in the HR waiting area (other employees would vacate the chair by the plant when they saw him arrive) but he liked the people who worked there. They didn't feel the same way about him, of course, but he didn't know that and just assumed they were being coy and mysterious.

"Hey, mate! How are things?" Martin appeared in the kitchen area with an unfeasibly broad smile.

Martin and Tom were childhood friends as well as work colleagues and Tom knew Martin well enough by now to realise that his smile meant he had some ridiculously trivial triumph from the weekend to gloat about. Martin and his wife Irma had so far produced two children – both boys – and Martin was forever sharing random and completely pointless things that one of these two little human nightmares had said or done.

"Hi, Martin," said Tom with more enthusiasm than he thought he'd be able to generate given his hangover and the fact that he didn't really care what happened in his friend's home life. "How are Irma and the boys?"

"Well mate, it's funny you should ask. Since Max turned five, he's become a lot more boisterous and on Saturday he tried to set Ben on fire."

"Wow!" said Tom with genuine enthusiasm for once. Finally, something genuinely interesting was happening rather than something that only Martin found interesting.

In a bid to retain his sanity and avoid the never-ending stream of pictures of the boys eating, running around the house and shitting – often all at the same time – Tom had turned down repeated friend requests on Facebook from Martin and Irma.

When Ben had been born just over three years ago, they'd even set up a 'cute' joint account called "BenMax" to showcase the more mundane aspects of the boys' lives. Although 'cute' wasn't the exact word Tom thought of when Martin told him about it for the first time; 'nause-ating' was his choice, but Martin was unmoved and still thought it was cute.

"How did he set him on fire?" Tom asked.

"Well, we had the family round and Irma's sister left a lighter on the table. Max just picked it up and started playing with it. The next thing we knew, Ben's trousers were smoking," replied Martin.

"Shit!" said Tom.

"Exactly. We stopped it before it did any major damage but his trousers were ruined so we had to throw them out. Although we then had to throw out Max's trousers as well," Martin explained.

"Why?"

"Irma likes to dress the boys in the same clothes every day so we can spot them both when we're out if they try to run off. Unfortunately, if one of them ruins a t-shirt or some trousers we need to get rid of the other boy's t-shirt or trousers as well. Ben's blue trousers were ruined so Irma threw out Max's blue trousers too," Martin clarified. "I wish my kids would stop setting each other on fire. It's costing us a fortune in new clothes."

"That's a bit odd. So, if one of them broke a leg – just as an example – would you have to deliberately injure the other one's leg so they both had matching plaster casts?" Tom asked, quite reasonably he thought.

"Of course not! We're not monsters!" Martin said in-dignantly, staring at Tom for a few seconds and then storming out of the kitchen and going back to his desk.

"At least you'd be able to spot them when you were out," Tom called out as Martin left. "Although they probably wouldn't be running anywhere if you'd given them both matching broken legs."

After pouring his coffee, Tom went back to his desk and decided to keep quiet for a while until Martin had calmed down. They had been best friends for many years since Tom's parents had moved into the street where Martin was already living. Tom had been 8 and Martin 6 when they first met and they grew up together as part of a larger group of children of different ages.

After initially going their separate ways career-wise, the two had eventually found themselves working together in the IT department of a large British clothing retailer almost a year ago when Martin joined and they were gradually coming to terms with a new dynamic in their relationship. This was especially worrying for Martin as he had an unfortunate nickname he didn't want anyone at his new job to know about. Tom knew about it — mainly because he'd given it to him when they were teenagers — and Martin had been stuck with it ever since. Even his parents sometimes used it and Martin was dreading the day it came out in a work environment, which it surely would.

Martin had recently had his 30th birthday but still couldn't shake his nickname and, while he appreciated this new job that Tom had helped him get, he still felt a sense of anxiety every time the office conversation turned towards certain subjects.

"You're happy to be back at work after a week off," Martin said sarcastically once he'd recovered his composure.

"Not really," replied Tom. "To be honest, I'm not really feeling it today after a few late nights."

"You'll be fine once you've had a few more coffees," said Martin, turning back to his screen and getting his headphones out of his incredibly messy desk drawer.

Tom watched him put his headphones in to drown out the background office noise and thought about tidying up Martin's drawer just to mess with his system of organised chaos. It was taking his friend a long time to put his headphones in and select a playlist...surely, he must be done by now.

"Dopey bastard," Tom whispered to himself.

"Hey! I haven't selected my playlist yet. At least wait until I can't hear you before you insult me."

Tom apologised and Martin gave him a cheesy thumbs-up signal that had come directly from the 1980s before selecting what he proudly called his 'Sexy Women of Country' playlist. Given that some of these artists were long dead and most of the others were well into their 70s, everyone on the team was worried about Martin's taste in women – especially those who'd met his wife Irma.

Tom turned back to his laptop wondering how long it took for somebody to select a playlist. It seemed to take Martin forever to sort his songs into the perfect order for the day ahead, only to be called away for a meeting two minutes later. Tom thought about suggesting the 'shuffle' option but he was worried Martin would then give him another creepy thumbs-up gesture; if he did that, Tom would have strangled him right there and then with his headphone wire.

Also, who still used wires? Weren't those wireless ear-buds that looked suspiciously like miniature tampons the way forward? Martin had never been at the forefront of technology – or anything else for that matter – and Tom suspected he still had a VCR at home. Maybe he'd send him a fax later and ask him.

Luckily for Martin, he turned back to his computer and got on with whatever it was he was paid a lot of money to do (and not very well, in Tom's opinion) and narrowly avoided a Monday morning strangling. Tom was never happy to be back at work after a week off, so the team tried to keep out of his way for the first couple of hours.

As Tom grumbled his way through the first part of his day, he began to think that mornings were stupid. Also, nobody liked Mondays – apart from old people – although most of them never seemed to know what day it was judging by the number of pensioners in the super-markets every Saturday and Sunday.

He'd never understood why people who'd had all week to themselves with very little to do other than drink tea, talk about the war and forget the names of their grandchildren waited until the weekend to do their food shopping. That was the only time that people who worked all week could go so Tom had decided that one day he'd get revenge by taking a Monday off work, visiting his local post office and standing in the queue in front of them all morning. Old people spent a lot of time in the post office so that would be a great place to get back at them for clogging the shops up on the only days when he and his generation were able to go out.

That would teach them – especially if he took Martin's unruly kids with him and got them to run around getting in everyone's way and setting their trousers on fire.

Chapter 2

Brighton, UK

The HR department was the heart of the company where Tom and Martin worked and the only department that spanned both the UK operation in Brighton and the fledgling US operation in Atlanta, Georgia. The company sold traditional British outdoor clothing to high-end department stores and also on its own website. The garments were typically the kind that somebody might wear while enjoying a long weekend in the country, fishing, hiking or whatever other outdoor pursuits interested the type of people who had a lot of money, very little fashion sense and enjoyed being out in the rain all day.

Most of the clothing options were dark green or khaki and, being a British company that catered primarily for British outdoor pursuits, everything had to be made of waterproof materials. Anybody visiting Britain – or locals holidaying in their own country because they were too cheap to go abroad – had to be mindful of the weather at all times of the year and this was something that Classic Country Clothing Ltd. had always been keen to capitalise on. The more rain there was, the more waterproof jackets, hats, gloves and boots they sold. For people who took their dogs out in the rain, they even sold an extensive range of obscenely-priced waterproof dog jackets.

The company had been founded in 1949 and was originally headquartered on a farm in the Sussex Downs, a beautifully scenic part of Southern England. Unfortunately, the business had been forced to move to new premises in 1988 after a disastrous incident with a flock of sheep, an office door that had been left open and a pile of sales orders for the upcoming season.

Having lost most of their sales orders for 1988, along with Margaret, a timid, softly spoken sales manager who nobody remembered employing but had been there since day one, the company decided to move to a more urban setting where they were less likely to be bothered by sheep devouring their paperwork.

Margaret had not personally been attacked by the sheep but did not make the move with the rest of the company due to an aversion to commuting to work. She had always walked to work and didn't see why she should ever have to change, so she gave this as the reason for her sudden retirement at the age of what seemed to most people to be at least 90 but, in reality, was only 63.

The move to new offices in Brighton on the Sussex coast, the introduction of primitive computers and a large talent pool of eager employees allowed the company to grow exponentially over the next few years and it now employed more than 200 staff in the UK. It also owned two manufacturing companies in Vietnam where, in a bid to stimulate the local economy, it had offered low-skilled jobs to some of the youngest members of Vietnamese society. This also helped to keep their costs lower than their more ethical competitors.

As the business expanded, they set up a Marketing department in 1990 whose first task was to design a new company logo. They had produced a line art drawing of a hooded outdoor jacket beneath the three capital 'C's taken from the company name. Unfortunately, the jacket looked like something a medieval executioner would wear and the arrangement of the three letters made them look like a badly made set of handcuffs designed for people with a particular sexual fetish – and an extra arm.

Just over a year ago, one of the new junior managers in the Marketing department had suggested the business adopt a 'new and hip brand identity' by changing its name to 'Klassic Kountry Klothing', which would both 'disrupt the market' and at the same time be more 'funky and edgy' for today's 'switched on, internet-savvy, cash rich but time poor consumers.'

Initially, this was not well-received by the directors as the company took great pride in being a traditional purveyor of clothing for the more discerning high-end customer but the Marketing department pushed ahead regardless, with commendable enthusiasm but very little support from around the business.

A new logo was designed and subsequently revealed at a board meeting to what the marketing people hoped would be a triumphant reception. The department had since re-invented itself as 'Global Corporate Branding' but was still staffed by four hyperactive university graduates and overseen by two junior managers who looked like they had to be up early for school the next day.

Unfortunately, the response to their creation was far less enthusiastic than the pony-tailed hipsters in Global Corporate Branding had hoped for. All but one of the board members present were horrified by what they saw, with only the Global Production & Logistics Director – known to everyone in the company as Racist Roy – expressing any positive views. At this point, the Marketing department accepted defeat when it was pointed out to them that a logo of 'KKK' and a hooded coat was less than ideal – especially given the company's plans to establish a new location in Atlanta, the birthplace of the American civil rights movement.

The heavily pregnant HR Director was the first to express her concern by swooning face down at the table in the Company's boardroom, her head narrowly missing her responsibly sourced coffee that she carried around in her environmentally friendly coffee mug.

She had subsequently taken a leave of absence to recover from the trauma and started her maternity leave without coming back to work. Having successfully negotiated her pregnancy and delivered a healthy baby boy, she had only just returned to work the previous Tuesday to pick up where she'd left off and was already regretting it.

Today was the beginning of only her second week back at work but she had just received an extremely worrying email from the US operation in Atlanta and, as she scanned her calendar for the day ahead, she noticed a familiar name on her list of appointments. She suddenly felt like she'd never been away and called out to her assistant, Debbie, in the open-plan area just outside her office.

"Hi, Louisa, is there anything wrong?" Debbie asked as she popped her head around the door.

"I'm looking at my list of appointments for today and I see Tom from the IT department is on it again."

"Yes," said Debbie. "You told me before you went off that you wanted any future transgressions of his to be dealt with at director level."

"I know," said Louisa. "Why are we still employing him?"

"Well, he's by far the best Project Manager we've got," Debbie replied.

"Maybe," said Louisa, shaking her head. "But before I went off on maternity leave, he seemed to spend more time up here than he did in his own department. Are these things still happening?"

"On and off, yes. We still have a few inappropriate comments and he does make some of the staff feel uncomfortable," Debbie confirmed.

"The female staff have a right to be protected in the workplace," said Louisa. "This is the 21st century, not the dark days of the 1970s."

19

"Some of his male colleagues find him a bit much too," offered Debbie. "He's just incessantly cheerful and makes a lot of jokes. They don't tend to like that in IT as most of them are still recovering from their personality bypass operations."

"So, what's he done this time?" Louisa asked with a weary sigh.

"He made a few comments on our last charity dress-down day just before Easter. We had to wait for him to come back from a week's leave before calling him in."

"Well, whatever he said, I'm pretty sure it would have been unacceptable so I think we'll have to deal with him once and for all this time."

"Ahh…before you do that, it may have been partly our fault," Debbie said gingerly.

"Our fault? How could it have possibly been our fault?!"

"A couple of weeks before you returned to work, the 'Rocky Horror Picture Show' was in town at the Theatre Royal. Most of the staff had tickets for it on the Friday night so we thought it would be an ideal costume theme for charity because they could then go straight from work. It was meant to be easier and more environmentally responsible than everybody leaving early, going home to change and then coming back again," Debbie elaborated.

"The 'Rocky Horror Picture Show'? Is that the one where the audience all dress up in a burlesque style?"

"Yes," said Debbie.

"So…let me get this right," said Louisa. "We actively encouraged our female staff to come to work in basques, corsets and fishnet stockings for charity?"

"Yes," Debbie admitted, looking down at the floor.

The rest of the department had realised the mistake within a few minutes of the first few staff members arriving so Debbie had fully expected Louisa to notice it when they told her.

"I bet the men had a great time ogling the women in basques and suspenders all day!"

"Yes, they did," Debbie said sheepishly, growing more uncomfortable by the second.

Louisa rolled her eyes and then stared up at the ceiling for several seconds. She could not believe what she was hearing.

"Some of the men were also dressed up," said Debbie, more brightly than she should have and then immediately blushed.

"It just keeps getting better," said Louisa. "So, what is Tom accused of? Actually, don't worry about it, I'm sure we both know that whatever it was he definitely did it."

"Various inappropriate comments mainly," said Debbie.

"Anything else?"

"Well, he dressed up as well and his outfit upset two of the women on his team."

"How?" asked Louisa, dreading the answer.

"They said he looked better in a basque and stockings than they did."

Louisa looked out of the window and tried to regain her composure. Her long blonde hair was in its customary ponytail and Debbie watched as she played with the hair band that was holding it together. She recognised this as a symptom of stress and had seen it many times before.

"I imagine the whole day was total chaos then?" Louisa asked, turning back around and looking even more exasperated as Debbie shuffled uncomfortably from one foot to the other trying to avoid her gaze.

This was not what she'd expected when she'd returned from maternity leave. Couldn't these people be left alone for five minutes to run things in her absence? For somebody only five feet tall, Louisa was fierce and didn't take any prisoners when she was fired up. She wasn't angry with Debbie, despite it being her who had overseen this travesty of an idea; she was angry with the laid-back attitude of the rest of the directors who only seemed to act on any staffing indiscretions when they threatened the company's existence.

"Not the whole day, fortunately. We were receiving reports that it was causing a few concerns, so we sent those who were in costume home at lunchtime to get changed into something more appropriate. Unfortunately, it was the start of the Easter holidays so the roads were busier than normal and none of them made it back into work by the end of the day."

"What?! So, we lost most of our staff for half a day because of this?" Louisa questioned angrily, becoming more agitated by the second.

"Unfortunately, yes. But it gets worse."

"How on Earth could it get any worse?!"

"Well, you know how we normally collect the money at 4 pm for the charities we sponsor?"

"Yes."

"Unfortunately, nobody made it back in time…" Debbie began.

"…so nobody was here to pay for the right to dress down, so we didn't make any money at all for the charity?" Louisa finished for her, throwing her arms up into the air as she did so.

"Yes."

"What a complete and utter shambles!"

Louisa was now apoplectic. This was becoming the worst day she'd had at the company since she started ten years ago and it wasn't even 11 am yet. At this rate, she'd be going to the pub at lunchtime and staying there all afternoon. She briefly thought about her time on maternity leave where she'd spent much of her day sitting at home watching children's TV while covered in baby vomit. That life was becoming more appealing by the second and she was now considering jumping on her husband as soon as she got home so she could have another few months away from this circus of a company.

Louisa got up from her desk, walked over to the window and banged her fist on the windowsill before staring down at the street five storeys below. Debbie could see she was lost in thought and went to leave but Louisa beckoned for her to stay. Louisa stayed motionless for well over a minute, far away in her thoughts until suddenly snapping back into the room.

"I have an idea that might solve two problems at once," she said. "Let me think about it."

Debbie left Louisa's office and returned to her desk wondering what her potential miracle cure would be. She and Tom had always got on well because he wasn't like most of the other socially awkward people in the IT department. He was fun and a bit cheeky – although that might be why he was always up in HR explaining his actions while the rest of his department were downstairs at their desks doing what they were paid to do without causing any problems.

She hoped he wouldn't be fired but knew it was now a strong possibility. Whatever happened, he would at least be getting another warning.

Chapter 3

Brighton, UK

Every Monday morning at 11 am, the Project team got together for the first of their many weekly meetings which, in the fast-moving world of IT, were known as 'stand-ups' and allowed (or forced) everyone to gather round one of the large tables in the office and take turns to update each other on the status of their work. While each person was speaking, the rest of the team would try to look interested while thinking about what they were having for lunch.

In a bid to generate team spirit, time was also allowed at the end for a brief discussion about the weekend and what people had been up to – although this attempt at forced personal interaction did not always work as well as intended. Normally Katrina would begin by telling people about her yoga and her disruptive teenage son before Colin took centre stage and updated everyone on one of his latest home improvement failures. These were often the source of great amusement – especially if he had fallen off something or broken something expensive – but lately they had become less exciting and amounted to little more than him arguing with his wife about paint colours for their spare bedroom.

Sue would then deliver a 5-minute soliloquy on her dogs and how much better they were than most humans and Tom would then regale them all with stories of his weekend or, in this case, his week off. Martin normally concluded the session by recounting in meticulous and painful detail every single inconsequential thing that each of his boys had said, done, eaten, drunk or shat out of their bodies. Katrina purposefully made him go last so she could wrap things up if too many of the team started to glaze over or look like they were about to murder him.

Occasionally Martin would mention his love of photography as well, although there was nothing on that subject this week because he'd just bought himself a new camera and was still trying to work out how to use it. Martin was an enthusiast who had very little aptitude – or 'all the gear, but no idea' as Tom had called it. The cameras he used were generally of the 'rangefinder' type which meant when he was taking the picture he was not looking directly through the lens and had been known on many occasions to unknowingly take multiple pictures with the lens cap still on.

He would always be immensely proud of what he'd shot on the day but then completely distraught when he got the photos back from the developer and find most of them were completely black. To save money and embarrassment, he'd once built a darkroom in the garage to develop the pictures himself, although Tom often threatened to go to his house and open the door to let all the 'dark' out. Martin eventually moved over to cameras with SD cards which allowed him to delete any accidental close-ups of the lens cap and this also had the happy side-effect of annoying Tom, who now had one less way to make fun of him.

"I'm so glad that's over for another week," Martin said to Tom as they returned to their desks via the kitchen.

"I think we all are," Tom replied.

"I always wonder if people are a bit bored hearing about the boys all the time."

Tom remained silent as they made their hot drinks and headed back across the large, open-plan office to the corner where the rest of the team were already settling back into their work. When they got back to their desks, they were just in time for Colin to tell them something he'd forgotten to share at the meeting. As it wasn't about home improvement – or home destruction in Colin's case – it was understandable that he hadn't remembered.

"Guys, I forgot to tell you I bought a new car on Saturday. It's a few years old and nothing fancy but it's newer than my previous one."

"Cool," said Tom. "What is it?"

"A Seat. It's eleven years old but it's only got 60,000 miles on the clock."

"What colour is it?" Sue asked.

"It's yellow," Colin replied sheepishly.

"Why didn't you get a normal colour?" Tom asked.

"It is a normal colour, I think," Colin said with slightly less enthusiasm than before.

"It sounds great, Colin. Are you pleased with it so far?" asked Katrina.

"Yes, I am, thanks."

"Except it's yellow," Tom added.

"Yes," said Colin.

Out of the corner of his eye, Tom could see Martin shifting uncomfortably in his chair. Tom knew exactly why this was and how it related to Martin's unfortunate nickname. Every time the topic of cars was brought up in any work or social situation, Martin's mind inevitably went back to the day he bought his first car from his cousin, Graham. It then moved forward to the day he first drove it.

When Martin was 18, he'd started taking driving lessons and his father, Brian, had seen it as an ideal opportunity to also learn to drive, so they devised a family competition to see which of them would pass first. They both ultimately had their driving tests booked for the same week; Martin failed his on Tuesday and Brian followed this up by failing his on Thursday.

Two months later, they were each ready for their second test and Brian, in a commendable show of consistency, managed to fail again. Unfortunately for him – and all the other local road users – Martin passed a couple of days later and immediately started to look for a car. As luck would have it, his cousin had a car he was looking to sell, so they arranged to meet the following weekend. On the day Graham came round with the car, Tom was waiting with Martin.

"How much does he want for it, Martin?" Tom asked before Graham arrived.

"I don't know, but I've got £2,000 saved up so hopefully it won't be any more than that."

"Here he comes now," said Tom as a light blue car came wheezing up the cul-de-sac where they both lived and shuddered to a halt next to them.

Graham switched off the engine of the battered old Ford and got out. Martin immediately went to greet him and they spent a few minutes catching up on family news before Martin proceeded to walk around the car and kick each of the tyres in turn.

"Why are you kicking the tyres?" Graham asked.

"Because that's what you're supposed to do," said Martin.

"Are you?"

"Well, I've seen it done on television and my dad told me to."

"So, what have you learned from that?" Tom asked, looking at Graham with both young men now having smirks on their faces.

"I don't know," admitted Martin. "But my dad might be watching from the window and he'll shout at me if I don't kick the tyres."

"Don't kick them too hard or the car might fall apart!" said Tom, laughing at the percentage of rust compared to the amount of original metal.

"Oh, shut up. It's better than your car," Martin replied as he got in and sat in the driver's seat.

Martin took the car for a short test drive leaving Graham and Tom to await his return. After about 20 minutes, the car came wheezing up the cul-de-sac again sounding like the last one standing in a demolition derby. Martin got out and asked Graham how much he wanted for it.

"I'm upgrading to a brand new one so I need £1,500 from this for the deposit."

"Oh, that's okay," said Martin. "I've got £2,000 saved up."

"That's fine," said Graham. "You've got yourself a new car! Let me have the two thousand by the end of the week and I'll bring the car over on Saturday morning."

They shook hands and Martin went in to tell his dad that he'd bought the car. Graham drove off and Tom went back to his house wondering what he'd just witnessed.

A few days later Graham delivered the car and Martin became the proud owner of his first vehicle, having managed to negotiate the price up by a third. His first task was to drive his annoying 10-year-old sister Emily to the library, which proved to be the last time anyone would get in a car with him for a very long time.

Tom watched the two siblings drive off from his bedroom window. He couldn't hear the day's first crunch of metal against another hard, unyielding material but he certainly saw it as he watched Martin scrape the right side of the car along the small wall that separated his parents' house from their neighbours. Undeterred, Martin began his journey and Tom saw the car swerving slowly down the street as Martin struggled to remember that turning the steering wheel left made the car go left while turning it right made the car go right.

When Martin returned, Tom went over to his house to see how he'd got on. As he walked up the path, he couldn't fail to notice that the car looked a lot different from the one he'd seen earlier.

"Why is the car so battered? I saw you scrape the wall but that doesn't explain the damage to the left side or the back," Tom asked. "Did you kick the tyres too hard?"

"Very funny. I was driving Emily to the library and another car was coming towards me. I moved over to the left a bit to let him pass but misjudged it and scraped the side of a parked car," Martin replied, sighing as he walked around the car to inspect the damage.

"Did you stop and leave a note or try to find the owner?"

"We were late and the library was closing for lunch so I was going to do it on the way back," said Martin.

"That sounds fair enough. What did the owner say?" Tom asked.

"I don't know. We came back by a different route so I forgot."

"What happened to the back?"

"When we got to the library, I was trying to park and reversed into a concrete post by mistake."

"Well, you wouldn't do it deliberately."

"No," said Martin. "Graham is coming round tomorrow to help me tidy the bodywork up a bit."

"Is he going to charge you?" Tom asked.

"I don't know," said Martin.

"Well, if he does, make sure you don't offer to pay extra like you did when you bought it," Tom replied, enjoying the whole situation. "You're so dopey sometimes, you're like Captain Dumbfuck, leader of all the dopey bastards in the world."

"Captain Dumbfuck! Captain Dumbfuck!" sang Emily, hearing Tom's comment as she walked past the open front door of their house.

"Oh crap," said Martin.

"I'm telling everyone!" she squealed with the kind of glee that can only be mustered by a sibling when their brother or sister does something stupid.

"Oh no," Martin said with a groan. "This is going to stick, isn't it?"

"Probably," said Tom. "Can I go and kick the tyres now?"

"No."

"Have you taken any photos of your car yet?" Tom asked.

"No," said Martin, suddenly distracted by the sight of his sister running around his car excitedly kicking the tyres and singing his new nickname at the top of her voice.

Tom took this as his cue to leave and go back to the relative calm and serenity of his own house. Growing up as an only child definitely had its advantages sometimes.

Chapter 4

Brighton, UK

"I see you have a meeting with HR today, Tom," said Katrina, once the small amount of interest in Colin's new car had died down.

Martin breathed a sigh of relief that Tom hadn't mentioned the story of his first car purchase and his subsequent unwitting attempts to wreck it on the first day he drove it.

"Is it anything I should be worried about?" Katrina continued.

"Not really. They only invite me up there because they like me," said Tom. "I mean, who wouldn't?!"

Everyone on the team looked at Tom and started laughing. At 32 years old, of average height, average build, average attractiveness and with slightly thinning brown hair, he was not most women's first choice. Or second choice for that matter. His most recent girlfriend had said he was very nearly a solid five out of ten – although she had been drunk at the time so it wasn't clear whether she was overstating it or understating it. A previous girlfriend had once referred to him as a 'placeholder' and he'd never been quite sure if that had been a compliment or not but, as an eternal optimist, he'd decided that it must have been.

Either way, Tom was undaunted and had the philosophy that if Captain Dumbfuck could find a job, get married, have kids and be happy, anything in the universe was possible. Confidence was the key – even if, in most cases, his was badly misplaced.

"I'm sure it's more of a summons than an invite," said Martin, laughing harder than everyone else and feeling relieved that the subject had been changed away from cars and his secret had been preserved for another day.

"I think it's something to do with the last dress-down day we had," said Tom.

"I missed that one," said Colin. "I heard it was quite a day."

"We're all trying very hard to forget it, Colin," said Katrina.

"Hopefully they'll be another one soon," Tom said brightly. "Maybe we can have a toga party?"

"I'd need a big toga," said Martin, prompting everyone to lower their heads and focus on their work again.

Martin had always struggled with his weight but it had never bothered him and he often made jokes about it. Growing up in less sensitive times had exposed him to some unpleasant comments as a boy but he wasn't fazed by anything. He'd always enjoyed his food and had ultimately married a woman who'd trained as a chef and had a habit of trying out new recipes on him.

Martin was enjoying his life, had everything that he'd ever wanted and was one of the few people Tom knew who could genuinely say they were truly happy. The bastard. And he had thicker hair than Tom. Double bastard.

***

Tom looked back at his screen and saw an email arrive from Karen in the American office. He looked at the clock and saw that it was just after 12:30 pm which meant it was only 7:30 am in Atlanta; she'd clearly arrived at work a lot earlier than normal.

"Hi, Tom, I hope you had a good break from work. We may have an issue with a data breach over here – I'm sure your people will share it with you sometime today but we could use your help later. Warm regards, Karen."

Karen was the IT manager of the American division in Atlanta and had been recruited to run that department as the business started to sell its clothing in various high-end stores in the USA. The American office had only been set up a few weeks when she joined so she was both the newest member of that division and, at 35, the youngest.

Classic Country Clothing (UK) Inc. had been formed so the company could reach a whole new market of American consumers who had the same surplus of money and shortage of fashion taste as their British counterparts. The location in Atlanta, Georgia had been chosen partly to limit the time differences that would have made dealing with a west coast site almost impossible but primarily because Atlanta was known as 'the city in a forest' which suited the company's image. There was no faulting the logic behind the decision and the new office had now been up and running for six months.

So far, the company had departments for Sales and Marketing, Customer Services, Shipping and Logistics and IT. They also had various levels of management, with each level proving to be more incompetent and ineffective than the one below. In the same way as the UK original, the US company sold its clothing to high-end stores and was now selling items online through its website and a dedicated smartphone app as well.

Setting up an overseas company from the UK had not been easy and, when the warehouse operation experienced some issues they couldn't resolve locally, there was no alternative but to fly the Global Production & Logistics Director over to help with the warehousing and shipping issues.

Before the UK company had grown and new departments had been formed to segregate the increasing workloads, Roy White had overseen production, warehousing, logistics and IT and was just about the most knowledgeable person in the business. As time passed, however, his internal empire had reduced to just warehousing and logistics but his breadth of knowledge was unmatched by anybody else so he was the obvious, but rather unfortunate choice to go to Atlanta.

Roy was nearing retirement and had spent his whole career upsetting people of various backgrounds and beliefs. He was short-tempered, grumpy, narrow-minded and – unsurprisingly – single. Change was not a welcome feature in his life. He hated large cities, meeting new people, trying new things or accepting new ideas.

The move to Brighton (the unofficial LGBTQ capital of the UK) had not sat well with Roy and many of the staff had guessed it would be a step too far for his outdated and unpleasant attitudes. He struggled with the bohemian atmosphere at first but then realised that given the choice between doing a job he liked in a company he was settled in was preferable to taking his chances at a company where he would almost certainly be required to learn new things and deal with new people. He therefore accepted his fate and decided to stay in his current role until he retired.

Everyone in the company knew Roy was just about the most intolerant human being alive but, while they initially accepted it, as time went on and attitudes changed, more and more people found him offensive. Some of his colleagues ultimately began to make fun of his prejudices and, each time the company recruited someone who didn't look or think like Roy, the rest of the staff would relish his growing discomfort.

When the news came out that Roy was being sent to resolve the issues in the American warehouse it was greeted with a mixture of horror and delight. After just two days in Atlanta (a city of over 5.5 million people with a racial mix of 40% white and 60% black, Asian and other races) Roy was struggling. When this was combined with the highest LGBTQ population per capita in the USA and a local populace who were friendly, polite and welcoming, Roy found himself so far outside his comfort zone that he paid for an early flight home.

When he returned to the office, he was challenged by the CEO. After keeping him waiting for a couple of hours, he went up and promptly resigned, citing a mystery incident in a local bar on the second night in Atlanta as the reason. He left the business immediately and was never seen or heard from again.

Despite the loss of Roy's knowledge, the Atlanta warehouse was eventually set up, local staff were recruited and a new security system was installed. Unfortunately, because this had taken longer than expected, the first shipment of clothing arrived from the manufacturers in Vietnam before the security system had been fully implemented and – two days after the stock arrived – there was a break-in and some of it was stolen.

Nobody was sure why the thieves had left behind more clothes than they'd taken, although the staff assumed that because they didn't like the clothing, nobody else would either. The newly appointed Logistics Director, Hank, had spoken for everyone when he'd said, 'this British stuff ain't worth shit – why would some fool want to steal any of it?'

Tom stared at the screen and read Karen's email again. It wasn't like her to be in the office that early and it certainly wasn't like her to be concise. Normally her emails were at least two pages long and – while any phone call with her would initially start on topic – it would soon go off on a tangent as she rambled on and on about some minor injustice or other that had affected her.

She always had a complaint about something. Sometimes it was quite reasonable like the weather or the traffic or the slow service at her local coffee shop, but other times it was more specific like her mother calling her while she was eating dinner, the neighbours having a baby or her sister Wendy working out the identity of the killer on a TV crime show before she did.

Unfortunately for Karen, her sister Wendy had recently moved in with her and brought along four cats and some unusually fussy dietary requirements. This change to her living arrangements had not improved Karen's already volatile temperament.

On the day after the break-in at the Atlanta warehouse, Karen's first complaint to Tom when she called him was that the thieves had not taken her co-worker's ugly, purple and mustard patterned jacket that had been on the coat rack in the office.

"They must have seen it!" she'd said. "It's one hell of an ugly ass jacket. Maybe that's what scared them off?!

They probably saw it and it gave them the creeps. I was so pissed when I came in and found it was still there. If I'd gotten in first, I would've just thrown it in the trash and told her the thieves took it."

"Maybe they only wanted the quality, waterproof garments we sell," Tom suggested.

"Oh, man! I love your British cuteness, but the only quality of these garments is poor!" she'd said with a booming laugh that had echoed around Tom's skull for several seconds before he could reply.

Tom liked Karen; she was fun and loud and always made him laugh. Tom often wondered if she actually needed the phone to communicate with him and was convinced that she could just shout from the top of her building and he'd be able to hear her just as well. Martin had spoken to her too, as had Katrina, and they both liked her as well. Everybody in the UK that had dealt with her liked her – in fact, the only person that hadn't liked her was no longer with the company.

Racist Roy had taken an instant dislike to the confident, young, mixed-race woman in charge of IT when he'd visited Atlanta – as well as almost everyone else in the company and across the city. He'd started by complaining about the local accents ('it was like being in a cowboy film') before moving on to the food ('I couldn't get fish and chips anywhere'), the good manners ('why do they have to call everyone 'sir' all the time?') and finally ending up criticising the local sayings ('why does everyone I talk to say, "bless your heart" to me?').

When he arrived at the building on the first day, Roy was immediately dismayed and said it was 'too big – just like everything else in America' and when he saw the ethnically-diverse group of staff ready to welcome him, he made up his tiny, uncultured mind that he didn't like anyone or anything the country had to offer.

Two days after arriving, he took a flight home at his own expense and by the end of the week he'd left the company completely. He'd quite liked that woman's purple and mustard patterned jacket though.

Chapter 5

Brighton, UK

Tom returned from his lunch break wondering what Karen was referring to in her email about the data breach and how serious it could be. He knew they were building up customer mailing lists and trying to get more retailers across the USA to stock the company's products, but it didn't seem as if there could be much more to it than that. No doubt the team would be given more details later, but it was approaching two o'clock and he had to prepare for his meeting with HR.

"Good luck mate!" said Martin as Tom returned to his desk and picked up his laptop.

"It was nice knowing you," said Colin cheerily.

"I wouldn't go that far," said Martin. "I've known him for 25 years and it's been average at best."

"Thanks, Captain Dumbfuck," said Tom as he walked away from the team, out into the corridor and headed towards the stairs that led to HR.

Martin put his head down and hoped nobody had heard what Tom had said. Luckily, they hadn't and his embarrassing nickname was safe for another day, although he was beginning to wonder if he should just let everyone know to save the embarrassment later. That would be a sensible approach – although if Tom got fired today Martin would be safe. He decided to cross his fingers and hope for the best – or the worst if he was seeing it from Tom's perspective.

The HR department was situated on the top floor of the building near the directors' offices, three floors above the IT department. Whether being on the top floor was meant to be intimidating to the other staff members was never quite explained but the HR Director had always argued that it gave her staff a degree of privacy they wouldn't have enjoyed if they'd been downstairs with the plebs.

As Tom walked up the stairs, the warm spring sunshine came streaming through the windows and he could see the myriad particles of dust floating in the air. Living and working in a bustling seaside city in the south of England was a real bonus and he couldn't imagine living anywhere else – unless he got fired and had to move back in with his parents.

The HR office was an oasis of calm away from the often-argumentative IT department where most of the staff considered themselves to be 'alpha males' – especially the women – and where heated debates over how best to implement a technology solution were often won by the person with the loudest voice and the longest staying power rather than by the person whose solution had the most merit or was the most cost-effective.

Meetings over which email program the company should use and how often the employees must change their passwords could take hours to resolve and usually became a war of attrition. They often went on late into the evening so managers had to have strong bladders, unwavering voices and no need for food or drink. If somebody stopped talking, suggested a coffee break or went to the toilet they were effectively 'out' and the debate raged on with one less competitor. This continued until all but one voice had been silenced and their idea was adopted while everyone else wearily made their way home broken, defeated and with suspicious wet stains on the front of their trousers.

Most people in the IT department liked the challenging environment they'd created because it brought the best out of everybody but Tom preferred to visit other areas of the company and get to know different people. One thing that had always struck him about HR was the overwhelming number of female staff working there compared to most of the other departments. It was definitely an area he'd like to work in one day, although he knew the only way the HR Director would have him working there would be so she could keep a closer eye on him. He could accept that, though, so each time he was called upstairs he harboured a faint hope that it would be the time when he was asked to move upstairs permanently.

Tom headed towards Debbie's desk and smiled at some of the women as he walked through the office.

They all knew him and he enjoyed what he called 'celebrity status' in that department, even though most of them didn't return his smile and immediately turned back to their work with a shudder.

"Good afternoon, Debbie, how are things with you today?" Tom asked brightly as he arrived at the HR waiting area.

The area where unfortunate employees waited to be called into Louisa's office to learn their fate contained four chairs lined up against one wall, with a filtered water machine at one end and a large potted plant at the other. Debbie's desk was situated at the front of this area and the layout made her seem like a modern-day Cerberus, the mythological Greek gatekeeper of the underworld – but without the three heads and the loud bark.

"Hi, Tom. Did you have a good week off?" Debbie asked as he approached her desk.

"Not bad, thanks. I had a few late nights and had to visit my grandfather a couple of times too. He's taken a turn for the worse in the nursing home."

"Oh, I'm sorry to hear that," said Debbie. "What's his condition like these days?"

"Much the same, although dementia is beginning to kick in a bit now. He's stopped chasing the nurses around and making lewd comments to them so he's clearly not himself anymore."

"I'm sure they will look after him as well as they can. I guess that's where you get it from?"

"Haha! Maybe," said Tom. "I'm sure if granddad was working here, you'd be seeing him more often than me."

"I think you'd both be up here equally," said Debbie, breaking into a broad smile. "You'd be fighting over that seat by the plant," she laughed.

"Oh no, that would be his seat. He'd outrank me in that area. I'm a bit scared of him so I'd just let him sit where he wanted."

The two laughed as Tom took his customary seat by the potted plant and waited for Louisa. It seemed she was running late so Debbie offered him a coffee, which he willingly accepted.

"Thanks, Debbie. I only come up here for the coffee; it's much better than ours."

"I thought you came up because our department is full of young women?"

"That too, of course," said Tom. "The IT department is full of smelly middle-aged men who spend hours arguing which font we should all use for our email signatures."

"I'm sure it isn't that bad down there," said Debbie, who was quite sure it was every bit as bad as that down there.

"As we get into the summer and the weather gets warmer, most of the men seem to forget that they're allowed to use deodorant. Up here everything is far more fragrant – although I was expecting to see a lot more sundresses and summer clothes today."

47

"I think they knew you were coming up so they dressed more conservatively," Debbie explained, only half-joking.

"That's not fair!" said Tom with mock indignation. "I'll just come up unannounced next time," he added, just as Louisa came out of her office, her high heels clicking on the wooden floor to announce her arrival.

"I think we see you far too often as it is without you coming up without an appointment," said Louisa. "Come into my office, we've got a lot to talk about," she continued, before turning on her heel and heading back through the open door with her long blonde ponytail swinging behind her.

Tom picked up his coffee and laptop and followed Louisa into her office, looking back and nodding to Debbie as he went through the door. Debbie smiled back, hoping this wouldn't be the last time she saw him.

"Sit down," said Louisa. "We have a problem."

"Oh?" Tom queried, sitting in the chair Louisa had indicated while she remained standing.

"Katrina tells me you are working on the main project for safeguarding the personal details of UK customers on our mailing lists. Is that right?"

"Yes, it's a significant upgrade to our data collection and storage processes to keep us compliant with the latest legislation," said Tom, slightly thrown off balance and wondering when he would be disciplined for the dress-down charity day issues. No doubt Louisa was building up to that but he didn't want to rush her in case she forgot.

"You know some of our people in Atlanta have been working on a similar thing for the American customer mailing lists I presume?" Louisa continued.

"Yes. Their rules are slightly different so I think there have been some complications with the secure storage and one or two issues with the data being collected."

"Well…" Louisa paused and then sat down.

Louisa's face darkened and she exhaled loudly. There was clearly something major happening over in the Atlanta office and Tom wondered if this was what Karen had alluded to in her email.

"We have a bit of a problem over there. There's been a data breach and we have lost some of our customer data," said Louisa, almost spitting the words from her mouth. "It came to light over the weekend and they're now looking to establish how the breach happened and what we can do about it."

"I understand," said Tom. "Do they need to use parts of our solution to improve theirs?"

"Possibly. But we have a much bigger problem," said Louisa, seemingly not wanting to get to the point in the vain hope that it wouldn't prove to be true if it wasn't spoken aloud.

"What else?" Tom asked. Maybe this was so big he wouldn't be getting disciplined at all. Surely, she wouldn't be telling him all this if she was planning to fire him?

Louisa got up and walked over to the window. Four hours ago, she was looking out of this same window wondering what to do about the employee who was now sitting in her office. Every muscle and bone in her body wanted to throw him out and watch as his body crashed down onto the hard, paved street below but she knew that the problem in the US could easily blow up and the company needed its best people on it to develop the solution.

Unfortunately, one of the company's best people was sitting in her office now, unaware of both the grisly fate she had originally imagined for him and the new fate she would soon be handing out. She hoped Tom had a valid passport as she turned back to him.

"There have been some errors in the data collection process. The software we originally used was bought from another company and came highly recommended by the former IT director there," Louisa explained. "He adapted it for us and it seemed to work well, but then the supplier went into liquidation and we weren't able to get any technical support so we had to modify it ourselves."

"Was that Johnny Pervert, the guy that came over here a while back?" Tom asked. "He was a bit dodgy. But well-named."

"His surname was Perver," said Louisa. "But you're right, in a way," continued Louisa.

"We all knew him as Johnny Pervert. What a name...and what a guy," said Tom, trying not to chuckle.

"Anyway, it seems that Mr Perver's chief contribution to the business was to recommend this data collection software, make some changes to the settings and then leave without sharing his knowledge with anyone," said Louisa.

"Why did he leave? Were the rumours true?" Tom asked.

"They had to let him go because they found him in the office watching certain materials on his computer," Louisa replied guardedly.

"We heard rumours that he'd been masturbating to porn in the office and the cleaner caught him after everyone else had gone home," said Tom.

"Well – and this is strictly confidential – there might be some truth in that," the HR Director admitted, turning her face to the window to avoid direct eye contact.

"Apparently she made him clean his own office that night."

"Whatever," said Louisa in disgust. She didn't want to think about that now – or, in fact, ever.

"We all knew he was dodgy. First the name, then the comments about British women when he visited us and the fact that he wanted to spend every night of his visit in a strip club. Total legend, that guy," said Tom.

Louisa looked at him blankly. Why couldn't she just throw him out of the window, forget the data breach in Atlanta and just go home and drink as much gin as her body would take until she passed out?

"I mean legend in a bad way, of course," Tom added, noticing that Louisa didn't appear to agree with him on Johnny Pervert's legendary status. Luckily, she didn't seem interested in knowing who had taken him to the strip club every night – although if she had, she would have found the culprit sitting right in front of her. Good times, great name, dodgy individual. What more could you want from a night out with someone?

Louisa sat back down and put her head in her hands. She held it there for several seconds before looking straight at Tom, seemingly staring into his very soul. It creeped him out a bit. Well, quite a lot actually.

"The software that we installed on his recommendation worked with an app on the customer's smartphones to build up a picture of their habits and preferences. Every time they went out it would access their location, the local weather and whether there was a store locally that sold our clothing. It would then make recommendations and give them discount vouchers if they had spent more than a certain amount with us," Louisa elaborated.

"That's ahead of what the UK version does," said Tom. "It sounds perfect."

"It sounds perfect, but it isn't," said a deep voice from Louisa's office door. "Sorry I'm late, but we're still trying to understand the damage here."

Tom recognised the voice as belonging to Keith, the IT Director. He was a tall, white-haired man in his late 50s with the deepest voice Tom had ever heard. Keith oversaw the whole of the IT department and was also Katrina's boss. He often sat in on meetings so he knew Tom, Martin and the rest of their team well and the whole department agreed that if he ever changed career, he would be the obvious choice to take over from the person who did the voice-overs for all of those Hollywood movie trailers.

"No problem," said Louisa. "Would you like to go over the technical issues for us?"

Chapter 6

Brighton, UK

The streets of Brighton were bustling with both tourists and locals enjoying the April sunshine, heading down to the beach or sitting in one of the many bars and restaurants around the city. Almost every establishment had tables and chairs outside it to entice weary shoppers and visitors to rest for a few minutes with a coffee and a panini, a cake or even a cocktail. On any given day, someone could throw a stone anywhere in the centre of Brighton and hit someone else who was eating or drinking. It wasn't something the tourism department suggested, but it could be done.

The vibrant south coast city attracts more than 11 million visitors each year, many of whom flock to the pebbled beach, the famous Victorian pier and the Royal Pavilion. On warm spring days, there were few better places to be in Britain – unless you were sitting a few floors above street level in the HR office of a company that had just discovered a major security breach that threatened its very existence.

Keith sat down next to Tom, nodded a greeting and continued where Louisa had left off.

"The app they developed was a giant technical leap forward in terms of the data it collected about people. It managed to bypass a lot of the controls and restrictions on people's phones and did things like checking the user's location at school pick-up times to work out if they had children or not so it could recommend kids clothing to them if appropriate."

"Impressive," said Tom.

"In a technical way, yes. But it wasn't altogether legal. It also checked all of their social media accounts and stored details of their contacts and cross-referenced them against any other information it could find to work out the age and date of birth of everyone the user knew so it could recommend products as birthday presents," Keith continued.

Louisa looked a little lost with the technical details but was pleased to see that Tom had a good grasp of what Keith was saying. Maybe throwing him out of her window could wait until after this crisis had been resolved.

"A lot of apps do stuff like that though," said Tom, cutting through Louisa's silent musings.

"Yes, they do, however this went much further. The app had screen-reading functionality too so if the user had a banking app on their phone, whenever they opened it, the app would record the screen and use optical character recognition software to look at the figures and make recommendations for more or less expensive items according to how much money they had."

"That's cool. Scary, but cool," said Tom.

"Unfortunately, it gets worse. Far worse..." said Louisa, her voice tailing off to a whisper.

"How?" Tom asked, now on the edge of his seat learning about the capabilities of the American version of their shopping app which were awesome and terrifying in equal parts. This was getting more exciting by the second and it seemed that the HR Director had forgotten the main reason for his visit, which was even better.

Louisa paused and looked at Keith.

"It reviewed their browser history," she said. "The software automatically recorded details of the customers' internet searches and fed it into our main database," she went on.

"Browser history?! Oh no. That's not good," Tom said with a slight smile.

"It's not amusing, Tom," Louisa admonished.

"No, it's not," Keith agreed. "They sent us some examples. Not only do we know that Martha from Connecticut bought one of our 'Stay Warm and Toasty' range of jackets, but we also know that she's single with no kids, has a brother in New York she hasn't called or messaged for at least a year, likes hiking on three trails near her home and is behind on her mortgage payments."

"That's not so bad," said Tom.

"Agreed," said Keith. "However, we also know that Martha watches several hours of lesbian porn on her phone each week and has purchased three vibrators online in the last month."

"If she's behind on her mortgage, maybe she needs some relief?" Tom suggested.

"It's not funny," said Louisa, privately admitting to herself that Tom could actually be quite funny sometimes.

"We also know that Bill from Tennessee is married, has been watching a lot of threesome sex videos online, spends far too much time around schools for a man with no children of his own and has recently bought some pills to make his penis bigger," Keith added.

"Do we know where he got the pills from?" Tom asked.

"What?"

"Asking for a friend," said Tom.

"Moving swiftly on, we know from the salary deposits into his bank account that Bill also works as a data security officer at one of the stores that sell our products," said Louisa.

"Which means he's the type of person that would be likely to request a copy of the data we currently hold," Keith explained.

"And if he does that and then takes it to the media..." Louisa continued, not needing to finish her sentence.

Louisa picked up a printout of an email received from Karen, the IT manager in Atlanta who was currently leading the investigation while a new IT Director was being recruited.

"Keith and I received an email this morning giving a handful of examples like this but Karen says there could be many thousands of compromised accounts," she told them, letting out a long sigh of despair.

"We know the full browsing history, location information, family situation, sexual preferences and purchasing history of adult products for all our American customers?" Tom asked.

"All products bought online are included," said Keith. "We know their tastes in books, films, video games, music, kitchen appliances, clothing...in fact, everything our customers have bought online over the last 3 months has been captured by the app and stored in our database – along with every website they've visited."

"That's not good," said Tom.

"The loss of this data has also highlighted security issues within the database itself and it seems that none of the data was encrypted or hidden from view. Anyone accessing our website on a computer could just add the words 'customer data' to the end of the URL and see everything."

"So, we use the app to steal their data and then accidentally publish it online?"

"Yes."

The room fell silent, with only the gentle hubbub of noise from the street below coming up through the open window. All three of them looked at the printed email Louisa had since put back down on her desk, none of them knowing what to say next. Louisa broke the silence.

"There have been a lot of meetings here today about this. We have just set up a quarterly email of offers and discounts on all of our products – along with other products from what used to be carefully selected partners. Unfortunately, the software system has corrupted our smartphone app and decided that every business our customers have recently purchased something from or even just visited online is now a carefully selected partner," she said.

Tom was beginning to grasp the seriousness of the situation and looked wide-eyed at Louisa and Keith.

"The emails are scheduled to go out at the end of next month but we can't send our customers a list of offers from inappropriate retailers," said Keith.

"So we're worried that Martha will get one voucher for a 20% discount with us and another for a 15% discount off a vibrator or a lesbian couples' weekend retreat?" Tom asked.

"Yes," said Keith.

"And Bill will get the same, only his email will include vouchers for car parks near schools, invitations to three-way sex parties and penis enlargement pills? That's going to be difficult to explain to his wife," said Tom.

"Exactly," said Louisa.

"What's our plan of action?" Tom asked, leaning forward as his interest level increased further and now feeling reasonably sure he wasn't getting fired today.

"We have two issues," said Keith. "First, our data collection has been far too rigorous so we need to stop that and delete the data we've already collected before the email goes out offering discounts on inappropriate products. Customers would question where we got our data from and that would cause us a major headache."

"That seems an obvious place to start," Tom agreed.

"We then need to re-write the code so it behaves properly in future," Keith added.

"So far, so good," said Tom.

"The other part is to focus on the data breach itself. We don't want thousands of our customers being contacted by malicious third parties and blackmailed over their browsing history."

"Most people have a dodgy browsing history," said Tom.

"I'm sure they do...although maybe some more than others," Louisa replied slowly, looking Tom straight in the eye and creeping him out for the second time that day. "But they certainly wouldn't want their families and friends finding out about it."

Tom accepted this and looked down at the floor, partly out of embarrassment at his own browser history and partly because he was worried that if Louisa stared at him a third time it might turn him to stone. And he certainly didn't want that — almost as much as their dodgy customers didn't want their families to know what kind of shady things they'd been looking at online.

"The Atlanta office doesn't have the IT skills to sort this out internally so we'll be sending a small team over there for a couple of weeks to find out what's gone wrong with the data collection and storage side. We will need to set up new data collection rules for the future and delete all of the unnecessary data we currently hold," said Keith.

"Would I be right in guessing that I'll be part of this team?" Tom asked.

"Yes. We need to fix this as soon as possible," Louisa interjected. "It needs to be completed before the promotional emails are sent out next month so I'm hoping you have a passport."

"Yes, of course. Although can't we just stop the emails from going out?"

"Sadly not," said Keith. "They're sent by a third party and our contract with them means we have to pay whether they go out or not. There is also a financial penalty if we delay them so we need to stick to the schedule."

During a short pause in the conversation, Tom looked out of the window as a seagull flew past with a loud squawk before returning his gaze to the room as Louisa began speaking again.

"The Global Corporate Branding department wants to send out details of the summer range before Memorial Day at the end of May," said Louisa. "It's seen as the start of summer over there and they want to take advantage of that to boost sales," she added.

"Are sales more important than the company's good reputation?" Tom asked, unable to hide his bemusement.

"No, but sales haven't been as good as expected so far and we need them to pick up soon or the future of the American division will be in doubt. Unfortunately, the whole of the Global Corporate Branding team has been promised a weekend away if they hit their targets."

"Where are they going?" Tom asked.

"Dresden in Germany," said Louisa.

"Dresden?! It's not exactly the tourism capital of Europe. Why don't they go somewhere good? What are they going to do in Dresden?"

"I have no idea, but they seem very keen to go, which is why we need you to focus on fixing the data collection and storage issues before they start marketing to all of our customers again and sending them vouchers for things they'd prefer us not to know they're interested in."

Louisa stood up and adjusted the blinds as the sun started to shine directly in her face.

"What about the data breach?" Tom asked.

"We're going to try and sort that from here. We've hired a specialist security firm to do that so your job will just be to focus on the data collection and storage problems," Keith explained.

"You'll be the Project Manager, but we haven't finalised who else is going yet. We'll let you know as soon as possible," Louisa added.

"This is awesome! When are we going?" Tom asked failing to keep his excitement concealed.

"Firstly, it's not awesome that we could be heavily fined for collecting highly sensitive and embarrassing data about our customers. It's also not awesome that we allowed our database to be hacked so that every customer's personal data is now available to people who may try to exploit it," said Louisa as patiently as she could. "And we all know what a litigious bunch the Americans can be. If this gets out, we could be sued for millions and it would ruin the company."

"Those bits aren't quite as awesome," Tom agreed.

"You'll be going this Saturday. Tarquin's assistant is booking the flights and hotels today," Louisa continued. "You'll get the weekend to relax and acclimatise and then you'll start work at 8 am on Monday. There will probably be four of you and Karen will be your contact over there," said Louisa.

"Okay, I'll speak to her later," said Tom, getting up and heading towards the door.

Louisa walked over to where Tom was standing as he tried to leave the office.

"Just one more thing," she said, standing a lot closer to Tom than he would have expected. "Don't screw this up."

"I won't," said Tom, trembling slightly.

"Don't do anything stupid and don't upset, embarrass or insult any of the female staff over there. If I hear of anything inappropriate, you'll be fired immediately and I will personally re-book your flight ticket home so you have to go through Iran, Somalia and North Korea."

"I'll be on my best behaviour," Tom promised

Louisa walked back to her desk, hoping she'd made herself clear before softening her tone.

"You'll need a visa for entry into the USA if you haven't got one. I think it's called an ESTA and you can apply online. We'll reimburse you for the cost of course."

"I've already got one. I was in Las Vegas over New Year so it should still be valid."

"I didn't know you went to Vegas," said Keith.

"Well, you know what they say – what happens in Vegas stays in Vegas," Tom replied with a smile.

"I've heard that," Keith chuckled.

"In my case, I brought it back with me but a course of antibiotics and some cream from the doctor soon cleared it up."

Louisa grimaced and started to wonder if this was really the best option they had. Deep down she knew there were no alternatives and could only hope that Tom and the team could get the job done without making things worse. She had scheduled a conference call with Karen and Keith later that day to discuss exactly what was needed and how to cover the resource requirements with as few people as possible but couldn't help worrying.

This had all happened so suddenly that the company hadn't had a lot of time to react, but it was clear they needed their best Project Manager involved and Tom's name was unfortunately at the top of the list.

The bonus to sending him out of the country for a while was that the staff in the UK office would get a break from him – even if it was only for a couple of weeks. Also, as a lot of Americans carried guns, she was quite hopeful that he'd upset someone to the point that they'd shoot him – and if they could do that after he'd fixed everything it would be perfect.

Chapter 7

Brighton, UK

Tom spoke briefly to Debbie after he left Louisa's office and told her of his upcoming trip to Atlanta. She wished him luck and was visibly pleased that he hadn't been fired. Tom said goodbye and made his way back downstairs where he saw Katrina walking towards him as he crossed the office.

"Hi, Tom, I've had an email from HR telling me you'll be going to Atlanta next week. Are you okay with that?" she asked.

"I can't wait! It will be brilliant to meet Karen and the rest of the team over there. You know I love travelling so I'm really looking forward to it."

"That's good," said Katrina. "But if you change your mind let me know as soon as possible."

"Don't worry, Katrina, I'm excited about going."

"I'm sure you're excited to fix the problem they have. We've just had an email from our CEO explaining what's happened. I suggest you read it before you speak to Karen."

"I will."

"Just remember it's not a holiday…you're going over to resolve a major issue."

"It's still exciting. I'd much rather be fixing an issue in sunny Atlanta than in a grim, featureless data centre on a grey industrial estate somewhere in Siberia," said Tom. "Or Birmingham."

Tom returned to his desk and noticed a buzz around the team; in fact, the whole office was full of excited chatter. He put his laptop back into its docking station and waited a few seconds for his monitors to switch on before opening the email from the CEO.

Dear colleagues,

It is with great regret that I must inform you of an incident that has occurred at our Atlanta office in the last few days.

As you will be aware, we operate in a highly sophisticated digital world which – while delivering many advantages – also brings with it several risks. One of these risks is data loss and it appears that we may have been the subject of an attack by a malicious third party. The result of this is that our customer data has been compromised and may now be available to the criminal fraternity or any other nefarious individuals seeking to profit from this information.

Whilst this is a serious enough issue itself, we have also discovered that the customer data we were collecting and storing went far beyond what would reasonably be expected – or indeed allowed by law – and every aspect of our customers' lives, including financial records, family details and even their internet browsing history has been captured in error.

It is this data that has been breached and we will now be working with the relevant authorities in both countries to mitigate the damage, correct our systems and implement new processes to ensure it does not happen again.

You are formally instructed to not discuss this with anyone outside our company; if you are contacted by any media outlets, please refer them to our Communications Department.

I will contact you all again when we know what the next steps are, but until then it is business as usual and you should go about your roles with the same passion and diligence as always.

Warm regards,

Tarquin Fotherington-Smythe

CEO

Classic Country Clothing Ltd.'

Tom stared blankly at his screen for a minute. Reading about the problem in an email from the CEO had somehow made it more real, even though the tone of the email was rather pompous. Upstairs in HR, it had just seemed like a problem that had to be solved, but after reading the email and hearing the nervous chatter from his colleagues it brought home the fact that the company had a serious problem and he was being asked to fix it.

Suddenly his desk phone rang. He could see the international code 001 followed by the Atlanta area code of 470 so he guessed it would be Karen.

"Hello, Tom speaking," he answered.

"Hi, y'all! How are you guys doing over there today?" came the cheery and surprisingly upbeat voice.

"Hi, Karen, I'm good thanks. How are you?"

"Oh, man, things ain't too good over here. We just got a copy of the email the CEO sent so I'm guessing you've been clued in on this situation too?" she said, sounding slightly less upbeat than a moment ago.

"Yeah, I just read it too," Tom confirmed.

"Well, the way I hear it, they're sending some of you people over here to help us fix things up."

"That's right. I got Georgia on my mind!"

"No way, man! For real? They're sending you?!"

Tom wasn't sure if this was being said in a welcoming way because they were finally getting to meet and it would be great to put a face to the voice or a slightly disappointed way because Karen wasn't convinced of his credentials to solve this particular crisis. Or to help in any way at all. Or at least to not make things any worse than they currently were. He soon got his answer.

"Why the hell are they sending your sorry ass over here?!" Karen asked, followed by a huge belly laugh. "I mean, don't they have anyone else? Like anyone AT ALL?!!"

The laughter went down Karen's phone line, travelled more than 4000 miles across the Atlantic Ocean, came up the phone line to the receiver by Tom's ear and out across the team. Sue and Martin sat closest to him and they both could hear Karen's booming laugh so they immediately started to laugh as well.

"It sounds like Karen's finding something funny," said Sue.

"Tom probably sent her a dick pic," said Martin, beginning to laugh harder.

"Ewww, that's gross," said Katrina. "Why would anyone ever send something like that? And why would she be laughing?"

"Maybe it wasn't very impressive?" Sue suggested as the whole team erupted into laughter.

Tom was getting laughed at on all sides as well as from the other end of the phone. This was some achievement – even for him – but he regained his composure and changed the subject.

"How was your weekend, Karen? Apart from letting everyone around the world know what kind of kinky stuff our customers are into."

"That wasn't me," Karen protested, amidst more laughter. "And I can't control what those folks look at in their spare time."

"What exactly do they look at in their spare time? We were given a couple of examples but I bet there are lots more."

"Well, we got these big-ass spreadsheets here with all the data on by state. There must be more than 50,000 names in total and you can filter the data columns and find out almost anything about anyone who has ever installed our app. Some people are into some freaky shit. It's the married ones who are the worst – especially the women."

"That's a surprise. I thought it would be lonely, single men that were the worst," said Tom.

"Like you? I bet you're glad you didn't buy anything from us!" said Karen and sent yet more booming laughter down the phone line towards the UK office.

Once again, Karen's laugh could be heard across the team.

"He's probably just sent her another picture," Martin said cheerfully, generating renewed laughter.

"Anyhow, yeah my weekend was good," said Karen. "Except for my dumbass sister moving in with me last week with all of her stupid cats. We spent most of this weekend clearing away her crap."

"Why has she moved in?" Tom asked.

"She got fired from her job a couple of weeks ago for being a lazy ass bitch. I always worried that she'd lose her job someday and move in here if she couldn't afford to pay her rent."

"That's not good," Tom sympathised. "Why did she get fired?"

"She was a receptionist at one of the museums here but she hates talking to strangers on the phone. She has a real phobia about it," Karen continued.

"Some people prefer to communicate by text," said Tom.

"I get that, but when you're the receptionist and you've got people calling you up for opening hours and shit you have to answer the damned phone. People don't send text messages for that stuff. It's just strangers though because she can talk to family and friends just fine."

"That's weird," said Tom.

"She's a weird one, that girl. Anyway, she told them she had a phobia of answering the phone so they fired her ass."

"Why did she take the job in the first place if she doesn't like talking on the phone?"

"She didn't. There used to be two of them working there – Wendy worked at the front desk and Edna answered the phones. Edna was 65 years old and liked to sit down all day while Wendy likes meeting people face-to-face so it worked out well."

"Presumably Edna retired?" Tom asked.

"No, she died in an armed robbery."

"Oh wow! That's so sad. Was it at the museum?"

"No, it was at a convenience store in Midtown."

"It's still sad to be caught up in something like that at her age," Tom said, with genuine sympathy.

"Yeah, the cops took her out as she left the store. She received three bullets to the chest as she opened fire on them."

"What?!" exclaimed Tom, more than loud enough to attract the attention of the rest of the team.

"Edna and her husband had knocked off a string of convenience stores to help prepare for their retirement but they finally got unlucky and the cops were waiting outside for them."

Tom was silenced for a moment. As Karen had been telling the story he'd had a vision of a sweet, white-haired old lady accidentally being in the wrong place at the wrong time, getting caught up in a robbery and dying of a heart attack due to the stress of the situation. Instead, she'd been one of the gun-toting perpetrators and had died in a hail of bullets like one half of a geriatric version of Bonnie and Clyde.

"So, what happened to Wendy?" Tom asked.

"They told her to answer the phones while the security guard covered reception duties but she didn't want to, so they fired her."

"That's a shame."

"Well, it sure is a damned shame for me now that I've got her sorry ass and her four stupid cats living with me. I swear that girl went out and bought a load of extra crap before she moved in just to mess with me. My house looks like there's been an explosion in a factory that sells a whole bunch of useless shit."

"What has she got?" Tom asked, visualising a mad cat lady moving in with piles of clothes, shoes, ornaments and pictures.

"What ain't she got?" said Karen, becoming less up-beat as the call went on. "A whole bunch of clothes, a ton of stuff for her cats and a lot of strange craft stuff. She thinks she can make a living as an artist selling crappy painted plates, knitted blankets in different colours, dreamcatchers and all sorts of crazy shit you'd normally just throw in the trash."

"That sounds like fun."

"Yeah...well, it ain't. And don't go getting me started on her eating habits. Man, I knew she was weird but she's got this crazy diet thing going on and she just does not shut the hell up about it. I mean, ever."

"Is she a vegan?" Tom asked.

"Yes! How did you know?"

"Just a lucky guess."

"Well, she bored the britches off my neighbour Justine yesterday. She was talking about her food for nearly an hour in the heat. I felt so sorry for Justine. She looked like she'd aged 5 years by the time Wendy let her go and Justine's the type who would have told her husband everything just so he didn't miss out on any of that misery either," Karen said.

Karen and Tom both broke into laughter and then said goodbye. It was almost home time in the UK while Karen was thinking about going out to get some lunch and as Tom put the phone down he began to reflect on the day and how it had delivered a trip to Atlanta, some important work that he'd presumably get a bonus for (assuming that he and whoever he went with could fix the problems) and the knowledge that everyone on the team thought he routinely sent inappropriate pictures to people.

This had become a far more interesting and successful day than he'd been expecting when he woke up.

**

"So, you're off to Atlanta then?" Martin said to his friend as the team were packing up for the day.

"Yes, it's going to be awesome. First-class flights, luxury accommodation, a generous expense account and two weeks of hot Georgia sunshine and fine Southern food," Tom replied, gloating as much as he possibly could.

"Don't get too carried away," Katrina warned him. "The company is not known for its generosity with these things. Last year Roy went to Vietnam to check on the main factories there and said it was a horrible experience."

"Yeah, but Racist Roy didn't like anywhere that was different," said Tom. "He didn't even like that company conference we had in Worthing and that was only 15 miles away."

"True," Katrina agreed. "Was that the one where they served pizza and pasta for lunch and he stormed off to get some fish and chips instead?"

"That was the one."

"Didn't he end up in a hotel that was full of Chinese backpackers when he went to Vietnam?" asked Sue.

"Yes," said Katrina. "He hated it and complained about the food, the staff, the other guests, the weather, the difference in time zones, the language and just about everything else."

"It couldn't have happened to a nicer person," said Tom.

Murmurs of agreement came from everyone on the team. Roy had been universally disliked and everyone in the company was happy that he'd left. Sending him to Vietnam and the American deep south was always going to challenge his unpleasant beliefs and his former colleagues all assumed he'd be murdered by somebody he offended one day – although they were disappointed that if it did now happen, they wouldn't get to hear about it.

"So, what are you doing this evening?" Martin asked as he did every day when they were about to leave work.

"I was thinking of walking the dog," said Tom. "But I'm not sure now because I need to pack for my trip."

"I didn't know you had a dog!" Sue said excitedly. "What breed is it? Have you got any pictures? Is it a boy or a girl? How old is it?"

As the team's resident dog-lover, her eyes lit up when she heard this and she suddenly found Tom slightly less obnoxious than normal.

"He doesn't have a dog of his own," Martin clarified. "He walks his neighbour's dog a couple of nights each week to try to pick up women in the local park."

"That's terrible!" Sue exclaimed as her feelings about Tom returned to their normal level with this disheartening development.

"It's genius," said Colin. "It shows women he has a caring side and likes animals."

"But it's false!" moaned Sue. "What do they do when they find out he hasn't got a dog?!"

"Well, it hasn't worked yet so I think the local women are safe," Martin said with a grin.

"Can't you get your own dog, Tom?" Sue asked. "At least then you'll be genuine and dogs are such good company."

"I know, but I don't like the idea of picking up their shit and carrying it around in a plastic bag all afternoon."

"What do you do when the dog you borrow has to do its business?"

"I just leave it there," said Tom. "It's not my shit. It's not even my dog."

"That's disgusting! No wonder you haven't met anybody," she said, totally horrified.

"I did meet somebody once," Tom protested. "A few weeks ago, I met a nice girl called Jane, or maybe Julie. I can't remember now."

"And what happened?" Sue asked.

"It didn't work out."

"You know why it didn't work out though, don't you?" said Martin, a smirk beginning to creep across his face.

"Maybe," said Tom.

"What happened?" asked Colin, who was as transfixed as everyone else on the team.

"Well…." Tom began.

"They got up from a bench they'd been sitting on together and she was about to give him her number when she stepped in a big pile of shit that the dog had just deposited," Martin told them gleefully.

"Yuk!" said Colin as everyone on the team stared open-mouthed.

"She was wearing sandals," said Tom sheepishly. "And the shit came up over the sides of her feet and went in between her toes. It was only on one foot to start with but there was quite a lot of it and it oozed onto the other one. I couldn't believe it when he crapped it all out a few minutes before because it's not as if it's a big dog. How much shit can one tiny little dog have inside it?"

"You didn't get her number then?" asked Sue.

"No, I have a feeling that might have put her off."

The whole team began laughing. This had become a common theme today and Tom wasn't enjoying it. He much preferred it when they were laughing at somebody else so he said goodnight and went home.

As he left, Tom heard Katrina calling Martin over to one of the meeting tables – presumably to tell the dopey bastard off about something – but he didn't stay to find out what. He had to get ready for his trip to Atlanta at the end of the week and needed to start organising things

so would definitely be giving the dog-walking a miss this
evening.

Chapter 8

Brighton, UK

Tom arrived home, took out a frozen pizza and put it in the oven. While it was heating up, he got his suitcase out ready to pack for what he was now calling his free holiday to Atlanta. Admittedly he'd have to do some work, but he was confident that it could be knocked out in a few hours each day leaving him and the others (who-ever they were) to enjoy their evenings. Hopefully, they would do most of the work for him and he could just 'oversee' it.

He was particularly looking forward to the first week-end where there would be no work expected from him at all – just him and some colleagues out on the town for a day and a half of drunken debauchery. He'd heard that American women loved British accents so he was looking forward to sweeping some of them off their feet – and potentially into his hotel room. That could be an interest-ing bonus because it had been a long time since he'd swept anyone anywhere and, since that incident in the park with the dog, most of the local women were keeping their distance.

Tom turned his attention back to the oven and got his pizza out. He'd also got himself a beer and had just cut the pizza into slices and sat down to eat it when his phone rang. He looked at the screen and saw the name

'Captain Dumbfuck' displayed above a picture of a potato. Tom's heart sank as Martin only normally called to tell him of something mind-numbingly mundane that one of his kids had done. Why couldn't this wait until tomorrow?

"Hi, Martin. How's it going?" he said, shovelling the first piece of pizza into his mouth.

"Hi, mate, it's going great. In fact, it's going all the way to Atlanta!" said Martin, unable to contain his enthusiasm.

Tom was immediately sceptical about travelling with his oldest friend as Martin had been to Disney World in Florida a month ago with some of Irma's family and friends and it was fair to say that it hadn't gone smoothly and their villa had soon been dubbed 'The Unhappiest Place on Earth.' The nightmare group of eight people included Irma's parents who hated fun of any kind and two of her female friends who were last-minute additions and didn't know anyone else in the group.

The trip hadn't started well as eight people were sharing a villa that was only meant for six and each of them proved to be incredibly lazy and refused to clean up after themselves. This led to a week of heated arguments over what a tip the place was becoming and whose fault it was. Eventually, it transpired that while everyone wanted the place to be kept clean and tidy, nobody actually wanted to put any effort in to keep it clean and tidy, so an uneasy truce was reached where nobody would do anything and they'd agree to pay a clean-up fee when they left.

Martin had called Tom after three days and told him the villa resembled the aftermath of a teenager's first house party where the only thing missing was an uninvited stranger lying face down in the pool, either drunk or dead.

When they returned, Martin insisted he'd never go away with Irma's family again and she agreed that it was a good idea. It wasn't clear whether she agreed that the four of them wouldn't go away with the others or if it was just Martin who wouldn't be going. He would doubtless discover which way she'd meant it the next time they went to book a holiday – but he did have a slight suspicion that he'd be flying solo from now on.

"Cool! It'll be just like the old days," said Tom, immediately looking back to the time they went to Spain when they were younger.

"As long as I don't fall off a moped again," Martin replied, with a nervous laugh.

"Definitely! Or drop your camera in the sea," said Tom, joining in the laughter. This discussion wasn't going to end well for Martin.

"I was gutted about that," Martin said dejectedly. "That camera cost a lot of money."

"I know, that's what made it funny! Hopefully, you won't lose your wallet, get kicked up the arse by a horse or crack your head open on the swimming pool diving board again," Tom added, warming to the task of re-counting Martin's multiple mishaps.

"I don't know why people call them the good old days. I spent most of my time in the local hospitals," said Martin. "I hope Atlanta is better."

"It will be," said Tom. "Going to Florida with Irma's family was alright once you got away from the villa."

"Mostly," said Martin. "Apart from when that roller-coaster broke down with a few of us at the top."

"I'd forgotten about that," said Tom. "But they got you down eventually."

"It took an hour and a half," said Martin, with a slight shudder.

"Well, there you are. I bet the view was good from up there though," said Tom.

"It might have been...but we were upside-down the whole time," Martin moaned.

Tom continued to eat his pizza while Martin complained about the rollercoaster incident. It would be good to have him along – not only as a friend but also because Martin enjoyed doing all the boring data analysis work which would save Tom from doing it. He guessed that there would also be a programmer going over to fix any bugs in the data-capturing software and re-program everything properly.

"Stuart and Bhavna are going too," said Martin as Tom began his second slice.

"That makes sense," he mumbled through a mouthful of dough.

"There will be four of us. Katrina wants me to review the data, you to design the approach to the fixes and the programmers to implement them. You, me and Karen will then test them once we're finished."

"Sounds good, Martin," said Tom. "What does Irma think?"

"She's got no idea. She can't even work her phone properly so she wouldn't be much help on something like this."

"I mean about you going to Atlanta, not the data problem."

Tom sighed. Martin was not quite as dopey as he'd been when they were kids, but he still had his moments.

"Oh, right. After the problems we had in Florida she's quite keen for me to go away on my own," said Martin.

"How do you feel about leaving the boys?"

"I'll miss them but I'm sure they won't change too much in a couple of weeks," said Martin. "I'll bring them something nice back. What is Atlanta famous for?"

"Infectious diseases and zombies I think," Tom replied.

"What?"

"Well, that's where they have the CDC which some of the locals call the disease factory."

"I'm sure they don't manufacture diseases," said Martin. "Or do they?"

"Who knows? I think they monitor diseases and try to find cures for them."

"But what if they can't? What happens to the people that are infected?" Martin asked, sounding significantly less comfortable about the trip than he had done a few minutes earlier.

"I think they probably shoot them."

"Fair enough," said Martin. "What about the zombies?"

"They definitely shoot them," Tom said, beginning to see some of the 'old' Martin shining through.

"Will we need guns when we go over there?"

"To shoot the zombies? I think they have specially-trained people to do that."

"I mean to protect ourselves," said Martin, knowing that Tom was just being difficult.

"It might be worth getting one," said Tom. "Although the security people might not let you take it on the plane."

"Good point. So, what should we do?"

"You could always go out for a walk once we've settled into the hotel. There must be a dodgy part of the city where some guy on a street corner will sell you one," Tom suggested, helpfully he thought.

"Maybe," said Martin, sounding uncertain. "I'll speak to the hotel receptionists when we get there and see if they know anyone who can help us out."

"Good idea," said Tom. "See you tomorrow."

Tom finished his pizza wondering if Martin had regressed to the time when he'd bought his first car or if he had just been messing with him. People often thought Martin was messing with them because they didn't think anyone could be that dim, but Tom had known him a long time and could confirm to anyone who asked that yes, he absolutely could be that dim.

After getting another beer from the kitchen, Tom continued with his evening. There was no dog-walking on the agenda tonight so he started sorting through his clothes and toiletries. While he didn't really care about anything or anyone outside his own limited sphere of influence, he prided himself on being well-prepared and wanted to impress the people of Atlanta – both at work and during his free time.

As a teenager, Tom had recognised that boyish good looks, a winning smile and a charming personality weren't going to get him far in life – especially as he didn't actually possess any of those things. Not only did he recognise the lack of these things in himself, but everyone he knew also recognised it and reminded him on a painfully regular basis.

Instead of breezing his way through life with a smile that unlocked doors, Tom realised that study, preparation and hard work were the only things that would help him. He consequently spent a lot of time outside work researching different things to give him an edge and help him keep up with the hand-shakers and the arse-lickers that seemed to blight large parts of the corporate world he'd chosen to make his living in.

Once he had an idea of what he needed to pack for his upcoming trip – which included a selection of Leeds United football shirts to confuse the locals who'd probably never heard of them – he settled down in front of his laptop and researched the history and culture of Atlanta, the layout of the city, the tourist attractions and – most importantly – the best restaurants and bars.

As he scoured the various travel resources available on the internet, Tom learned the city had been founded in 1836 when the state of Georgia had decided to use Atlanta as the railway terminus for a line being built to the Midwest – wherever that was. He looked at an online map and found it was a ramshackle collection of what were termed 'flyover states' in what most normal countries would have called the North Central rather than the Midwest.

Putting aside his own ideas of how the various geographical regions of the United States should be divided up and what they should be called, he delved into the history of the city and discovered that Atlanta was once a major distribution hub for the 'South' in the American civil war, the birthplace of Dr Martin Luther King Jr. and the home of the civil rights movement.

He also learned that it was the world headquarters of Coca-Cola and that the Olympic Games had been held there in 1996. The city also counted CNN as one of its major corporations.

Finally, he saw that Atlanta was the home of the largest aquarium in the United States and, while this wasn't perhaps the most earth-shattering fact he'd discovered, he was a big fan of aquariums so this was the cherry on the top as far as he was concerned. It sounded like a great city and Tom immediately knew it would be a place he'd enjoy visiting, provided they didn't want him to do too much actual work while he was there. That would be a downer.

Chapter 9

Atlanta, USA

Karen looked at the clock and saw it was nearly 5 pm. This meant it was officially quitting time, so she shut down her computer and got ready to head home. She enjoyed her job but wasn't yet convinced that this random British company had what it took to survive in retail America.

The first concern she had was over the quality of the garments they were selling. As far as she could tell, there were two factories – one in Ho Chi Minh City and one in Hanoi – with all garments for the US operation coming from the Hanoi factory while the UK received garments from both, although primarily the one in Ho Chi Minh City. This might explain why the UK office didn't get as many complaints as they did and why the Customer Services department in Atlanta was the fastest-growing part of the company.

When Karen had started, the conversion of the warehouse was still being finished and the stock had just begun to arrive. Most of it was green and brown and all the staff had laughed at it, so it wasn't a big surprise that the thieves who broke in shortly after had left far more behind than they'd actually taken.

"What type of fools do they think are going to buy this shit?" she'd said to her co-workers on her second day on the job and was greeted with murmurs of thoughtful agreement from the older staff and raucous laughter from the ones closer to her age.

"I'd rather get wet than wear any of this," said Delores, whose own lack of fashion taste was proven every day by the appearance of a purple and mustard patterned jacket wrapped around her as she walked through the office door.

Fortunately for Karen and her co-workers (although maybe not for the customers) the clothing had sold in sufficient numbers to keep them all employed. Returns had become a problem, however, as the customers who'd rushed to buy the clothing in the first three months realised that many of the garments weren't of good quality and returned them for refunds.

The recent data breach had shaken everyone in the company and now Karen seriously began to wonder if she wanted to remain working for them as she packed her laptop into her bag. There was only one good thing about this job and that was that it paid the bills; well, it had so far but what would happen now that her airheaded sister Wendy had moved in was anybody's guess. Fortunately, her employer hadn't made her move into Johnny Pervert's old office when he was fired so that was definitely a positive as well.

Nobody had wanted his old office even though it had been cleaned and disinfected thoroughly; hopefully, the new IT director would get it and nobody would tell him what had happened in there. Everyone knew Johnny had been a big fan of Louis Armstrong and Duke Ellington so the office had now become known as 'The House of Jizz.' It gave Karen the creeps just thinking about it as she walked past it on her way to the main door and temporary freedom for the evening.

***

Once she'd left the building and was outside in the late afternoon sun, Karen got into her car to begin the 20-minute drive home north on the I-75 towards Cumberland where she had – until last week – enjoyed living alone. Her normally pristine house had always been her sanctuary from the world until her sister recently moved in with her four cats. Karen's small, three-bedroomed home was now a mess as the two of them struggled to combine two lots of furniture into one space and she didn't want to consider what state it would be in when she got home that evening. She thought about going for a drive just to delay getting home. Possibly to Mexico.

As Karen got closer to her house, she began to look back over the events of the last couple of days. First the data breach and then the knowledge that head office was sending a team of people over to fix it. She didn't care too much about the breach because it wasn't her fault; all she wanted was for people to continue buying their clothing so she'd still be employed and could pay her bills. It was none of her business if a single mother from Des

Moines was buying a suspiciously high number of cucumbers. Although she'd rather not know what she was doing with them.

Karen was currently focused on the impending visit from Tom and the others – whoever they were – at the end of the week. After spending several weeks talking and laughing, she knew she would get on well with Tom but she was curious to see what the rest of them were like. She wondered if he would be wearing a three-piece pinstripe suit with a bowler hat and carrying a briefcase and umbrella. Either way, he had to be better than the previous person they'd sent over who'd only lasted two days.

As Karen pulled up outside her house and got out of the car, everything seemed normal. There were no obvious signs of damage and no flames coming from anywhere, so she braced herself and went inside.

"Hey, sis!" said Wendy as she heard the door open. "Did you have a good day?"

"Hi, Wendy. Not bad, thanks."

"Good. You'll be pleased to know that me and the girls have finally settled in and unpacked all of our stuff," said Wendy, walking over to hug her older sister.

"The girls?" Karen asked.

"My cats. I've always called them my girls," Wendy explained.

"But one of them is a boy," said Karen, looking at Wendy like a mother who had just been told her 15-year-old child had scored the lowest-ever mark on a school test and was now being sent back to kindergarten.

"Well, technically that may be true," Wendy agreed. "But I used to have three girl cats and I can't stop calling them my girls just because one of them is a boy."

"But they're not all girls," complained Karen. "You can't call them girls if they ain't all girls. That's just wrong."

"They're my cats so I'll call them whatever I want," said Wendy and went into the kitchen.

"Well, you're my sister so that means I can call you a dumbass."

"I love you too, sis!"

Karen stared at the space Wendy had just vacated. This was going to be a long...she stopped herself. How long was Wendy planning on staying? She'd arrived less than a week ago and already the whole place was chaotic with four cats, noise (why couldn't she ever stop singing?) and random crap on just about every free surface in each room.

If things didn't improve soon, Karen would be looking online for a solution. She wasn't sure if she should be looking for a rent-free apartment for Wendy, a pair of noise-cancelling headphones for herself or an unemployed former Mafia hitman to provide a more permanent solution. Each of these options had distinct benefits and she'd favoured each one at different times during the last few days, although one of them was now in her head far more often than the other two.

Karen sighed as Wendy came back from the kitchen. Life wasn't like those movies from the 1940s where if you needed someone whacked you just went into a bar with an envelope of cash and found someone to do it. These days there were just far too many rules – not just against murdering someone which, to be fair, had always been frowned upon – but also covering the health and safety of any potential assassin she hired. The way the country was going with all the new rules designed to protect employees, she'd probably need to provide healthcare and dental coverage before anyone would even think about taking the job on. It would be far too much hassle getting rid of Wendy so she wearily resigned herself to her current fate.

"I made you some coffee," said Wendy.

"Thanks," said Karen, taking a mug from Wendy that she didn't recognise. "Are these mugs new? What happened to my green ones?"

"Yes, I got them yesterday. I have a phobia about the colour green so I can't use your mugs. These are mine but you can use them while I'm here."

"You have a phobia about a colour?!"

"Sure. I got drunk one night a couple of months back and passed out in a park. When I woke up there was grass everywhere and I freaked out. I didn't know where I was and my therapist thinks that's where I got the phobia. There was literally green stuff everywhere."

"Your therapist must be a rich man by now," said Karen. "You spend more time on his couch than you do anywhere else. You could have moved into his office instead of coming here."

"I can't help having a few phobias. I think I may have been dropped on my head as a baby – maybe more than once."

"That would explain a lot of things," Karen said, laughing so hard that she almost spilled her coffee as she went to put it down on the table beside her. "So how do you go anywhere?"

"I don't have a problem with going out."

"But what about when there's trees and grass and shit? Doesn't that mess with your head?"

"I'm okay if the trees and grass stay away from me. It's just when there's something green right in my face that I have a problem."

"You're weird," said Karen.

"Thanks, sis! Anyway, I heard there's a new free phobia workshop starting up this week that might help. They meet on Tuesdays and Fridays so I'm going along to talk about my shit with people that suffer from similar things. Hopefully, they'll be more sympathetic than some people I know," said Wendy, looking straight at her sister.

"Which day are you going?"

"I'm going to go both days. I've got a lot of phobias so I don't think we'll have time to cover them all in just one session – especially if I have to sit and listen to everybody else's crap first."

"That's very public-spirited of you," said Karen. "Where is it?"

"Just around the corner near the Braves' stadium," said Wendy. "I'm super excited to meet up with some like-minded people for a change."

"You mean other weirdos like you?"

"Exactly!" Wendy said triumphantly.

"It sounds good, Wendy. When you've done that, maybe you can start looking for a new job and a place to live."

"I can only focus properly on one thing at a time. You know I have a fear of multitasking," Wendy replied as she left the room and went upstairs, leaving four pairs of hungry eyes looking at Karen from the sofa.

"Have you got a phobia about feeding your stupid cats too?" Karen shouted up at Wendy, but a sudden attack of selective hearing had kicked in and there was no reply. Karen sighed and went into the kitchen to feed them, just as she had every other evening since Wendy had moved in.

Once Karen had fed all of Wendy's cats, she began fixing something for herself and her sister, who was fast becoming the most difficult person to feed in the entire world. Karen had a very simple diet and generally ate fried chicken, gumbo, jambalaya, pizza, pasta, fish, Chinese food and burgers. Although she ate a lot of fruit and vegetables, she was basically a carnivore who also had a love of dairy products.

Karen had vaguely known about Wendy's veganism for a long time, but until she moved in a few days ago had not really considered the practicalities and had just assumed that a selection of vegetables and fruit would be sufficient and that Wendy would cook for herself. For the first few days, Karen had been out with different friends for dinner so tonight was the first time she was cooking for her sister. She chose a vegan-friendly meal with plenty of vegetables and a vegan-friendly spicy sauce; that would be simple enough, or so she'd assumed.

Wendy came into the kitchen, saw what Karen was cooking and stopped her in mid-flow.

"You know I have a phobia of the colour green, don't you?" Wendy said.

"What? I thought that was just coffee mugs and grass. How are you supposed to eat vegetables if you can't eat anything green?"

"It's not easy," Wendy admitted.

"So, what do you eat?"

"Tomatoes, mostly. And corn."

"What about nuts?" Karen asked.

"I have a nut allergy so that rules them out."

For the first time in a while, the two sisters were standing next to one another and Karen looked Wendy up and down. She was wearing one of her trademark baggy t-shirts and a pair of skinny jeans and Karen couldn't help but notice how thin she was.

"How do you eat and maintain your strength?" she asked.

"It's quite difficult, but it means I can get into the clothes I wore in high school, so there's that."

"But that shit went out of fashion ten years ago."

"Style is always in fashion, sis, and I'm the most stylish person I know," Wendy boasted.

"You obviously don't know that many stylish people then," Karen replied as she opened the kitchen door to let one of Wendy's cats out.

Wendy went to close the door after the cat had left but as she did so a gust of wind blew in and knocked her off balance.

"Oh, man! What's wrong with you Wendy?!"

"It's this baggy t-shirt. It got caught in the wind and nearly knocked me over."

"Does this happen a lot?" Karen asked.

"More often than I'd like," Wendy replied sadly.

Karen turned back to where the food was being prepared and sighed. This was going to be an even longer week...month? year? than she'd first thought.

"Let me cook something tonight," Wendy said brightly. "I can show you how it's done so it'll be easier for you in the future."

"The future? Just how long are you planning to keep your lazy ass here?" Karen asked.

"Just until my business gets up and running," said Wendy. "I'm going to start selling craft items online. You know...blankets, hats, scarves, feather earrings and all that cool stuff. There's a big market for it out there."

"Really?" Karen asked dubiously.

Her face was frozen in a mixture of surprise, horror and fear. Was her airheaded sister seriously thinking she could sell craft stuff on the internet and make enough money to pay rent somewhere? And what type of fools were buying that crap?

"There are loads of weirdos out there if you know where to find them," said Wendy.

"I bet there are – and you'd certainly know where to find them."

Wendy ignored her sister and began to cook. To break the silence, she Karen asked about her day at work.

"Well, we had a data breach over the weekend and they're sending some Brits over to fix it for us. They think we can't clear up our own shit," Karen complained, stepping over two of Wendy's cats to get to the sink.

"Can you clear up your own shit?"

"Well, no, we can't – but that ain't the point."

"When are they coming over?" Wendy asked, chopping up a selection of non-green vegetables and putting them in a wok with some oil.

"They're coming on Saturday, but they won't start work until Monday morning. I've been told I have to babysit their asses."

"That sounds nasty," said Wendy. "Is your friend Tom coming with them?"

"He's not my friend!" Karen replied, a little more firmly than she'd meant to. She also felt a hot flush on her cheeks.

"I swear you're blushing behind me, sis!" Wendy said with a giggle and turned round to see if her assumption was correct.

"Oh, shut your mouth and cook your stupid tomatoes and shit," said Karen as she walked out of the room.

"How long are they here for?"

"About two weeks," came the reply from the living room.

"Are you going out with them in the evenings?"

"What the hell is this? Jeopardy? Leave me alone and just focus on that pan of hot rabbit food you're making."

"Well don't bring any of them home. I have a phobia of foreigners," said Wendy.

"A what? You seem to have a phobia of just about every damned thing on this planet. How do you manage to get through your day?"

"With more difficulty than you'd think."

Wendy turned round and went back to stirring her pan of tomatoes, corn and whatever that purple vegetable was. She knew it had a name that didn't suit it and had even used the emoji of it on her phone – although she'd never used that particular emoji to represent food.

Chapter 10

Brighton, UK

Tom arrived at work on Tuesday morning with a spring in his step, knowing he only had four days before they left for Atlanta. Going with Martin would be good and he'd worked with Stuart before and knew he was cool, although he did have an unruly beard that seemed to take over more and more of his face each week. As far as he was aware, Bhavna did not have a beard and wasn't planning to grow one. He'd never worked with her but had heard she could be a little pedantic at times.

As Tom sat down at his desk with his first coffee of the day, Martin was even more cheerful than usual so the idea of being away from his family for a couple of weeks wasn't troubling him as much as it would some people.

"So, you two are off on a jolly to Atlanta then," said Sue, trying – and failing – to hide the jealousy in her voice.

"We certainly are! We're flying out on Saturday, although we're so awesome we'll probably have this whole thing wrapped up in a couple of days," Tom answered. "It's the dream team on tour!"

"Please try to remember that you're supposed to be doing some work while you're over there," said Katrina.

"Yes, boss," said Martin as he and Tom both mockingly saluted Katrina.

"I'm not sure they're taking it very seriously," said Colin.

"Well, they should," said Katrina. "The eyes of the whole company will be on them."

"How come they get to have all the fun?" Sue moaned.

"They don't. The rest of us have a special treat lined up," said Katrina, standing up so she could be seen more easily over the monitors and fans that cluttered everyone's desks.

"What will we be missing out on?" Tom asked.

"There is a team-building event next week for the whole IT department," said Katrina.

"Phew! I'm glad we're missing that," said Tom. "We've dodged a bullet there. Maybe a whole hail of bullets."

"Why?" asked Colin. "I always think they're good fun because you get to bond more closely with your colleagues in a different environment. What's not to like about that?"

"They're not fun at all," said Tom. "Everyone hates them because they're stupid and they force you to do pointless things you don't want to do with people you can't stand. It just puts everyone in a bad mood and makes them want to kill each other."

"I still like them."

"It might just be me then," Tom admitted.

As the oldest member of the team – and some would say the laziest – Colin enjoyed meetings, workshops, team-building events and anything that got him away from his desk and prevented him from doing any actual work. He was counting down his last few years to retirement and was effectively working at 50% capacity or less. Most of the team saw him as an 'uncle' figure, only without the lewd comments and inappropriate touching at family gatherings.

"We were hoping you would be our official photographer, Martin, but now you're going to Atlanta we'll need to find someone else," said Katrina.

"That's a shame. I would have enjoyed that," Martin said disappointedly.

"Have you thought about Alan from the network team?" Tom suggested. "He's always taking pictures of people."

"He's no longer with us," said Sue.

"He died?!" asked Colin, clearly alarmed.

"No, he got arrested."

"What for?"

"For taking pictures of people without their knowledge or consent," Sue explained. "You might have seen it on the news a couple of weeks ago."

"Was that the guy the local newspaper called 'Upskirt Alan'? I didn't realise he was our Alan," said Tom. "The company kept that quiet."

"Well, they would, wouldn't they?" said Katrina. "It's not good for our reputation."

"I guess not," said Tom. "So, he's not available for the team-building event then?"

"No, he isn't. But I'm sure they'll find someone else."

"What's the event this year?" Colin asked.

"It's a surprise at the moment, but we'll all be told on the day," Katrina promised. "I'm reliably informed that it will be a lot less terrible than last year."

Sue and Colin perked up even more at this news but Tom remained unconvinced and was glad he and Martin were going to miss it. Although Martin was so dopey, he probably would have enjoyed it, no matter how bad it proved to be.

"What happened last year?" Martin asked. "That must have been before I started."

"The first exercise involved everyone picking three people at random and telling them something we liked about them and something we thought they could improve upon. They called it 'Good News, Bad News' or something like that," Tom began.

"Oh...that sounds like something that could easily go wrong," said Martin.

"It went very wrong," Tom continued, warming to his tale. "Not everyone was as tactful as they could have been and after a few minutes there were arguments and tears."

"And a fight," added Sue. "George in the facilities team told Upskirt Alan that while his ability to keep the network up and running during bad weather was excellent, he wasn't quite so keen on him taking pictures of his

105

wife under her desk every time he went up to the Finance department to fix her computer."

"What happened next?" Martin asked expectantly.

"Alan pushed him backwards and then George kicked him in the balls."

"Ouch," said Martin.

"They ended up rolling around on the floor trying to grab each other. It wasn't like one of those fights you often see in the movies where good, clean punches are traded, it was more like two blind men trying to swat an invisible bee," Tom explained.

"Would it matter that the bee was invisible if the two men were blind?" Sue queried.

"I guess not, but you know what I mean."

"Most of the staff were left in tears or in shock so the event was curtailed," said Katrina, trying to bring an air of calm to what had suddenly become a very animated discussion.

"I'm sorry I missed that," said Martin.

"You also missed the one before," said Tom.

"What happened at that one?" Martin asked, perking up at the thought of another office brawl.

"I don't think we need to go into that one," said Katrina.

"Maybe not, but it would serve as an important lesson for Martin in case he was ever asked to organise a team-building event of his own," said Tom.

"I'm sure Martin won't ever organise a team-building event, but you may as well carry on as I know you'll probably tell him outside work anyway."

"One of the exercises was a trust test – like when someone falls backwards and you're supposed to catch them."

"What do you mean you're 'supposed' to catch them?!" Sue asked. "Surely, you definitely have to catch them?"

"I expect it depends on whether you like them or not," said Colin.

"Anyway, getting back to the subject, we were at a hotel out in the country and there was a food-tasting challenge where people were paired up and one was blindfolded while the other put different foods in their mouth; the 'eater' had to guess what each mystery food was."

"Did someone bite another person's finger off?" Martin asked, looking quite worried. "I don't think I would trust anyone enough to put my finger in their mouth."

"Not quite. One of the guys fed the Marketing Director's assistant a peanut. Nobody knew about her severe nut allergy and she had an anaphylactic shock," said Tom.

"Shit," said Martin. "What happened?"

"An ambulance was called but sadly she died on the way to the hospital," said Katrina.

"So, the team event continued even though somebody had died?" Martin asked, completely horrified.

"Yes," said Katrina. "It had been paid for in advance and we didn't know she'd died until the following day when her job was announced on the internal vacancies list."

"But the rest of the day went well," Sue said brightly. "Apart from her team being one person short for the rest of the activities. That did unbalance the events a bit and I felt sorry for them being one person down – especially when we were all told to build a human pyramid to climb over a wall."

"That was tough to watch," said Tom. "They weren't the tallest team to begin with and trying to reach the top of the wall with one person less meant they had no chance."

"Didn't one of the guys try leaping up from the top of the pyramid to grab onto the top of the wall?" Sue asked.

"He tried, yes. That was the guy that fell and broke his arm, remember?" said Colin.

"Oh yes," said Sue with a chuckle. "It's all coming back to me now. I know there was someone who broke their arm at one of these events but couldn't remember who."

"That wasn't him," said Tom. "He only broke his wrist. It was the guy he landed on who broke an arm."

"You're right," Colin chuckled. "Good times."

The rest of the team started teasing Colin about his age and poor memory. As with most office teams, the oldest man is usually the butt of the jokes about age and forgetfulness (until one of the younger ones needs some practical advice about home improvements or car maintenance) while the oldest woman is normally the shoulder to cry on if anyone has any personal problems they want to talk about. She also tends to make most of the tea.

***

Tom and Martin went off to get another coffee. When they returned to their desks, the team had already settled down into the seemingly endless cycle of reading emails, replying to messages and putting PowerPoint presentations together to show how much progress they were making on each project. As they both sat down, Tom's phone rang and the display showed a familiar international number.

"Good morning, Tom speaking."

"Hey, Tom. How are y'all doing today?"

"Hi, Karen, I'm good thanks. How are you?"

"It'll be a hot one over here today," Karen replied. "I hope you can all cope with the Georgia heat because the folks at the local weather channel reckon it'll be in the high 80s every day next week."

"Wow! What's that on the normal temperature scale?" Tom asked.

"I have no idea but it's going to be too damned hot for you pale-skinned Brits. The trees over here are going to start bribing the dogs soon."

Karen's laugh once again came straight down the phone, went in Tom's left ear, reverberated around his skull for a few seconds and then went out through his right ear so the rest of the team could enjoy it too. He changed the subject before they all started laughing at him like they had yesterday.

"How's it working out with your sister?"

"It's not good. She's so messy and those damned cats of hers are just getting everywhere," said Karen, now with a serious tone.

"How long will she be there?" Tom asked.

"I have no idea. She wants to make hats and scarves and crap like that to sell on the internet to folks with more money than sense. A bit like our customers. Hey, maybe we can give her the data about our customers who like that kind of shit?"

"I'm not sure we're allowed to, but if that would help her get a job and leave you in peace, I'll email her a copy of it today."

"That would be appreciated because I don't think she'll ever move out."

"That's bad news. Can't she get a proper job?"

"I don't know. She's got so many phobias it makes it difficult for her to go anywhere. She's even afraid of foreigners now," Karen said with a weary sigh.

"Wow! We'll have to meet her and freak her out," said Tom.

"Oh, man! I would love that! Maybe you could scare her into getting herself a job and moving into her own place," Karen roared down the phone, the laughter echoing across Tom's open-plan office, through the open windows and out into the busy streets of Brighton.

"It's a deal then. I'll wear a t-shirt with a picture of our Royal Family on it and Martin can wear a beret he got himself in France."

"You guys have got to do that! She won't know what hit her. How can anyone have a fear of foreigners? It ain't like we're living in some kind of bubble over here. I'm sure she's just making most of these phobias up," said Karen.

The conversation then moved to work matters, IT reports and how they were going to approach the problem next week. Tom told Karen it had already been decided that Martin would analyse the data that had been collected, Stuart and Bhavna would look at where it was stored and he would oversee everything and discuss the solution with senior managers in both offices. Once it was agreed, Stuart and Bhavna would take care of the reprogramming and then Tom, Martin and Karen would re-analyse the data and ensure it was no longer capturing every aspect of their customers' lives – especially the more sordid ones.

"That seems like a good plan," said Karen. "Although I don't see a whole bunch of work with your name against it."

"I've got to design the solution, discuss it with the directors, make sure everything works properly and then test it. That's a big responsibility."

"Hmmm," said Karen, not entirely convinced. "What about your day job over there? Who's going to cover that?"

"I don't do that much over here so I'm sure it'll be fine," said Tom.

Katrina and Sue both looked up, which then made Colin look up too. Martin was lost in his music and oblivious to Tom's admission and the furrowed brows it had generated across the rest of the team.

"What I mean to say, Karen, is that I do a lot of highly-skilled and valuable work but I'm so good at it that I make it look effortless. Most normal people could be forgiven for thinking that I don't do much," Tom added loudly.

"The rest of your team are looking at you, aren't they?!"

"Yes," said Tom as the human-sized meerkats across from him lowered their heads and went back to their work and Karen's laughter came gushing down the phone line once again.

"One good thing has come out of this though," Tom continued. "We don't have to go on a shitty corporate team-building event they've got planned while we're away."

"Oh, man! Do you have those things there too? They can be horrific!"

"I know! That's what I've been telling everyone here."

The rest of the team looked up at Tom again as it seemed he was about to tell Karen about the disasters that had befallen the company's two most recent team-building events and were preparing to mentally tune out, although Tom initially fell silent.

"We had one at my old company once," said Karen. "We all had to go out in the woods in teams of ten with just a map, a compass and a few crappy flashlights. They took our cell phones from us so we couldn't use GPS because they said it would be good for us to experience what things were like in the days before technology got to where it is now."

"Ouch," said Tom.

"I know, right? Each team was dropped off in a different spot and had to find their way back to a hunting lodge where we were staying overnight."

"That sounds both fun and terrifying," said Tom.

"It sure does. There were six teams and each team was abandoned five miles in a straight line away from the lodge. It was 2 pm and they told us we should be back by 5 pm at the latest."

"What happened?" Tom asked, knowing that Martin would love to hear this too.

"Well, the fools just left us to it and everyone in our team started arguing about which way we should go. One of the managers said he would take charge so he took the map, picked a random direction and walked off."

"What did the rest of you do?"

"We couldn't do anything without a map so we just trudged along behind his dumb ass until we reached a small river that he couldn't find anywhere on the map."

"You'd gone off course?" Tom was loving this and couldn't wait to tell the rest of the team – especially Colin, who particularly disliked the countryside. Hopefully, the team-building event next week would be outdoors and Colin would hate it.

"We were miles off course!" Karen confirmed, followed by her trademark laugh. "Eventually, the fool in charge accidentally found a road so we walked along it for about an hour until we reached a gas station and used their phone to call a bunch of taxis to take us back to the lodge."

"That sounds terrible," said Tom, unable to disguise the excitement in his voice.

"I know, right!" Karen laughed. "We got back to the lodge well after five o'clock when most of the other teams were already getting ready for dinner."

"Were you the last team back?"

"No, we weren't. One of the teams came in about 8:30 pm," said Karen. "The worst thing was there were only nine of them when they returned because they'd lost Gerry, one of their sales guys."

"They lost him?"

"Yeah. That's why they were so late back. They'd been wandering around the forest for hours and when they finally saw the lights of the lodge, they had a group hug out of relief and noticed he wasn't with them. So, they re-traced their tracks a bit to look for him but it started to rain and they were worried about getting lost again so they gave up."

"What did the organisers say?"

"The group didn't tell them at first because they were cold and wet and just wanted to be somewhere dry with some hot food. Also, nobody liked Gerry so they didn't want to have to go out looking for him in the dark."

"I guess they mentioned it eventually?" Tom asked.

"Yeah. When they got their participation trophies, the Sales Director asked where Gerry was and it came out that he'd been lost for a few hours so they called the Forest Service to send some guys out to look for him."

"That's good news, at least. So how did Gerry take it all?"

"We don't know," said Karen. "They never found him."

"Oh crap! What did the company do?"

"They immediately advertised his job because there was a big sales convention coming up the following week and they needed a full team."

"Poor Gerry," said Tom.

"Poor Sales," said Karen. "The guy they hired to replace him was a total loser so they had to fire him and hire someone else a few weeks later."

At the end of the call, Tom put down the phone and looked across the desk at Katrina, Sue and Colin. They had all been following his half of the conversation with interest and were desperate to hear the other half. Martin was still listening to his music so Tom nudged him.

"What's up?" said Martin.

"I've just been talking to Karen about team-building events. You're going to love hearing about the one she went to. It's brilliant!" said Tom as he re-told Karen's story to them all and was met with four shocked faces.

"That's hilarious!" said Martin once Tom had finished.

"I think it's more tragic than hilarious," Katrina chided them.

"Of course. It's certainly tragic, but it's hilarious too. Let's go to the pier and get some lunch," Tom said to Martin.

The two friends got up from their desks while the rest of the team carried on with their work.

"That was a tragic story," said Katrina.
"Very sad," Sue agreed. "Poor Gerry."
"Definitely," said Colin looking to his right where he could see both Katrina's and Sue's shoulders shaking as they tried to contain their laughter.

Chapter 11

Atlanta, USA

After chatting with Tom, Karen called her sister Wendy to confirm she was still going to the phobia workshop. Wendy had a habit of saying she would do something or go somewhere and then not following through, so Karen took it upon herself to give her a kick sometimes.

"Hi, sis! Are you checking up on me?" Wendy asked breezily.

"Hell, yeah! I know what you're like for committing to stuff but not doing it."

"It's okay, I'm just outside the building, although I'm worried I'll be the weirdest one there."

"Probably. Just don't let it bother you and you'll be fine. You could let the others speak first so you can judge how weird your shit is compared to theirs and just tell them the tame parts."

"Thanks, Karen, I love how you're always looking out for me."

"Don't thank me. I know for sure you'll be the weirdest one there. I'm more worried about those other poor fools."

Karen's laugh was just as loud when she was talking to family and friends as it was at work and Wendy had learned long ago to hold the phone away from her ear whenever she sensed it coming.

"I'll talk to you later."

"Good luck," said Karen and ended the call.

As Wendy walked towards the building, she saw a young blonde woman standing in front of the door staring at it. She was about Wendy's age but a few inches taller than her.

"Excuse me," said Wendy. "I need to get in there."

"Me too!" said the tall blonde. "I'm Sadie. I'm here for the phobia workshop."

"Hi, Sadie, it's nice to meet you. I'm Wendy and I'm here for the workshop too. Why aren't you going in?"

"I have a phobia of opening doors," said Sadie.

"Okay. Let me get that for you," said Wendy with a smile as she opened the door to allow them both to enter the building.

Once inside, the two of them approached the registration desk where a surly octogenarian looked at them before pointing at a dilapidated book and a pen with a chewed end. He scowled at them both before gesturing for them to sign in.

"He seems nice," said Sadie as they walked into the main hall.

"I might ask him for his number later," Wendy said with a giggle, instantly liking Sadie.

"You'll have to fight me for him!" Sadie replied.

As the two entered, they were greeted with a warm smile by Lloyd, the workshop organiser. He was a tall, broad, immaculately-dressed African-American man in his mid-sixties and shook each of their hands in turn.

"Good morning," he said. "Welcome to the first of our bi-weekly phobia workshops. Please help yourselves to some coffee, sweet tea or water from the table at the back and then, if you'd like to take a seat, we'll introduce ourselves once everyone has arrived."

Wendy greeted Lloyd and then went to get some coffee. She liked Sadie but there was something different about her that she couldn't quite grasp. Sadie was certainly a lot taller than her – maybe approaching six feet – but there was something else. Wendy poured some coffee and headed towards the chairs that had been arranged in the centre of the room, thinking nothing further of it.

"Good morning to you all," Lloyd began, now standing opposite the semicircle of chairs where five eager participants had seated themselves. "Thank you all for attending. My name is Lloyd and I will be your guide as we talk about our phobias, try to understand where they came from and support each other on our respective journeys."

Wendy looked at Sadie and the others as Lloyd's voice boomed out across the room.

"Let us begin by introducing ourselves and telling the group a little about our background and our phobias,"

Lloyd went on. "Let's start with you and work our way along the line," he said, pointing to a young man at the opposite end of the row from where Wendy and Sadie were sitting.

"Hi, everyone. My name is Lucas."

"Hi, Lucas," said Lloyd and the rest of the group in unison.

"Hi. Again. Well, I'm 21 and I live with my parents but I have a phobia of authority," Lucas began. "I can't get a job because I get violent when people tell me what to do."

"Come now," said Lloyd, smiling in encouragement. "I just asked you to introduce yourself and you did. That could be seen as a form of authority by some."

"I know. I'm thinking of punching you in the throat."

Lloyd was immediately taken aback while the others looked shocked and Wendy spat some of her coffee out on the floor in front of her.

"So why didn't you act on your impulse, Lucas?" Lloyd asked, regaining his composure but taking a slight step back in case Lucas attacked him.

"Well, I'm afraid of physical contact as well," added Lucas. "That's another reason why I can't get a job because if I went to an interview the hiring manager would want to shake hands with me and I wouldn't be able to do it."

The group looked at Lucas and then looked at Lloyd, who appeared to have lost some of his previous composure.

"I see," said Lloyd, relieved that the threat of physical violence appeared to have now passed, although theoretically there was nothing to stop Lucas from throwing a chair at him.

Lloyd made a mental note to move back another few steps before he spoke to Lucas again and addressed the young woman sitting next to him in the hope that it would calm his nerves a little.

"My name is Alisha and I have two phobias; one of them is clowns and the other is birthday parties where there may be clowns in attendance."

"Hi, Alisha," said everybody.

"Welcome, Alisha. Are you sure that's not just one phobia?" Lloyd asked.

"No, it's definitely two. I fear clowns and I also fear parties that may have clowns there, like a children's birthday party. They always have clowns."

"What about parties where there aren't clowns?"

"I don't know. I never go to parties in case they have clowns."

Lloyd was struggling to fully see what Alisha meant but thanked her anyway and moved along the row to the next member of the group.

"Hi, everyone, I'm Dave and I have a phobia of water...as well as spiders, snakes, insects, fish, birds, wild animals, pets and zoos."

"Hi, Dave," said the group.

"Welcome, Dave. It seems that you're afraid of all animals, fish, birds, insects and reptiles," said Lloyd.

"No," said Dave. "I like dolphins."

"Anything else?" Lloyd asked.

"No. Just dolphins," Dave confirmed.

"Thank you, Dave. Now let's move on to these two young ladies at the end," said Lloyd.

"I also have a fear of heights so I live in my parents' basement. They keep asking me to move into the main house but I prefer things on ground level or underground."

"Thank you again, Dave. Ladies, please would you now share your phobias with us."

Sadie was next to speak and from what Wendy had already heard she was hoping Sadie would have more than one phobia or she'd be embarrassed when it came to her turn. Wendy had been worried about being the weirdest one there and, so far, it was proving to be true. While the others were sharing just one or two phobias, Wendy's mind was busy organising a whole list.

"Hi there, everyone – I'm Sadie! It's great to know y'all," she began.

"Hi, Sadie," said the group, growing less enthusiastic with each introduction.

122

"What can I tell you about myself?! I'm 29 years old and I am currently couch-surfing at some of my friends' houses. I used to be Steve and drive a truck but then I had an operation and now I'm Sadie. I work as a hooker offering comfort and support to Atlanta's poor and homeless and have a phobia of opening doors because you never know what's on the other side. I also have a phobia of television and I don't like boats or handcuffs."

Lloyd looked aghast. They seemed to be getting worse as he moved from left to right along the line. He briefly looked at the other members of the group and they were all equally shocked, except for the mixed-race woman who had come in with Sadie. It was possible they were friends – although she seemed to look more relieved than anything else. Did that mean she was just as bad? Lloyd hoped not.

"Welcome, Sadie. You seem to have led a very interesting life," Lloyd said as diplomatically as he could.

"Thank you, Lloyd! It's certainly been a fun ride and I'm not just talking about sitting on top of a homeless guy behind a dumpster on a cold winter's night," she said, with a level of vitality and enthusiasm normally only found in the very young.

"I'm sure it has. May I just clarify something?"

"Sure thing, Lloyd."

"Did you mention that you used to be called Steve?"

"Yes, before I got the operation," said Sadie. "I was a trucker but I never felt comfortable as a man so they just snipped that thing right off and now here I am!"

"Thank you, Sadie. And now for our final friend," Lloyd said, turning his head towards Wendy.

Wendy shuffled in her seat and put her coffee on the floor beside her before she continued, finally having an answer to the query she'd earlier had about Sadie.

"Good morning, everyone. I'm Wendy and it's great to be here!"

"Hi, Wendy," mumbled the group, still in shock over Sadie's surprisingly candid introduction.

"So, what phobia do you have Wendy?" Lloyd prompted.

"Well, I have more than one," Wendy replied. "I have a phobia of talking to strangers on the phone and I recently lost my job because of it."

"That seems a little unfair," said Lloyd.

"It was, but I was a receptionist at a museum and they said it was the main part of my job so if I didn't do it, they'd have to fire me."

"I see," said Lloyd. "Please continue."

"I also have a phobia of foreigners, the colour green and multitasking. The last one also helped me get fired because I can't do two things at once," said Wendy. "I'm a vegan as well so maybe I have a phobia of meat and dairy products too."

"Maybe I'm a vegan too because I don't like animals," said Dave.

"Maybe," said Wendy.

"I couldn't go without meat," said Sadie. "That would be no fun at all."

"I'm sure," said Lloyd.

"I do love a good steak," said Dave. "Fried chicken as well."

"You're probably not completely vegan then," said Wendy.

Lloyd rolled his eyes and began to question some of his recent life choices. What was he doing here with these people? How could any of them function to the standard required to have actually got themselves here today without a significant amount of adult supervision? What had he done to deserve this?

A neighbour had recently told him to join the local church to help fill his time now that he had retired. He could run workshops that would help people in the local community, she said. It would be fun, she said. Today was the first of Lloyd's workshops and, so far, it had been the complete opposite of fun.

As Lloyd contemplated the best way to kill his neighbour for suggesting this and began to put together a shortlist of remote locations where he could hide her body, Wendy started talking about her phobias again.

"I also have a fear of children and I don't like the moon," she began.

"You have a fear of children?" Dave asked. "Why?"

"They're too short," said Wendy. "It freaks me out the way they run around being all short and full of noise. They make more noise per inch than any other creature on Earth. I don't mind them once they've grown up – it's just the little, short, noisy bastards that mess with my head."

"I hate them too," Sadie agreed. "Also, the parents who think they're so perfect and encourage them to do stuff make me want to puke."

"Like what?" Dave asked.

"Well, you know how every time little Jenny or Johnny draws or paints some lame picture and the parents immediately put it up on the front of their refrigerator like it's some important work of art? That shit sucks," said Sadie.

"It really does," Wendy agreed. "That's why you don't see any parents with young kids working as art gallery curators."

"Why is that?" asked Lucas from the far end of the row.

"People with kids don't know shit about art or they wouldn't put all those crappy pictures up on their refrigerators. If they were in charge of displaying pictures in an art gallery, what do you think they'd put up? It wouldn't be the Mona Lisa or a picture of dogs playing poker, it would be a stupid finger painting of a fish with three legs or a family where the mother is twice as tall as everyone else and both parents have a penis. No offence, Sadie."

"None taken," Sadie replied.

Lloyd had stood motionless for several minutes staring into space while the conversation meandered from children's paintings to veganism and touched on just about everything else in between. He snapped out of his trance-like state at the mention of the moon. As a keen astronomer, he was interested in what the group might have to say on this subject.

"Why don't you like the moon, Wendy?" Lloyd asked her when he sensed a gap during her rant about children's paintings.

"It's just too bright and it comes and goes all the time. It freaks me out."

"I know what you mean!" Sadie agreed. "Sometimes, when I'm with one of my clients under the overpass downtown it's all dark and romantic but then suddenly that bitch is up there shining her light down on everything and the cops see us and I get arrested."

"That might just be the clouds moving across it," said Alisha.

"The moon should either be there all the time or not at all," Sadie insisted. "There have been times when I've been trying to find a good spot for my client but the moon has come out and shone its light on a dead body right behind us. It's just creepy. It kills the mood, too."

"So how many dead bodies have you seen?" Dave asked.

"More than I want to," said Sadie. "Working in the seedier parts of the city means I get to see a whole bunch of stuff that most folks don't."

"Is it dangerous?" Wendy asked.

"It can be but I can look after myself."

"I bet," said Wendy.

"Although it's not all fun," she continued. "I get arrested quite a lot so I think that might be where my fear of handcuffs comes from. Or maybe it was that time two guys handcuffed me to a boat in San Diego and ran away with my purse. I was there all night until the police saw me the following morning and arrested me."

"What did they do?" Dave asked.

"Well, they released me from the handcuffs on the boat but then they immediately put me back in some more handcuffs."

As the other group members listened to Sadie with a mixture of awe and horror, Wendy felt a pang of admiration for her. Not only had she had the courage to have gender realignment surgery but she also did a 'job' that she enjoyed – if you could call it a job. She had no problem with Sadie's profession, but she seemed to offer her services for free which didn't seem very profitable. Whether she was earning money or not, it was her choice and her life. It might be a mixture of couch-surfing and having sex with homeless bums but she clearly enjoyed it and Wendy supported that. She probably wouldn't tell Karen too much about her though.

***

Lloyd walked across to the other side of the room and found himself a chair. He brought it back to where the group were still in an animated discussion about handcuffs and tried to bring some semblance of order back to the workshop. He started by delving into each person's phobias more thoroughly, although without any of the enthusiasm he'd opened the session with. He just wanted to go home, strangle his neighbour who'd suggested this, then sit on his porch and ask his wife Millicent to bring him a glass of sweet, iced tea.

How many sessions had he signed up to run? This first one was already proving to be one too many. He'd have to find a way of getting out of doing them but first, he needed to bring this one to a close and there was no time like the present so he stood up and addressed the group.

"Thank you all so much for your contributions today. I think we can all agree it has been most illuminating," he said. "I hope to see you all back here next Tuesday morning at the same time although I, for my sins, am running a second workshop on Friday mornings as well."

"I might come along to that one," said Wendy. "I have a few more things I need to talk about."

"That sounds fun!" said Sadie. "I'll join you. Anyone else?"

Lucas and Alisha both looked at the floor in front of them and said nothing while Dave mumbled that he might come along. Lloyd looked up at the ceiling as if imploring something or someone to strike him down with a bolt of lightning. Or possibly strike the others down. Maybe it could strike his neighbour down too for suggesting he set up these sessions in the first place.

"Good," said Lloyd, meaning the complete opposite. "I will see some of you again on Friday and the rest of you next Tuesday. But please do not feel obligated to come to these sessions when they no longer serve your needs."

While a mentally beaten Lloyd was vainly trying to sow the seeds of future non-attendance in their minds, everybody else got up and headed towards the door to leave. Sadie reached the door first and stopped in her tracks, causing everyone else to stop too.

"Sorry," she said. "It's my door phobia again."

Wendy reached forward and opened the door so they could all leave and while Lucas and Alisha nearly sprinted out of the open door, Dave hesitated.

"Hey, Sadie, I'm sure I recognise you from some-where," he began.

"That old line!" said Sadie. "It never worked for me as a man and it's never worked on me as a woman," she said with a hearty laugh.

"I've been arrested a few times too; I wonder if I've seen you at one of the local police stations," Dave continued.

"Maybe. They usually take me to Zone 5 or CNN."

"I'm usually in Zone 5 or Fulton County. The guys at Zone 5 are pretty cool."

"Why do you get arrested?" Wendy asked Dave.

This was turning out to be a great day and she'd finally met some people who were as weird as her. Well, almost as weird as her.

"I get drunk a lot when I go out and me and my buddies can get a bit boisterous sometimes."

"Do you all get arrested?" Sadie asked.

"No, it's just me usually."

"Why?"

"Well, they normally run off as soon as any trouble starts but I just keep drinking so I'm the only one who gets caught. Also, they've all got responsible jobs so they can't get a police record or they'll get fired," Dave explained

"What do you do?" Wendy asked.

"Mainly odd jobs here and there. I just started as a swimming instructor."

"Didn't you say you had a phobia of water?" Sadie asked.

"Yeah...I can't swim either. At the moment I'm just winging it from the side of the pool."

"How's that working out?"

"It's going well so far. For the first three lessons, I just put all the kids on chairs and make them wave their arms about a bit and shake their legs to simulate swimming without any danger of getting wet. It might get tougher when they want to get in an actual pool though."

"That doesn't sound like the best job you could do," said Wendy.

"No, but it pays ten bucks per kid and it's not the worst one I've had. Last year I tried out as a stuntman for a local production company who were producing a movie about zombies. It was a spin-off from that TV show they filmed here."

"What happened?" Sadie asked.

"Their office was in a glass-fronted building near Centennial Park and I had to walk down a bunch of steps to get to the entrance. I was rushing because I was late and tripped on the top step and fell all the way down and crashed head-first straight through their huge front window."

"Oh no!" said Wendy. "What happened?"

"They all cheered and gave me the job immediately," Dave said proudly. "But I couldn't start work because of my injuries. It was a real bummer."

Sadie and Wendy looked at one another not knowing whether to laugh or not. Dave sensed their dilemma and started laughing himself as a prompt for them to join in.

The two women duly obliged and, as the three of them left the building, they swapped phone numbers and arranged to see each other again on Friday at the next workshop.

Wendy got in her car and drove back to Karen's house. It had been quite a morning so far and she couldn't wait to tell her sister about it. Karen would love the stories she'd just heard, although she'd be judgemental of course. What was it with older sisters that made them like that? At least she was there for her and Karen's house was in a far better location than her apartment had been so she couldn't complain. She certainly couldn't complain as much as Karen did. Nobody could.

As Wendy pulled up outside Karen's house, she looked forward to a couple of hours of peace before her sister got home and started complaining about some trivial thing or other. Wendy often wondered if she'd been on a course called 'How to Complain' and imagined all the attendees being given name badges on their first day with spaces for stars like employees in fast food restaurants.

Wendy sat for a few seconds staring down the street and imagined Karen earning three stars on the first morning and then being asked to run the course from the second day. She giggled to herself before getting out of her car and going into the house to reunite herself with her cats, hoping they hadn't pooped anywhere they shouldn't have done.

Chapter 12

Atlanta, USA

Sitting at her desk, Karen was bored. She had a lot of work to do but the last week had seen her sister move in (temporarily, she hoped) and a major IT breach at the company where she was the IT manager. Some security experts in the UK were investigating it, while the mothership – as they all called the UK office – was sending a team over to help them clear up the mess they were in.

She began to wonder how her life had suddenly become so busy. Just over a week ago, everything had been moving along at a nice, relaxing pace but now it was complete chaos. She needed to clear her head and do what she always did when faced with a crisis – get back to nature. She promised herself a trip to her favourite hiking trail at nearby Stone Mountain Park this weekend and maybe she'd invite those Brits that were coming over – that would probably toughen them up. Or kill them.

As she started to lose herself in thoughts of cable cars, views stretching for up to 60 miles and some fresh Georgia air, her phone rang. She jumped out of her daydream and saw the caller was the person she was most looking forward to meeting.

"Hi, Karen. It's me again," said Tom.
"Hey! How are y'all doing?"

"I'm good thanks; the company is making arrangements for our flights and stuff. We'll be staying in the downtown area of the city at a place called the Ocean Hotel."

"The Ocean Hotel? There ain't no ocean within 200 miles of here!" Karen said, laughing loudly. "Are you sure they're not sending you to Atlantic City instead of Atlanta?"

"I didn't think the Ocean Hotel sounded very likely," Tom agreed. "But I checked and it's not named after the actual ocean, it's named after the owner. Anyway, how's your day going so far?"

"It's all good here. I haven't heard of that hotel though, maybe it's an old one that's just been given a new name."

"Maybe. How's life with your sister?"

"Don't ask. She's got so many damned phobias and weird hang-ups I'm thinking of kicking her ass to the kerb," said Karen. "She's at some kind of phobia workshop for weirdos today and she's worried she'll be the weirdest one there."

"And will she be?" Tom asked, knowing exactly what was coming next and moving the phone away from his ear in preparation.

"Hell, yeah!" came the reply, followed by Karen's distinctive laugh.

"She sounds like a bit of a character with all her phobias and dietary issues."

"Ain't that the truth!" said Karen, still laughing.

"How is the food part of it going? Do you have to cook at different times?"

"I've told her she needs to cook for herself from now on because she says she can't be in the kitchen when I'm cooking a steak or some fried chicken. She's been on this vegan diet for the last two months."

"Has she lost any weight?"

"Not that I can tell; there's hardly anything of her as it is."

"Martin's been on a diet recently," Tom added. "He's lost 8 pounds so far."

"Good for him," said Karen.

"Unfortunately, most of it was personality."

"Oh, man!"

Tom moved the phone quickly away from his ear again as Karen's laugh got louder, prompting the rest of the team to look up at him.

"You two should get a room," said Martin, able to hear the laughter between the songs he was listening to but missing Tom's insult.

Martin was starting to wonder what he was letting himself in for on their upcoming trip to Atlanta. He just wanted to go over, get the job done as quickly as possible, take a few photos of the city and get back home to his family without any incidents or excitement. Tom had told him there was an American football museum there and, as a big fan of the sport, it was the only attraction Martin wanted to visit.

Martin didn't like excitement. He'd never been full of confidence and often made mistakes that resulted in people laughing at him – like buying a car for £2,000 when his cousin had only wanted £1,500 for it – so he kept to a small circle of friends and family. He liked his job, his family and his photography and that was about it. He'd never really understood those people who enjoyed jetting off all over the world visiting new places and trying new things. Martin preferred routine and liked his family to be around him whenever he went anywhere new, although after a few up-and-down weeks at home with Irma, this trip had come at the right time and he was now quite excited to get away. He was also glad he'd have his best friend with him.

***

Tom and Karen ended their conversation and the UK project team then went into another of their weekly meetings. Karen put the phone down to get on with her day but first decided to call her sister to find out how the workshop had gone. Hopefully, she would have met a millionaire who'd instantly fallen in love with her and invited her to move in with him immediately, although knowing Wendy it was more likely she'd have met a couple of unhinged drifters and brought them home. The drifters would probably both have cats as well.

"Hey, sis!" said Wendy as she answered her phone.
"Hi, Wendy, how did your meeting go?" Karen asked gingerly.

"It was great," said Wendy. "I met some interesting people there and I wasn't the weirdest one."

"Really?"

"Well, I'm sure I have the most phobias…"

"I knew it!"

"…but there were a couple of people there who are both as quirky as me so that was pretty cool," said Wendy.

"That is cool," Karen echoed, somewhat dubiously. "Are you sure they're as messed up as you?"

"I prefer the term 'quirky' but yes – although in different ways. One guy keeps getting arrested for being drunk and boisterous and is scared of every animal, bird and fish in the world apart from dolphins. He's quite cute actually."

"He's afraid of every living thing on this planet apart from people and dolphins?"

"Pretty much. He's also afraid of water."

"Does he ever take a bath?" Karen asked.

"I don't know. I haven't got close enough to smell him yet," said Wendy.

"Yet? Are you fixing to make a move on a guy who always gets arrested and never showers?"

"We'll see how it goes," Wendy replied, with a smile Karen could almost hear over the phone.

"But he won't like your cats."

"That could be a problem, although we also met a hooker called Sadie who used to be a truck driver called Steve. She keeps getting arrested as well and she's hilarious."

"I see what you mean about them all being as messed up as you."

"I'll tell you more when I get home as I have to go and do some stuff now and I won't be back until late tonight as I'm going to see some friends."

"Okay, I'll catch you when I see you; I got some stuff to do here at this stupid office."

"They want you to actually do some work?" Wendy asked.

"If I didn't, this whole damned place would fall apart," Karen replied with a laugh before saying goodbye and returning to her work, happy that Wendy was now making some new friends who'd embrace her weirdness and hopefully take the strain off of her.

The rest of the day dragged by and Karen had very little motivation to do any work. All the excitement and stress of the week so far had started to take its toll and she was now feeling both mentally and physically tired. Having Wendy and her four cats in the house didn't help either, so she decided to leave work early, go home, take a long hot bath and go to bed early with her favourite book and a large whiskey. She might even take the bottle upstairs to enjoy while she read about a group of assassins who travelled the world eliminating people. Maybe one of them could come over to Atlanta and take some of her co-workers out for her.

***

A few miles from where Karen worked, down in the Midtown part of Atlanta, an elderly man was enjoying his afternoon walk around Piedmont Park. He was comfortable in the heat and loved to be outside seeing people enjoying themselves in the afternoon sun. On one memorable occasion last week he'd stumbled across a young couple enjoying themselves (and one another) in some bushes near the tennis courts; they hadn't seen him but he'd certainly seen a lot of them.

Every day seemed to bring him a new and interesting experience and he was glad he'd decided to make Atlanta his home. It wasn't as humid as other places he'd lived but the temperature at this time of year was ideal and the greenery reminded him of his former home. Piedmont Park was his favourite place in the city and walking around different sections of this 75-hectare green space with its lake and plentiful foliage was always the perfect end to his day.

Chapter 13

Brighton, UK

Tom arrived at his desk earlier than usual on Thursday morning as he had a lot to do before jetting off on his corporate jolly the day after tomorrow. The company had given the four of them the day off on Friday as compensation for losing a day of their weekend flying to Atlanta and, while there was an expectation that they would use it to plan their approach, Tom was planning to go to the beach all day while Irma had a list of jobs around the house for Martin to do before he left.

Tom walked across the large open-plan room like a rock star, saying 'good morning' to his legion of fans who were naturally envious of his new-found status as an International Trouble-shooter and Fire Putter-Outer. When he returned in a couple of weeks, he would probably need to update his business cards to reflect his new level of awesomeness. He might also need security to keep his fans at a distance too, although walking through the office this morning it seemed like most people were ignoring him. They must have been starstruck.

"Hello, mate," Martin greeted him as he reached his desk.

"Hi, Martin. Are you all ready to go on Saturday?"

"Yep! I'm looking forward to it. We're having an early party for Irma tomorrow because it's her birthday next week and I won't be here."

"Cool. What have you bought her?"

"I'll pick something nice up in Atlanta but for the moment I've got her a new iron," Martin replied.

"A what?!" asked Sue.

"A new iron. She needs one with the amount of ironing she does. The boys have so many clothes these days and she's always at it," Martin explained.

"Do you think that's the most romantic present you could get her?" Katrina asked.

"I'll get her something in Atlanta as well. She's always drinking Coke so I could get her a t-shirt from the Coca-Cola Museum."

"Why not buy her some nice things in Atlanta and then wait until you get back before you give her the iron? That way you could hide the iron among the good presents," Tom suggested.

"That wouldn't really work," said Martin. "It always takes her a few goes before she gets the hang of using anything new so I want her to practice on her own clothes before she irons any of mine. I'll have a lot of ironing when I come back so I want her to know what she's doing."

The team were stunned into silence. Martin must be living back in the 1950s but there was no point in arguing with him as his domestic arrangements were none of their business; even so, Katrina and Sue both made mental notes to call Irma with details of potential new husbands while he was away.

"I'll need your number, Tom," said Katrina. "Keith and Louisa have asked for daily progress reports so we'll need to keep in touch."

"Okay," said Tom. "Don't call me when we're out partying though!"

"Hopefully you won't be partying, you'll be working."

"Of course. What time will you be calling?" Tom asked.

"The directors want to meet with me every lunchtime so once I've seen them, I'll call you to give you any new instructions and get an update from your end. It'll probably be just as you start work each day, around 8:30 am your time."

"Why aren't we using the office phones?"

"Let's get some coffee," said Katrina, picking up her cup and beckoning Tom to follow her to the kitchen.

"What's going on?" Tom asked when they were alone.

"Keith isn't sure where the problem is. The data breach is likely to have been instigated by a third party but it may also have been internal, in which case it could have come from our end or theirs. While you're over there we'll need you to check if there is anything unusual with their setup."

"In what way?"

"Stuart and Bhavna have been told to look for anything unusual in the system but Louisa wants you to keep an eye on the staff over there. Don't tell Martin, Karen or anyone else because we don't know if the data has been leaked from an internal source or if it was an outsider hacking into the systems."

"So, I'm like an undercover agent as well?!" Tom asked excitedly but in a hushed tone.

"Something like that. Just be available between 8 am and 9 am each morning to let me know what's happening in that area. Anything else can be discussed normally during the day."

"Okay, Katrina," said Tom. "You can rely on me."

"I hope so. This could significantly elevate your standing in the company if it works out. There are a couple of very high-profile programmes of work coming up that need a Programme Manager to oversee them. Let's not get ahead of ourselves yet, but this could be a great opportunity for you if you get it done."

Tom and Katrina went back to their desks and their individual routines of analysis, checking emails and attending meetings. There was a meeting scheduled with HR for Tom, Martin, Stuart and Bhavna later that afternoon to finalise the travel and accommodation arrangements and clarify the expenses policy. Until then, Tom and Martin just busied themselves as usual, with Tom making witty comments (most of which were inappropriate for work) and Martin listening to his various country music playlists.

Just after lunchtime, Tom received an email from Karen asking for his phone number so she could get in touch when they were in Atlanta to make the arrangements for arriving at the office on Monday morning. Tom emailed his number to her and, a few seconds later, his phone buzzed and he saw the familiar green notification icon from his messaging app and an American number he didn't recognise.

"Hi, Tom, just letting you have my number. I'm in a ton of meetings today and I know you're off tomorrow so have a great flight on Saturday and we'll catch up soon. Do you guys want to meet up for lunch on Sunday? Let me know! Karen."

Tom stared at the screen for a few moments and was about to reply but then thought of the others on the team. Would they want to go or not? It didn't matter — the weekends were their own time and they didn't need to spend it together so he replied:

"Hi, Karen, that sounds great! I'll certainly be there and I'll ask the others today. I'll let you know when we get to our hotel on Saturday night and we can organise something then. See you soon."

Just over 4000 miles away across the Atlantic, Karen saw the message come through and was pleased she'd get to meet Tom and the others informally before they had to start working together. It would make things far easier on Monday if they could get straight on with what they were doing without wasting time going through all the introductions.

Chapter 14

Brighton, UK

After a day at leisure on the beach and a relatively early night, it was now a cool, clear and dark Saturday morning that greeted Tom as he went to pick Martin up and drive them both to Heathrow Airport. When he arrived at Martin's house, he asked his friend to double-check he had his passport and everything else he needed before setting off.

"I'm not that dopey," said Martin.

"I just don't want you to forget anything," Tom reiterated.

"I went to Florida last month without you fussing over me," Martin replied, immediately regretting it.

"I remember that," said Tom. "Did you forget anything?"

"Irma," Martin admitted. "But it wasn't my fault. She told me to put the suitcases in the car while she put the boys in their booster seats. She then got in the car and I heard her shut the door. When I finished, I just got in the car and drove off without looking across at the passenger seat. How was I supposed to know she'd gone back in the house for something? It was dark and I was half-asleep."

"Just like this morning?"

"Yeah...a bit," Martin acknowledged.

Tom checked Martin had everything he needed, including his passport, laptop, voltage adapter, phone and wallet. If he was missing anything else he'd have to go to Walmart and buy it; maybe he could get himself a gun there as well. Once they were satisfied they both had everything, Martin said goodbye to Irma and got in the car for their journey to the airport.

"Hold on," said Martin as they got to the end of his road. "I've forgotten something."
"What?"
"My camera. I need it to take pictures of the city because I'm entering a competition at my photography club."

After going back and collecting Martin's new camera, they were finally on the road and heading north to the airport.

"What time do we get there, mate?" Martin asked as they drove up the M23, passing Gatwick Airport as they approached the M25 that would lead them towards Heathrow.
"About 5:30 pm I think. Which will be 10:30 pm our time and then we have to go through customs and get to the hotel."
"It will probably be time for bed by then," said Martin.
"Well, not really," Tom argued. "We'll probably get to the hotel around 7 o'clock local time so I'm planning on

going out for a beer and a burger. We might as well make the most of our first weekend."

"I suppose so," said Martin, feeling slightly unsure. The last time he and Tom had been out things hadn't ended well and Martin's luck on holiday had never been good.

"Are you still thinking back to that night in London last year?" Tom asked.

"Yeah. I have a lasting souvenir of it."

"But you always said you wanted a tattoo," said Tom.

"Not on my arse. And not of a pink unicorn."

"It was the only colour the guy had. It was quite late and he'd run out of all the normal colours."

"That's because we went back to his house. He probably had loads at his studio."

"But his studio wasn't open. It was 2 am. You can't expect him to be open at 2 am. Everyone needs some time away from work."

"Why didn't we wait until morning then?" Martin asked.

"Because you were insistent you wanted a tattoo and didn't want to wait."

"I was drunk," said Martin. "You should have stopped me."

"I was drunk too," Tom replied.

"So was the tattoo artist."

"Yeah, he was absolutely wasted," Tom agreed, laughing at the memory of the tattoo artist's hand shaking as he tried to ink the outline. "It didn't look much like a prancing horse, did it?"

"No, it didn't. I wanted a majestic prancing horse – just like the Ferrari logo but in bright red," said Martin. "Instead, I got a pink fucking unicorn!"

Tom began to laugh uncontrollably. He could see out of the corner of his eye that Martin didn't share his mirth but continued anyway.

"Irma liked it though," he said, trying to be supportive.

"Yeah...she did, to be fair. Once she'd stopped laughing," Martin admitted.

"Well, there you go then. No harm done."

"I suppose not. But I'm not getting any tattoos in Atlanta."

"You say that now..." Tom began, but Martin had turned his head towards the side window and was no longer listening.

Tom continued driving and turned onto the M25 which would take them the remaining 30 miles or so northwest to Heathrow. They had arranged to meet Stuart and Bhavna outside the terminal as those two both lived in a different part of Sussex. Also, Stuart's beard had a strange smell to it and Tom didn't want it in his car.

"What do you think of the others?" Martin asked.

"Stuart and Bhavna? They're alright. Bhavna knows her stuff and works all the hours she can, which will take the pressure off us and Stuart is a tenacious bastard so if there's a problem with some code he'll find it," Tom replied.

"They certainly picked the 'Dream Team' for this trip," said Martin.

"I just hope we don't have to eat with them too often."

"Why?"

"Well, Stuart's beard traps bits of food that drop out of his mouth and I've never had the heart to tell him," Tom explained.

"Perhaps he's saving it for a mid-afternoon snack?"

"Maybe, but his beard is like the roof of a thatched cottage. There could be all sorts of small animals living in it. I'm sure I saw a tiny mouse come out of it, grab a crumb of mince pie and then scuttle back in again at the last Christmas party."

"I'm sure he wouldn't have a mouse living in his beard," said Martin. "It would be difficult to sleep at night with all the scurrying that mice do."

"True. I don't know if he's married or not but I wouldn't think he'd be able to attract too many women with a family of mice living in his beard. Some women can be a bit fussy about having rodents in their bed. I guess that's the problem with having a beard that's bigger than your own face."

"What about Bhavna?"

"I don't think she has a beard. Certainly not one bigger than her face."

"I meant does she have annoying habits?"

"None that I can remember. She's quite uptight and serious and I think she might slurp her soup."

"Have you ever seen her slurp her soup?" Martin asked.

"No. I just think it's the type of thing she'd probably do. She's got the mouth for it."

"I know what you mean. Let's make sure we don't eat with them too often then," Martin agreed.

"Well, we'll be eating with Karen tomorrow. She's invited us out for lunch."

"Really? That's good," said Martin. "Has she invited all of us?"

"What do you mean?"

"It's no secret you two get on well and you're always laughing on the phone. We just wondered if you were planning some 'alone time' together?"

"Who is 'we'?" Tom asked, turning his head to look at Martin, who had his trademark stupid grin on his face.

"The team. We've got a sweepstake going."

"A sweepstake?"

"Yeah. Katrina thinks you'll ask her out and fall flat on your face, Sue thinks you'll ask her out but she'll realise you're a dick and Colin thinks she'll realise you're a dick before you ask her out."

"Well thanks, mate; that really makes me feel good," said Tom. "And what about you? What have you got your money on?"

"I think you'll have sex with her and then she'll hate herself forever and it will make things so awkward that the project will be ruined, we'll all get sent home early and you'll be fired," Martin replied. "I've got £10 riding on that one."

"Thanks for your support," said Tom, slightly hurt but also pleased that Martin thought he'd be having sex with Karen. It wasn't something he'd thought about himself but the idea was now in his head and he'd certainly think about it while he was on the plane.

"I just want to get back as soon as possible," Martin added.

"Why do you want to get back early? This trip will be great, even if you don't win your bet about me getting together with Karen."

"I just want to be back with Irma and the boys. Well, the boys mainly."

"You're rubbish at being on holiday," said Tom.

"Probably. I don't like going away because I'm too accident-prone. I always feel safer at home."

"Do you have accidents at home?"

"Yeah...but Irma has a first aid kit so she fixes me up and there's a hospital just across the road if I get any serious injuries."

"How often are you in the A&E department?"

"No more than once a month usually," said Martin.

"That's quite a lot."

"At least I don't have my own seat in the waiting room like you have in HR," Martin replied.

"That's probably for the best," said Tom.

"Why?"

"Because you'd probably fall off it and break a leg or something."

The first signpost for the airport came into view as the morning sun rose across west London. Tom followed the GPS directions, turning the volume up to drown out any more conversation from Martin and they were soon pulling into their pre-booked airport car park. Tom brought the car to a stop so they could get out and opened the boot so they could get their luggage out. He looked at his bright blue suitcase. He then looked quizzically at Martin's bright blue suitcase right next to it.

"Why have you got the same suitcase as me?" Tom asked. "We're going to look like a right pair of idiots walking through the airport with matching luggage."

"You told me it was good when you bought it last year."

"I know. But I didn't expect you to buy one exactly the same."

"Well, I didn't expect to be going away with you," said Martin. "I've got a yellow ribbon on mine to identify it on the baggage claim though."

"So have I," said Tom.

"Great minds think alike," Martin said cheerily.

"What a twat," Tom replied under his breath.

They took out their cases without further comment and made their way towards the bus stop where the bus would soon arrive to take them to Terminal 3 where Stuart and Bhavna would be waiting. They would then check in and go for some breakfast. Tom reminded himself to sit next to Stuart rather than opposite him so his eye wasn't drawn to the food dropping down into his beard that would later be eaten by the family of tiny mice that undoubtedly lived there and were about to go on their first trip out of the country.

The arrival of the bus jolted Tom out of his thoughts. There were a handful of other passengers ahead of them in the queue but they all eventually got on for the ten-minute ride to the terminal. As they approached the building, Stuart and Bhavna were waiting and greeted them warmly.

"Hi, guys! It's great to see you. How are things?" said Stuart.

"Good morning to you both," Bhavna added. "I am very pleased that we are all together now as I was worried that one half of the team might be delayed. Not our half, of course, as we were very well-prepared and have been here for some time."

"We're good thanks. Let's rock and roll," said Martin, without any clear intention to rock or roll.

"Good morning," said Tom. "How long have you been here?"

"Two and a half hours," Stuart replied despondently.

"It is far better to be two hours early than one minute late," argued Bhavna.

"Two and a half," Stuart corrected her.

"You could have got here half an hour early," suggested Tom.

"That's what I suggested," said Stuart.

"I see you have matching cases," said Bhavna, changing the subject. "We didn't get the memo, did we Stuart?"

"No. I'm glad about that though as it would have been embarrassing," Stuart added as they headed inside to find the check-in desks.

"I told you," Tom said, glaring at Martin. "I think one of us should buy a new case; probably you, because I had mine first."

"You won't be able to until we have passed through security and by then it will be too late," Bhavna told him, rather unhelpfully.

"Let's just get this done and get some food," said Tom, heading towards the check-in.

After check-in and bag drop came the usual rigmarole of security where they all removed their belts, jackets and shoes to go through the scanner. Tom noticed an attractive young female security agent and deliberately left some coins in the front pocket of his jeans. Hopefully, the machine would beep and she'd come over to frisk him.

Beep.

"Over here please," the attractive young female security agent called over to Tom after the machine had sounded its warning.

"Certainly!" said Tom as he quickly walked over to where she was standing.

"It'll just be a minute," she said as she called her colleague Sergei over.

Sergei arrived and towered over Tom. He was well over six feet tall and was built like a tank that had just swallowed another tank. Tom looked up and gulped. Where was the young female agent he'd been hoping would pat him down?

Sergei picked up an electronic body scanner and moved it up and down Tom's arms, legs and torso as his female colleague did the same with a female traveller a few feet away. After a rigorous pat down of some body parts that Tom had been hoping the female agent would be patting down, Sergei satisfied himself that this traveller was more of an idiot than a terrorist and waved him through, noticing that all the other young men in the queue were now emptying their pockets of any loose change that was likely to set off the metal detectors.

"I'm glad that's over," said Tom as he joined the others.

"Did you deliberately make the machine beep so a pretty young girl would touch you up?" Bhavna asked with a grin.

"No," Tom said defensively.

"You should know that they have agents of different genders for that very reason," she replied.

The rest of the team laughed as they walked off to find a restaurant leaving Tom in their wake, who subsequently arrived last and saw the only seat left was opposite Stuart. He reluctantly sat down, noticing a wry smile on Martin's face as he'd taken the only seat without a direct view of the impressive, but unruly beard. Breakfast was every bit as bad as Tom had feared, with at least four pieces of scrambled egg and a generous portion of toast crumbs finding their way into Stuart's beard. That should keep the mouse family going for a couple of days.

Finishing their breakfasts, they left the restaurant and made their way to the departure gate where they sat and waited for their flight to be called.

"Here we go," said Martin. "I'm on the early plane to Georgia," he half said and half sang.

"That doesn't have quite the same ring as the midnight train," said Tom.

"Well, no," said Martin.

"It would be impossible to go there by train from here," said Bhavna.

"We know," said Tom, thinking to himself that Bhavna was going to be hard work on this trip if she took everything so literally. Maybe there was a way that she could be sent somewhere else instead – like the moon. She sucked all the atmosphere out of a room whenever she started talking so she'd fit right in there.

A few minutes later, the four of them got up, joined the queue and boarded their flight to Atlanta. As Tom settled into his seat and looked out of the window, he wondered what lay ahead. Did the rest of his team really have a sweepstake on what would happen between him and Karen? Thoughts of the work ahead of them, how they would spend their free time in Atlanta and who would win the bet about him and Karen swirled around his mind as his eyes began to close and sleep overtook him.

In the next seat, Martin had already plugged his headphones into his music player and was also about to drift off to sleep. Two rows in front, Bhavna had instructed Stuart to swap seats with her so she could have the aisle seat and he was unceremoniously moved to the middle one. Bhavna then began talking about the job they needed to do in Atlanta in great detail so Stuart closed his eyes and pretended to be asleep. Soon he actually was asleep, leaving Bhavna talking to herself as the plane took off.

PART TWO

Chapter 15

Atlanta, USA

It had been an uneventful Saturday morning in the IT department of Classic Country Clothing (UK) Inc. in Atlanta and Karen had found nothing to do with her time other than stare at her co-worker's ugly coat that was currently resting on the back of the chair next to her. If the weather improved in the afternoons, Delores would often leave it there some days; she claimed to forget it but Karen was sure it was done deliberately just to annoy her, although the following morning Delores would turn up wearing something almost as ugly and would then have to take two jackets home. That served her right.

One of the many other things that annoyed Karen about her daily life was having to work every second Saturday to provide IT support to those customers that were dumb enough to use the company's app on their smartphones. It was well below her pay grade and experience level so most of the time she just told them to restart their phones and hope they didn't call back. This generally worked, although she always made sure one of her colleagues took the call if the customer did come back.

Since the recent data capture incident, however, she was tempted to look up their names on her spreadsheet and ask them what they liked doing with bananas and honey in their spare time, although, after having seen a lot of the data, she knew she wouldn't enjoy some of the answers.

As morning turned to afternoon, Karen realised she was bored; this was partly because there was little she could do until the UK team came over and sorted the data capture issues out and partly from apprehension. She was expecting the team to arrive just as she was going home for the night and would give Tom and the others a couple of hours to get to their hotel and settle down before she messaged them about meeting up tomorrow lunchtime. They were staying downtown so she'd probably arrange to meet them at their hotel and they could find somewhere for lunch from there.

As 5 pm got closer, the skeleton staff employed on Saturdays started to drift off home so Karen packed up and left too. Why was she so nervous? She got in her car and selected a different route back to her house. For the first time since Wendy arrived, she was quite glad her sister was staying with her as it would give her someone to talk to this evening; for some reason she didn't understand and couldn't explain, she had suddenly become a bundle of nerves.

The journey home passed uneventfully but Karen barely remembered any of the drive. Her mind was somewhere else and she almost walked into Wendy as she went through her front door.

"Hey, sis! Watch where you're going!" said Wendy. "You nearly knocked me over!"

"Sorry, Wendy. I'm not totally with it today."

"Is that because your British guy is coming over to see you?" Wendy teased, making kissing noises to annoy her older sister just a little bit more.

"No!" Karen protested, knowing the answer was the exact opposite.

"When are you all meeting up?"

"I'm going downtown to meet them for lunch tomorrow. There are four of them coming over to rake through our shit so it's all strictly professional."

"Are you happy about that?"

"Hell no! If it's got to be done, then it's got to be done, but I wish they'd trusted us to fix it first rather than sending a bunch of Brits over to get all up in our business."

"I bet there's one of them who you'd love to be getting all up in your business," Wendy teased her, laughing as she picked up one of her cats and deposited it in the kitchen where its food was waiting.

Karen went to sit in her favourite chair only to find another of Wendy's cats already sitting there.

"I don't know what you're talking about," she said, blushing slightly and ushering the cat to get out of her chair. "You know, sometimes I wonder if we came from the same mother – what with you being all flighty and shit and me being all sensible and mature."

"You mean boring?" Wendy asked, extending the word boring for a good three seconds.

"Whatever," said Karen. "Just hurry up and make your stupid rabbit food so I can get in there and cook a nice juicy steak."

Wendy was about to reply when Karen's phone rang. She noticed Karen's face light up as she looked at the screen. It was an expression she hadn't seen since they were teenagers and she'd caught her sneaking a boy into her room late one night while their parents were sleeping.

"Hey! How are y'all doing?" Karen began. "Did you have a good flight?"

"Hi, Karen. Yes thanks – we were delayed for a while but we're finally at the hotel," Tom replied.

"What's your hotel like?" Karen asked.

"It's not the best, to be fair. There's a car park with some big bins outside and a few homeless people sitting by them."

"That's hilarious!" Karen's booming laugh erupted across her living room, taking Wendy by surprise and scaring those cats that hadn't yet realised their food was waiting for them in the kitchen.

"Where is it?"

"I don't know but it's a couple of streets behind a big Ferris wheel."

"That's the Skyview. And we call them 'blocks' over here," said Karen. "Those bins you see are called dumpsters," she added, seeing Wendy pretending to kiss an imaginary person in front of her.

"One of them is on fire," said Tom.

"That sounds like a real fancy hotel you've been given there. Don't worry about it; I know someone whose whole life is one big dumpster fire," Karen replied, turning her head to look straight at Wendy like a velociraptor eyeing its prey.

"The inside of the hotel isn't great either and there are a lot of flies in the rooms."

"Ewww. That ain't good," said Karen. "It sounds like the company is sparing no expense with you guys."

"Yeah, it's a bit disappointing. Anyway, I have a question."

"Shoot," said Karen.

"We're all meant to be meeting up tomorrow but are you free tonight?" Tom asked. "The other three aren't exactly party animals and I'm going to struggle to get them to leave the hotel unless I pull the fire alarm or throw them out of their bedroom windows."

Karen paused for a second or two. She hadn't been expecting this but she had no plans for the evening and it would at least get the awkward introductions out of the way sooner rather than later so she gestured to Wendy to invite her along too.

163

"That'll be awesome!" Wendy said excitedly.

"Hey, Tom, how do you feel about my dumbass sister coming down too?"

"Wendy? That'll be great! She does know we're foreigners, doesn't she?"

"Yeah, I told her you're just like Americans but a lot quieter. Like a lite version of a soda so she thinks she'll be able to cope."

"That sounds good," said Tom.

"We'll meet you at the Skyview Ferris wheel at eight and then grab some food somewhere," said Karen.

"Cool! I'll tell the others and some of us will see you at eight!"

Karen looked at Wendy who was now dancing around the room with one of her cats singing a made-up song that seemed to only have one line – 'Karen's gonna get it tonight, oh yes she is, she's gonna get it real good.'

Karen ignored her sister and went upstairs to get ready. This wasn't how she thought her night would pan out when she'd left the office just over an hour ago but she was excited to meet the others – and at least it would be a night away from Wendy's stupid cats.

"Why did you invite me along?" Wendy shouted up the stairs. "You know I have a phobia of foreigners."

"They used to own this country a couple of hundred years ago so just think of them as distant cousins."

"I can do that, but I thought you'd want to go and meet Tom alone."

"If you think I'm going down there to meet these fools on my own you're dead wrong so just get your lazy ass ready."

***

Just over an hour later, the two warring sisters got out of Karen's car in downtown Atlanta and walked along the main road towards the Skyview where Tom and the others were supposed to be waiting, although when Karen and Wendy arrived, they were nowhere to be seen.

"So where are those damned fools at?" Karen asked as they stood waiting and looking around.

"Maybe they have a phobia of being on time," suggested Wendy. "Do you know what they look like?"

"Yeah, Tom and I connected on LinkedIn so I've seen his picture."

"Hey, Karen!"

Karen and Wendy looked round to where the voice had come from and saw two excited people getting out of one of the cars on the Ferris wheel and heading towards them; they were followed by two other people who looked slightly unwell.

"Hey, guys! How are y'all doing tonight?" said Karen warmly as the two groups approached each other.

"We're great! Well, I am and so is Bhavna, but Martin and Stuart didn't like the Ferris wheel," Tom said with a grin as he extended his hand towards her.

"What the hell is that?" Karen asked, pushing Tom's hand away and hugging him instead.

"Woah!" said Tom as they embraced, noticing Wendy had a grin on her face.

"That's how you greet people Southern-style," Karen told him and then laughed at his surprise.

Everyone introduced themselves with hugs apart from Stuart whose face had turned green from a combination of jet lag, the Ferris wheel and Bhavna talking his ears off at 39,000 feet for most of their nine-hour flight. Karen then led them all down a side street towards a restaurant she and Wendy used to go to when they both worked in the downtown area a few years ago.

"What do you think of Atlanta so far?" Wendy asked.

"I feel sick," said Stuart.

"I took the time and trouble to read up on the city and familiarise myself with the layout and the history so there have been no surprises for me," Bhavna added.

"I want to visit the College Football Hall of Fame," said Martin. "I also need to buy my wife a Coca-Cola t-shirt for her birthday."

"Is that her main gift?" Wendy asked.

"No, he bought her an iron before we came away," said Tom, laughing his head off. "How did she take it, Martin?"

"She wasn't impressed but it might grow on her," Martin replied, generating raucous laughter. "Unfortunately, I'm not allowed to spend too much money without telling her what I'm spending it on."

"Why not?" Wendy asked.

"When we got married, she said we should each have a discretionary spend limit each month so we can buy things up to that limit without telling the other one what they are."

"That sounds fun! How much is the limit?" Wendy said with an encouraging smile.

"Her limit is £500."

"That could buy a lot more than an iron."

"That's her limit...mine is £40."

"Oh, man! You should have saved up your allowance for a few months because she's gonna ram that thing right up your ass when you get home," said Karen as her booming laugh filled the night air for six blocks in every direction.

The group reached the restaurant still laughing and were soon seated at a large round table in the window. The place had seen better days but it had been a favourite of Karen's so Tom didn't question it. Also, Stuart had perked up a little and his beard seemed to have come back to life and Tom wondered what the mice had thought of the Ferris wheel. Luckily, this time he was sitting next to Stuart so wouldn't have to see the beard while he ate, although being that close did mean that if there were any small creatures living in it, they might take an interest in Tom's food too.

"Why don't we all tell everybody something random and embarrassing about ourselves," Wendy suggested after they'd all ordered.

"Hell no!" said Karen. "These good people don't want to know that shit about us."

"I don't mind," said Tom. "Although it might be more fun if we told the group something about somebody else."

"Now we're talking," said Karen.

"Oh shit," said Martin, knowing exactly what Tom's story would be about.

"Who agrees?" Wendy asked.

Tom and Karen said 'yes' but everyone else looked down at the table so they went with Wendy's original plan of saying something about themselves.

"That's a bit of a shame," said Tom, seeing the relief on Martin's face. "But never mind. I was once with someone who paid £2,000 for a £1,500 car!"

"Oh crap," said Martin as the table exploded into laughter.

"You've got to tell us who that fool was," Karen said excitedly, already guessing his identity.

"It was me," Martin admitted. "It was years ago and when my cousin told me how much he wanted for his car, it sort of slipped out that I had a bit more saved up than that, so he took it."

"What was the vehicle like?" asked Bhavna. "Were you ultimately pleased with its performance despite the actual price you paid being considerably higher than the price you needed to pay?"

"It was okay."

"He crashed it three times on the first day during a two-mile drive," said Tom.

"Oh my! This is too funny!" said Wendy, sitting next to Martin with tears streaming down her face. "You're a legend, Martin," she said as she gave him a big hug.

"Thanks. At least I don't borrow my neighbour's dog to go to the park and pick up women."

"Who does that?!" Karen screamed.

"Tom does," said Martin. "It doesn't work because any woman who's unlucky enough to be approached by him ends up with shit in her shoes because he doesn't clean up after his dog."

"As I've said before, it's not my dog so technically it's not my shit to clean up."

More laughter erupted as the food arrived and the table then descended into relative quiet. As is usual when groups go out to eat, everyone started looking at everyone else's plates.

"What have you got there, Wendy?" Tom asked.

"It's a vegan-friendly meal of tomatoes, corn and mushrooms," she said proudly.

"I told you Wendy's a vegan and it turns out that she has a phobia of the colour green so she can't eat 90% of the vegetables in the world."

"I get by, sis," said Wendy.

"Only just. There ain't nothing of you. What do you weigh, about 30 pounds?"

"A little more than that," Wendy said indignantly, but with a laugh. "Maybe we should go back to telling each other something about ourselves rather than other people?"

"Okay. Well, I'm 32 and I'm single," said Tom, meeting Karen's eye opposite him and noticing her looking away quickly. "I have been in my current job for four years and outside work, I love travelling and video games. I also watch a lot of sport on TV because I'm too lazy to play."

"But you like walking your neighbour's dog?" Wendy asked.

"Yeah, but the park is literally next door to his house," said Martin. "But that's only to pick up women and it doesn't even work."

"I think we are getting a flavour of Tom now," said Bhavna. "I will go next. I am 29 years old and I am originally from India. I love computer programming and coding and I am a very hard worker."

"What do you do for fun?" Wendy asked.

"As I said, I love computer programming and coding. I find it immensely fulfilling and love to code late into the night. I also have three cats and love spending time with them."

"I have four cats!" exclaimed Wendy. "My girls are wonderful!"

"Except one of them is a boy," Karen corrected her.

"Technically, yes, but he's still a girl to me. Just like that Sadie I met at the phobia workshop. She's a woman that used to be a man. I'm sure it's the same with cats."

"But your cat hasn't had gender realignment surgery," said Karen.

"Well, no. Not yet, but I'm looking into it."

It was the group's turn to laugh at Wendy now as the waiter arrived with dessert menus. Karen turned to take one from him and as she did so, she looked out of the window and saw two police officers escorting a woman to a patrol car that was parked just across the street from the restaurant. That woman was wearing one ugly ass coat, she thought. It reminded her of the one Delores wore to work – in fact, now that she looked, she could see that it was Delores from work.

"Hey, guys, you know I mentioned one of my co-workers always wears a real ugly purple and mustard patterned jacket?"

"Yes," said Tom. "I can't wait to see it on Monday."

"You can see it right now because she's just gone and gotten herself arrested outside."

Everyone at the table, including the waiter, turned to look out of the window. Just across the street was a woman wearing the ugliest jacket they'd ever seen slowly disappearing into the back of a police car.

"I wonder what she got arrested for," said Tom.

"Probably wearing that jacket in public. That'd be a misdemeanour without her having to commit any actual crime," said Karen as her laugh boomed around the restaurant.

"Irma's got a coat like that," said Martin, to howls of laughter from everyone else.

"Her taste in men isn't much better," Tom added.

"Don't be so mean to him," Wendy chided. "Martin, tell us more about yourself."

"I'm married to Irma and we have two boys aged five and three. I do data analysis at work but I love taking pictures of things so I've brought my camera over. I want to go out late at night and take some photos of the empty city streets and the buildings."

"Just be careful, Martin. It can be dangerous in some areas," Wendy warned. "Why not take Tom with you?"

"I don't want to get shot!" Tom protested.

"You probably won't get shot," said Wendy.

"Probably?"

"Well, almost definitely."

"Can you guarantee it?"

"Not totally."

"There you are then. Anyway, Martin has already nearly been killed once today. As we left the hotel, we started to cross the street but he forgot to look the right way and got blasted by an ambulance so he probably won't survive long enough to worry about getting shot later."

"At least he would have been in good hands if he'd been hit by an ambulance," said Stuart.

"You are correct but the American healthcare system is very different from our own and he would have had to pay for his treatment, however minor it may have been," Bhavna added.

Tom, Martin and Stuart looked down at the table to see if there were any bread rolls remaining that they could wedge into Bhavna's mouth to stop her from talking. Luckily for Bhavna, there weren't and the desserts arrived to distract everybody again.

As the group started on their desserts, Martin told them about his love of country music and food before boring them all to death (in Tom's opinion) with tales of his kids. Stuart then took over and gave them all some dull facts about his life before the four from the UK office turned to the two locals.

"So, you all know I'm Karen and I'm the IT Manager..."

"...and single," interrupted a slightly drunk Wendy, who was now on her fourth whiskey.

"As I was trying to say, I've been working for this dumb British company that sells a range of ugly, poor quality, green and brown coats, hats and other shit," she continued to much laughter.

"Go Karen!" said Wendy, almost on the floor now. "But don't ever get me one of those green coats. It would probably explode my head."

"As I was saying, AGAIN, I love nature and walking in the forest. I also used to enjoy the peace and quiet of living alone until my dumbass sister lost her damned job, couldn't pay her rent and had to move in with me."

"I love you, sis," Wendy dribbled into her now empty whiskey glass.

"How about you show me how much you love me by getting yourself a job and moving into a place of your own?"

Wendy was now face down on the table so Karen said she'd have to take her home. Tom and the others were also fading as the time difference was beginning to hit them, so they left the restaurant with Stuart and Martin helping to support Wendy on the way to Karen's car.

"Are we going to meet up tomorrow as well?" Karen asked.

"If that's alright with you, I'd love to," said Tom. "We want to go to see a few of the touristy things in the morning, so could we meet later in the day?"

"That works for me. Wendy won't be awake until noon if she's drunk. How about we meet y'all at 3 o'clock? We could go to Piedmont Park for some fresh air. There's a nice tavern there too so we can eat."

"Sounds perfect," said Tom as they reached Karen's car.

"Right, just let me get this drunken reprobate home and I'll call you tomorrow," said Karen and gave Tom another hug – this one slightly longer and a lot tighter.

"Cool. I'm getting excited already," said Tom.

"I know," said Karen as she pulled away.

The group said goodbye and the four visitors watched Karen drive off with a severely inebriated Wendy waving out of the passenger window and screaming unintelligible things to anyone in earshot. They then turned around and went to find their hotel. It was only just after ten but they were all exhausted and looking forward to a good night's rest – hopefully without too many flies buzzing around them as they slept. Maybe they'd all settle down for the night in Stuart's beard.

Chapter 16

Atlanta, USA

Sunday had always been one of Tom's two favourite days of the week and he never understood why office workers the world over loved Fridays when they were a day of work while Saturdays and Sundays were days of rest and nights of partying. Friday nights were good, obviously, but the day part still sucked as much as any other workday. Weekends were awesome – Saturdays were better, but Sundays were sort of okay as well.

On this particular Sunday, he woke up in a strange bed in a strange place and it took him a second or two to remember where he was. Atlanta. Did he really go out with Karen and her sister last night? It was still a bit of a blur so he'd ask Martin at breakfast in case he'd taken pictures – as long as the dopey bastard had remembered to remove the lens cap first.

Tom showered, got dressed, picked up what he needed for the day and then went to find Martin's room at the other end of the hotel corridor. He banged on the door and when Martin opened it Tom saw that he was just as annoyingly bright-eyed and enthusiastic as he usually was in the mornings.

"Morning!" Martin greeted him cheerily.

"Alright?" Tom mumbled, slightly tired but not too badly hungover.

"Are you going down for breakfast?"

"Yeah...let's get the others. I told Karen we'd meet them at 3 o'clock today so we can go to the aquarium and Coca-Cola first."

"Okay," said Martin. "Where are we going later?"

"Some bar near a place called Piedmont Park. Apparently, it does good food and then we can chill out in the park after."

"Sounds good. Let's grab the others and get some breakfast."

"How do you feel?"

"I'm okay," said Martin. "Although I'm not sure what we ate last night. I was in the toilet a couple of times."

"Really? Me too," Tom admitted.

"Maybe it was just jet lag and excitement," Martin suggested.

The two friends found the stairs and went down one floor to where Stuart and Bhavna had their rooms. Tom knocked on Bhavna's door while Martin knocked on Stuart's which was directly opposite but neither got a reply, so they knocked again. Still no replies.

"They're probably downstairs already," said Tom.

"I hope there's a buffet," Martin added as they went down the remaining stairs to the hotel lobby.

As they walked into the restaurant Tom looked around but could see no sign of Stuart or Bhavna anywhere. Martin headed to the buffet while Tom found a four-top table for them all. As Martin came back with his first plate of food, Tom's phone buzzed and he saw a message from Stuart.

"Hi, guys. I'm not sure what I ate last night but I'm feeling terrible. I think it could be food poisoning. I heard someone else throwing up all night across the corridor – it might be Bhavna. I'm staying in bed today. Stuart."

"Stuart says he's got food poisoning and is staying in bed all day," Tom told Martin. "Bhavna might be ill too."

"Shit. That's not good. What did they eat?"

"Wasn't it some kind of Thai curry?"

"That's it – they both had the same because Stuart complained Bhavna's portion was bigger than his and she laughed at him," Martin remembered.

"Well, if that's what did it, she won't be laughing now. I'll message her."

Tom sent a message to Stuart telling him to look after himself and message him if he needed anything and then sent one to Bhavna before visiting the buffet. As he sat back down, a reply came through from Bhavna.

"Good morning. I am sorry but I am feeling a little poorly today. I believe there may have been some issues with the food I ate last night so I will get some rest here today and try to join you this evening. Warmest regards, Bhavna."

Tom had a mouthful of food so he just held up his phone to show Martin the message. It looked like today would be just like old times now there were only two of them. Good, he thought. Stuart was boring and Bhavna was a pain in the arse – at least Martin was fun. And his accident-prone nature meant there was always a chance he'd fall down a sinkhole or get picked up by a really small tornado and hurled into a trailer park.

As they continued eating, Karen called to check they'd all got back safely and Tom explained that Stuart and Bhavna were ill which meant there'd just be two of them later on.

"What did those two eat last night?" Karen asked.

"They both had Thai curry. Maybe there was something wrong with it; although we both suffered a bit in the night too."

"You did? I'm sorry to hear that. I'm fine but Wendy is still hungover on the couch with two of her cats."

"Are the cats hungover as well?"

"No, they aren't. What kind of a dumb question is that?!" Karen asked. "You Brits have some strange habits if you take your cats out drinking with you; there are laws against that kind of stuff over here."

Martin looked up as he heard Karen's laugh come through Tom's phone and across the table. It was just like being at work and he wondered if he'd win the office sweepstake about the two of them. Stuart was the official adjudicator because Katrina and the rest of the team had said there'd be a conflict of interest if Martin was reporting on what happened and also had money on one of the outcomes. Unfortunately, with Stuart currently confined to his room, Martin would have to let them all know what

179

transpired and was now wondering if he should take some pictures – although that might be seen as a bit creepy.

Tom finished his call with Karen and turned back to Martin, who was now messaging Irma and had received a photo from her of the two boys playing with a hosepipe in the garden. It looked like total carnage with everything covered in water and, while he was sad that he wasn't with them, it looked like a real mess and he knew who'd be in charge of cleaning everything up if he were there.

"What's this?" Martin asked, pointing at a strangely coloured, porridge-like substance on his plate.

"I've no idea," said Tom. "It doesn't look very nice though."

"A woman at the buffet said it was called grits and I should try it because it's a true Southern food. She said I'd love it."

"Do you love it?"

"No, it's disgusting. It's gooey and bland."

"What does it taste like?"

"Disappointment and sadness."

"Maybe we should find her and ask her why she hates you so much."

"I'll just leave it here; maybe they can use it to fill in those cracks in the wall behind you before they paint over them."

"Let's make our escape and get started," said Tom. "We'll head over to the aquarium and then the Coca-Cola Museum next door."

"What about the College Football Hall of Fame?"

"Maybe next weekend? We've got two days so we could do that on one of them and then go to Stone Mountain on the other. It's a big old rock in the middle of nowhere with a cable car that takes you to the top."

"That sounds like a plan," Martin agreed as they left the restaurant. "I'll go up and get my camera then meet you here in a few minutes," he said as he disappeared up the stairs, glad that Tom would be handling their entertainment arrangements.

A few minutes later, they were both outside in the mid-morning sunshine, heading over to the far side of Centennial Park to see the wonders of the aquatic world at the Georgia Aquarium and then buy Irma a t-shirt with the name of her favourite fizzy drink on. It wasn't the most inspiring of birthday presents, Tom thought, but this was Captain Dumbfuck and at least it was better than the iron he'd already bought her. Marginally.

"Martin, have you thought about how thrilled Irma is going to be when she uses her new iron on her new Coca-Cola t-shirt?" Tom asked, wondering to himself if Martin would notice his sarcasm.

"No, I hadn't thought of that. It's a good point though."

"She'll be ecstatic seeing both of her birthday presents working in harmony with one another."

"Yeah, she will," Martin said enthusiastically.

"I wouldn't be surprised if there's an addition to the family nine months after you get home."

"Really? Do you think she'll be that pleased? I hadn't thought about that. Maybe I'll get her a keyring instead."

"Why? Don't you want any more mini versions of you in the world?"

"Not really," said Martin. "Three of us is probably enough."

Tom started to laugh as they walked past the Fountain of Rings where a dozen or so young children were running in and out of the water.

"If the boys were here now, Max would probably be waterboarding Ben in those fountains," Martin said grimly as they walked past and headed across the green towards the aquarium.

"From what you say they can be a bit of a handful."

"Ben's okay; it's Max. He's mad."

"I'm trying to think of a nickname for him now," said Tom.

"Yeah, I know. We call him that. There's something not quite right about his temperament and I think we might need to seek professional help."

"What, like a hitman?"

"No! A child psychologist. Although your idea might be cheaper in the long run because Irma thinks it will take

182

months of work. And of course, she won't let one boy do anything without the other one doing it too."

"I thought that was just clothes?" Tom queried.

"No, it's everything. If one of them has a shit the other one gets taken up to have one as well."

"That's a bit weird," said Tom.

"Yeah...I'm worried that if we take Max and get him sorted out, Irma will insist on taking Ben too and we'll mess him up."

"That might happen. Have you thought about eBay?"

"To find a child psychologist? I don't think you can buy one of those on there."

"No, to sell Max. I think they have a specific category for small pets and unwanted family members. Normally it's just for grandparents who have outlived their usefulness and don't have any more stories about the war to bore people with, but you might be able to put Max on there."

"I'll have a look," said Martin. "But I'm not sure how Irma would react. She thinks more of the boys than she does of me."

"That's probably natural."

"For all women – or just for the one I'm with?" Martin asked, now looking directly at Tom.

"Oh look, we're here," said Tom brightly as he joined the queue to buy tickets from the machine outside the main building.

After purchasing their tickets, they joined the queue for the entrance to the aquarium and what Tom was convinced would be the highlight of his trip to Atlanta. Martin enjoyed anything from the natural world and while he wasn't the world's biggest fan of animal captivity, he was happy to be out and about doing something different. Also, he could buy some soft toys for the boys while he was there.

***

Just over 12 miles north of the Georgia Aquarium in a small, three-bedroomed house belonging to her sister, Wendy was gradually regaining consciousness face-down on Karen's couch with one of her cats licking her ear. She struggled to open her eyes, but she eventually did and was greeted with a small furry face less than an inch from her nose, followed by another one and then a third. The final cat then jumped up on her legs and startled her.

"Ouch! Leave me alone, girls."

"They've been bothering me all morning, sleepy-head," said Karen from the chair opposite.

"What time is it? Why am I down here?"

"It's just after eleven and your drunk ass passed out on my couch last night,"

"Did I have a good time?"

"Hell yeah…certainly if you judge it by the number of empty whiskey glasses in front of you on the table."

"Did I do anything stupid?"

Karen looked at her and said nothing but Wendy knew herself well enough to know she'd probably done something and Karen was trying to protect her with her silence.

"What did I do?" Wendy asked.

"Well, first you hugged one of those Brits that you're supposed to have a phobia about, then you got drunk and passed out on the table and told everyone I was single."

"Maybe my phobia has gone! That's a good thing, right?"

"That's if it was even there in the first damned place. I'm thinking of feeding you some green beans later to find out if that phobia is real too," Karen said, only half joking.

"They're all real. What else did I do? Why have I only got one shoe on?"

"We pulled up at a stop light and you saw a guy you liked the look of coming out of a liquor store," said Karen. "You shouted some unintelligible shit about being Cinderella and threw your shoe at him; you told him if he could find you and bring your shoe back then you'd marry his ass."

"That doesn't sound like me," said Wendy.

"You sure as hell did it though."

"What did he say?"

"He said you were a drunk, crazy bitch who should go home and sleep it off."

"That part sounds like me," Wendy admitted.

"Then he threw your shoe at the car as we drove off and it hit my back window."

"He must have had a good aim. Good for him, sis!"

Karen got up to make some coffee while Wendy sat up on the couch and started to talk to her cats. Coffee would be welcome and then a shower.

"Here's your coffee," said Karen, handing her a hot drink in a green mug.

"It's green. You know I have a phobia about the colour green."

"Yeah, right. I also know you have a phobia of foreigners but you had a good time last night, so just drink it. You need to wake yourself up because we're going out this afternoon."

"Where are we going?"

"We're meeting the others for a late lunch in a bar near Piedmont Park."

"I'm not sure if I can make that," said Wendy. "I'm meant to be seeing Sadie and Dave from the phobia workshop later."

"Just bring them along; unless they've got phobias of meeting people's sisters?"

"Dave doesn't get on well with water," said Wendy.

"We won't push him in the lake then."

"I'm not sure I can just change the plans at short notice."

"Sure, you can. Just tell them to meet us at that bar outside Piedmont Park at three o'clock. Two of the Brits won't be coming because they've got some kind of food poisoning shit going on today. They've just got weak ass stomachs if you ask me."

"Which two are coming?" Wendy asked with a slight smile. "Will Tom be there?"

"Yes, he will. Martin will be there too but the others are sick."

"Good," said Wendy as she got up and went upstairs to get dressed and message Sadie and Dave with details of the new plan.

Chapter 17

Atlanta, USA

Martin left Georgia Aquarium laden down with soft toys and t-shirts for his two boys. His camera was also given a good workout and, apart from a small number of shots of the inside of the lens cap that should have been pictures of African Penguins, he was happy with how his first morning in Atlanta had gone. Tom was also happy because he'd seen some dolphins and some turtles and had got talking to an attractive young woman in the gift shop who'd given him her number.

"What did you think?" Tom asked Martin as they walked the short distance across Pemberton Place to their next destination.

"It was brilliant; I enjoyed it a lot more than I thought I would. I like anything to do with animals and fish. Not birds though – they're a bit annoying."

"I meant Lucille in the gift shop."

"She sounds like the type of woman who'd leave you with 400 children and a crop in the field," Martin laughed.

"What do you mean?"

"You know the old song where everyone thought the words were 400 children instead of four hungry children?"

"I have no idea, Martin. You probably need to listen to some more modern music."

"I like what I like."

"What do you want to know about Lucille?" Tom asked.

"She looked okay. Quite tall though."

"She gave me her number," said Tom, showing Martin his phone.

Martin stopped in mid-stride and took the phone. He looked at the screen, looked at it for a second and then gave it back to Tom with a broad grin.

"What's going on?" Tom asked him.

"Oh, mate! This is a classic. I can't wait to tell Karen and Wendy about this later," Martin continued. "Can you see the area code 555?"

"Yes," said Tom, looking at his phone but still not seeing what Martin saw.

"Do you ever pay attention to American TV programmes or films?"

"Not really," said Tom. "I don't pay attention to many things to be honest."

"Well, if you did, you'd see they always give out numbers with 555 in them. It's to stop people calling them in real life."

"Oh," Tom said disappointedly.

"And to protect innocent American women from horny British visitors."

"At least I didn't take a load of photos with the lens cap on."

"Yeah...I thought I might have done that. One good thing has come out of this though."

"What's that?" Tom asked suspiciously as they entered the Coca-Cola Museum.

"The next time you talk to a random woman and she gives you a number with '555' in it you'll know she's not interested immediately rather than having to wait until you call her and get the 'out of service' tone."

"Good point. It'll save a bit of time so I should consider that a win."

Martin rolled his eyes and walked off wondering which one of them was more worthy of the name 'Captain Dumbfuck'. He'd always known it was him, but sometimes Tom seemed to be just as deserving.

***

Karen and Wendy were getting ready for their afternoon out and were arguing about bathroom usage, who should feed the cats and which one of them was going to drive when Wendy's phone buzzed. It was a message from Sadie confirming that she and Dave would meet them at the bar later and that they were looking forward to meeting Karen and the two English guys.

The message went on to say that neither of them had ever met anyone from England before and that Dave wanted to know if they spoke English. Wendy messaged back that they did and that they were good guys so it should be a fun afternoon. She then read the message again.

"Hey, sis, look at this," said Wendy, showing Karen her phone.

"What's that?" Karen asked.

"It's this message from Sadie. She says that she will be there with Dave at three o'clock today."

"That's good, isn't it?"

"I guess. But she's answering for Dave when he's not even there."

"Maybe she's with him and they're coming together."

"But…" Wendy began.

"Maybe they've hooked up," Karen suggested, catching the look of disappointment on Wendy's face as she turned away and headed into the bathroom.

"It's possible, I guess. They do go well together – almost as well as a certain sister of mine and a certain British guy."

"What are you talking about?!" Karen shouted from the bathroom.

"I saw the way he kept looking at you."

"He looks at everyone like that. He looked at the server like that, the hostess and a couple of women on the table next to us. Hell, he'd probably even look at one of your damned cats like that."

Karen's laughter carried across the hallway as she walked back to her bedroom to finish getting ready, leaving Wendy to wonder what whoever was controlling her romantic life had in store for her now that Dave was probably with Sadie. Hopefully, there would be some

191

new weirdos for her to talk to at the next phobia work-shop. Or she could just get there before Sadie and shut all the doors so she couldn't get in.

***

"That was good," said Martin. "And I got Irma a t-shirt for her birthday."

"Did you get the right size?" Tom asked as they waited to be served in the gift shop.

"Yeah...I think so. Why?"

"Well, Irma's got big boobs. Is that t-shirt going to hold them in?"

"Why do you know so much about my wife's boobs?" Martin asked.

"It's impossible not to notice them."

"True. She's certainly well-endowed. Maybe I'll get the next size up."

"Don't you know what size your own wife takes in clothing?"

"No. That's why I usually buy her household appli-ances. I got her a microwave for Christmas."

"What did she say?" Tom asked, expecting something quite insulting.

"Nothing."

"Nothing?"

"Yeah...she just threw the box at me."

"Why don't you buy her some jewellery or something personal for her to cherish?"

"She spends most of her time doing stuff around the house and looking after the kids and says she never wants anything fancy," Martin explained.

"Which is exactly why you should buy her something nice...to show her that you see her as more than a wife and mother. Let's speak to Karen and find out if there's a nice jewellery shop locally so you can surprise Irma when you get back."

"That's a good idea. As long as she doesn't expect the same next year; I don't want to set a precedent."

They left the museum and took a long walk around Centennial Park on the way back to their hotel. Martin took a few pictures of the fountains, the College Football Hall of Fame and the Ferris wheel from a distance before crossing over to the CNN building. Just as he stepped into the road, he heard some people shouting. Martin spun round to see two burly young men on cycles heading straight for him just as he felt a hand grab his arm and pull him towards the kerb.

"You're going to get yourself killed if you don't look the right way," said Tom. "That's twice you've nearly been killed and we've only been here a day."

"Yeah...the cyclists seem a bit militant over here," Martin said sheepishly.

"If you want to get yourself killed, at least wait until we've sorted this data breach out."

"Is that the only reason?" Martin asked.

"It's the main reason. Also, I don't want to have to tell Irma that you got killed by a bloke on a bike. Getting shot would be cool but being hit by a bike is a bit lame."

"You're right," Martin reluctantly agreed.

"It's not the most glorious of deaths, is it? Although I could invent something a bit more heroic if you wanted."

"You're loving this aren't you?"

"I just don't want to have to go to your house and tell Irma that you got hit by a toddler on a tricycle and died."

"You just want to go round and stare at her boobs."

"I hadn't thought of that," said Tom. "Maybe I should stop saving your life so it will give me an excuse to go and see her. For the moment, though, let's just go back to the hotel so you can dump your stuff and then we'll get an Uber to the bar and meet the others. Karen just sent me the details."

***

The sun was high in the sky and the temperature was hotter than either Tom or Martin had expected as their Uber pulled up outside the bar Karen had suggested. As they got out, they both immediately made for the shade of some nearby trees.

"This is seriously warm," said Tom, not necessarily to Martin but he answered anyway.

"Yeah...I had a message from Irma a few minutes ago. She says it's raining at home."

"That's good," said Tom. "I hate it when I go on holiday and the weather at home is nice. You get everyone saying, 'the weather was great here; you should have stayed at home' even though I've been sightseeing all day and partying all night while they've been chained to their desks."

"That's what you said to me when I came back from Florida," Martin pointed out.

"Did I?"

"Yeah...you said you'd had hot sunny weather all day, every day and I'd have been better off not going to Orlando."

"Was I right?"

"Yeah," said Martin. "I didn't really enjoy it with Irma's family but that's not the point; the weather was good."

"But the holiday was crap."

"A bit."

"I still think it's you. You've always been rubbish at being on holiday."

"Hey, y'all!" came a loud American voice from behind them.

"Hi, Karen! Hi, Wendy! How are you guys coping with the heat today?" said Tom, turning to face the two women who were walking towards them.

"Hi, girls," said Martin as they all embraced.

"I've heard it's raining in England," Tom told them.

"No shit! It's always raining over there," said Karen, her laugh not seeming quite as loud now they were outside.

"We had a hot summer in 1976," Tom offered.

"And you're all still talking about that a hundred years later?"

"Yeah," said Tom and Martin in unison, to more laughter from the Americans.

Looking at the four of them as they walked to the bar, anyone passing would have thought they were two couples who had been friends for years. The laughter and the smiles appeared so easily whenever one of them said anything and there were now playful arm punches and slaps between one of the 'couples' too.

"What happened to Stuart and Bhavna?" Karen asked as they entered the bar.

"They both seem to have food poisoning," Tom replied.

"Are you sure they ain't hooking up?" Karen asked wickedly.

"I hadn't thought of that," said Tom. "What about you, Martin?"

"I doubt it; Bhavna is hard work and Stuart isn't much fun. They just seem to bicker all the time."

"Well, that's it then. They're just like an old married couple," said Wendy. "I bet they're at it right now," she added to a combination of laughter and disgust from the rest of the group.

"Ewww," said Tom. "Can you imagine that beard?"

"Oh, shut up!" said Karen. "I'm going to eat soon; I don't want to be thinking about that damned thing going anywhere near anyone."

More laughter filled the bar as the hostess escorted them to their table.

"I'm sorry, but we'll need a bigger table," said Wendy. "We have two more coming soon."

"Two more?" Tom asked as they were escorted to another part of the bar.

"Yes, I met a couple of really cool people at my phobia workshop last week so I invited them along. You'll love them!"

"Cool. The more the merrier!"

As the hostess showed them to a more suitable table, Dave and Sadie were making their way through Piedmont Park. They had spent the night together, but not in the traditional way. They had both been arrested in separate locations and had been taken to the same police station downtown where they'd both been held overnight. When Sadie had been released this morning, she'd seen Dave standing outside and had gone over to him.

"Hey, Dave! It's so great to see you! What were you in for?" she asked.

"Hi, Sadie! Just the usual drunk and disorderly conduct. No big deal. What about you?"

"I got caught in the parking lot near the stadium. There's a new bunch of homeless guys living under the bridge so I thought I'd make their Friday night for them."

"And you got arrested?"

"Yeah, it's a bummer but they're super friendly at this station, aren't they? Michael and Lauren are both quite cool."

"You know them by name?" Dave asked.

"I've been here a lot," Sadie admitted. "They even know how I like my coffee."

"I guess that's one benefit of being a regular. I'm not usually downtown on Saturday nights; I normally only get brought here on Sundays."

"Maybe we'll see each other tonight then?" Sadie began to laugh but then suddenly stopped as her attention was caught by someone else coming out of the police station.

"What is it?" Dave asked.

"Did you see that woman's coat? That's the most disgusting thing I've ever seen," said Sadie.

"That purple and mustard patterned one over there. I wish I hadn't seen that; I'm still hungover and I think I'm going to be sick now."

"Do you think she got arrested for wearing it?" Sadie asked.

"No. If she had, they would have kept it as evidence and destroyed it."

They were both laughing and about to go off their separate ways when Wendy's message had come through.

Sadie had responded on behalf of them both and Dave had invited her back to the house he shared with his parents to hang out before meeting up with the others.

"I live quite close to that bar. We could both go back to my basement and you could take a shower and get freshened up there."

"You're inviting me back to your basement? That sounds a bit creepy," Sadie said with a grin.

"I know," said Dave. "It sounded alright in my head though."

"It's okay. I've got some clothes in my bag; it will be quicker than going back to where I've been staying this week."

They took a bus to Midtown where Dave's parents lived and walked the rest of the way swapping stories of their various arrests, the standard of coffee in the different police stations they'd been taken to and the level of fines they'd each had to pay. Once they'd reached Dave's basement, showered and made themselves presentable, these two people who'd only met a few days earlier started to walk through Piedmont Park towards a bar to meet up with someone else they'd only known for a few days and three random people they'd hadn't yet met – two of whom were British. What a strange world, Sadie thought, as she stood at the entrance to the bar and waited for Dave to open the door for her.

Chapter 18

Atlanta, USA

Dave opened the door to let Sadie into the bar and they made themselves known to the hostess. They could hear Wendy and the others long before they saw them and Wendy immediately got up and greeted them both like old friends.

"Hey! How are you guys?!" she immediately asked them both.

"I'm good thanks, but I can't speak for Sadie," said Dave.

"I'm good too!" said Sadie. "We were both in the same jail last night. What a coincidence!"

"That's so cool!" said Wendy, slightly relieved that Sadie and Dave weren't properly together, but still upset at the level of comfort they already seemed to have with one another.

Undeterred, Wendy introduced them both to the rest of the group.

"That's my big sister Karen, who suggested I come and stay with her."

"What are you talking about?" Karen asked a split second ahead of her booming laugh. "I never invited you, Wendy; you invited yourself. And you brought a houseful of stupid cats with you."

"Anyway...sitting suspiciously close to my wonderful sister Karen is Tom from England and this is Martin who works with Tom and they've also been friends since kindergarten. Do you guys have kindergarten over there?"

"Yes, but we call it infant school," said Tom as he got up to shake hands with the newcomers. "And I didn't know Martin then or I would have flushed his head down the toilet every day."

Dave and Sadie introduced themselves and sat down in the booth with the others. Wendy was happy that Dave sat down beside her and she was now in between two men and opposite her sister.

"So, tell us about your jail time last night," said Karen.

"I got arrested for being a bit too drunk, " Dave said, laughing. "I think I should get some kind of loyalty card from the Atlanta Police so every time I get arrested, I get a stamp on it."

"What would happen after you got arrested ten times?" Tom asked.

"I haven't thought that all the way through yet; maybe I could get a free go in the electric chair? At a low voltage of course. I don't like too much pain."

As everybody laughed, Tom looked at Dave and saw what he thought was a typical American redneck – a baseball cap, faded jeans, a white t-shirt and a few days of beard growth. He also got drunk and arrested a lot. He decided he liked him and then looked across at Sadie, who used to be a truck driver called Steve in a former life, according to Wendy. She kept looking at Dave and laughing at his comments so she probably liked him too – but in a different way. They were probably at it, he thought. Or soon would be.

"I got arrested down behind the stadium giving some much-needed comfort to some of Atlanta's homeless men," Sadie explained.

"Oh my!" said Tom, shocked at this admission. "That doesn't sound right."

"I know!" said Sadie, completely missing Tom's meaning. "I offered the policemen something special if they'd let me go but they wouldn't go for it. Boring cops."

"Maybe they just want to protect and serve?" Karen suggested.

"Maybe," said Sadie. "It's still a bummer though and I had to pay another fine."

A goth waitress came over to take their drink orders while they looked at the menus. She was young, had dyed black hair and had a personality that sparkled like a piece of damp cardboard.

"So how are you two liking Atlanta so far?" Sadie asked Martin and Tom.

"It's cool," Martin replied. "There are four of us here but the others got food poisoning last night so they're recovering in the hotel. I'm enjoying it so far, although we have to work tomorrow so it'll be a bit less fun then.

"Me too," added Tom. "I just love the place and the people I've met so far. It's such a vibrant city and there's so much to see and do."

"It is pretty cool here," Dave agreed.

"We went to the aquarium and the Coca-Cola Museum earlier and Martin got his wife a t-shirt for her birthday."

"A t-shirt?" Dave asked. "Is that all?"

Tom, Karen and Wendy began to laugh as they knew what was coming next.

"I bought her an iron before I came over," Martin said quietly, expecting the worst and getting it.

"An iron! That's terrible!" said Dave, although hardly anyone heard him over the laughter and the arrival of the waitress with their drinks.

"I'll probably have to get her something else as well," Martin admitted.

"You think?!" said Dave.

"That's if he makes it home," said Tom. "He keeps forgetting to look the right way when we cross the road and has nearly been wiped out twice since last night."

"That's so funny!" said Sadie. "Has anyone else ever done something really dumb that made their partner mad?"

"Well," Dave began. "I was married once. My wife was putting on a dress she hadn't worn for a few months and asked me if it still fitted her properly."

"You didn't say 'no' did you?" Karen asked, already beginning to sense how this was going to end.

"No of course not – I'm not that dumb. But I did hesitate a bit."

"Uh-oh," said Karen.

"It was only for a fraction of a second!"

"That'll do it. What happened?"

"She went apeshit and threw her shoes at me. One of her heels caught me in the eye and it started bleeding so we had to call 911," said Dave, beginning to laugh.

"You got off easy," said Tom. "My old boss did that once. His wife got angry and he told her to calm down."

"Big mistake," Karen and Wendy said together.

"They never did find all of his body parts."

"That serves him right if you ask me," Karen said, turning towards him and realising their faces were now only inches apart.

The waitress returned with their food order and the noise level began to reduce as they started to eat – much to the relief of everyone else in the bar.

"Martin's worried about getting shot while we're over here," said Tom, who didn't like awkward silences and was always ready to embarrass Martin if he could.

"No way," said Dave. "You should be fine until June 1st."

"What happens then?" Martin asked, now getting slightly worried.

"That's shooting season. All Brits and Europeans become fair game."

"Do they?"

"Sure. We give y'all special t-shirts to wear with archery targets on them to make it easier for us to spot you. And for scoring purposes."

"Scoring?"

"Yeah. We get ten points for the heart, 9 points for a vital organ and so on."

"Shit," said Martin, looking down at the steak he'd ordered. "We'd better get this work finished soon."

As he looked back up, he was just in time to see five faces exploding with laughter at him and he realised he'd been set up. Standing right behind them was their waitress who was beginning to regret coming to work today.

"What about getting run over by a bike?" Tom asked. "Martin nearly got hit by two cyclists this morning outside the CNN building."

"Did he?" Wendy asked. "You poor thing," she said to Martin and briefly squeezed his knee under the table.

"At least he would have made the news. If something happened outside their front door, they'd probably run the story all day," said Dave. "Especially if he lost a leg or an arm."

"I once saw a guy with one leg in a bicycle store," said Sadie.

"Was he buying a bike?" Tom asked. "Surely he'd just ride around in circles?"

205

"I don't know; I was in there trying to pick up some paying clients. The homeless guys are very grateful but they don't have any money. I need to get some paying clients soon and make some money or I'll be couch-surfing forever."

"Or you could get a partner?" Dave suggested.

"Oh, I had a boyfriend for a while but that ended a few weeks back."

"What happened?"

"I dumped him when he told me he had a phobia of opening doors too. We can't both have the same phobia or we'd never be able to go anywhere. Not anywhere that had a door anyway."

"Hey, Wendy, what happened to that guy you were dating a few months ago? Wasn't he a police detective?" Karen asked.

"Schrödinger? He wasn't talkative enough. I like a guy who talks a lot but he was almost monosyllabic and hardly spoke at all unless it was about work so I ended it."

"What did he say?" Tom asked.

"Nothing."

"Nothing at all?"

"Nope. He just walked out the door. He never was a big talker."

"Did he have a first name?"

"I found out near the end that it was Pete. I only knew his surname for most of the relationship."

"How did you know his last name was Schrödinger?" Martin asked.

"I saw it on the citation he gave me when he stopped me for jay-walking while intoxicated."

"She dated him for two months and never knew his first name!" said Karen. "That's typical Wendy," she added as she began to laugh again.

"He wasn't a detective at the time. He was just a regular cop but he was so nice to me that I asked him out."

"Did he say anything?" Tom asked, to more laughter from Karen.

"Not at the time, but he did call me later that day and we went out a few times."

"That's nice," said Sadie.

"It was cool for a couple of months but then he got promoted to detective and became even more serious so I dumped him. I don't have anything against cops, but if I dated another one I'd want someone more talkative."

"Maybe you should knock off a bank," Tom suggested. "you'd meet a load of cops then."

"That would work."

"Good grief," mumbled the waitress under her breath as she put some more napkins on their table and went back to the kitchen.

***

Less than a mile away from where this unlikely group of new friends were enjoying their late afternoon lunch, Norman Henry Normanson was enjoying his afternoon coffee. It was a ritual he had been following for the last few weeks because it helped keep his bowels regular and today's coffee was just as welcome as every other cup he'd had.

Norman was sitting in the same chair he always sat in and was watching the same channel on TV that he always watched. The birds were singing in the garden outside the open window to his left and everything was normal. He'd shortly be going out for his late afternoon walk and then he'd come back, have a late dinner and settle down in front of the TV for the rest of the evening.

He walked around Piedmont Park most days because he loved to watch people enjoying themselves in the warm sunshine. On cooler days, he'd sometimes walk along the Beltline, although it had a lack of benches to sit on and fewer trees to take shade beneath so that was a walk he only took when he wanted a change of scenery. He had already decided that it would be Piedmont Park today.

Norman thought about the calm, smooth routine his life had recently settled into. He got up each morning, enjoyed a light breakfast, watched some TV before lunch and then watched some more in the afternoon before going for his walk. Some people would call it dull but he enjoyed it and, as a man of advanced years, it brought him peace and contentment. This evening, however, Norman's life was about to get a whole lot more exciting.

It was also going to end.

***

"How's it going at table six this afternoon, Becci?" asked the duty manager.

"It's okay, I guess. They're a bit loud though and they just laugh all the time. It's really pissing me off."

"You don't like people laughing?"

"I'm a goth."

"I see. Are they celebrating something?"

"Not that I can tell," said Becci. "Unless they're celebrating being idiots. From what I can tell there are two arguing sisters – one of whom has a bunch of cats that the other one doesn't like, a transgender hooker, a drunken jailbird and a couple of guys from Britain."

"Two British guys? That sucks. Make sure you don't give them the check."

"Why?"

"Because they don't have the same tipping culture in the UK so you won't make much if they pay it. Give it to the two warring sisters – hopefully, they'll fight so much over who's paying that they'll tip you twice."

Becci took the bill and the credit card machine over to table six and checked once again that everything had been alright with their meals. As she reached the table, she caught the tail end of what seemed to be a horrific story that she would forever remember as 'grand theft baby'. What did people in Britain get up to in their spare time?!

"You got banned from all of the grocery stores across the whole country?" Sadie asked.

"Yes!" said Tom, looking pleased with himself. "Although you have to understand that it was only from one chain of stores. We do have several others so I'm not going to starve."

"That's good to know. What did you do? Was it something gross involving fresh produce?"

"No, nothing like that."

"That's a shame," said Dave, provoking much laughter from the table and increasing levels of concern from Becci as she stood there not wanting to listen any further but unable to tear herself away.

"Well, you know how you sometimes grab something out of a random person's trolley and put it in somebody else's trolley for a laugh…" Tom began.

"No," said the whole table in unison.

"Oh, you must have done it! You can then imagine the other person getting home with a frozen turkey that they didn't think they wanted."

"I haven't," said Dave. "And I've done some pretty messed up stuff in my time."

"Me neither," said Sadie.

"What about you, Wendy?" Karen asked.

"I don't think so...but I don't want to confirm or deny anything at this stage. Tom, by 'trolley' do you mean shopping cart?"

"Yes, I do," said Tom. "Anyway, I was on a dare from somebody who gave me ten seconds to grab something from the trolley of a woman in a blue dress who had just passed us and put it in someone else's trolley."

"Did you do it?" Dave asked.

"I had to because it was a dare, but she'd only just started shopping so there wasn't much in her trolley and I panicked and grabbed the first thing I could."

"What was it?" Karen asked as the eyes of the Americans were all on Tom, including Becci's.

"It was a baby. It was sitting in the little trolley seat so I just picked it up and put it in another woman's trolley."

"What??!!"

An explosion of laughter from the people seated around the table reverberated around the bar while Becci the goth waitress stood frozen to the spot in horror – as if she had stared at Medusa's face for slightly longer than the recommended time limit.

"I made sure I put it in the trolley of another woman rather than some weird old man," Tom added, trying to justify his actions.

"What happened next?" Wendy asked.

"A security guard was called and he showed us to the door. I'm not allowed to shop there ever again," said Tom dejectedly. "It's a shame because it's only a couple of minutes from my house."

"What about the woman with the baby?" Karen asked.

"Oh, she's still allowed to shop in there. I often see her while I'm walking past."

"Does she recognise you?"

"I don't know...but she runs off every time she sees me so it's possible."

"I don't blame her," said Wendy.

"I blame the person who dared me," said Tom. "It's probably more his fault than mine."

"Who was it?" Karen asked.

Tom went quiet and looked at the person directly opposite him, who had remained quiet during the telling of this whole story. He could also see the waitress hadn't left as she clearly wanted to know who'd set him up too.

"It's not my fault," said Martin. "There was another woman wearing a blue dress who had loads of stuff in her trolley. She wouldn't have missed a tin of soup. If you'd have done it properly, we wouldn't have both been banned."

"Have you been banned too?" Karen asked in mid-laugh.

"Yes. They have a superstore close to where I live but they have my picture on the door to let the staff know I'm not allowed in."

As the idiots at table six began to laugh at each other once again, Becci went back to her station and told her duty manager she was traumatised and wanted to lie down. The duty manager went over to take the payment and purposely looked back and forth between the two sisters as the group discussed their options.

Eventually, the older of the two women pulled out her credit card and muttered something that sounded like 'it's about time you got yourself a damned job' to the woman opposite her. Once the transaction was complete and they began to leave, the duty manager saw they'd left a healthy tip. That should make Becci smile, he thought. Although knowing her as he did, it probably wouldn't.

Chapter 19

Atlanta, USA

Piedmont Park has been enjoyed by the good people of Atlanta and its visitors since 1887. Situated just over a mile north-east of the downtown area, it was originally opened to host two major expositions, housed the first professional baseball team in the city and also served as a major athletic centre. Over the years, it had been expanded and improved and was now a popular choice for both locals and visitors to relax in. It had also become Norman Henry Normanson's favourite place to walk before his evening meal each day.

Whenever he chose Piedmont Park for his walk, he would walk up the street, turn left at the high school, then turn right, cross over the main road and he was there. He loved the green space, the lake and the trees; seeing young families playing and cycling gave him pleasure as he reminisced on his own life, his youth, the choices he'd made and the chances he'd taken. They had all led him to this point – his final day on Earth.

Norman reached the park and began to walk towards Lake Clara Meer – his favourite spot in the whole of Atlanta. The park wasn't as busy as usual but as he continued his slow walk around the lake, he could hear the sound of a group of high-spirited young people. He paused briefly, took off his hat for a second or two to mop his brow and looked over to his left. He saw what looked like five – no, it was six – people sitting on the grass talking and laughing. They were having a good time but it sounded like they'd been in a bar all afternoon.

As a reformed alcoholic, Norman had not had a drink for over 20 years. He'd been tempted a few times but had never succumbed. He wasn't anti-alcohol and could understand why people enjoyed it, but it wasn't something he wanted or needed in his life. Besides, some people made complete fools of themselves after too much alcohol and he'd seen enough drink-fuelled fights in his younger days to last a lifetime. To be fair, Norman had started most of them, but he still counted them as fights he'd seen.

The six young people Norman had briefly studied began to fade from his mind as he walked around the lake to look for a bench to rest on. At his age he was no longer young and sprightly and, although getting old was bad, the alternative was worse. He envied the young people with their whole lives ahead of them and that group of six people he'd just seen were certainly living their lives to the full. Norman approved of this. But did they have to be quite so loud about it?

The bench that appeared a short way ahead of him was a very welcome sight and he sat down to survey the scene. Norman sat for longer than he normally did and continued to look back on his life. Maybe it was the group of young people he'd just seen, but he suddenly missed his youth and would give anything to be back in his 20s or 30s again – but with all of the opportunities today's young people had. He would certainly want to have a lot more sex than he'd had the first time around.

After a few more minutes of reverie, Norman got up and made his way back to the house he lived in. The sun would later set on both Atlanta and on his own life – although at this precise moment, he was only expecting one of those two things to happen. He turned to look back at the park for what would prove to be his final time and then headed home.

***

"Did you see that old guy looking at us?" Sadie asked the group as they sat in the middle of the park.

"No," said Tom. "Which old guy?"

"Just some random dude walking past. He stopped and looked at us for a few minutes and then walked off," said Wendy. "He had a small head."

"Did he have a small body to match?"

"Not especially. He was kind of average build, quite tall but with a small head. He was wearing a cap that looked way too big for him."

"How do you know he had a small head?" Tom asked.

"He took his cap off for a second and I saw his head. It just seemed smaller than normal."

"I didn't see him. Was he looking at all of us?"

"I think so. He just looked at us and then moved on."

"Perhaps he was just looking at Karen," Wendy suggested. "You've got some competition now Tom!"

"What the hell do you mean?!" Karen asked her.

"Oh, come on sis! I'm sure you only caused that problem at work so you could get Tom over here," she laughed, taking another drink from her water bottle that Karen was beginning to suspect didn't have water in it.

"Just shut your mouth or you and your stupid cats can move out," Karen said forcefully. "You could move in with that creepy old guy who's just walked past; although I wouldn't wish that on anyone," she said, laughing as she did so.

"I was just saying, that's all."

"Maybe you should wait until you've got something important to say like you've got yourself a job and you're moving out."

"What job are you looking for?" Sadie asked.

"She used to be a telephone operator at one of the museums here but her phobia of speaking to strangers on the phone got her fired," Karen told them.

"I need something more exciting," said Wendy. "But I don't know what."

"Maybe we could think of something for you. What do you like doing?" Sadie asked.

"She likes being a pain in the ass, eating my food, pointing at shit, telling people how to live their lives and having her head up in the clouds the whole time. What kind of job fits that particular set of qualifications?"

"If she likes pointing at things, she could be a weather presenter on TV," Martin suggested. "All they do is stand there and point at stuff. It's probably quite easy over here where it's sunny and warm most of the time. She could also be in Marketing as those people have always got their heads up in the clouds."

"What about a job for someone who's got their head up their ass the whole time?" Wendy asked, laughing and looking at her sister. "Maybe Karen could be a courtroom judge because she likes bossing people about."

"You're such a disappointment," said Karen. "Come on, let's go for a walk. I'm seizing up sitting here."

"I'd like to take some pictures of the park and the skyline as the sun goes down," Martin said.

"Well, don't walk too far because there's a road that goes through the park up there. Tom says you keep getting hit by trucks and bikes."

"I don't keep getting hit. I keep nearly getting hit. There's a big difference."

Everyone got up and gathered their belongings so Karen could show them around the park. As a nature lover, she enjoyed nothing more than being outside amongst the trees, lakes and open spaces. It was normally peaceful, but today she had these fools with her so she wasn't sure if she'd enjoy it as much, although she could always push them into the lake if they became too annoying.

Making their way around the park was slow because Martin kept stopping to take pictures. He took pictures of the lake, the skyline and the group of them; he also managed a few shots of the inside of his lens cap, much to everyone's hilarity. They could see the lens cap still covering the lens as he lined up the first shot but, just as Wendy was about to warn him, Tom had nudged her to keep quiet.

Word soon reached Sadie and Dave what was going on and every time Martin lined them all up the laughter increased. Martin wondered about the hilarity but assumed it had been caused by the beer and whatever it was in Wendy's water bottle. Eventually, Tom told him so he could get some actual pictures of them – not necessarily for Martin's sake, but because he wanted some pictures to remind him of the new friends they'd made and couldn't be bothered to take any himself.

***

A few streets away from this happy band of new friends, Norman Henry Normanson had just finished his final meal and was looking forward to watching whatever crime dramas the American TV networks had scheduled for that evening. He wouldn't get to see any of them, but he didn't know that yet.

***

"Hey, Wendy," said Sadie as they walked past the tennis courts in the northern section of the park. "What's the worst job you've ever had?"

"Probably having Karen as my older sister. That's really hard work," Wendy replied. "Also, working in a fast-food shop late at night and dealing with all the drunks. No offence, Dave."

"None taken," Dave said with a grin. "I've been known to tear it up a bit when I've had a few too many. It can't be easy working in those places, especially when people like me come in."

"Do you ever go back the next day and apologise?" Tom asked. "We apologise for everything in the UK, even if we haven't done anything wrong. We're a bit like Canadians."

"I would do, but I can't always remember anything about where I've been or what I've gotten up to when I wake up in jail the next morning."

"That's fair enough," Tom nodded.

"I worked in a fast-food restaurant once," Martin piped up while getting his camera ready to take some more pictures.

"They called him 'Johnny No Stars' while he was there," Tom added.

"I'd forgotten about that," Martin admitted.

"Why did they call you that?" Wendy asked.

"You know they all have stars on their name badges to show how proficient they are? I was there for three years and didn't earn any stars."

"But they give you a star for making it through the first day without setting the place on fire, don't they?" Wendy asked.

"Yeah...about that..." Martin began, but couldn't finish due to the laughter coming from all sides.

"Guys, I've known Martin for 25 years and he has a unique level of stupidity in some things. It's not something you can teach. He was born with it."

"It's a gift," Martin agreed.

The six of them continued their walk around the park swapping stories of all the bad jobs they'd had as the sun began to set.

"I was once a tattoo artist," Dave began as they sat on the steps in front of the gates that separated Piedmont Park from the Atlanta Botanical Gardens.

"You could get another tattoo, Martin," Tom suggested.

"No thanks," said Martin.

"Did you enjoy it, Dave?" Sadie asked.

"Yeah, I did but I had to leave."

"Why?"

"It wasn't my fault...really," Dave said with a grin.

"Tell us more!" Sadie begged him.

"A guy came in one day and wanted a tattoo of a teardrop. I was quite new so the owner said I could do it because teardrops are easy."

"Don't they signify you've killed someone?" Karen asked.

"Yeah, the guy had just come out of prison for killing his boss for telling him to do overtime on a Saturday."

"I think we could have all been there at some point," said Karen.

"I hear you. But this guy had a really bad stutter and I'd just come back from my lunch break in the bar next door."

"What happened?" Sadie asked.

"I was a bit drunk and he was stuttering and asked for a teardrop like 17 times. So, I gave him 17 teardrops."

"Oh, man!" said Karen.

"Yeah...he was on his phone and wasn't concentrating and I was drunk so I wasn't concentrating either. When I finished and he saw what I'd done he went mad and shouted, 'I look like a fucking serial killer now!' and walked out without paying. I didn't get a tip either."

"What did the owner say?"

"He fired me and told me if he ever saw me again he'd be the one needing a teardrop tattoo."

Darkness was now beginning to engulf them as Martin and Tom let the others go on ahead so Martin could continue taking pictures of the trees silhouetted against the skyline of the buildings in Midtown. The sky had turned from light blue to orange as the sun went down and was now a deep blue as night approached.

Martin had a look of frustration on his face that meant he was struggling with something that most normal people would have no problem at all doing.

"Are you alright, Martin?"

"Yeah, mate...it's just my hands have been a bit sweaty because of this heat and every time I go to adjust my camera or put it in its case, I accidentally press the button and take a picture. It's really annoying."

"Aren't cameras all very similar?"

"Mostly, yes, but this is new and I haven't got used to it yet. It's too easy to press the button and accidentally take a picture. I'll be alright in a few days."

"What do you think of it other than that?"

"It's the second one I've had that's got an SD card. I used to prefer traditional rolls of film, but with this one I can take a lot more shots in case I mess a few up."

"Or take a few with the lens cap on."

"Yeah, that too," Martin agreed.

"Isn't it too dark now for landscape shots?"

"It is a bit."

"Can you take a couple of me so I can use them on my online dating profile when I get home? I want people to think I'm well-travelled and sophisticated and this twilight will make me look dark and mysterious as well."

"But you're none of those things."

"I know, but I still want people to think I am."

"Okay, stand over there under that lamppost by this wall and I'll…"

"MOVE!!" Tom shouted suddenly, grabbing Martin and pulling him onto the path.

As Martin had stepped back onto one of the internal roads in the park to take the pictures Tom had asked for, a car had come hurtling around the corner and almost ran them both down. Martin had seen Tom jump forward to grab him and had also jumped back instinctively, dropped his new camera and fallen over a small stone wall as the car disappeared into the night.

"How fast was he going?!" Martin asked. "He could have killed us both."

"I know," said Tom as the others turned back to see what the commotion was about.

"Hey, y'all. Are you guys okay?" Karen shouted.

"I think so. Some maniac in a car tried to kill us!" said Tom.

"I'm sure they didn't try to kill you on purpose. They don't know you well enough yet," said Karen.

"That's true," Tom agreed.

"Give them a few days and then you can start getting worried."

"Thanks, Karen. That makes us feel a lot better."

"I'm just messing with y'all," she replied. "Come on, let's get out of here so you can get back to your hotel. Try not to get assassinated on the way back."

"That's good advice in any situation," said Tom as they prepared to make their way back through the park.

Martin hesitated for a few moments to check his camera was still working but it was too dark now so he was suddenly anxious to get back to the hotel to check it. He also remembered he'd promised to call Irma; she wouldn't be happy but at least he was halfway around the world from her. If they were in the same room and he hadn't done something she'd told him to then a broken camera would be the least of his worries.

"Hey, guys, what's that?" Wendy asked. "Just there by the water. It looks like…"

"Where?" Dave asked.

"I see it," said Karen.

"It looks like…"

"A dead body," said Dave, following his observation with a low whistle.

"Is it a dead hooker?!" Tom asked excitedly. "I've heard a lot about them."

"No, sadly," said Dave.

"What do you mean 'sadly'?" Sadie asked, getting upset. "Are you a fan of dead hookers?"

"No, of course not. I meant it would be a shame for Tom if he's always wanted to see one."

"Oh yeah, definitely. That would be a shame."

"I haven't always wanted to see one…it's just something you hear a lot about on TV cop shows and in the movies," said Tom. "I'd be almost as happy to not see one."

"That's not what you said on the plane," said Martin.

"Is that the thanks I get for saving your life three times since we've been here?"

"It's only twice; the first time you just laughed and the second time you were more interested in going round to my house to tell Irma's boobs I'd been killed by a little kid on a tricycle."

225

Dave and Wendy approached the edge of the lake to get closer to the object that looked like a dead body and discovered that was exactly what it was. It also had a smaller-than-average head.

"I know it's quite dark but it looks like he's got a small head," said Dave.

"Maybe it's that creepy old guy from earlier," Sadie suggested.

"Whoever it is, we'd better call the cops," said Karen as she reached for her phone.

Chapter 20

Atlanta, USA

The warm, yellow glow of the ornamental lamp posts in Piedmont Park was punctured by the flashing blue lights of two dark blue patrol cars as they made their way across a small bridge that led from the city streets to the centre of the park. As they stopped their vehicles and got out, the four uniformed officers were greeted by six civilians and what looked like a corpse just behind them.

"Can somebody tell me what happened here?" the first officer addressed the group.

"We were just walking through the park and we stumbled across this body," said Karen, electing herself as the official spokesperson.

"I see," said the officer. "Go on."

"We'd been out for lunch, walking around and generally having a good time. As soon as we decided to leave, we saw what looked like a body and called you guys."

"Did you notice anything suspicious at the time?" asked a second officer, leaning over the body for a closer look.

"Not really. Although these two guys nearly got mowed down by a speeding car just before we found it," Karen replied, pointing at Tom and Martin.

"What was that?" the first officer asked just as he was about to examine the body but then stopping and turning to face the group instead.

227

"We were hanging back a bit checking out my camera when someone came speeding towards us and nearly killed us," said Martin. "I jumped back and fell over a wall," he added.

"I saved his life," said Tom. "That's twice today so far. I think I should get a medal."

"How long was it between this incident and your discovery of the body?" asked the first officer, trying to keep the conversation on track.

"A couple of minutes, I think. The car came from down this way and then headed off in the direction you came from," said Martin.

"To confirm, you're saying that while you were back there, a car came from this direction at high speed and almost ran you down. Then you caught up with your friends to continue your walk and came across the body a couple of minutes later?"

"Yes," said Martin.

"Did you get a look at the vehicle?"

"Not really. It all happened so fast but it looked like an old car. Like one of those classic American cars from the 1950s. It wasn't anything we'd have in the UK," said Tom.

"Did you get a colour?"

"It was a dark colour; maybe black or brown or a dark blue or green. Sorry, I didn't see it clearly."

"And what about you?"

"Sorry," said Martin. "I was facing the other way as it came around the corner from behind me. I didn't see it until it was practically on top of us. It wasn't a Cadillac though."

"How do you know that?"

"It didn't have any tail fins. Cadillacs have tail fins according to an old Johnny Cash song."

"Okay. Thank you...I think," said the first officer before turning to address the rest of the group. "Does anyone have anything else to add at this time? Anything useful, that is."

The six of them looked at each other and mumbled incoherently before confirming they didn't have any other information that could be construed as remotely useful apart from noticing that the victim looked like he had quite a small head and they'd seen a man walking around the park earlier with a similarly small head.

"Can you describe the man you saw earlier? Was he doing anything suspicious?" the first officer asked.

"He was just walking around the park. He stopped and looked across at us from the path but then moved on," said Wendy. "He took his cap off and I noticed his head was quite small."

"Did you get a good look at him?"

"Not really, he was too far away for us to see his face, although he seemed quite tall and looked old. We did have a look at the dead guy here but his face is pretty bashed in so I can't tell if it's the same guy or not."

"The victim does appear to be an elderly gentleman and – if it is the same person – it might indicate that he lived locally and had walked to the park. We'll investigate this but we'll need you all to come to the station so we can take statements."

"Cool," said Tom. I've never been in a police station."

"They're so cool," said Sadie. "I'm thinking of reviewing them on Trip Advisor. I could score them on friendliness, space in the cells and the quality of the coffee."

"What about free Wi-Fi?" Dave asked. "That's always good to know."

"Oh yes! Of course."

"Why would you want to review police stations?" the second police officer asked, rubbing the back of his head in bemusement at this ramshackle group of what could only loosely be called witnesses.

"Well, it would let people know the best places to get arrested. It would also help the local economy," Sadie added.

"How would it help the local economy?" asked the same officer.

"Easy," said Dave. "I get arrested a lot for being drunk and I get taken to the nearest police station. If I knew which police stations were the nicest..."

"...the most perp-friendly?" the officer interjected.

"Yes! If I knew which ones were the most welcoming, I'd make sure I drank in the bars closest to that particular station and that would generate more income for them."

"I hate to admit it, but that's a good point," the officer acknowledged.

"We could run 'Officer of the Month' contests from the perspective of the public," said Sadie.

"Do we get to vote out the ones we don't like?" Dave asked.

"That would be even better. There's one officer that books me in sometimes who's always so mean. She treats me like a criminal."

"If you're arrested and charged with a crime that would technically make you a criminal. There's a clue in the word," said the first officer.

"I know, but they don't have to be so mean about it," Sadie complained.

"Have you tried not committing crimes?"

"But then I'd miss the free coffee."

***

The two officers from the second patrol car were sealing off the crime scene as the medical examiner arrived. He went to investigate the body and immediately advised the uniformed officers that the cause of death appeared to be blunt force trauma to the head, although there were some inconsistencies in terms of the shape of the murder weapon and the depth of some of the indentations it had made. Also, the victim had a smaller-than-average head.

"What do you think could have caused the injuries?" asked the first officer.

"It's hard to say. There are quite a lot of indentations where I would usually expect them to be of a similar

231

shape and size. This victim has a lot of fairly shallow wounds – and I mean a lot – as well as a few deeper ones so it's likely he was struck by two different objects," said Dr Brownstein.

"Really?"

"Yes. I'm not sure why the murderer needed to give him so many blows to the head. Normally one or two would suffice. I'm guessing here, but I'd say whoever did this wasn't very strong so they had to hit him multiple times."

"A woman then?"

"It's possible, but not conclusive. It could be someone very young, slight of build or even someone old. The sheer number of shallow blows suggests somebody really hated the victim but there's also a second pattern that must have been caused by another weapon."

"Could two people have killed him, doc?"

"Again, anything is possible," Dr Brownstein replied.

"I'll call it in so they can assign a detective to the case and take the witness statements at the station."

"Don't worry officer, I already have. Detective Schrödinger will be here shortly."

The medical examiner continued to review the body while the four officers secured the scene and checked the immediate area. There were no tyre tracks, no discarded personal items and nothing unusual. They would stay and work through the night but weren't confident of spotting anything until daylight, which still several hours away.

As the officers alternated between speaking to Dr Brownstein, securing the area and searching for clues, Tom, Martin and the others waited by a bench a few yards from the scene and were the first to see the lights of more patrol cars emerge from the darkness. Once the vehicles had stopped it was clear that there were three of them.

"How many police officers do they need?" Tom asked. "It's just like in the movies where they bring two hundred cars and a thousand officers to arrest someone who has gone up and taken a free drink refill in a restaurant that doesn't offer them."

"They like to be thorough over here," said Dave. "Whenever I get arrested there are usually at least six officers present."

"Why do they need so many?"

"Well...I don't tend to go quietly. When I've had my fill, I get a bit on the rambunctious side so if they try to arrest me, I fight back."

"Do you assault the officers?" Wendy asked.

"I try to, but I don't usually succeed because I'm usually too wasted to know what I'm doing. I've punched myself in the face a few times by mistake," Dave explained and started to laugh.

"That's brilliant!" said Tom. "That's the type of thing you'd do, Martin."

"I've done it before," Martin admitted. "Normally when Irma is helping me out of a tight t-shirt or sweatshirt. Sometimes she pulls the sleeves and I'm pulling my arms and I smack myself in the face by accident."

"You two are awesome!" said Wendy. "This has been such a great day."

"Apart from the dead guy," Karen reminded her. "It's probably not been a great day for him."

"I guess not," said Wendy. "But I'm sure he's laughing with us wherever he is."

"He's over there under a tarpaulin. I don't hear him laughing."

"He's probably laughing on the inside," Wendy replied undaunted, reaching for her water bottle again.

"Good evening," said a loud voice approaching the bench where they were congregated.

"Hi, Pete!" said Wendy, getting up from her seat. "How are you doing?"

"Oh. Hi, Wendy," said Detective Schrödinger. "I'm good thanks. How are you?"

"We're all cool. This is my sister Karen, her friends Tom and Martin from England and these two are Dave and Sadie who I met at a phobia workshop."

"Good evening, everybody. I am Detective Schrödinger from Atlanta PD and I will be leading the investigation on this case. I understand you found the body?"

"We sure did, Pete," said Wendy.

"Wendy, as this is official business, I'll need you to call me by my proper title. How did you know my first name anyway?"

"I looked in your wallet and checked your ID one morning while you were in the shower. Why do you still have a Blockbuster Video membership card?"

"Let's just get on with trying to find out what happened here. Can one of you tell me what happened and what you saw from the time you arrived at the park until the time you found the body of the victim? Not you, Wendy."

"Sorry, Pete. Just one thing though – why are they called victims and not 'murderees'? It would make more sense if you had a murderer and a murderee. Just like employers and employees."

Detective Schrödinger sighed and looked back at the uniformed officers who were examining the area around the body as he tried to regain his focus.

"I need somebody to go through your movements this afternoon," he said with increasing exasperation.

"Hey, Detective, I'm Karen. The six of us had been out for the afternoon and we'd had lunch at the bar at the entrance of the park and then just sat around and walked and talked."

"Do you have a receipt for your lunch?"

"Yes, I do. We were there until sometime after five o'clock and then we hung out in the park enjoying the sunshine."

Schrödinger started to take notes as Karen told the story of their afternoon with the occasional interruption from Wendy. She then handed over to Tom to tell the part of the story where he and Martin had nearly been hit by the speeding car before Wendy took over to finish the story and explain how she'd been the first one to see the body and had pointed it out to the others. She also mentioned that her cats were good at solving murders as they often hissed at people on TV shows and at least part of the time the person they'd hissed at ultimately proved to be the murderer.

The detective let them speak without asking questions and took copious notes. He was a methodical man, taller than each of them and a lot more serious. He had short black hair and a Latino complexion; as he was talking, Karen could see that he and Wendy would not have been a good match. Whatever complaints her sister may have had about him being too quiet and serious, he would have had the same number of issues with her being too loud and flighty.

"Thank you all," Schrödinger said when they had finished. "I will need you to attend the police station in Midtown tomorrow to give formal statements but in the meantime, I will need your contact details."

"We are staying at The Ocean Hotel," said Martin.

"You have my sympathies," said Schrödinger. "Room numbers?"

"I'm in 204 and Tom's in 212."

"Thanks."

"I'm staying with Karen in Cumberland," said Wendy as she gave Schrödinger the address.

"I'm staying with Dave in Virginia-Hyland," said Sadie.

"Are you?" Dave asked.

"It would be much easier. Especially as we can't skip town now because we're witnesses to a major crime."

"Okay," said Dave. "I live with my parents in their basement."

"You all live in their basement?"

"No. They live upstairs. I live in the basement."

"He invited me to his basement earlier – but not in a creepy way," said Sadie as Dave showed Detective Schrödinger his ID with the address of his parents' house.

"Thanks," said Schrödinger. "That will be enough for tonight. I will need you all at the Midtown police station at 8 am tomorrow. Have a good night."

Detective Schrödinger walked back towards the flashing lights of the patrol cars to rejoin his uniformed colleagues and the medical examiner as they scoured the scene, leaving the six witnesses sitting together in an eerie silence.

"It's been quite an interesting day," said Tom.

"Yep," Martin agreed. "Aren't we supposed to be at work tomorrow sorting the data breach out?"

"Probably. But I think this is more important."

"Katrina will go mad."

"She will."

"Just tell her that you're both at the police station. It won't be a big surprise," said Karen, using her laugh for the first time in a couple of hours.

"I did think we might end up in jail at some point on this trip," Tom admitted. "But I thought it might be for one of us killing Bhavna."

"Hell yeah! You know she'd be complaining about how you weren't doing it in the most efficient way while you were murdering her though, don't you?"

"She'd be all like, 'if you severed my carotid artery with a steak knife instead of trying to beat me to death with a can of diet Coke it would be much quicker for both of us' while Googling if there were any other methods that were even more efficient."

"Can you beat someone to death with a can of Coke?" Martin asked as the laughter intensified.

"I had a buddy who knocked himself out with a beer can once," said Dave.

"That's cool," said Tom, clearly impressed.

"Not really. Frank was driving his truck and was coming to pick me up to go fishing. He'd had a couple of beers on the way over and as he got close to where I was standing, he smacked an empty can against his forehead to crush it. Unfortunately, the fool wasn't concentrating and picked up a full can instead of an empty one, hit himself too hard and gave himself a concussion."

"That's terrible!" said Sadie. "Was he alright?"

"He was, but I wasn't. When he knocked himself out, he lost control of his truck and it headed straight towards me. I ran away but the truck kept coming so I jumped over a fence into somebody's yard and got chased by their dog. I was getting bitten by this damned mutt while unconscious Frank and his stupid truck rolled right on past me into the river without a care in the world."

Laughter once again filled the air a few yards away from where Schrödinger and his team were discussing the body. The police considered murder a serious business even if this bunch of drunks and misfits didn't. He felt confident he and his team would get to the bottom of this crime and it would then be another step on the way to his next promotion, although finding out his ex-girlfriend was one of the key witnesses – or potentially a suspect – was not something he would have chosen.

Maybe he could just pin the murder on her and her friends. Wendy and her laughing sister would go away for a long time, the other two Americans looked like they already knew what the inside of a jail cell looked like and the two British guys could be sent back home to the Kingdom of United Britain-land or whatever those people called themselves over there.

As Schrödinger smiled to himself, he could see in the distance that this group of drunks and misfits had got up from their bench and were now making their way out of the park. He was left with a team of uniformed officers and now had the task of establishing the identity, last movements and murderer of the person whose body they had just sent to the city morgue.

The medical examiner's vehicle pulled away from the crime scene and the body of 81-year-old Norman Henry Normanson left its favourite place in Atlanta for the final time.

Chapter 21

Atlanta, USA

Karen had offered to drive Tom and Martin back to their hotel so they said goodbye to Dave and Sadie at the edge of the park and walked to Karen's car.

"I need to get some gas first," she said as they reached the vehicle.

"I've never been to an American petrol station," said Tom. "What are they like?"

"Just the same as yours, I guess. You pump your gas and you can buy all sorts of overpriced shit that you don't need in the store."

"Some of them sell food," added Wendy. "Although the quality varies. I remember being invited over to meet Pete's parents for the first time at a potluck lunch."

"What's that?" Martin asked.

"Oh my! Don't you have them over there?"

"We might call it something different."

"Well, y'all get together and take a dish of homemade food for everyone to enjoy," Wendy explained. "It's so much fun!"

"Do you want to know how it all turned out?" Karen asked, threatening to deafen them all with her laugh. "Tell them, Wendy."

"It wasn't all my fault. I was running out of time so I bought some sushi from the gas station."

"Gas station sushi?" Tom asked. "That doesn't sound good."

"It wasn't the best," Wendy admitted. "Everybody got food poisoning and Pete was off work for a week in the middle of a big murder investigation. I think the killer got away but I'm sure they'll catch him next time. I hope so, anyway."

"What about you?"

"I was okay because I don't eat sushi. I got my food from the deli."

Karen pulled up at the pump and noticed the woman opposite was checking the display before paying.

"That woman there has just put $1 of gas in at pump two. How far does she think she'll get on that? Pump three?"

"Maybe she's poor?" Martin suggested.

"She's driving a big-ass truck for a poor person."

"Maybe she stole it?"

"Well, she ain't going to get far on a dollar of gas if the police start chasing her. I'd be filling up so I could make it to the state border."

Karen sighed with frustration and got out of the car. Tom noticed that she filled up and thought it was a good idea – especially if the police suspected they'd had anything to do with the murder of that man with the small head.

"Stuart and Bhavna won't be very happy to have missed all the excitement," Martin suggested as Karen returned to the car and they headed downtown to the hotel.

"Maybe they were the ones who killed him. We haven't seen them all day," said Tom.

"Why would they kill some random man in a foreign country?"

"Maybe he wouldn't accept Bhavna's opinion on something trivial."

"The medical examiner said there were two different types of wounds on his head so maybe Bhavna hit him a few times with her shoe and then Stuart finished him off with his laptop," Martin suggested.

"Hey, y'all. Do you need me to pick you up tomorrow morning or are you going to make your own way to the police station?" Karen asked during a break in the conversation.

"We'll get a taxi," said Tom. "I don't want you to have to come downtown in all the traffic. We'll see you there at 8 am."

"Okay, that's cool."

The car soon pulled up by the hotel and the two English friends got out. Tom went to the driver's window and thanked Karen for driving them back. Her arm was leaning on the door through the open window so he squeezed it for a second; she laid her other hand on his and smiled. It had been a fun day – maybe not quite as much fun for the guy who'd died – but certainly for the rest of them and she was already looking forward to seeing him again tomorrow.

Tom and Martin said goodnight and walked into their hotel lobby as Karen and Wendy drove home. Stuart and Bhavna were sitting in the bar and looked up as they walked in. Neither of them looked particularly happy — or healthy — but at least they'd left their rooms.

"How are you both feeling?" Tom asked brightly as he went to sit down with them.

"We do not feel very good and we are also unhappy," said Bhavna.

"Why is that?" Tom asked as Martin went off to the bar to order some beers.

"The food last night was terrible and we have wasted the day in bed today. We came down to the bar this evening and I have been talking to Stuart about the work we have to do this week but he says he feels worse now."

"It's true," Stuart agreed. "I feel a lot worse after having to listen to Bhavna talking to me about work for four hours on a Sunday."

"I am very disappointed that you two were not here to listen to my plans to resolve this problem."

"It's been a long day, Bhavna. Also, I'm the Project Manager so you report to me for this and there is no way I am going to get into a long discussion about work on our day off. If I'd been here this evening I would have felt just as bad as Stuart having to listen to you talk about work all night."

"Also, we were involved in a murder," Martin added, rather more cheerfully than most people would consider polite.

"What?!" said Stuart. "You're kidding."

"We were in the park with Karen and some others and found a dead body. The police asked us loads of questions and we have to attend the police station tomorrow to give formal statements," Tom explained.

"I'm not sure I believe this story," Bhavna said, clearly doubting every word they were saying.

"Well, here is Detective Schrödinger's card and the address of the police station we have to go to tomorrow."

"With a name like Schrödinger, how do we know he even exists?"

"I'll ask him for a picture of his cat if that helps. We need to be at the police station by 8 am and then I presume Karen will take us to work from there. Maybe you guys should go on ahead and have a look at some of the data first? We'll meet you at the office when we're done.

"That sounds good," said Stuart, looking straight at Bhavna. "And it didn't take you four hours to give us our instructions."

"Tell us about this so-called murder you say you were involved in," said Bhavna, deliberately not returning Stuart's gaze.

Tom and Martin looked at one another, took sips of their drinks and began the story of their day, from the aquarium and the museum in the morning to the long

245

lunch and the walk around Piedmont Park in the afternoon. No detail was spared and Stuart began to think that Tom and Martin were just a bit too excited telling it – especially considering an old man had lost his life earlier that day.

When they finished their story, Bhavna sat open-mouthed while Stuart had a blank look on the part of his face that was visible above his beard. Tom went to order some more beers and was met with a barrage of questions from Bhavna when he returned. Once she was satisfied that she knew as much about their day as they did, the conversation slowed down so they agreed to meet for breakfast the next morning before heading upstairs to their rooms for the night.

***

The Georgia sun was shining through the Atlanta skyscrapers on Monday morning as Tom and the others woke and prepared themselves for the day ahead. For Tom and Martin, it was a trip to the police station to give witness statements, while Stuart and Bhavna would be going straight to the Atlanta office of Classic Country Clothing (UK) Inc. to start work.

It was clear from the night before that Bhavna didn't believe there had even been a murder but hopefully, with Karen corroborating his and Martin's story, she would have to believe them. Or maybe she still wouldn't – although it didn't matter what she thought because it had been a great day yesterday and Tom was looking forward to seeing what today would bring.

"Morning!" Martin shouted from the hotel corridor as he knocked on Tom's door.

"Just give me a minute to get my shit together," Tom replied. "I had a bit of a restless night."

"Me too. It's probably due to all the excitement we had yesterday. I'll grab the others and meet you at breakfast," Martin shouted again, much to the annoyance of the guests still sleeping in the nearby rooms.

Tom finished his morning ablutions and made his way downstairs. He had a slight pain in his foot from an accident the night before as he got into bed but was hoping it wouldn't need a trip to the hospital. If it did, all he'd need is for the hotel to catch fire and his bingo card for interactions with the emergency services would be full.

"Are you okay?" Stuart asked when he saw Tom limping slightly.

"Yes. Just a minor accident last night," Tom replied as he joined them all at the breakfast table. "Where is the buffet?"

"They only have it at weekends, apparently," said Martin.

"Bummer," Tom said with a loud sigh.

"What's the plan today?" Martin asked.

"Karen and the others will be meeting us at the police station while Stuart and Bhavna will go straight to the office and meet with Delores and her delightful jacket."

"What time do you think you will be joining us?" Bhavna asked, still not convinced that there had actually been a murder.

"I wouldn't think it would take more than a couple of hours but they might interview each of us separately to see if our stories match."

"Do you think we should go over our stories first?" Martin asked, looking worried.

"No. We'll just tell them what we saw. Our experience will be slightly different from the others because we've got the car to talk about."

"Okay, you're probably right."

"It seems that you will be having fun at the police station with your friends while you send us to do all the work," said Bhavna.

"I don't make the rules," said Tom.

"You literally just made that rule," said Stuart.

"It's just common sense. There's no point in you two hanging around here waiting for us. Just crack on and we'll be with you as soon as possible."

After finishing their breakfast, they made their way upstairs to collect their laptops and bags and then asked reception to call them two taxis. As Tom watched Stuart and Bhavna get into the first taxi, he couldn't help but wonder if Bhavna would survive this trip.

"She's a pain in the arse, isn't she?"

"Definitely," Martin agreed. "But she knows her stuff."

"I know that once she gets cracking on the work, we won't hear another word from her until the end of the day but at the moment she's just doing my head in."

"Could we get her a dodgy kebab for lunch so she'll get food poisoning again?"

"I like your thinking, but unfortunately we need her," said Tom. "I wish they'd sent Sarah instead."

"Which one's she?"

"The one with the big boobs," Tom replied.

"Do you mean the one with the excellent computer skills?" Martin asked.

"Yes, but she's got big boobs as well. It's just my way of identifying her from the rest of the people on that team."

"The rest of her team are men."

"And none of them have got big boobs. I rest my case."

"What about Gordon? He's got big man boobs."

"Fair point," Tom agreed as they made their way outside.

The taxi arrived and soon deposited them at the police station in Midtown where Karen, Wendy, Dave and Sadie were waiting outside. They'd all had a restless night and an early start so their greetings were more muted than before and they immediately headed inside and reported to the reception desk.

The officer took their names and pointed to a waiting area where they were told to sit and wait for Detective

249

Schrödinger to arrive. Tom chose a seat next to a large plant as it reminded him of his seat in the HR waiting room. Hopefully, the coffee here would be as good as it was in HR.

"Thank you all for coming this morning," said a deep voice to his right. "Please follow me to the interview rooms."

"It's good to see you again, Detective," said Wendy, emphasizing the last word in response to Schrödinger's insistence that she stopped calling him Pete.

Schrödinger led the group through a door and ushered Tom and Martin into one room and the four Americans into another where a colleague was waiting. Turning back to the first room, Schrödinger joined Tom and Martin and told them to sit down. A young, uniformed officer asked if they wanted coffee and they all accepted.

"I believe you two were slightly behind the rest of the group immediately before the body was discovered?"

"Yes, we were," said Tom, deciding it would be better if he did all the talking.

Martin wasn't as dopey as he had been when they were younger, but if he let him say too much there was a good chance they'd be in the electric chair by the end of the day.

"What is your relationship to the others?" Schrödinger asked.

"We work for a company in England and have been sent over to investigate a data breach that has affected the Atlanta office. Karen is our contact there so we decided to meet up on Saturday night for a beer to get to know each other. We had a great time together so we decided to meet up again yesterday for lunch."

"Is the company called Classic Country Clothing (UK) Inc.?" asked Schrödinger, referring to a notepad on the desk in front of him.

"Yes. There's been a data breach and we have guys in the UK looking at the technical side of it while we've been sent over here to check the data, find out what went wrong and implement some new controls."

"I hope you'll be vigilant because I bought one of your coats online and I take my data privacy very seriously. In fact, I take everything very seriously."

"We will be," said Tom as Schrödinger looked down at his notepad.

Tom made a mental note to check out Detective Schrödinger's browsing history when he got to the office to see what kind of things he'd been looking at – just in case they got arrested and needed some leverage to get out of jail.

"So, you work with Karen, but what about the others?" Schrödinger asked, turning his gaze towards Martin for the first time.

"Wendy is Karen's sister. She came along on Saturday night, but the other two are friends of hers and we met them for the first time yesterday," Martin answered.

"Are there any other people in the group that travelled over here?"

"Yes. We have two people who came with us but they both got food poisoning on Saturday so they didn't come out on Sunday."

"I see," said Schrödinger as he paused once again to take notes. "Tell me what happened from the time you met Wendy and the others until the time the police arrived."

The coffees arrived and Tom gave Detective Schrödinger a detailed explanation of the day with Martin chipping in whenever Tom took a sip of his drink. So far, so good. There was no electric chair in sight, but they'd only reached the part where the car had nearly hit them so there was plenty of time for Martin to say something that would condemn them both to a shocking – but arguably half-deserved – end. Maybe Georgia didn't have the death penalty? He probably should have researched this before they'd come over as he could never be certain of getting home in one piece when he went anywhere with Martin.

"You told me last night that the car was a dark colour. Do you remember any more details?"

"I'm sorry, but no. It was definitely an old car and I'd say it was black or dark blue but I don't want to rule anything out."

"That's okay. We'll check the database and see if we can match classic vehicles in the Atlanta area. Did you see the driver or the licence plate?"

"Sorry again. It all happened so fast and the headlights were full on. Martin was taking some photos of me for my dating profile when we got home so I probably saw more than he did, but I hardly saw anything."

"You looked like a serial killer in the first photo I took," Martin added. "You should smile more."

"But then I look like a psychopath."

"True."

"Please continue telling me what happened during the rest of the evening," said Schrödinger, hoping their coffees had accidentally been poisoned.

Martin picked up the story with Tom interjecting this time. They reached the part where Wendy had called them over to check the body when Detective Schrödinger stopped them.

"Was it definitely Wendy who called out to you?"

"Yes. We were about 20 metres away from them," Tom added.

"20 metres? That's about 65 feet?"

"I'm not sure, but it sounds about right."

"So, you both joined the others, saw the body and called 911. Is that right?"

"Yes. Karen called the police and then we stood around waiting for them to arrive," said Tom.

"Do you think the incidents are connected? Martin asked.

"Almost certainly. It's likely that the perpetrator had just committed the crime and was fleeing the scene as you all arrived. That would explain the vehicle travelling at high speed towards you. If someone commits a crime, they don't usually keep to the posted speed limits, especially when leaving the crime scene."

"It could have been a triple homicide as you guys say over here," Tom suggested.

"If you had both been hit by the vehicle, potentially yes."

"Cool," said Tom and took another sip of his coffee.

Detective Schrödinger looked at Tom in the same way a cat might look at a cucumber. Were they all like this where these two came from? His cousin was a big fan of the Beatles and had once visited Liverpool to soak up the history of their home city. When he returned to Atlanta, he'd complained that he couldn't understand a word anyone was saying. This case was slightly different because Schrödinger could certainly understand what Tom was saying – he just couldn't understand why he was saying it.

"Thank you for your time. We have your contact details on file and I will be in touch again if we need you. If you think of anything else in the meantime, please contact me."

"We will," said Tom.

"How long are you here for?" Schrödinger asked.

"Two weeks initially."

"Okay. You won't be able to leave the country without permission so, if we haven't spoken again, please check in with me before you leave. You will need authorisation from us or they will stop you at the airport."

"Awesome. Are we free to go?"

"Sure, but please call if you remember anything else, no matter how insignificant it may appear."

Chapter 22

Atlanta, USA

Tom and Martin were shown out of the police station and sat on the wall outside while they waited for the others. Tom's phone had buzzed a few times while they were in with Detective Schrödinger and he now had the chance to check it. There were three missed calls from Katrina on his messaging app so he called her back immediately.

"Good morning to you. How was the flight?" Katrina asked.

"Hi, Katrina. The flight was good but the hotel isn't the best; they said it's being demolished in a few weeks due to repeated public health code violations."

"I'm sorry to hear that, but you know what the company is like when it comes to spending money on anything. How are you all getting on?"

"It's been great so far. We're at the police station at the moment," Tom replied.

"What?!"

"We're at the police station. I'm with Martin and Karen, plus her sister and two of her friends."

"What the hell are you doing at a police station?! It's only your second full day there. Couldn't you keep out of trouble for five minutes?!"

"It's not us. We're witnesses to a murder," Tom said brightly.

"Did one of you kill Bhavna? We thought it might be a possibility so we started a sweepstake. I've got £10 on Stuart."

"No, we were in the park yesterday and found a dead body so we reported it and the police have been taking statements from us this morning. Stuart and Bhavna weren't involved because they had food poisoning so they've gone on ahead and should be at the office – unless he's killed her in the taxi and the driver is helping him bury her body."

At the other end of the phone, Katrina sighed. The initial shock had subsided and she was slightly calmer now she knew that two of the team hadn't been arrested and the third one hadn't killed the fourth.

"When will you be doing some actual work?" she asked.

"We're waiting for Karen and should be going up soon. It's just after 9 am here and it's only a few minutes away."

"Okay," said Katrina. "I'll call you tomorrow but let me know if you find anything out before then."

"I will," said Tom as he saw Karen and the others coming out of the police station.

Tom ended the call and walked back over to Martin. Karen had already offered to drive them to the office while Wendy, Dave and Sadie stayed downtown so they all said goodbye.

"Do you all want to meet up tonight?" Sadie asked. "It's Dave's birthday!"

"Hey! Happy birthday, Dave," said Wendy, followed by a chorus of 'Happy Birthdays' from the others.

"It's no big deal," said Dave. "I mean, why do we congratulate someone for not doing anything dumb enough to get themselves killed over the last 12 months?"

"From what you've told me about your life so far it's a pretty big deal for you to not get yourself killed over the course of a year," said Sadie.

"Yeah...you've got me there."

"It's a big deal for Martin as well," Tom added. "He's always falling over, breaking himself or getting stuck in mechanical things. I was trying to stop him from saying too much during the interview in case we ended up in the electric chair."

"We do it by lethal injection these days," said Karen. "It's more humane."

"Why do they care about being humane when they're killing someone?" Martin asked.

"They just do. Something about lawsuits probably. Or maybe they didn't pay their power bill."

"The one about the power bill makes sense," said Tom. "You wouldn't want to pull the switch and find that only 15 volts came out. It would take forever to fry someone with that."

"Oh, man! Where did you come from?!" Karen asked. "Is everyone in England like you? I'm going to have to come over and visit someday."

"Most people aren't like him," said Martin. "Most people are normal."

"Maybe I'll go over one day," Karen replied. "But in the meantime, we need to get to work. I'll call you later, Wendy. It would be great to go out tonight for Dave's birthday if everyone's free?"

"I'm not free," said Dave. "I have to do family shit. But tomorrow would be good."

"That's fine. Let's talk about it later and we can meet up tomorrow. And let's hope we don't find any more dead bodies or the police will start thinking these two have come over on some kind of murdering spree," said Karen. "We thought we'd got rid of them in Boston by throwing all their tea in the harbour but the fools keep coming back."

"We want revenge," said Tom. "We take our tea very seriously in Britain."

Looking down at the six from the vantage point of an upstairs window, Detective Schrödinger couldn't imagine any of them as murderers. All they seemed to do was talk and laugh the whole time and he couldn't see any of them being serious enough for long enough to do something as grave as murdering somebody. He could see them annoying someone to death, but bludgeoning them seemed unlikely.

Down on the street, unaware of Schrödinger's favourable appraisal of them, the group of six separated into two groups of three and parted company. Wendy,

Dave and Sadie went to get some breakfast, while Karen led Tom and Martin to her car for the short drive north to the office.

***

Stuart and Bhavna were busy interrogating the internal code of the system that had caused the company so much trouble when the others arrived. They were absorbed in their tasks and Bhavna was particularly pleased to be doing some actual work rather than having to socialise with the others. She knew she was the odd one out in terms of her work ethic, but doing a good job meant more to her than going out and filling her face with food and drink – especially after the food poisoning incident on Saturday night.

Stuart was less pleased to be working but from the sound of what was happening with Tom, Martin and Karen he was much safer in front of a computer than he would be in the bars of Atlanta and had already thought of his excuse for the next time they invited him out. He never thought that people working in IT could be so noisy; normally the only noise that came from them was the tapping of their keyboards. As if to prove his point, the main door suddenly opened to a cacophony of noise and laughter as Karen breezed in, followed by Tom and Martin.

"Hey, y'all! Happy Monday, everyone!" she shouted as she walked across the office.

"Good morning, Karen," said Bhavna as she approached the desks where she and Stuart were sitting. "I understand that there may have been an unsavoury incident yesterday?"

"Hell yeah! A real live dead body right in front of us! Can you imagine that?"

"I cannot."

"What?"

"I cannot imagine a real live dead body. A dead body is, by its very definition, dead, so I cannot imagine a live dead body."

Karen went to the kitchen to make some coffee and offered to give Tom and Martin a tour of the building.

"What the hell is wrong with that woman?" Karen asked Tom once they were out of Bhavna's earshot.

"She's a bit anal, isn't she?"

"More than a bit."

"She's just as bad in England," offered Martin. "She's great at her job but far too serious."

"If she took that stick out of her ass then she might be okay," Karen agreed. "But I somehow doubt it."

A few minutes after leaving the main office, Tom and Martin reappeared and went to sit at some spare desks near Stuart and Bhavna. As the American division of the company was still growing, there was still plenty of space in the main office where most people sat and spare desks were easy to find. It was hoped that within a few months the whole of the ground floor – or the first floor as Karen had called it – would be occupied and they would then need to move the directors and senior managers upstairs to the second floor (or the first floor as Tom and Martin had called it).

"How is it going?" Tom asked as he and Martin sat down.

"We're just getting into the system now and it does seem to be capturing a lot more data than you'd expect," said Stuart. "We can isolate certain data fields and tell the system not to capture them in future, but why this has happened is a mystery at the moment."

"It sounds like Johnny Pervert wanted to know a bit more about the customers than he had any right to," Tom suggested.

"Firing him was the best thing they did. Do they think he could be behind the data breach?"

"I don't know. Keith is dealing with that and they're not ruling anything out."

"How did the meeting at the police station go?" Bhavna asked, seemingly satisfied that there had actually been a murder now that Karen had confirmed it.

"They asked for our statements and we told them what we saw – or rather didn't see. It was dark so all we saw was a dark car whizzing past us and then a dead body by the lake."

"I am sure the police will do their work and establish the identity of the murderer."

"Let's hope so. If they saw us, then we might be next," said Tom.

"What do you mean?" Martin asked, suddenly worried about his safety.

"Well, you know how it is. Murderers like to tie up all the loose ends. We should probably avoid that park for the rest of our trip."

"Yeah...probably. I told you we should have brought some guns with us."

"You did," said Tom. "Maybe I should listen to you occasionally. Not often, but occasionally."

Martin laughed and set up his laptop. Karen came over and logged them in to spare computers and gave them both USB data sticks to allow them to transfer data from the main computers to their laptops. She then went back to her desk to speak to Delores, whose trademark purple and mustard jacket was thankfully missing due to the warm weather. Karen hoped she wouldn't now see it again until October.

"Hey, Delores. Did you have a good weekend?"

"Just the usual," Delores answered, not looking up.

"You get arrested every weekend?!"

"What do you mean by that?"

"We were in a restaurant downtown and saw you being bundled into the back of a squad car."

"What made you think that was me?" Delores asked defensively.

"You were wearing that ugly ass coat of yours. Nobody else has a coat like that."

"That's because nobody else has the same taste in clothes as me."

"You've got that right. Why did they arrest you? As your manager, I need to be sure you're not some kind of master criminal."

"It was nothing. I had some two-dollar bills and I went to pay for some medicine with them. The cashier at the drug store refused to take them and I got angry because I needed the meds."

"Two-dollar bills are legal tender though."

"That's what I said. But they accused me of fraud and called the cops."

"What happened then?"

"The cops came and they also disputed that two-dollar bills were legal tender so they put me in the back of a patrol car. Once we got to the station the sergeant on duty told them that two-dollar bills were legal and they had to release me. They were about to let me go but one of them commented on my coat."

"Was it a positive comment?" Karen asked, trying not to laugh.

"No, it was not a positive comment. He said I shouldn't wear it near a school in case I scared the kids and gave them nightmares."

"What did you do?"

"I slapped that young man right around his head. That's when they arrested me and kept me in overnight."

Across the other side of the room, Tom and the others were busy looking at different sets of computer data when an explosion of laughter reached them. It was impossible to concentrate when Karen was laughing and – after being at work for almost ten minutes – Tom was now ready for a break and walked over to find out what was going on. Delores explained the story of her arrest and what the police officer had said about her coat and Tom duly relayed this to the others when he got back to his desk.

Martin and Stuart both found the tale amusing but Bhavna was either not impressed or had left her sense of humour at home and immediately put her headphones back in. Tom noticed she was another one still using wires; what was wrong with these people? Tom got out his wireless headphones, logged in to the company's Wi-Fi network and followed the rest of the team in getting down to what it was they were being paid to do. He did wonder about the murder though and hoped they hadn't heard the last of it.

***

Across the city, Wendy was spending the afternoon at The King Center with her new friends Sadie and Dave. Sitting on a bench by the cobalt blue waters of the reflecting pool, Wendy felt a sense of much-needed calm and tranquillity. She saw herself as a free spirit and, while she had a list of phobias as long as the terms and conditions in an iPhone software update, she tried not to let things get to her. This felt different, however, and brought with it a huge sense of loss that somehow seemed personal.

Two weeks ago, Wendy had been working in a museum and living in her own apartment. Since then, she'd lost her job, been forced to give up her apartment to move in with her sister and had now seen the body of a man who had just lost his life. Seeing Pete Schrödinger again had brought back the memories of her relationship with him and its eventual end – resulting in more loss. Living with Karen couldn't last forever and she knew that once the excitement of the murder had subsided and the British guys had gone home, there would be another hole in both of their lives.

Wendy gazed into the peaceful waters surrounding Martin Luther King's tomb as she waited for Dave and Sadie to come back from the gift shop and still didn't know if the other two were together or not. They certainly seemed to get on well, but then all three of them got on well so it was hard to tell, although with Sadie now effectively living with Dave there was a fair chance that they were becoming a couple.

She was snapped out of her thoughts by a group of tourists asking her to take a picture of them by the Eternal Flame that burned in a small area opposite Dr King's tomb. As Wendy took the photo for them, she heard a male voice call her and turned around to see Dave's grinning face.

"Hi, Dave. Where's Sadie?"

"She's in the bathroom. She's been there a while so she's either taking a huge dump or she's waiting for someone to open the door for her. We were going to get something to eat soon if you want to come along. It's a bit early but I've got this birthday thing later with my folks so I need to get some food in my stomach to soak up all the beer I'll be forced to drink."

"Forced?" Wendy asked, raising one eyebrow.

"Well, no," Dave replied. "I'm always happy to drink beer. I'm pretty good at it too."

"Normally I'd say yes but the last couple of days have been a bit full on so I think I'll just head home."

"What's up, Wendy?" Sadie asked, arriving from the bathroom.

"I'm thinking of heading home and crashing on the couch for the evening. Last night was a bit intense."

"It was cool, wasn't it?" Sadie said excitedly.

"That's not the word I would have used."

"I guess not. But it's been a while since I've seen a dead body. I'm trying to clean up my life a bit and get away from that world if I can."

"That's great news," said Wendy.

"I'm helping her," Dave added, blushing as Sadie squeezed his arm.

"Well, you two kids have fun now," Wendy said. "I'm going to call an Uber and go back to Karen's and drink the biggest bottle of wine I can find."

Sadie and Dave hugged Wendy and then watched her walk back up the slope that ran alongside the reflecting pool to the exit before deciding where they were going to eat.

Chapter 23

Atlanta, USA

It was late afternoon and Detective Schrödinger was going over the notes from the two sets of interviews held earlier that day. Having interviewed the two British witnesses himself, he'd studied their nuances of speech and body language and could just about conclusively prove they were too immature to have been involved in anything like murder. He also knew Wendy was not capable of murder and her sister Karen seemed like the only sensible one in the whole group so he could probably rule her out too.

The other two each had a list of arrests for minor misdemeanours but again, nothing that would point to murder and he was sure that even if they had been involved, at least one of the others would have slipped up and said something. It looked like this was a genuine case of innocent people finding a dead body in a park. It was not an everyday occurrence in this city but it probably did happen somewhere. Maybe in Britain? Any country that drives on the wrong side of the road must have something wrong with it.

As Schrödinger re-focused on his case notes, he looked at the coroner's report. The autopsy had been performed but nothing conclusive had come back yet. The head wounds were inflicted by two separate objects and, according to Dr Brownstein, there were more than 20 shallow indentations in the victim's head in the shape of what appeared to be a cooking ladle. Who kills somebody with a giant spoon? This was the one thing that prevented him from ruling out Wendy's friends completely as that would be exactly the type of thing they'd try to do.

The other wounds were deeper, but there were only two of them – one to the face and the other to the side of the head. It looked like whoever had tried to kill the victim with a ladle had either found something more substantial to finish the job off with or had received help from someone with an altogether more serious approach to bashing people's heads in.

Detective Schrödinger got up and looked out of the window to clear his head for a second. The streets were beginning to fill up with the usual evening traffic as the commuters from downtown made their way back home to their families in the suburbs. Living alone, Schrödinger often felt lonely and having his own office cut him off from the rest of the department and made it worse. He wasn't the most talkative of people but did miss the company of others, even if it was just to pass the time of day with or talk about the latest sports game. He didn't miss their inane chatter though. The phone on his desk rang and the number on the display showed him the caller was from Dr Brownstein's office.

"Schrödinger."
"Hey, Pete, it's Bill."

"Hi, Bill. What have you got for me?

"The guy with the small head and the multiple murder weapons..." Brownstein began.

"Yes?"

"We think we know what the second weapon was."

"That's good progress. What is it?"

"It's a sandwich grill."

"A sandwich grill?"

"You know, you get some bread, add some cheese and tomato and then grill it. My wife bought one a while back and makes excellent toasted sandwiches and paninis."

"I know what it is. I have one too, although I'm not sure I want to use it again now I know it can be used as a murder weapon."

"Yeah, about that. It looks like somebody attacked the victim with the ladle and bashed his head in pretty well with multiple blows to the back, sides and front. The sandwich grill was used afterwards, possibly to finish him off when they realised the ladle wasn't quite doing it. We've got some iron fragments in the skull from the ladle and plastic fragments from the sandwich grill."

"Are you sure?"

"Almost 100%. Technically, the sandwich grill is the murder weapon as there were no wounds inflicted post-mortem."

"So, let me think," said Schrödinger. "Both of these items are kitchen implements so we could work on the possibility that the murder happened in the home – most likely the kitchen."

"That would be my guess too," Bill agreed.

"The wounds are shallow but there are a whole bunch of them. This would indicate someone without a lot of strength but with a lot of anger."

"That makes sense, although they did have the strength to carry the body from the house – if he was killed in a house – to the car and then from the car to the side of the lake."

"That's confusing."

"It sure is," Brownstein agreed. "It seems you could be looking for someone strong enough to move a body but not strong enough to kill with a single blow."

"Or two people," said Schrödinger.

"Or multiple people," Brownstein added.

"True. The victim was a senior citizen and if we think the murder probably took place in the home it could mean the killer was his wife or another family member."

"That would be the first place I'd focus on. You could be looking at a family where one person beat the guy up with a ladle – possibly the wife, as the wounds are quite shallow which would be consistent with a woman of advanced years – and then another family member cleans his clock with a sandwich grill and disposes of the body for her."

"That works," said the detective. "Do you have an ID on the victim yet?"

"Nothing at all."

"Why not?"

"He's not in the system. He had no ID, no wallet, no cell phone...nothing. Dental records have come up blank too."

"So he's not a US citizen?" Schrödinger asked.

"That was what I'm thinking, Pete. He was definitely a Caucasian but doesn't seem to have spent any time in the US. Also, his skin shows signs of sun damage so he's likely to have come from somewhere more tropical."

"What's he doing here in Atlanta? Surely, he didn't move here in the hope of getting killed by a combination of a ladle and a sandwich grill?"

"It's unlikely," Bill said, laughing at the absurdity. "But we've got the corpse of an old man in his 70s or 80s who possibly lived here because your witnesses saw him walking around the same park a few hours earlier in the day."

"Are we sure it's the same guy?" Schrödinger asked.

"Pretty sure. The height and age, along with your witnesses' description of a smaller-than-average head would suggest it is. You're probably looking at an old, white guy who has moved to Atlanta after spending most of his life in another country. He lived close enough to Piedmont Park to walk there in the afternoon but then finds himself dead in the evening."

"That's about it. Although he could have driven to the park in the afternoon and then gone for a walk," Schrödinger added. "He could have lived just about anywhere."

"Good point. I'm glad you're the one that has to solve this and not me," Brownstein chuckled.

"Thanks. Just one more thing. How do you know it was a sandwich grill that killed him and not something like a toaster?"

"The two final blows to the victim's head left two distinct impressions. One was the corner of the grill and the other was the patterned ridges inside. It looks like the top half may have broken off with the impact of the first blow and the second blow was with the inside of the machine. The pattern is very clear. I can even tell you the brand and model number but I'll put it all in my report and email it to you by the end of the day."

"Thanks, Bill, I appreciate it."

"No problem, Pete. Have a good evening."

Schrödinger put the phone down, left his office and headed to the kitchen to make some more coffee. On his way, he thought about what Bill had told him. Who kills someone with a large spoon and a sandwich grill? What happened to the old days when a couple of slugs to the chest would do it? Were today's murderers becoming more creative? Or was it some kind of environmentally responsible way of killing people by not using bullets in case they increased the rate of climate change?

He picked up the coffee pot and poured the strong black liquid into his mug. He'd got this for Christmas from Wendy. She'd had it personalised to say, 'My Favorite Detective' and it also had a picture of some handcuffs on it. He wasn't sure whether the picture referred to his job or their personal life but it made him smile. If only Wendy hadn't been such an airhead, their relationship could have gone somewhere. He needed someone who took life as seriously as he did but Wendy wasn't that person, although seeing her twice in two days had made him think about her again.

Schrödinger walked back to his office and turned his mind back to the case. From what he'd seen and from what Bill had just told him, it sounded like a simple domestic homicide. In cases like this, a family member would ordinarily be the chief suspect – particularly given this particular victim's age – but so far, he had no idea who the victim actually was.

***

"Hey, sis! How was your day?" Wendy asked as soon as she saw Karen walk through the front door.

"Hi, Wendy, it was good thanks. The British guys have been staring at computer data all day so I just got on with my regular work," Karen replied.

"I went out with Dave and Sadie today but we didn't find any more dead bodies."

"That's a blessing. Try not to find too many more or your ex-boyfriend will think you're a serial killer."

"How can I be a serial killer? I haven't even killed one person yet."

"Try to keep it like that," Karen suggested with a smile.

"I will. But it's probably best if you don't annoy me – just in case," said Wendy, picking up one of her cats and stroking its head.

"What random shit are you having for your dinner tonight?"

"Tofu."

"What the hell is tofu?" Karen asked. "Is that some kind of hippie vegan stuff?"

"It's coagulated soy milk."

"What the...? Never mind. I don't even want to know. I'm just going to enjoy a meat feast pizza."

"Are you seeing Tom and the others tonight?" Wendy asked as they made their way into the kitchen to prepare their separate meals.

"No, I've been stuck looking at those fools for most of the day so I need a break from them tonight."

"Are we going out with Dave and Sadie tomorrow?"

"Sure. I'll ask the others, but I'll wait until Tom and Martin are alone."

"What's wrong with the other Brits?" Wendy asked.

"The woman – Bhavna – is so pedantic; even if you say something simple, she'll correct you to fifteen decimal places and Stuart has a beard twice the size of my head. Tom says he's seen insects and small rodents moving about in it."

Karen's laugh scared two of the cats out of the kitchen so Wendy went to collect them. As she went to find them, she checked her phone and saw a missed call from Pete – or Detective Schrödinger as he now wanted to be called. She took the phone up to her bedroom and called him back.

There was no answer at first so she went back downstairs, checked to make sure Karen wasn't trying to scare any more of her cats with her laugh and tried again. Still no answer.

"What's up?" Karen asked.

"Pete called but now he won't answer my calls. I'll have to keep trying."

"Why can't you just leave him?"

"He wouldn't call if it wasn't important and I don't want him to think I'm ignoring him because he might need my help to solve the case."

"Do you think it will be about the murder or the two of you?"

"It could be either. He wasn't the most talkative person when I was dating him so he's difficult to read. Hold on, my phone's ringing."

"Hi, Pete, how are you?"

"I'm good thanks, Wendy. I was thinking about something you said yesterday about meeting Dave and Sadie at a phobia workshop."

"Yes, that's right."

"How long ago did you meet them?"

"Last week. It was my first session."

"I was thinking about coming along. What day does it run?"

"Tuesdays and Fridays," Wendy told him. "We'll be going again tomorrow."

"That works for me. Tuesday is my day off. Can you text me the details?"

"Sure, Pete. It's up near the Braves stadium so I'll text you the address and the time."

"Thanks. I'll see you tomorrow," said Schrödinger as he ended the call.

"Pete's coming to the phobia workshop tomorrow. Maybe I can get some details of the murder from him."

"What's he got a phobia of? Apart from dumbasses like you," Karen replied, with her accompanying laugh causing Wendy to look at her cats and prepare to reassure them.

"The only one I know of is loud noises, but he might have more."

"Maybe you two fools are made for one another after all," said Karen as she took her pizza out of the oven and carried it to the table.

"You eat a lot of pizza."

"I like pizza."

"You'll end up looking like a pizza soon," said Wendy.

"And if you don't shut your damned mouth, you'll end up looking like that guy we found in the park yesterday."

***

The Ocean Hotel was a small hotel with a terrible reputation in the heart of downtown Atlanta. It was about to be demolished and the owner was trying to make as much money as he could before that happened. Tonight was the third consecutive night that a group of noisy and slightly clueless business travellers from Britain had been staying and it looked like this would be the first time they would be spending their whole evening in the bar.

Stuart bought the first round of drinks and the conversation started with the data analysis work Martin had been doing before flowing into Stuart and Bhavna's investigation of the data storage problems.

"What can you tell us then, Martin?" Tom asked once they had all settled down at the table with their drinks and their laptops.

"Well, mate, it looks like the program Johnny Pervert installed was grabbing every piece of data from the user's phone if they had the app."

"I believe that the gentleman's name was Johnathan Perver," Bhavna corrected him.

"We know," said Tom. "But given what we know about him and the data being collected by the software he recommended, bought and oversaw, we're going to continue calling him Johnny Pervert."

"That is fair," Bhavna agreed. "Please continue, Martin."

"If a user installed our app, it would monitor everything they browsed, typed, messaged or looked at and then store it on the database. There are thousands of photos on there, copies of emails, texts and browsing histories."

"Are there loads of annoying pictures of people's kids eating?" Tom asked.

"Of course," Martin replied as the inference went completely over his head. "Every social media post was captured from the time they installed the app. To be honest, it's horrifying."

The four of them paused and took sips of their drinks. Tom and Martin had bottles of beer, Stuart had a large rum while Bhavna contented herself with a small orange juice as she didn't drink alcohol.

"How about you guys?" Tom asked. "What did you find?"

"We found a lot of random data stored in a database on the server, including everything Martin found. It's not great news but we can certainly delete it," Stuart began.

"That would be the most favourable option," Bhavna added.

"Can you break it down into categories so I can go to the directors and the data security team to agree on what needs to be deleted and what can stay?" Tom asked.

"Yes, of course. It's sorted by app so it should be simple enough to delete anything it took from other apps such as social media, texts, emails and their internet browser and just keep the data from our own app."

Martin leaned over to the next table to grab some menus for everyone and they took a few moments to decide what they were having to eat before the server came over and took their orders.

"Bhavna just said the data is stored according to the app it was taken from. Is that how you see it too?" Tom asked Martin when the server had left.

"Yeah...whenever the user opens an app, the program hidden in our app just seems to scrape all the data from that app and store it somewhere."

"It stores it neatly in app folders so we could easily set up a list of apps we want to keep data from and remove the rest," Stuart added.

"What apps would we need to keep data from?" Tom asked

"Firstly, our own app, so we know what they've looked at and bought already but also any others from similar retailers. If the customer looks at our app, browses hats for example but then buys a hat from a competitor, we could keep that data and send them offers on hats so they buy their next one from us instead."

"Okay, that sounds sensible. What about internet browsing?"

"We could set it up so it only captures data from other retailers and holiday websites," Stuart suggested.

"Holiday websites?"

"If a customer looks at a yachting holiday website, we might want to capture that and send them offers for wet weather clothes and anything else that might be useful on a boat."

"That sounds good," said Tom. "Can you give me a list of the type of apps we should keep data from and I'll speak to the directors tomorrow?"

"I can do that for you," said Bhavna.

"Thanks," said Tom as the food arrived and the conversation moved away from work and onto the murder because Stuart wanted to know every detail of the police interviews that morning.

Chapter 24

Atlanta, USA

The Tuesday morning sun shone down on Atlanta as Tom, Martin, Stuart and Bhavna made their way by taxi to the offices of Classic Country Clothing (UK) Inc. As the taxi pulled up outside the building, Tom's phone rang so he excused himself while the others went inside.

"Hi, Katrina, how are you?"

"Hi, Tom. I'm good thanks; I hope you're not in police custody again?!" she teased.

"Not yet, although the day is still young over here and we're all going out tonight so who knows."

"Please don't get arrested," said Katrina.

"I'll try not to. Anyway, we've made good progress and we now know that the software powering the app was effectively scraping every bit of data from people's phones and storing it in folders on our database."

"Everything?" Katrina asked.

"Literally everything – from photos of their kids to private texts to their wives or husbands."

"Or somebody else's wife or husband."

"Exactly."

"It's every bit as bad as we'd feared," said Katrina.

"Yes, it is, but the good news is the data is stored very simply and Stuart can remove it from the database just as simply. We just need the directors' permission to capture data from certain apps but ignore it from others. I'll email you a summary when I'm set up at my desk."

"That will be great, thanks. Do you just need a 'yes' or 'no' against each app?"

"Yes," said Tom.

"Then you can delete the data we've captured and stop it from capturing anything else from those apps?"

"Yes. If we don't want data from their banking app or their emails just let me know and what we've got already will be deleted and we won't capture any more in the future."

"That's a huge weight off my mind. I know Louisa and Keith will be pleased. Have you managed to find anything else out?"

"Nothing at all. Everyone here is just as surprised as we were. None of them seems the type to do anything like that and half of them aren't bright enough, to be honest. Their fashion sense leaves a lot to be desired, too."

"What about Karen?"

"She's indifferent to the whole thing. She wasn't involved in any of the setting up of the app or the software and doesn't care enough about the company either way to be bothered if it steals people's data or not."

"I'm not sure if that's a good thing or a bad thing," said Katrina.

"I've asked Stuart and Bhavna to stay late tonight and delve into everyone's computers when they've all gone home so we should find out if there is anything amiss tomorrow morning."

"That's good. Well done, Tom. I knew I could trust you to do a good job on this."

"Thanks, Katrina. Maybe we'll solve the murder too while we're at it."

"Maybe, but please focus on the data breach first," Katrina said as they ended the call and Tom made his way into the building.

***

"Good morning to you, sir. My name is Lloyd. Are you here for the phobia workshop?"

"Yes. I'm quite nervous though," said the heavy-set young man before him with brown hair and fierce eyes. "I'm Vinny and I have a phobia of groups of people. I'm from Brooklyn originally, but it was too crowded there so I moved down here to Atlanta."

"It's good to meet you, Vinny. We are all friends here so please don't be nervous. There is no judgement," said Lloyd, trying to reassure the newest member of the group.

"Thanks. I'm sorry I'm a few minutes early but I've got a phobia of being late."

"That is perfectly acceptable. The others will no doubt be joining us shortly."

"I hope they're not late because I've also got a phobia of other people being late."

"I'm sure they'll be here on time," said Lloyd.

"I hope so," Vinny growled. "For their sakes."

"Please help yourself to refreshments and take a seat. We have coffee, sweet tea and water on the table over there next to the fire exit."

"Thanks," said Vinny as he went to pour himself some coffee before finding a seat.

Outside the building, Sadie and Dave were waiting for Wendy. When she arrived, she told them that Detective Schrödinger would be joining them so they waited for him. A few minutes later, a shiny black car pulled up and Schrödinger got out.

"Hey, Pete! You made it," said Wendy as the detective approached the group.

"Good morning to you all. I'm sorry if I'm late."

"Good morning, everybody," said a deep voice behind them. "I recognise three of you but you, sir, are one of our new friends, I take it? My name is Lloyd and I run these workshops."

"Good day, Lloyd. I am Detective Pete Schrödinger."

"My word, Detective! We are not in any kind of trouble, are we?"

"Not at all. I am just here for the workshop. Wendy suggested I came along."

"That's a relief," Lloyd replied, leading them into the building. "We have another new friend who has already arrived. His name is Vinny and he has a phobia of groups of people so please be kind to him."

"Is that him running out of the fire exit?" Wendy asked.

"Yes...that was him," Lloyd said sadly. "Anyway, please help yourselves to the refreshments on the table that Vinny almost knocked over in his haste to leave and we will begin."

The four of them poured themselves some coffee and returned to the centre of the room where the seats had been set out. As Lloyd watched them, he wondered if he could move to a remote village in another country far away and change his name so nobody would ever find him. The session last Friday had been curtailed after only ten minutes due to the fire alarm accidentally going off and causing them to evacuate the building. He could only hope the alarm would go off again today – although maybe the calming presence of a police detective would bring some normality to proceedings this time.

"Good morning, everyone and welcome to today's phobia workshop. As you all know, my name is Lloyd and while I always start by saying we are all friends, it seems that this is particularly true this week. You all know each other from this workshop or from outside in the real world so maybe we should begin immediately."

"Good morning, Lloyd," said the group.

"As we have one new friend with us, maybe you could go first. Please tell me why you are here and what you have a phobia of."

"Certainly," said Schrödinger, clearing his throat. "I have a fear of loud noises which has proved to be limiting in my line of work."

"In what way?" Lloyd asked.

"I don't like gunfire so I prefer not to fire my weapon if possible."

"Well, that's admirable Detective Schrödinger. Or may I call you Pete?"

"Pete is fine," said Schrödinger. "But only when I'm off duty," he added, looking sternly at Wendy, Dave and Sadie.

"What you suffer from is called phonophobia, Pete. Do you know when your fear of loud noises began?" Lloyd asked, trying to get the conversation back to this fairly common phobia.

"It began some years ago when I was a rookie. One of the senior officers in my division was killed in the performance of his duty so there was a full police funeral with a guard of honour and a three-volley salute."

"I'm sorry, Pete. I'm not familiar with that term."

"Funerals of senior officers and those that served our country usually incorporate a three-volley salute where three rounds of ammunition are fired into the air to represent duty, honour and sacrifice."

"Thank you. Please continue."

"I was one of the officers taking part in the salute but I was slow to raise my rifle."

"What happened?"

"The rest of my team fired before I was ready and the noise of their shots gave me a start. I accidentally discharged my rifle and the bullet went into the coffin of the deceased officer."

"I see," said Lloyd, beginning to question his earlier assumption that the presence of a police officer might keep today's meeting on a more sensible footing.

"Everyone said the bullet would have killed him if he hadn't been dead already."

"I see," said Lloyd again, wondering who exactly this officer was protecting and serving.

"Ever since then, loud noises have bothered me," said Schrödinger.

"I can understand that. Is there anything else?"

"Not at the moment."

The fire exit suddenly opened and a heavy-set young man gingerly put his head into the room.

"Is that Vinny again?" Wendy asked.

"It appears so," said Lloyd. "Vinny! Won't you come and join us?"

"I'm sorry Lloyd. There are too many of you. I'll come back next week — unless you do one-to-one sessions?"

"I'm sorry, Vinny. These are strictly group sessions on Tuesdays and Fridays."

"Okay, I'm sorry. There's a guy out here that wants to come in but he says he's scared of chairs and wants to stand up. What should I tell him?"

"You may tell him that he is welcome to come in and stand with us."

"But he's also scared of being late, just like me. That's how we got to talking."

"How long have you two been talking?"

"I saw him here when I ran out and we just started talking about being late."

"So…he was on time until he met you?" Lloyd asked.

"Sure," said Vinny. "But then we started talking and now he's late."

"That doesn't matter; tell him that he is welcome to attend and can stand up if he prefers."

"I'll try but I don't know what he'll say. Also, he's late. In Brooklyn, we wouldn't allow this type of thing,"

"Please tell him to come in."

"He said he's happy to stand up but he's scared you'll give him a hard time because he's late."

"You can assure him that we won't give him a hard time," said Lloyd.

"I'd give him a hard time if I were you."

"But you are not me, Vinny. Please tell our friend that he is more than welcome to come in."

"Do you want me to beat his ass for being late?"

"Why would I want a thing like that?" Lloyd asked, wondering how his day had taken such a wrong turn.

"To teach him a lesson for being late."

"But he has a phobia of being late."

"Maybe if I beat his ass, he won't be able to sit down and that will cure two problems at once."

"Vinny, we are here to help each other. I'm sure he's sorry he's late – even though it wasn't technically his fault."

"He doesn't look too repentant," said Vinny. "Do you want me to whack him?"

"No! I do not want you to whack him."

"Have you got anyone else you want me to whack?"

"No! I don't want you to whack anyone."

"They'd have to be on their own though. I wouldn't be able to take anyone out who was part of a group."

Detective Schrödinger stood up and walked towards the fire exit where Vinny was gesticulating to a timid man standing by a dumpster. It looked like he was dragging his finger across his throat while his target was frozen to the spot in fear. Schrödinger showed Vinny his badge.

"Listen to me, sir. I need you to go home right now or I will arrest you for threatening behaviour."

"I ain't done nothing," Vinny protested. "Are you going to arrest me for nothing?"

"Maybe I won't arrest you," said Schrödinger. "But I could do something far worse."

"Like what?"

"See that structure over there? That's Truist Park where the Atlanta Braves play baseball. Later today, that place will be teeming with thousands of people going to the game. How about I take you there and leave you in the middle of the crowd?"

"No way!" said Vinny. "I'm going. I won't cause you any trouble."

Schrödinger took a step forward and Vinny quickly ran off. The timid man had already disappeared in the opposite direction so Schrödinger went back through the fire exit and into the room. As soon as he entered, he could see someone was missing. It was Lloyd.

"Where did Lloyd go?"

"He said he had to leave urgently," said Dave.

"They weren't his exact words," Wendy clarified. "His exact words were 'What the fuck is wrong with you people?' and then he walked out."

"Does that mean there won't be a workshop on Friday?"

"Probably not. He looked like he was going to lock himself away in a dark room for the rest of the day."

"Maybe he has a phobia of people with phobias," suggested Sadie. "That would be fun."

"But then he'd be afraid of himself if he had a phobia," said Dave.

"That would suck," said Sadie. "No wonder he had to leave."

"I need to go," said Schrödinger.

"How's the case going, Detective?" Sadie asked.

"You know I can't talk about active investigations but we do have an idea about the two murder weapons."

"That's a good start, isn't it?" Dave asked.

"Yes, but unfortunately we don't have any concrete leads and we can't ID the victim because he's not in the system.

"What does that mean, Pete? I mean 'Detective'," Wendy asked.

"It means he was probably a foreign national. Look, I'll be honest with you, Wendy. We have no idea who he is or where he came from so unless someone reports him missing, I can see this case sliding down the list of priorities. I'm sorry but that's just the way it is."

"That doesn't seem fair."

"I know, but this appears to be an isolated domestic homicide and we aren't expecting any further killings. Currently, he's just another John Doe that will be buried at the city's expense. It's harsh but we don't have much to go on at the moment."

"Did you say there were two murder weapons?" Dave asked.

"Yes. Strictly between us – and I'm counting on you to not spread this around – he was attacked multiple times with a large metal spoon or ladle and finally killed with a sandwich grill."

"A sandwich grill?"

"Yes."

"One of those appliances that are advertised on TV shopping channels that old people buy, use once and then put at the back of the cabinet?"

"Yes."

"Old people are great, aren't they?" Sadie laughed.

"They're like young people but they've been around a long time," said Dave. "Like dinosaurs."

"Would dinosaurs use a sandwich grill?" Wendy asked.

"Not the T-Rex," Dave answered, carefully considering the matter. "They've only got little arms so I doubt they'd be able to plug it in."

"Good point," said Sadie. "Did they have electricity when the dinosaurs were around?"

"I'm not sure, but even if they did, the sandwich grill wouldn't have been much use to them if they had small arms."

"And if they didn't have electricity, they wouldn't have been able to buy one anyway because there would have been no TV to advertise them on," Wendy added.

"You're right. Although only old people buy them and I'm not sure they would have moved into a retirement community near a dinosaur habitat," said Dave.

"Can we stop talking about dinosaurs?!" said Schrödinger. "Some of us have work to do."

"Detective?"

"Yes, Dave."

"Seeing as we're all valuable witnesses in a major Georgia murder investigation would you be able to help me out with some outstanding citations?"

"No."

"My brother used to date a police officer up in Cobb County and I used to ask him all the time to ask her to help me get out of tickets."

"And did she?"

"No, sir, she did not. I was a bit disappointed, to be truthful. I always thought that having a cop in the family would help me get out of jail."

"The best way to get out of jail is to not be in jail in the first place and the best way to achieve that is to not commit petty crimes."

"Are you sure, Detective?"

"Positive. Without people like you, we'd have a lot less to do."

"You mean you'd be bored?"

"I have to go," said an exasperated Schrödinger.

As he turned away, Schrödinger wondered how he kept getting into these random conversations. Maybe he could pin the murder on these idiots after all, for the sake of his sanity. He'd ask the District Attorney for the death penalty and administer the injection himself if needed. And on his day off if he had to.

"See you later, Pete. Maybe we can talk sometime?"

"Sure, Wendy. Have a good day, everyone."

Detective Schrödinger made his way across the room, went through the door and headed back to the sanctuary of his car. Wendy, Dave and Sadie were now alone in a room that was meant to be alive with people discussing their phobias and devising coping mechanisms for each other but which now felt curiously empty without Lloyd.

"Do you think Lloyd will be back on Friday?" Sadie asked optimistically.

"I can't be sure," said Wendy. "He didn't seem very happy when he left. When he was talking to Vinny it looked like all the life was slowly draining out of him and I think I saw his soul leave his body when Vinny offered to whack that other guy. Vinny seemed scary...I don't think I'll ever be able to forget him."

"I saw that too," said Sadie. "I need to get all my things from various friends and move them to your basement if that's okay Dave?"

"Sure. Just be back by seven o'clock so we can all go out," Dave replied.

"Definitely," said Sadie.

"I'll call Karen and her two British friends to see what they're doing tonight. Shall we go back to that bar we were at on Sunday? It could be our tribute to the guy that got murdered."

"Sounds great," Dave agreed as they made their way out of the building.

As they went their separate ways, somewhere across the city a goth waitress was getting ready for her first shift back at work after what had been a particularly traumatic Sunday afternoon, although at least that group from table six wouldn't be there again this evening. She looked in the mirror as she applied her darkest make-up and practised her best resting bitch face.

Chapter 25

Atlanta, USA

Stuart and Bhavna were working through the data that had been stored on the server and had separated it into two types – data that should be kept and data that should be deleted. Emails had been going backwards and forwards between Tom and Katrina all morning and, just after lunch, Tom had received the confirmation they needed to delete all of the unnecessary and highly sensitive data.

"I've just forwarded you confirmation from Louisa to delete everything captured from browsers, phone calls, texts, messaging programs and social media accounts," Tom said to Stuart

"Thanks," said Stuart. "I'll do that right away."

"Before you do, I need to check something."

"Sure. What do you need?"

"That detective told me he bought something from us so I think we should use him as a test case. A sort of 'before and after' snapshot."

"It makes a lot of sense to perform this test," Bhavna agreed. "But why do you wish to use him as the test subject? Are you hoping to find out more about him?"

"Of course."

"Let's have a look," Stuart said with a grin. "What's his name?"

"Pete Schrödinger. I presume he lives in Atlanta."

"Found him."

"That was quick," said Tom, surprised and pleased at the same time.

"It's an unusual name."

"Let's see what he's interested in."

"Well, he doesn't have a cat which is a bit of a shame. He's single, 40 years old and his hobbies are...." Stuart tailed off.

"Is it that juicy?!" Tom asked, moving closer to the computer screen.

"No, quite the opposite. Everything about him is just about average and there's nothing salacious at all. He likes walking, the Atlanta Braves baseball team, Star Wars and Leeds United. That's odd."

"How did some boring American cop hear about the mighty Leeds?" Tom asked. "I didn't think football was that big over here."

"Exactly. At least it will give you two something to talk about."

"I know, although I won't bring it up or he'll know we've looked into him. I'll just mention it casually."

"Why are you trying to befriend this police detective?" Bhavna asked.

"We just want to help if we can; we found the body, after all. If we help him out, we might get a Purple Heart or something."

"I think that's just for American military personnel who are killed or wounded in the line of duty," said Bhavna.

"There must be a similar medal for civilians."

"Perhaps there is, but you would have to do a lot more than snoop through a detective's browsing history to earn it."

"You're probably right, but it's worth a try."

Stuart and Bhavna buried themselves in their work and Tom went over to talk to Karen. Why did the woman sitting next to her still need to bring that disgusting purple and mustard patterned jacket in when the weather was so warm? She must be doing it to annoy Karen.

"Hey, Delores. That's a nice coat you've got there."

"Why, thank you, it's good of you to notice. At least somebody in this office shares the same taste in high-quality garments as me."

"Bless your heart, Delores," Tom added.

"Excuse me?"

"It's a British phrase. It means I agree with you."

"Oh, that's good! It means something a little different over here, but I guess you wouldn't have known that."

"Shall we get a coffee and have an update?" Karen asked, stifling her laughter as she got up.

"Good idea," said Tom and followed her to the kitchen.

"You know exactly what 'bless your heart' means down here and I know you hate that ugly ass jacket just as much as we all do," Karen said as they reached the kitchen, unable to contain her laughter any longer.

"I was just trying to be friendly," Tom replied with a cheeky grin.

"You make me laugh so much. It's great having you here."

"I love it in Atlanta and wish I could stay forever. We're getting through the work much quicker than expected and the murder was fun."

"Fun?" Karen asked, raising one eyebrow quizzically. "Maybe for some people, but certainly not for the guy we found with his head bashed in by a sandwich grill."

"What's that?"

"Don't you have those over there? It's a small appliance that you put bread and shit in and it makes a grilled sandwich for you."

"Like a toasted sandwich maker?"

"Does that do the same thing?"

"I think so."

"Well, that's apparently what killed the poor guy. Wendy just messaged me and said Schrödinger told them the guy was beaten up with a metal ladle and finished off with a sandwich grill. The spoon would have softened him up before the grill finished the job."

"Ouch," said Tom.

"Yeah, that would have hurt. She's been trying to find out all the juicy details from Schrödinger."

"Cool. What else did she find out?"

"She said she'd tell us tonight. Are you guys still on for Dave's birthday night out? Wendy says they're going to the same bar we went to on Sunday."

"Definitely, although I've got some stuff for Stuart and Bhavna to do tonight so they won't be able to make it."

"That's good," Karen said with a laugh as she turned to leave the kitchen.

"I wouldn't want to spoil Bhavna's fun by taking her away from her work."

"Good. Let's finish up here and we'll meet you at the bar later."

"Sounds great. I'll tell Martin when the others aren't around."

Tom and Karen went back to the main office and Tom called a meeting with the UK team to go through what progress they'd made so far. Stuart confirmed he'd deleted the sensitive data from the database and would test the 'before and after' scenarios with customers that were currently using the app while Bhavna added that she was re-programming the app to ensure it wouldn't capture any more sensitive data. Martin then confirmed he'd removed some of the storage folders on the database so there was nowhere for the software to store the data even if it did accidentally capture it again.

"It looks like we're in a good place so far. Martin, could you send an email to Katrina asking her if we can have the list of approved apps tomorrow morning?"

"No problem. I'll do it now," he replied and walked back to his desk where he'd left his laptop.

"Are you two happy to stay on tonight and check the systems here as we said? I'm not allowed to tell Martin, Karen or anyone else. Not even that woman with the disgusting jacket."

"It would be a pleasure to complete this task to establish which of these American staff is a cyber-criminal. It should not take too long," Bhavna beamed.

"Thanks," said Tom. "Let me know tomorrow what you find. Send me an email confirming it so we have a trail and copy Katrina and Keith in."

"Sure," said Stuart. "What are you two up to tonight?"

"We're going out with Karen and Wendy for an hour or so," said Tom, trying to play it down. "It was Dave's birthday yesterday – he was one of the people with us when we found that body."

"Just don't get too drunk. We'll probably just go to the hotel restaurant once we've finished here."

Martin returned to the meeting table they were using and confirmed the email had been sent and everyone then returned to their desks. Tom and Martin shut down their laptops and got ready to leave as the others buried their heads in their laptops.

"Bhavna and Stuart are staying late to finish some stuff and we're meeting Karen and the others later. We're going to the same place we were at on Sunday because Wendy wants to pay tribute to the dead man."

"That sounds a bit creepy," said Martin.

"It does, but it's food and beer so I'm not complaining."

"Food and beer are always good," Martin agreed as they waved goodbye to everyone in the office and waited outside for the taxi to take them back to their hotel.

***

Becci had just finished her break and had enjoyed her shift so far. The bar hadn't been too busy and most of the customers were senior citizens who didn't normally cause any trouble. She liked working weekdays – not that anyone could tell by looking at her – but inwardly she was happy, or what passed for being happy in her world. She was working until 10 pm tonight and was planning to meet up with some of her goth friends at a club and stand moodily in the corner scowling at everyone.

As she walked back to the bar from the recessed area by the kitchen where the staff took their breaks she froze in her tracks.

"Hey, Becci," said the duty manager. "Can you seat this group in your section? They've asked to sit by the window."

"Sure," said Becci reluctantly, giving her manager a death stare. "Good evening. Didn't I see you all here on Sunday?" she asked the group of customers waiting expectantly in front of her, although it was more of an accusation than a welcome.

"Yes," said Wendy. "After we left, we found a dead body so we thought we'd come back and honour the dead guy's memory."

"By eating, drinking and getting loud?"

"Exactly!"

"Follow me," said Becci and slowly led them to a round table by the window but wishing she could lead them to another bar instead.

The group made their way around the table to sit down and Martin was about to sit next to Karen when he felt his shirt being pulled from behind. He knew Tom well enough to know what that meant so he took another seat, leaving a space next to Karen. As Tom sat down, he noticed Karen move her chair slightly closer to his.

"Can I get you some drinks?" came a sullen voice from behind them.

"Shall we get a bucket of beers?" said Dave. "It's my birthday week so I feel like celebrating."

"That sounds perfect," Sadie added. "Let's get 12 to start with."

"Let's get a bucket of 20 instead," said Dave. "That way we can have a couple for the dead guy with the small head."

"Good idea. Do you think having a small head would stop him from drinking as much beer as other people?" Sadie asked.

"I don't think so," said Tom. "Every other part of him was probably a normal size."

"True," Dave admitted.

"I'd imagine him being dead would stop him from drinking beer more than the size of his head would," said Karen, to laughter from the group and panic from Becci as she realised that even the most sensible one of these idiots wasn't that much better than the rest of them.

"I'll be right back with your drinks."

"Is that the same table of weirdos you served on Sunday?" the duty manager asked her as she approached the bar.

"Yes. They've come back to honour a dead guy they found in the park by having a bucket of beers."

"What?"

"I want to go home."

"They gave you a $30 tip last time."

"I know. I'm putting it towards a therapy session."

"Maybe they'll give you another big tip tonight? That would help you pay for the whole session so these people could be a positive thing."

"They're causing the issues I need therapy for. I think I have a phobia of people."

"My neighbour runs a phobia workshop up in Cumberland near Truist Park. He might be able to help. It's free."

"Maybe I'll give it a go. I just don't want to see any of these people ever again after tonight."

Becci and the duty manager carried the bucket of beers to the table by the window and set them down. The six customers eagerly grabbed a beer each and one of them proposed a toast.

"To the dead guy!" said Dave. "Whoever he was!"

"I see what you mean," said the duty manager as he and Becci turned away.

"To Dave!" said Sadie. "Happy birthday for yesterday."

"To the dead guy and Dave!" said Wendy.

"Can't I be first?" Dave asked, looking hurt. "I'm still alive."

"To Dave and the dead guy," they all said, just as Becci returned to take their orders.

After they had ordered their food and some of them had reached into the bucket of beers for a second time, the conversation turned to the murder as Wendy was keen to tell Karen, Tom and Martin what Detective Schrödinger had told her at the phobia workshop.

"Pete said they don't know who he is but they know he was killed by a combination of a ladle and a sandwich grill."

"What a way to go," said Tom. "I think I'd rather be shot in the back of the head by a sniper just as I'm about to do something I don't want to do."

"Why?" asked Martin.

"Well, I wouldn't see the bullet coming if it was behind me and half a mile away and being dead would get me out of doing whatever it was I didn't want to do."

"Maybe you could hire someone to follow you around and shoot you if they see you doing something you don't want to do."

"Hmmm...but how would they know I didn't want to do it?" Tom asked.

"You could agree on some hand signals," Dave suggested. "If you wanted to be shot you could just scratch your right ear or something."

"But what if I just scratched my ear in normal life?"

"That's a chance you'd have to take I guess," Dave conceded. "You'd have to hope the sniper either didn't spot it or it was his day off."

"He wouldn't be a very good assassin if he wasn't concentrating and couldn't spot a signal," said Martin. "And what if the target was only available on that one day? Taking the day off would mean he'd miss his chance."

"True. We need to think about this a bit more," said Dave. "For Tom's sake."

"Thanks," said Tom. "I think."

"You get what you pay for with contract killers," said Martin.

"I don't want to pay too much," Tom said.

"But you'd soon be dead so you wouldn't need any money."

"Good point."

Becci had just arrived with their food and was passing the plates to each of them. As seemed to be the case every time she approached this table, the six of them were engaged in a surreal conversation that seemed to go every-where but nowhere. As she left, she scratched her right ear and hoped that somewhere across the park a sniper would see her signal and grant her a sweet release. While she waited for that blissful moment, she could hear the conversation starting up again behind her.

"Do you have anyone actively trying to kill you?" Dave asked. "That would complicate things a bit if there were two potential assassins. They'd get in each other's way."

"I don't think so," said Tom.

"Sometimes the people at work want to kill him," Martin admitted.

"Do they?" Karen asked. "I can believe that. What's stopping them?"

"Money. We've looked it up online and it costs too much. We had a collection one day but were still a bit short."

"How much were you short?" Tom asked, now becoming slightly concerned.

"Quite a bit, so we're now looking to crowdfund it."

"Pete was nearly murdered once," said Wendy.

"But he's a police officer; that goes with the job over here, doesn't it?" Tom asked. "At least his work colleagues aren't trying to kill him."

"In this case they were. Pete used to get a couple of donuts each morning and take them in for his breakfast. One day he arrested a guy dressed up as Santa in the local mall for selling drugs to the parents of the kids who were going in to see him. Mrs Claus was a cop and didn't take it too well."

"What did she do?"

"She got some poison and injected it into Pete's donuts while he went to make his coffee."

"Did he eat the donuts?" Tom asked.

"No. Luckily somebody got murdered right across the street so he had to run out and deal with that instead."

"That was lucky," Tom agreed as Becci walked away shaking her head.

Chapter 26

Atlanta, USA

Detective Schrödinger was working late and had just spoken to Bill Brownstein, the medical examiner dealing with the dead body found in Piedmont Park. Dr Brownstein had completed his final examination and had nothing further to report other than traces of an anti-malarial drug in the victim's system. Bill had said it was likely the victim had spent some time in the southern hemisphere recently, but couldn't be more specific – although if he'd spent much of his life there it could explain why he wasn't anywhere on any of the American databases.

Schrödinger looked at the pile of cases on his desk. He still preferred paper files despite the move towards greener working practices and was well-known for printing off every email, report or document that anybody sent him. It infuriated his colleagues but it allowed him to make notes and, if there was one thing Schrödinger enjoyed, it was making notes.

The murder of a visiting foreign businessman and two of his staff that morning had now taken precedence and this case had officially been classed as low priority. As a perfectionist, he wanted to solve every case that came across his desk, but the department had been told to focus on more important matters so it looked like this would be left until they had more time, which he knew would be never.

The clock in Schrödinger's office struck nine and he got up to leave. He took one final look at the picture of the victim. Who would kill someone with a sandwich grill? What was it that Wendy's friend Dave had said earlier? Something about sandwich grills being bought by old people on TV shopping channels. That would fit in with his theory that the murderer was not a strong individual and it was a domestic homicide, so it was more than likely that it was the victim's wife who'd killed him – although it didn't look like he was a local.

Schrödinger checked the autopsy report and the photos again. There was no mention of a wedding ring and no differences in the colour of the skin on the victim's ring finger. Did somebody else's wife kill him? Or maybe the husband of someone he was having an affair with? Did people in their late 70s or early 80s even have affairs?

He got up from his desk and made his way towards the door, leaving the file open as a reminder to have another look at it tomorrow. He wanted to solve the case for Wendy too as he realised he missed her. Given the choice, he'd rather not have her or any of her friends anywhere near one of his investigations, but seeing her again this week had stirred something inside him. Instead of being a vacuous airhead, perhaps she just had a happy-go-lucky side to her. His parents were always telling him to lighten up and maybe this was the type of woman he needed to help that happen. Although she might not be as interested in him when he told her that he'd been asked to drop the case.

***

The noise levels were increasing at the table in the window of the tavern by Piedmont Park. Becci, the goth waitress, had repeatedly tried to pass the table to a colleague but all of the other servers had declined, either politely ('That's okay, honey, you keep it') or more directly ('Oh crap, no') and, as she approached the table with another bucket of beers, she was wondering if she could fake her own death in the break area.

"I've always wanted to go to England," said Dave. "Would I get to see any of the Royal Family?"

"Probably not," said Tom. "They don't tend to socialise with us commoners much."

"Oh, that's a real shame. I love that it's so old and historic."

"We've got loads of castles and old buildings everywhere. Where we live there is a massive palace with onion domes on the roof. It was built as a seaside retreat for Prince George who later became King George IV."

"Was he the mad one?" Karen asked.

"Not as mad as some of the others. He was a bit mad, but not as much as his father George III. He was the one that lost America."

"So, if George III wasn't mad, we'd belong to you still?" Wendy asked.

"Who knows?" said Tom, turning to look at Karen. "It would be fun to have my very own American."

"Yes, sir, your royal awesomeness," said Dave, mockingly tugging his forelock as they all laughed.

"You could all be my butlers."

"If you think I'm going to wait on you like a servant you're mistaken," said Karen. "I'd give it a week at most."

"Until what?" Tom asked.

"Until I whooped your sorry ass and buried you in an unmarked grave."

"Is murder common over there?" Dave asked.

"Not as much as it is here, but we don't have the death penalty."

"If they don't take it as seriously as we do, does that mean you can get away with it a bit more?"

"Oh no, it's still frowned upon," Tom clarified. "If you murdered someone, you'd probably have your golf club membership cancelled and you wouldn't be invited to certain social gatherings."

"I get it," said Dave. "I've got a cousin like that in Tennessee. Nobody talks to him any more since that time with the preacher's daughter down by the river one Saturday night."

"What happened?" Sadie asked.

"Well, Cletus – that's my cousin – had just got himself married to Mary-Beth. That's another cousin but she lived in a different county so their parents and the preacher said it was okay. On their wedding night, they'd agreed to meet down by the river because they didn't have a place of their own yet so they were staying with Cletus's parents and wanted some privacy."

"That's understandable," said Tom.

"Yeah, well Cletus was at the river and it was dusk and he saw her standing by the riverbank. He just went right up behind her and had his way with her right there."

"That's so romantic!" Sadie exclaimed.

"Yeah, but his phone kept ringing while he was doing the deed and he ignored it."

"Well, you would, wouldn't you?" said Tom.

"Yeah, but it was Mary-Beth calling him from the other side of the river and she could see exactly what he was doing."

"Oh my!" Wendy laughed. "And the woman he was with was the preacher's daughter?"

"Yep. Mary-Beth wanted to know why he'd ignored her calls because her name and picture came up on his screen when she called him. He'd rested his phone on the other girl's back when she'd bent over and Mary-Beth could see him looking at it every time it rang."

"Ouch!" said Tom. "That's not easy to explain away."

"That wasn't the worst part. The preacher's daughter was tall, skinny and blonde while Mary-Beth was a short, pregnant brunette. Even a blind man with a bag over his head in a dark room in the middle of the night could have told those two apart."

"What happened to them?" Karen asked. Even Becci – now rooted to the spot just behind Dave – wanted to know how this ended.

"Well, Mary-Beth had her baby in the winter," said Dave. "And the preacher's daughter had her baby in the spring."

"What?!" said Becci, unable to control herself.

"I know! They both had their babies within a few months of one another," said Dave, turning round to address the additional audience member. "Cletus and Mary-Beth patched things up and he goes over to see his other family at the weekends but nobody in town talks to him anymore."

"I'm sorry," said a flustered Becci and walked away.

The server quickly made her way to the kitchen, took off her apron and continued her journey out of the back door and across the street to her car. Ten minutes later she was at home vowing to never go back.

"I'm not sure I'd ever want to get married," said Tom.

"I'm married," said Martin. "It's alright."

"What's good about it?" Wendy asked.

"You get someone to talk to and hang out with when all your friends are busy."

"Why would all your friends be busy?" Dave asked.

"Well, they might be out," Martin replied, slightly unsure.

"Yeah, we're all out enjoying ourselves because we're not married. We just don't always invite you because we know what Irma would say. We fear for your safety sometimes."

"That's a fair point. She can be a bit fierce," Martin admitted. "To be honest, I didn't know there was a wrong way to put the milk back in the fridge until I got married."

"Or have your hair cut?" Tom added.

"Yeah, that too."

"Being single and able to mingle is the way forward."

"It's not all it's cracked up to be though. What happened the last time you went out on a date?"

"Nothing."

"Exactly. At least I'm in with a chance of getting some each night."

"And do you get some each night?" Wendy asked.

"Not usually, no," said Martin, generating much mirth. "We've got two kids and she won't let me near her again until I've had the snip."

"There you go then. Single people often have sex more than married people," Tom said triumphantly.

"You might be right. Although I remember that last date you told me about didn't go too well."

"Which one?"

"The girl whose family were all in the navy," Martin elaborated.

"What happened, Tom?" Karen asked, enjoying the way Martin was making him squirm.

"I was sitting with her in a pizza restaurant and she blinked a lot so I just thought she had something wrong with her eyes."

"Did she?" Karen probed, sensing her booming laugh building inside her.

"No," said Martin. "She was blinking the words 'help me' in Morse code to an old man sitting behind Tom in the hope that he'd understand it and rescue her."

"Oh, man!" said Karen, spitting some of her drink out across the table. "Oh shit! I'm so sorry, guys."

Nobody could hear Karen's apology through the laughter that was making its way across the bar from their table. Becci was now safely at home so was spared this latest episode but the rest of the staff and most of the customers were starting to wonder what else might have been in that table's buckets aside from the beer.

Amidst the noise, the duty manager appeared at the table with the credit card machine to take their payment and was dismayed to see it was one of the British guys paying. This meant they'd not be leaving much of a tip, although now Becci had quit, all her tips were going to him so he'd take whatever he got.

Tom paid the bill using the company credit card they'd given him to use while he was here. He wasn't sure if it was meant to be used to pay for the food and drinks of non-employees but he could tell them that Stuart and Bhavna had come out. Also, he knew that solving the computer data breach problem would result in them erecting a statue of him in the company car park as a 'thank you' so a few extra dollars on a meal shouldn't be a big deal. He'd even left a 5% tip because he was generous like that. Especially when it wasn't his money.

Passing the credit card machine back to the duty manager – who suddenly looked surprisingly grumpy for an American working in customer service – Tom asked Karen if she would drive them back to the hotel so they could meet up with Stuart and Bhavna. The group of them went outside and said goodbye to Dave and Sadie before getting in Karen's car for the short ride downtown.

"I'll see you both in the morning," Karen shouted as Tom and Martin got out of her car.

"Goodnight! Hopefully, we can meet up again soon," said Tom.

"See y'all later," said Wendy as they pulled away.

"You like her, don't you?" Martin asked his friend as the two women drove off.

"Yeah," Tom admitted as they walked into the hotel and headed to the bar to find the others.

"Hey, guys!" Stuart shouted.

"Hi, Stuart. How did it go this evening?" Tom asked as Martin went to the bar.

"It went very well. I've sent you and Katrina an email and copied Keith and Louisa in. There isn't anything wrong at this end. Everything is fine apart from the software that Johnny Pervert landed them with."

"All of the systems and access permissions are correct and there is no unusual activity on any account in this office," Bhavna added. "We cannot find any evidence of a data breach or anything that would cause somebody to raise their eyebrows."

"Would you raise both eyebrows or just one?" Tom asked, trying to beat Bhavna at her pedantic game.

"It probably depends on how surprised you are," said Stuart. "You could theoretically raise one eyebrow in surprise and then – if things suddenly got more surprising – raise the other one."

"I guess," said Tom, too tired to argue but relieved that Karen hadn't been implicated in anything.

Martin returned with some drinks and then he and Tom started what was becoming a regular late-night ritual of discussing what they'd found out about the data breach and updating the others on the progress of the murder investigation – although there wasn't that much to say on the latter topic tonight and there was soon going to be even less to report.

***

"Hi, Pete!" said Wendy, answering her phone just as she and Karen got home. "Is everything okay?"

"Hi, Wendy. Yes, I'm fine thanks. Where are you?"

"I'm at Karen's house."

"Is it just the two of you?"

"Yes. And the girls of course!"

"The girls?"

"Her stupid cats!" Karen shouted at the phone. "And one of them is a boy anyway."

"I need to talk to both of you so could you put me on speakerphone?"

"Sure, Pete," said Wendy, setting the phone on the kitchen table.

"The case of the John Doe in Piedmont Park has unfortunately been classified as a low priority due to a series of high-profile homicides earlier today. We simply don't have the resources to tackle this at the moment so I've been assigned to the more pressing cases. I'll keep this one open and will keep having a look at it when I can, but I thought it only fair to tell you that the department is expecting us to focus all our efforts elsewhere for the time being."

"So the investigation is over?" Karen asked.

"Officially, yes. Unofficially I will still look at it in my spare time, but we have very little to go on. It looks like a domestic homicide but we don't even have an ID for the victim so we're at a dead end. I'm sorry."

"Thanks for letting us know, Pete. I'll talk to you soon," said Wendy.

"Goodnight," said Schrödinger and ended the call.

"That's a bummer," said Karen.

"Maybe we should investigate it ourselves," Wendy suggested.

"What the hell do you know about investigating a crime?"

"I watch a lot of cop shows on TV and I always know who the killer is before you. Well, the girls do."

"That's just TV. And most of those shows were reruns from the 80s so how do I know you ain't seen them all before anyway?"

"You're just mad because I'm smarter at these things than you are."

"Maybe I spend all my brain energy at work — do you know that word? It's something most people do. You should try it someday."

"I did try it," said Wendy. "But I didn't like it and it's more fun living here with you and the girls."

"They ain't all girls!" said Karen.

"Well, they should be. I'm going to ask Sadie where she had her operation done and see if they do cats as well as people."

"Can you even get a transgender cat?" Karen asked.

"I'll find out. But first, my girls need my help in solving a murder," said Wendy excitedly as she got up and headed upstairs to bed.

PART THREE

Chapter 27

Brighton, UK

It was a bright Wednesday morning in Brighton as Katrina walked along the beach towards the offices of Classic Country Clothing Ltd. During the summer, she usually parked her car about a mile away from the city centre under the famous Victorian arches in Madeira Drive so she could enjoy the walk along the seafront. Her grandfather had once been a driver on the Volk's Electric Railway that ran from Brighton Marina to the city centre and now, whenever she saw the distinctive brown and yellow carriages trundling along, it brought back fond memories of him.

The walk took 20 minutes or so each morning and gave her time to prepare herself for the day ahead. She enjoyed her job and the people she worked with but, as with any job, some days were more challenging than others and the last week had certainly been challenging. It had also been quiet. The loss of two people from any team would be noticeable but with Tom and Martin both gone it seemed to have sucked all of the energy out of the group. There was no good-natured banter (usually aimed at Colin), no embarrassing stories (often at Martin's expense) and no slightly inappropriate comments (always from Tom).

As Katrina reached the building in the heart of The Lanes – Brighton's lively centre that was full of boutique shops, restaurants and bars – she wondered if she missed having Tom around. He was less politically correct than most people, well everyone to be honest, but he did liven the place up and since he now had Martin as a foil, the interplay between them had certainly brought a new dynamic to the team. It had also earned him a few more visits to HR.

"Good morning, Sue," Katrina said as she reached her desk.

"Hi, Katrina," said Sue. "Colin called just now to say he'll be a bit late."

"Okay. Did he give a reason?"

"He said his car had been stolen."

"Oh no! He's only had it a week or two, hasn't he?"

"Yes. He was at the garage filling up with petrol and someone drove off with it while he was paying for his fuel and buying a bacon roll."

"That's terrible," said Katrina, holding her hands up to her face.

"He tried to run out and chase after them but the cashier stopped him because he hadn't yet paid. They thought it was a pre-planned robbery and called the police."

"What did they do?"

"They detained him and confiscated his bacon roll," said Sue.

"So that's another one of my team in the police station," Katrina said with a sigh, wishing that she could drive an electric train backwards and forwards along Brighton Beach all day instead of having to deal with all this drama.

"They let him go and he's on his way in," Sue added.

"Please tell me you don't have any plans to get arrested today," Katrina said as she turned her laptop on and waited for the screen to light up.

"Well, I was thinking of hanging around the train station later to see if I can earn a bit of spare cash," Sue said with a smile.

"Don't even joke about that," warned Katrina. "I need at least one person I can rely on."

Katrina's laptop had now come on and she immediately opened her emails. As she did so, she saw the IT director walking towards the team.

"Morning, Keith," she said.

"Hi, Katrina. Can we borrow you for a few minutes in HR? It's about the email from Stuart."

"Sure. I'll be right up."

Katrina followed Keith out of the main door and up the stairs to HR. They walked through the sparsely populated office and headed over to where Louisa was talking to Debbie. As they walked through the office, Katrina wondered if the reason for the relatively empty office was Tom's absence. If he wasn't walking around the building upsetting people then they wouldn't need as many HR staff to deal with the fallout. If he ever left – or, more likely, got fired – they could probably get rid of most of the HR team.

"Good morning," Louisa greeted Karen and Keith as they approached her office. "Can we talk about the email from Stuart and have a quick update on where we are with the Atlanta situation?"

"Sure," said Keith as they all went into Louisa's office.

"Firstly, the good news seems to be that nobody in Atlanta appears to be involved in the data breach," Louisa began. "I know we thought it might be connected to their previous IT director who originally recommended the system but, apart from that questionable choice, they seem to be entirely innocent over there."

"Agreed," said Keith. "I've had a few updates from Bhavna as well. I asked her to watch Tom and Karen to see if anything was going on. Katrina says they get on well and I wanted to be sure he didn't have a blind spot in that area."

"Good idea," Louisa acknowledged. "Bhavna was a good choice. Did she see anything?"

"Nothing at all. She noted that Tom and Martin have been out with Karen and some friends of hers a couple of times but during the working day it's been totally professional and he's even annoyed her a couple of times with some of his questions."

"That doesn't sound like Tom," said Louisa with mock surprise, drawing a laugh from Katrina.

"To add to that, he was the one who suggested Stuart and Bhavna check all the computers in the Atlanta office, so it seems that he had his own suspicions too."

"How can they check everyone else's computers?" Louisa asked.

"Everything each user does is stored in personal folders and saved in a central place. They have a program that effectively sweeps all of those folders and can check what programs are installed, what emails are sent or received and what websites the user browses. Apart from a few social media and online shopping visits, everyone was clear."

"That's good," said Louisa. "So where are we now?"

"We've deleted all of the data the app collected in error and the next step is to reprogramme the system to only collect the data we need," said Karen.

"Which means Debbie from Dallas will soon be able to use our app without any of her personal data being compromised?" Louisa asked.

"I think Debbie from Dallas may be busy doing other things, but yes," Keith said with a chuckle.

"I probably should have said Bonnie from Boston," Louisa admitted, blushing as she realised what she'd originally said.

"Stuart and Bhavna will begin the work today but it will take a couple of days," Katrina added, not understanding what the other two had found so funny and trying to bring the focus back to the task at hand.

"Do you think they could be finished by the end of the week?" Louisa asked.

"It's possible. They've covered a lot of ground so far."

"That's good to know. We need to clear this up before it becomes public knowledge. The last thing we need is a scandal when we're trying to break into a new market. What about the data breach?"

"We're currently working with an external security firm and I'm hoping for a report from them in the next day or so. They seem to think there is a security vulnerability in our system," Keith advised.

"In what way?" Louisa asked.

"It's basically a back door into our system. Sometimes systems are designed with these to let the programmers access them once they've been installed. If you build and install a system for a customer who promptly locks themselves out, the developers can access it remotely and get them back up and running again."

"So, it's a good thing?"

"Not always. It's like hiding a spare door key under a plant pot. It allows you to get into your house if you lock yourself out, but it also allows a criminal to get in if they find it."

"Has that happened here?"

"Broadly speaking, yes, but we don't yet know how it got there. It could have been sitting there since the system was upgraded just waiting for somebody to come along and execute a random cyber-attack against us. The other possibility is that it was a more recent addition and if that proves to be the case, then it's more likely that this was a targeted attack."

Louisa thought for a second, knowing the question she had to ask but not wanting to ask it.

"Which one do we think it is?" she asked, unsure of which answer she'd prefer.

"We don't know yet. The security firm should hopefully give us some answers tomorrow."

"We can confirm that we've fixed it," Katrina added.

"We've shut the back door?" Louisa asked.

"Yes; we've locked it too so it doesn't happen again," said Keith, who always enjoyed explaining technical things in an everyday way so non-technical people could understand them.

Louisa let out a sigh of relief at the positive progress the teams in both countries had been making and congratulated herself on not throwing Tom out of her office window the previous Monday afternoon.

"Thanks, Keith. Please let me know when you hear from the security firm. Katrina, I need you to let me know when the work in Atlanta is nearing completion. We may as well bring the team home rather than pay for them to stay another week in a fancy hotel."

"I will," Katrina acknowledged. "Although from what I hear from Tom, the word 'fancy' wasn't the first one that sprang to mind when they got to the hotel."

"Really? What was the word they used?"

"Shit hole."

"Technically that's two words," said Keith. "But I know the company is famously parsimonious when it comes to travel expenses. Did we fly them over in economy class or did we make them go in the hold with the luggage?"

"I didn't know that was an option or I might have put one of them down there – if only to give the female flight attendants some peace," said Louisa. "Thanks very much for the update. Let me know more when you have any more news."

"Thanks, Louisa," said Katrina as she and Keith got up and made their way out of her office and across the open-plan HR department towards the stairs.

***

Keith reached his office on the ground floor and found his assistant Sanjay waiting for him by the door with an excited look on his face. Sanjay was in charge of dealing with the external security firm so Keith was hoping this was good news.

"Hello, Sanjay. What can I do for you?" Keith asked.

"We have found more details of the security vulnerability and it is quite new," Sanjay babbled, almost incoherently.

"That's interesting," said Keith. "Go on, but...slow down."

"After lots and lots of searching," Sanjay took a breath to calm himself, "the security firm found some unusual changes. These were made at the time of the last security update but were not part of the update itself. It seems that the vulnerability appeared at the same time as the update."

"Are they saying that the back door arrived with the security update?"

"Not with it, but at the same time."

"We installed an update and it opened a back door?"

"Not exactly," Sanjay continued, his voice getting higher as he got more excited. "The new vulnerability was added just after the security update finished. It was added separately by another source."

"Where did it come from?"

"They don't know. All they know is that after the update some malicious code was also added to provide access to anyone who knew it was there. It was added at the end of February from this building."

"Who would have had the capability to do this?"

"Only senior members of the IT department and the directors."

"None of the directors would have the right level of IT knowledge," said Keith. "Most of them can't even work their phones properly so that means the focus falls on our department."

Sanjay could see that Keith was agitated and was trying to process this information so he said nothing.

"But I can't believe anyone here would have done something like that. How many people have that level of access?"

"Not many," said Sanjay. "You, me, John, Linda and Oleg."

"Well, it wasn't me," said Keith.

"Nor me," said Sanjay.

"I can't believe it would be one of the others either."

"There is one further possibility," Sanjay said quietly.

"Who?" asked Keith, mentally scanning the list of people in his department. "I can't think of anyone else in IT."

"At the end of February, we lost a director who had significant IT experience."

"Roy White?"

"Yes. Although the staff all called him Racist Roy."

"So did the directors," said Keith. "Would he have had the access needed for this?"

"Certainly. He would have kept his IT access permissions from his time running the department and, as a director, he could authorise any system changes."

"Okay. Talk to the security company again and see if they can confirm this came from the computer Roy used. I think you might be onto something."

"I'll get on it right away," said Sanjay as he hurried back to his desk.

Keith went into his office and called Louisa to let her know what Sanjay had just told him and what his current thinking was. They couldn't be sure yet, but it looked like they might have identified the culprit and, if that proved to be the case, Keith would be a very relieved man. It wasn't that he thought his staff weren't vindictive enough to do something like this – because they certainly were – but if it had been one of them, they would certainly have been fired and it might have cost him his job too.

**

"What happened to you this morning?" Katrina asked with a slight smile as Colin bustled his way into the office and sat down.

"Someone stole my car while I was filling up with petrol. What a cheek!" Colin replied, flustered and suddenly looking around for something he'd lost.

"What's the matter?"

"I haven't got my laptop."

"Where is it?" Katrina asked.

"In the car."

"Don't worry, I'll ask Keith to get you a spare one."

"Thanks."

"So, you were paying for your fuel and someone just ran up, jumped in your car and drove off?"

"That's about it," Colin acknowledged.

"Why did you leave your keys in the ignition?"

"I always do. It's a small local garage close to my house and they all know me and give me an extra piece of bacon in my bacon roll. I'm normally the only one in there at that time."

"Will the insurance company pay out?" Sue asked.

"They said they probably wouldn't because they think it's my fault."

"Leaving the keys to your new car in the ignition while you walked off to get a bacon roll is somehow your fault? I'm shocked," said Katrina, making a jazz hands gesture.

"Now you put it like that I can see their position," Colin admitted. "If they don't recover it, I'll have to get a new car. Although the police think it might be easy to find because it's bright yellow."

"Good point," said Sue. "Nobody in their right mind would want a bright yellow car."

"Hey!" said a hurt-looking Colin.

"I mean thieves, not normal people."

"I'll just wait to hear from them and see what they say before I go and buy another one. Diane will be pleased though."

"Why would your wife be pleased you had your car stolen?" Katrina asked.

"She didn't like the colour."

"Do you think she could be the criminal mastermind behind the theft? She may well have paid a couple of ne'er do wells to steal it so you'd have to buy a new one."

"I hadn't thought of that," Colin admitted. "Although she did say something on Saturday about wishing some-one would steal it."

"Well, there you are then; case solved," said Sue. "It's not just Tom and Martin that have had the chance to play amateur detectives. What are you going to do now?"

"I'll just keep buying yellow cars. She's got a short attention span so she'll eventually get bored and stop stealing them," Colin said smugly.

Chapter 28

Atlanta, USA

After a good night's sleep, Tom, Martin, Stuart and Bhavna had decided to mix up their morning routine and had forsaken the hotel breakfast and relocated to the diner across the street where they each ordered a strange, but hearty, full American breakfast.

This had involved eggs, bacon, shredded potato, pancakes, some fluffy scones that were called biscuits, gravy that looked like porridge, maple syrup and some strawberries – all of which were piled onto the same plate. Their plates also contained some butter and honey for reasons best known to the chef and the four of them carefully ate all of the savoury items first, before attempting the sweet ones.

After this 'interesting experience' as Stuart had called it, they took a taxi and arrived at work relatively enthusiastic about the day ahead.

The team had been entrusted with reviewing what customer data was being captured, deleting anything unnecessary or illegal and then ensuring the software didn't capture it again. So far, Martin had identified how the data capture process worked and Tom had obtained authorisation from the directors back in the UK to remove the data that wasn't needed. Stuart and Bhavna had now completed this work and were now working on repro-gramming the software so the problem didn't occur again.

Everything was going according to plan, so that was good news. Or was it? As the four of them settled down at their desks, Tom began to wonder if they were working too quickly; at this rate, they'd be finished by the end of the week and would probably be called home early. His life back home in Brighton didn't compare favourably against the few days he'd spent here so he was in no rush to go home. There was another reason he wanted to stay longer and that reason was just walking through the of-fice door.

"Good morning y'all. How are we all doing today? Happy Wednesday!"
"Hi, Karen," Tom said with a big smile.
"Hi, Tom. Do you and Martin want to get some cof-fee with me in the kitchen?"

Tom and Martin got up and followed her across the office. When they reached the kitchen, Karen told them about Wendy's conversation with Detective Schrödinger the previous night and how the police department no longer saw their murder case as a priority.

"Now Wendy and her damned cats think they're go-ing to solve the case themselves," Karen added as she be-gan to laugh.
"I'm not sure how helpful the cats will be," said Tom.

"They've got a better chance of solving it than Wendy has," Karen replied, laughing harder.

"Probably," Tom agreed. "It would be good to know what happened to that guy though. I wonder if we're next on the murderer's hit list. We did see their car speeding off."

"I'm sure you're safe."

"It's probably best to avoid the park for a while just in case we get our heads beaten in with a spatula or something," said Martin.

"Why a spatula?" Tom asked.

"The murderer might have run out of ladles."

Tom's phone rang and he excused himself – it was Katrina with her daily request for an update, except this time she had an update for Tom.

"Hi, Tom, I hope it's still going well over there," Katrina began. "We have some big news over here to share with you."

"Hi, Katrina. What's up?"

"Keith and Sanjay have been working with the security company and they think they've found the source of the data breach. Some malicious code was installed at the time of the last security patch and it opened a back door."

"Shit."

"Exactly."

"Do they know who did it? A back door suggests it wasn't a random cyber-criminal from Russia or China."

"They have a theory and are 99% sure. The external security consultants are here now checking one of the computers upstairs."

"Whose computer are they checking?" Tom asked, partly excited but also slightly worried that things were moving even faster than he'd feared and they'd soon be asked to go home.

Katrina's voice lowered and Tom could tell she was moving to another part of the office where she would have more privacy. This meant he was likely to get the name of the person responsible for this mess.

"They haven't confirmed it yet...but I saw them going into the office at the back of the Logistics Department."

"Wasn't that Racist Roy's old office?" Tom asked.

"I'm not allowed to confirm that at the moment, but it was the office right at the back that overlooked the car park."

"Roy's office overlooked the car park. He used to take great pleasure showing me his allocated parking space knowing that I had to pay to rent a space on somebody's drive."

"As I said before, I can't tell you exactly who it was but we'll know for certain by the end of the day."

"Cool. Will Roy be arrested?"

"Whoever did this has committed a crime so we'd expect the police to be involved at some point. How are you doing over there?"

"Well, we know there's no involvement from anyone here so it's just a case of reprogramming the software to ensure it doesn't happen again and then Karen and I will test it."

"It sounds like you might be finished earlier than we thought."

"I'll let you know how it goes."

"Thanks. I'll email you once we've confirmed who caused the data breach."

"Thanks, Katrina," Tom replied quietly.

"You don't sound very thrilled."

"Sorry, it's just that I'm enjoying what we're doing over here and the people are great so the thought of having to come back doesn't fill me with excitement."

"If you complete the work early, you'll have the satisfaction of a job well done and there might be a promotion coming up soon."

"I know," said Tom, not feeling any more excited.

"What if I told you Colin had his car stolen while he was buying a bacon roll? Would that cheer you up?"

"It totally would!"

"Well, it happened this morning," said Katrina and went on to explain the conversation she'd had with Sue and Colin earlier that day.

The tale of Colin's stolen car certainly cheered Tom up and once the call ended, he went straight over to tell the rest of the team. Tom knew how much Martin hated hearing car stories and watching the discomfort on his face whenever he started a conversation with 'I have a funny story about a car' would be even better, although since Martin had admitted what happened when he bought his first car it wouldn't be quite as humiliating for him. That was a shame.

***

As the working day in the UK ended, Tom received an email from Keith with details of the investigation into the data breach. Roy White had indeed been the culprit and the external security consultants were producing a file that would be passed to the company's legal team and then on to Sussex Police. The email left Tom in no doubt that the company would prosecute Roy to the fullest extent. There was also a non-disclosure agreement for Tom to digitally sign to confirm he would not pass this information on to anyone else.

Tom replied to the email to confirm his acceptance and then saw an email from Katrina advising that Colin's car had been found. It had been abandoned and set on fire on the nudist beach in Brighton and the local fire brigade was now on the scene – although from what Katrina had said, the beach had been quite busy so the firefighters had stayed on the scene for a long time after the fire had been extinguished.

"I bet the firefighters are loving their job right now," Tom said to Martin as he told him what had happened to Colin's car.

"Have you ever been on that nudist beach?"

"No. Have you?"

"We went once before the kids came along. Irma wanted to see what all the fuss was about."

"What was it like?" said Tom, imagining Irma lying naked on the beach and trying not to think of Martin lying next to her.

"Are you imagining Irma's boobs on the beach?" Martin asked.

"Yes," Tom admitted. "But go on, what was it like?"

"It was full of old men and a bit disappointing. If it's the same today, the firemen won't be happy. The female firemen might be though."

"I think they're all just called firefighters. I don't think you can have female firemen."

"I bet my dumbass sister Wendy could," said Karen, who had caught the end of the conversation on her way to the kitchen. "She's got a boy cat that she calls a girl. There's something not quite right with her."

"I think she's great," said Martin.

"Me too," Tom agreed. "Are you two free tonight, Karen?"

"Sure. I'll check with Wendy but we can meet up and do something. Do you guys like burgers?"

"Definitely," Tom and Martin replied simultaneously.

"Well, there's a place in Midtown that's really cool so we could go there."

"What about Wendy?" Tom asked. "Isn't she a vegan?"

"Yeah, but she recommended it. They do those impossible burgers – you know the ones without any meat in them that are supposed to taste like real food?"

"I've heard of them," said Martin. "Do they do normal burgers too?"

"Hell, yeah! They've got a bar in there as well so we can stay as long as we want."

"Brilliant. What about the other two?" Tom asked, pointing to Stuart and Bhavna who were over the other side of the office talking to the technician who maintained the computer equipment in the Atlanta office.

Karen and Martin's faces dropped as they turned to look at the others. None of the three of them wanted Bhavna there but they couldn't just invite Stuart.

"Can't you make them work late again?" Karen suggested. "Bhavna's a right pain in the ass and I don't think I could cope with her and Wendy together."

"I'll see what I can do," Tom assured her.

"Thanks," said Karen as she left the two of them and headed off to the kitchen.

"Can we finish a bit earlier today?" Martin asked. "I need to call Irma and she wants me to send her some of the photos I've taken so far."

"Sure. We'll make a move soon and chill out in the hotel bar for a bit."

"We'll probably have to ask the others if they want to come out with us."

"Maybe we could sneak out somehow," said Tom, trying to think of a way to avoid Stuart and Bhavna that evening. "You could pull the fire alarm and, in the confusion, everyone will run out of the front door while we sneak out the back."

"There's probably just one fire exit that you all have to go out of."

"I haven't seen any fire exits in our hotel, have you?"

"No. I haven't seen any fire alarms either," said Martin.

"That's good then."

"Well, not really. If there was a fire, we might all die."

"You've been making some good points since you've been over here," Tom admitted as Stuart and Bhavna came back to their desks. "Are you feeling okay?"

***

Wendy was sitting in Karen's house talking to her cats when her phone rang. She hated talking to strangers so she never answered unknown numbers but this time it was from a local number she knew well and took a chance that it would be the person she thought it was.

"Hello," said Wendy, hoping it was who she thought it was, but terrified in case it wasn't.

"Hi, Wendy. The guys are thinking of going out tonight. Would you be interested in a burger at that place in Midtown you took me to a while back?"

"Hey, sis! Sure. That way we won't need to cook."

"What do you mean by 'we'?! Usually, it's me doing everything while you just stand there talking to your damned cats and getting in my way."

"In that case, you won't have me getting in your way tonight while you're cooking, so we all win," Wendy replied cheerfully.

"What? Never mind," said Karen. "Do you want to message Dave and Sadie and tell them what we're doing? They'll probably want to come too."

"No problem, sis!" See you soon."

Karen ended the call and stared at her computer screen for a few seconds. She needed to find a way of getting Wendy out of her house. There was nothing inherently wrong with her sister, but her constant upbeat cheerfulness irritated her. Why are the dumbest people always the happiest ones? As she mulled this over, she saw the UK team make their way out of the building. Tom waved to her with a smile and Karen realised she was going to miss him when he went back home.

The taxi ride back to the hotel was spent deciding on what they were all doing that evening. Tom and Martin let Stuart and Bhavna go first and it turned out that Stuart was going to see a baseball game. He loved sport and was taking the opportunity to see his first live American sporting event. He admitted that he didn't know the rules but was just going for the spectacle and the hot dogs. One down, one to go.

Martin asked Bhavna what her plans were but she confessed to not having any so Tom had to invite her out with the rest of the group. Bhavna hesitated for a few seconds before deciding that she'd rather stay in the hotel and continue the work she was doing. She admitted that her preference was to complete everything as soon as possible and go home so she was happy to work in the evenings. Tom smiled to himself at this welcome development and he had a spring in his step as they got out of the taxi and headed to their rooms to freshen up.

***

An hour after arriving at the hotel, Tom walked into the bar and saw Martin sitting at a table examining his camera and laptop. He went up to the bar and ordered a couple of beers and then sat down where he saw his friend had a perplexed look on his face. Something technical was clearly bothering him. His laptop was probably upside down and he couldn't work out why the keyboard was above the screen.

"How's it going, Martin?"

"Not bad mate. I'm just loading up some pictures to the laptop so I can email them to Irma."

"Cool," said Tom as their drinks arrived.

"Cheers," said Martin, raising his glass. "Some of these pictures aren't as good as I'd hoped."

"Lens cap?" Tom asked, taking his first sip of what was supposed to be one of the most popular lite beers in

America but which actually tasted like fizzy urine – but without any of the flavour.

"There are a few of those, yeah. Why didn't anyone tell me?" Martin asked wearily.

"We don't know much about cameras," said Tom.

"Nor do I," Martin laughed. "I was hoping that buying an expensive model would make it easier but some of these pictures aren't that great. It's like my photography skills have deteriorated since I got here."

"Let's have a look," said Tom, moving his chair next to Martin so he could see his laptop screen.

"These first ones are very blue," Martin said glumly.

"You took them in the aquarium so that's probably understandable. Can't you manipulate them with some editing software when you get home?"

"Yeah, I think so. The ones I took at the Coca-Cola Museum and in the park are okay though."

"That's a good one," said Tom, pointing at the screen.

"The one where you've got your arm around Karen?" Martin said with a huge grin. "I know why you like that."

"I meant the composition. You did a good job there. Can you email it to me?"

"No worries, mate. The pictures of the park at sunset are quite good. The colours really come through."

"I'm glad you've got some good ones among all the close-up shots of the inside of the lens cap," Tom said encouragingly as Martin continued scrolling through them.

"I'm pleased with most of them," said Martin, just as he scrolled to another dark photo.

"And we're back," said Tom. "Another lens cap close-up!"

"Yeah," Martin agreed, realising that arguing was futile.

"You've got quite a collection of those. You should probably give them their own exhibition called 'Lens Caps Through the Years' and pay people to come and see it."

"Hold on," said Martin. "That one's not a lens cap, it's just a blurry image with some light bits."

"It looks like it's sideways as well," Tom added. "How much had you been drinking when you took that one?!"

"I don't remember taking it."

"What's the next picture of?"

"There aren't any more; that's the last one. I haven't used the camera since Sunday night."

"Turn the picture round the right way," Tom said, beginning to wonder what this mystery picture was that Martin couldn't remember taking.

"It looks like…" Martin began.

"The back of a car."

"Is that a number plate? Zoom in a bit."

Martin zoomed in on the image and lightened it as much as he could on the company laptop's rudimentary picture editing software. They both stared at the picture for a few seconds then looked at one another.

"If this was the last picture you took, it must have been taken at Piedmont Park. Look, you can see one of those ornamental lamp posts," Tom said, pointing at the screen.

"So, this was taken as we were almost run over?" Martin asked.

"Yes. That blurry mass must be the car that almost knocked us both over the wall. Zoom in a bit more on the back...it looks like a number plate."

"It's still a bit blurry," Martin complained.

"But you can see some numbers...it looks like 808 or 308. Can you send that to me and I'll send it to Karen? Maybe Wendy can give it to her detective friend."

Martin saved the image and emailed it to Tom before looking through the rest of his photos for decent ones to send to Irma. She wasn't a big fan of lens cap pictures so he deleted all of those and then sent her three emails with four pictures on each one, making sure they were all scenery shots and didn't include any of the women they'd befriended.

Tom received the picture of the car and immediately sent it to Karen with a message for her to ask Wendy to send it to Schrödinger. He then ordered another beer and looked up at the big screen TV behind the bar where the baseball game was being shown. He thought about Stuart being in the stadium and wondered if the broadcaster had a 'Beard Cam' which would show a close-up of Stuart in the same way they did with 'Kiss Cam' when they zoomed in on happy couples and forced them to kiss on live TV.

That would be an interesting twist he thought as he returned to Martin – although he had heard that there was one occasion when a guy was caught on the 'Kiss Cam' but was reluctant to kiss the girl he was sitting with because he was worried his other girlfriend might be watching the game at home on TV. Although Stuart wouldn't have that problem; with his beard growing longer and wider by the day, there wouldn't be room for anyone to sit within three seats of him in any direction.

Chapter 29

Atlanta, USA

Tom and Martin arrived at the restaurant suggested by Karen and found everyone else waiting outside, talking over each other excitedly. Martin's photo seemed to have had an effect and Karen came over to them as they got out of their taxi.

"Hey, y'all! You made it," she said, giving Tom an unexpected hug.

"Hi, Karen. I guess you got the photo I sent?"

"We sure did and Wendy sent it to Detective Schrödinger."

"Hi, guys," said Wendy as they approached the rest of the group. "Pete was very interested in that photo and he's going to get his tech people to enhance the image and see if they can match it to a vehicle."

"We should go inside in case the murderer takes us out in a drive-thru shooting," Martin suggested.

"It's called a drive-by," said Dave, trying to be helpful. He didn't have a lot of cash with him so the more people that survived the evening the less chance there was of him having to pay.

"What's the difference between a drive-by and a drive-thru?"

"A drive-thru is where you get food."

"What happens if you do a drive-by at a drive-thru?" Tom asked. "What would that be called?"

"Just go inside before one of the customers on these outdoor tables comes inside and does a drive-by on your ass," said Karen, noticing a familiar-looking young goth woman sitting with some friends and looking as if she was about to break down in tears. Or kill someone.

"Good idea," said Tom. "I don't mind getting shot after I've eaten but not before."

"I like your shirt," said Karen as they were shown to a table. What does 'LUFC' stand for?"

"It's my football team, Leeds United. You call it soccer here."

"Are they good?"

"I think they're excellent and they have a lot of awesome fans. They just don't win as much as they should."

"They take a lot of fans to their away games and make a ridiculous amount of noise. I've seen them play my local team a few times and it's deafening," said Martin.

"We can't help it if we're a collection of passionate individuals," Tom argued.

"You mean a bunch of noisy bastards," Martin corrected him.

"Are you both going to fight like a couple of racoons in an empty trash can all night?" Karen asked, interrupting them before they came to blows.

"We're okay," said Tom.

"That's good," said Karen. "Don't make me whip your ass."

Tom looked at Karen and she looked straight back at him. They each instinctively knew what the other was thinking and were trying to remain calm. The server came over with the menus and the tension subsided again. As she took the menu, Karen moved her chair closer to Tom's and rested her knee against his leg. He looked at her and smiled, hoping they'd get a chance to go out without the others one evening.

***

Half a mile away from Peachtree Street Northeast where burger menus were being reviewed, Detective Schrödinger was working late scanning the photo he'd received from Wendy. He'd called in a favour from one of the department's technical guys and together they sat in Schrödinger's office as his colleague Pat worked some magic on his laptop.

"There you are, Pete. It looks like quite an old licence plate, probably from the 1960s. The last 3 digits are 303 and there can't be that many classic automobiles around anymore."

"That ties in with the witness accounts of the vehicle being a vintage car. He was British so he couldn't identify a make or model so all we had was an old, dark-coloured car. This helps a lot."

Schrödinger turned to his desktop monitor and clicked on the shortcut to the software that was linked to the Department of Motor Vehicles database. He entered the last three digits of the licence plate along with the state of 'Georgia' and waited for the database to run the search. It would normally take a few minutes so he turned back to Pat but was immediately interrupted by a sound from his monitor.

"That was quick," said Pat. "Did you get a hit?"

"We've got two possible vehicles – both owned by women. We have a dark blue 1964 Hudson Hornet owned by Mary Normanson who lives close to Piedmont Park and a dark red 1963 Buick Wildcat convertible owned by Pastoress June Lawrence. She lives down in Riverdale."

"Who's your money on?" asked Pat, seeing a frown on Schrödinger's face.

"Mary Normanson lives close to where the body was found and the car fits the description given by the witness..." but Schrödinger then noticed something and his voice trailed off.

"So?"

"She's 74 years old."

"That might rule her out," said Pat. "What about the other woman?"

"She's 61 years old and a preacher. That's not the normal profile of a murderer; also, why would she drive all the way to the middle of Atlanta to dump a body when there are far better places close to where she lives?"

"People do crazy things when they're under pressure," said Pat.

"I know, but the witness said the car looked like a dark blue or black and this photo matches more with Mrs Normanson's car."

"I agree. Looking at this picture it looks more like a Hornet than a Buick and it looks more black or dark blue than red. Perhaps Mary Normanson loaned her car to someone else? Or maybe it was stolen?"

Schrödinger looked at Pat as he mulled all of this information over in his head. He had a very analytical mind and didn't like to work on anything other than hard facts and evidence. He didn't consider conjecture or 'hunches' to be helpful in the same way that many of his colleagues did and, while they now had two solid leads, he wouldn't rule either of them out just because of their age – even though neither seemed particularly likely to be killers.

"It hasn't been reported as stolen, but a family member may have borrowed it. I'm not convinced that either of these two could be murderers but I need to follow what we've got so I'll talk to each of them tomorrow."

"Sure," Pat agreed.

"Can you find me some pictures of the rear ends of each of those two makes of car and print off two copies of each? I'll see if the witnesses recognise either of them."

Wendy's phone buzzed and she saw a message from Pete asking where she was and if the British guys were with her. She messaged him back and told him where they all were and was surprised when he said he'd be there in a few minutes.

"Hey, everyone," Wendy said, during a gap in the middle of a particularly raucous conversation about unsuitable ex-partners. "Pete is coming down to see us shortly; he's got something he wants to show Tom and Martin."

"Cool," said Tom. "As long as it's not the inside of a jail cell."

"Why would he throw your ass in jail?" Karen asked.

"He's done a few questionable things in the past," Martin added. "I could easily write a list for the detective if that helps?"

"How long ago were these 'questionable things'?" Karen asked.

"A few years ago when we used to go on holiday together."

"Well, the statute of limitations has probably passed by now," Karen laughed. "You're going to need some more recent shit if you want to get him arrested. It would have to be local to Atlanta as well."

"Maybe we'll see you there," Sadie said to Tom. "Some of the police stations here are nicer than others, so make sure you get taken to a good one."

"Yeah," agreed Dave. "Although we haven't been arrested since we met up."

"That's good," said Wendy.

"Maybe," Sadie replied. "Police station coffee is better than the stuff Dave makes so it would be nice to have a decent cup occasionally."

"Good evening," said the now familiar official voice from behind Wendy and Sadie.

"Good evening, Detective," said Karen. "Would you like to join us?"

"Thank you, Karen, but I'm here on official business," Schrödinger replied, reaching into his pocket and fishing out four sheets of paper before turning to address Tom and Martin.

"I understand that you were the only witnesses to the car that left Piedmont Park last Sunday evening?"

"Yes, we were," said Tom.

"Please can you each look at these two pictures independently and let me know if either of them looks like the car you saw. Please don't confer with one another."

"No problem," said Tom, taking his two sheets while he saw Schrödinger pass two similar sheets to Martin.

"If either one of these car shapes is more recognisable than the other, please give me that picture back."

Tom studied the two pictures – one of them was a photograph of a dark blue car with a slightly smooth rear end that sloped downwards while the other was a dark red car with a squarer rear profile.

"I'm not sure," said Tom, handing one of the sheets back to Detective Schrödinger. "But I would say it was more likely to be this one."

"I'm going to say this one; it looks more like the picture I accidentally took and it seemed to have a sloping back," Martin said, handing the picture of the dark blue

Hudson Hornet to the detective, whose face immediately betrayed his frustration.

"Thank you both very much. We have a couple of leads that we are chasing down and I'm hoping we can solve the case if one of them pans out."

"Cool," said Tom, pleased that he and Martin had been able to help and looking forward to whatever privileges the City of Atlanta would shortly bestow on them.

"Just one more thing before I go," said Schrödinger. "I'm looking at your shirt; are you a Leeds United supporter?"

"Yes, I am. Since I was a kid."

"My father was in the US Air Force and was stationed in the UK in the early 1970s before he got married. He said they were the best soccer team in England at the time so he followed them."

"That's awesome, Detective."

"He passed away five years ago so I follow them on and off in his memory. I've not been to the UK but maybe I'll make it over to a match one day to see what all the fuss is about. Have a good evening, everyone. Wendy, can I talk to you outside?"

"Sure thing, Pete."

"Goodnight, everyone. Enjoy the rest of your evening."

Wendy and Schrödinger left the restaurant and went outside, leaving the others wondering if this was good news or bad. Whatever it was, Wendy had always said that

Schrödinger was not a big talker so it probably wouldn't take long.

"What car did you give him?" Martin asked.

"The red one," Tom replied.

"I gave him the blue one," said Martin, generating laughter around the table.

"At least we covered all the bases," Tom said. "That's the most important thing for witnesses."

"You two fools didn't witness shit," said Karen. "I'm surprised one of you didn't say you saw my damned car!"

"He's bound to believe Tom," Dave said. "They're besties now."

"No, we're not," Tom protested. "We support the same team, that's all."

"Maybe he'll fly over to the UK and they can go to games together," said Sadie. "Is he going to stay with you? It would protect you against home invasions if you had a detective living with you."

"No! He's not my best friend, he's not coming over to the UK and he's certainly not staying in my house," Tom protested, wondering why they all suddenly thought he was in a bromance with Detective Schrödinger.

"I'm with Tom on this one," said Martin. "There's only one person from Atlanta he'd want staying with him and it isn't Schrödinger."

"Who's that then?" said Sadie as all eyes focused on the person to Tom's right.

"Oh, shut the hell up, everyone," said Karen. "Do you see the skeleton sitting on that motorbike up there? Don't make me beat y'all to death with one of his bones."

They all looked up and saw a full-size, decorative skeleton above their heads, posed as if it were riding a motorbike just as Wendy walked back into the restaurant to join them.

"Hey, Wendy, come and save me from these fools."
"What are they doing?"
"Never mind. Is everything okay?"
"Pete said he wants to see me this weekend."
"Go Wendy!" said Sadie and Dave together, amidst cheers from the others at the table.
"Pete's got a couple of days off so he wants to see how we get on together."
"Do you think he'll talk?" Karen asked.
"I hope not. I'm in the middle of a dry spell so I hope he just gets on with it," Wendy replied, laughing as she sat down.
"Go Wendy!" said Sadie. "It'll be awesome."
"Seeing him work this case has changed my mind about him. He's got a serious job so he needs to be serious; maybe I should give him a second chance."
"I'm sure you'll have a great time," said Sadie. "We should get away for a night or two, Dave."
"I don't have much money at the moment, but I hear they're building a swanky new police station in Augusta.

We could go up there when they're done and I could start a fight and get us both arrested so we can try it out."

"I'm in if the coffee's good," said Sadie.

Chapter 30

Atlanta USA

Detective Schrödinger woke up at the usual time but not to the usual Atlanta weather. After a long period of clear skies and hot sun, this Thursday morning was dull and overcast. His first task was to check his phone for any calls, texts or emails that related to his active investigations, but there was nothing there this morning other than a text from Wendy with a single heart. He looked at the timestamp – just after midnight; she'd probably sent it at the end of the evening after a few whiskeys.

As someone who was tee-total, Schrödinger didn't understand the attraction of alcohol and, as a police officer, he'd seen the effects of it on people's behaviour first-hand and the impact it subsequently had on other people's lives. He began to question if seeing Wendy again socially was such a good idea after all and wondered if she took life seriously enough for him. Or did he take life too seriously for her?

The case of the body in Piedmont Park seemed to be nearing its conclusion and, once it was solved, he would have no need to see her again on a professional basis. If their upcoming weekend away together went well, they could move forwards towards a relationship but if it didn't, at least they wouldn't see one another again. If he could solve the case before tomorrow night it would make things a lot less complicated if the weekend didn't go well.

Schrödinger got ready for work and sat at his kitchen table drinking his coffee and watching the TV news. It was an established routine and the doom and gloom on the news always prepared him for the doom and gloom he would undoubtedly face during the day. His first task would be to see Mary Normanson; once he had interviewed her, he'd either visit the preacher in Riverdale or send a local uniformed officer to see her. He got up from his table, turned off the TV, put his empty cup in the sink and headed out to visit his first suspect – although he still wasn't convinced that either of these two women would prove to be the murderer.

The drive to Mary's house took less than 20 minutes and he was soon knocking on her front door. As he waited for the occupant to answer, Schrödinger cast his eye around the property; it was a two-storey house with a wide front porch where a table and two chairs had been set up. Potted plants formed a guard of honour on either side of the six steps he'd just walked up to reach the porch that he was now sheltering under as the rain began to fall. There was a driveway to the left with a garage at the end where a car would presumably be kept but, before he could investigate further, the door opened and a bright, cheerful old lady stood in front of him.

"Good morning, young man. How may I help you?"

"Good morning, ma'am," said Schrödinger, showing her his badge and police ID. "Are you Mrs Mary Normanson?"

"Why certainly," said Mary. "Won't you come in and have some tea?"

"Thank you, ma'am. I'd like that very much," said Schrödinger, following her into the house and towards the kitchen at the rear.

"Please take a seat, Detective," Mary said as she turned the kettle on. "I don't get many visitors these days so it's always nice to have some company. What can I do for you?"

"We're investigating an incident involving a classic automobile and are checking on anyone who might own such a car."

"Oh, this is so exciting!" Mary squealed as she poured them both some tea. "Would you like milk and sugar, Detective?"

"Just milk please," said Schrödinger. "Do you own such a vehicle?"

"Yes, I do. Well, I say I do but the car was always my late husband's. He passed away last year and I need to change the ownership papers. Is this what this is about? I really should have done it sooner but I've been so busy."

"What car do you have Mrs Normanson?"

"It's a Hudson Hornet. That door behind you leads to the garage; please feel free to have a look for yourself while I fetch you some cookies."

Schrödinger got up and went through the door Mary had indicated and pulled a cord inside the garage. An old strip light flickered into life and showed the garage in its entirety; directly in front of where he was standing was a dark blue Hudson Hornet. He walked around to the rear of the car, looked at the licence plate and saw the last three digits were 303. This was certainly not how he'd expected this visit to go.

"Thank you, Mrs Normanson," he said as he turned off the light, closed the door and returned to the kitchen where his tea was waiting. Something was bothering him.

"Is everything alright, Detective?"

"Everything's fine, thank you. Did you say your husband passed away last year?"

"Yes, my poor Walter passed last October. He was 81 years of age but had Alzheimer's for the last few years of his life. It was so very sad because he was such a lovely man."

"Do you have any pictures of the two of you together?" Schrödinger asked.

"Of course, Detective! If you'd care to follow me into the sitting room, there are plenty of them."

As they walked along the hallway, Schrödinger couldn't help but notice how sprightly Mary was for somebody in her mid-70s. She was certainly not frail and moved with the agility of somebody far younger. She also had an exceptionally clean house; in his experience, many older people had cluttered houses full of ornaments and photos collected over the many years of their existence. A lot of them weren't always that clean either. It was as if the occupants had decided that with relatively little time left on this earth, they would dispense with cleaning their houses and focus on enjoying themselves instead. Perhaps her sprightliness meant she had more energy to clean her house than most people he wondered, just as Mary began speaking again.

"There you are, Detective," said Mary, gesturing to an array of framed photographs on various shelves around the room before picking the nearest one up and handing it to him.

"Thank you," said Schrödinger as he looked at the photograph.

"This is the most recent one. That was taken last year on the fourth of July at a family party. It's hard to believe that just three months later he was gone."

"Can I ask how your husband died?"

"He had a heart attack, Detective. It was his second in two years. He was as strong as an ox in his younger days, but a few years into his retirement his body started to give up."

"I'm very sorry for your loss, Mrs Normanson."

"Thank you, Detective. What does Walter have to do with your investigation?"

"I'm not sure at the moment," said Schrödinger, lost in thought as he moved from one framed photograph to the next.

Schrödinger studied each of the pictures in turn. The facial features were the same as those of his John Doe back at the morgue and the smaller-than-average head confirmed his identity.

"I'm sorry to ask this, but did your late husband suffer from microcephaly?"

"I'm not sure Detective. He always knew his head was smaller than most people's but insisted that it wasn't microcephaly. He'd been examined by various doctors when he was younger but they said it was just nature giving him a small head. He made up for it by having a big heart."

"That's more important to a lot of people," said Schrödinger, suddenly thinking of Wendy.

Schrödinger's mind wandered for a second. Despite her shortcomings in other areas, Wendy had a big heart and it was only now he was in the presence of Mary – who was quite clearly missing her late husband – that he finally appreciated it.

"A heart full of love is much nicer than a head full of brains," Mary added, breaking him out of his reverie.

"Can I ask one more thing, Mrs Normanson?"

"Of course, Detective."

"Your husband died in October last year – is that correct?"

"Yes, he did. October 25th to be precise. I had him cremated on November 1st – the day after Halloween. Walter always loved Halloween and it was such a shame that he missed it. I wanted to cremate him on October 31st but the crematorium was closed that day so they did it the next day instead."

"And which service did you use for that?" Schrödinger asked.

"I can't remember the name but it was right by the golf course. Walter loved golf so it seemed fitting. I wish I could remember the name."

"Don't worry, I know the one you mean. I won't take up any more of your time today. Thank you for the tea."

"Oh, it was my pleasure, Detective."

"I must compliment you on your home, Mrs Normanson. It's exceptionally clean."

"I don't like dirt or dust of any kind. Walter always used to tease me and said I had a phobia of dirt and I should be more relaxed."

"I know there are several phobia workshops across the city, Mrs Normanson. A friend of mine goes to one to help her deal with the various issues she has."

"That sounds interesting, Detective. I might just look those up – although they'd have to be during the day because I don't like driving too far at night these days."

"I'm sure you'll find one that meets during daylight hours. There was one in the north of the city that met on Tuesdays and Fridays but there was an incident there recently so it may not be on anymore."

"What happened?" asked Mary.

"One member of the group offered to kill another member."

"Oh my, that's certainly not the type of place I would like to visit. I have a phobia of being killed, Detective. Although I guess a lot of other people might share that with me."

"I'm sure they might," Schrödinger agreed, turning to head out of the sitting room.

As he made his way towards the door, Schrödinger noticed a recessed shelf that he hadn't seen on his way in. It was full of trophies and photos of what looked like Mary Normanson in a leotard.

"Are these trophies all yours, Mrs Normanson?" Schrödinger asked. "They're very impressive."

"Thank you, Detective. I'm very proud of them."

"How did you win them all?"

"I was a wrestling champion when I was younger. It was a long time ago and it wasn't fully legal back in those days so I hope you won't arrest me. I enjoyed it, but I had to give it up when I got married to Walter because he didn't like the idea of me cavorting around in a leotard in front of other men."

"Don't worry," said Schrödinger with a warm smile. "I'm not here to arrest you for it; I think the statute of limitations has passed on that anyway."

"Thank goodness," said Mary.

"These trophies look relatively new."

"Oh, they are. I won these quite recently."

"You returned to wrestling?"

"Yes, I did, Detective. I've always kept myself fit and would have continued my career if I hadn't have got married. My Walter was a lovely man; he was kind, generous and always so very thoughtful. He gave me three wonderful children but didn't want me to carry on with my wrestling career, so I stopped out of respect for him,"

"But you started back up again recently?"

"Yes, I did. When he started suffering from Alzheimer's disease, he didn't know whether I was in the house or not so I would tell him I was going to the grocery store but joined a senior citizen's wrestling group instead."

"I see," said Schrödinger, not seeing at all.

"I won the Atlanta Seniors Wrestling Championship four years straight and the Georgia State Championship three times. I would have won last year as well but the tournament started the day after Walter died and it didn't seem right to leave his body here while I was competing."

"That's very noble of you."

"I know, Detective. That slutty bitch from Kirkwood won."

"Excuse me?" said Schrödinger, shocked at Mary's sudden descent into vulgar language.

"Mary-Lou Crowder. She flirts with the officials and wears revealing leotards to distract them from their jobs. I beat her in the final last year and the year before but she kept coming back for more."

"Will you enter next year's tournament?"

"I sure will. I'm going to grind her face into the dirt," said Mary, clearly animated.

Schrödinger was taken aback at this sudden turn in Mary's character. A sweet, kind old lady had now shown signs of becoming a raging demon. Wrestling appeared to bring out that side of her and, whoever the woman in Kirkwood was, he felt sorry for her.

"Well, thank you again, Mrs Normanson. I'll be in touch if I need any more information."

"You're very welcome, Detective," Mary replied as she opened the front door for him. "Please come back any time."

Schrödinger got into his car and drove along the street for a minute or so before pulling over. He had planned to visit the other suspect in Riverdale but suddenly Mary Normanson seemed a lot more likely to have committed the crime. She looked strong enough to move a body and had a fire inside her that could become a temper under the right provocation. Mary Normanson had now gone from being a person of interest to his main suspect. There was just one small problem – Mary's husband had been cremated in October but they'd found his body just last week, totally intact and with no signs of having been anywhere near a furnace.

The next stop that morning would be the crematorium but if that proved to be a dead end, he'd then ask a uniformed officer to visit the pastoress in Riverdale. The rain began to ease slightly as he pulled away from the side of the road and headed north, wondering if he was really

making any progress or if he was just telling himself he
was.

Chapter 31

Atlanta, USA

It was close to lunchtime but Tom had not yet received his daily call from Katrina so he presumed that something important was happening back in the UK. The last he'd heard was the police were involved and Racist Roy appeared to be the man they'd set their sights on. In the absence of any clear direction – and not looking to rush through the work and finish early in case they were called home early – he decided to hold a meeting. That would drag things out a bit.

He called the rest of the UK team together for an update and asked them all for individual progress reports. Stuart and Bhavna had come to the end of their reprogramming work and were now effectively finished and could potentially go home. Martin had also finished his work but Tom wanted him to help test the changes the other two had made. Looking down at the list of outstanding tasks he realised that, aside from confirming the system no longer captured and stored inappropriate customer data, there was nothing else left to do.

Tom planned to check the data capture part with Karen but he would also need Martin to check the data was stored correctly. This last task wasn't particularly difficult, but it was extremely boring and Martin enjoyed boring tasks. Or was it Stuart? Tom knew it was one of them but it didn't matter who because he was giving it to Martin. This would all be done tomorrow, so hopefully they'd be able to stay here for the weekend at least before flying home.

The four of them agreed to take an early lunch break and then spend the rest of the afternoon writing individual reports on what they had done. These would ultimately be combined and presented to the directors when they got back to the UK. Assuming the other three didn't mess things up, this would get Tom the promotion Katrina had mentioned. As the others returned to their desks, Tom called Katrina to update her on their progress before she left for the day.

"Hi, Tom, how's your day going?" Katrina said, through a lot of wind noise.

"Hi, Katrina, we're good thanks. Have I caught you at a bad time?"

"No, I'm just walking back to the car. It's been an intense day today and there have been a few more developments. Give me a moment to get to the car and I'll explain. Could you get the others and put me on speakerphone?"

"Sure thing, Katrina."

Tom called the others over and they headed towards an empty room where the call would not disturb the rest of the office. Just as they were about to go in, Karen shouted over to them.

"Hey, guys! I wouldn't go in there if I were you, that's the House of Jizz!" she half-shouted and half-laughed. "Try the room in the corner instead. There probably won't be as much jizz in that one."

"What do you mean 'there probably won't be as much'?" Tom asked, but she and the rest of her team had already started laughing – although most of her co-workers were upset that she'd warned them about the notorious room.

"Hello?" Katrina's voice came over the phone. "Is everyone there?"

"Yes, Katrina, we're just going into a quiet room."

"Thanks."

"Right, we're all here now. Martin, Stuart and Bhavna are with me."

"Hello, everyone, we've got some good news that you'll find interesting."

"Good afternoon from us and good evening to you," said Bhavna.

"Hi, Bhavna. Our security consultants have traced the source of the data breach. It seems that our old friend Roy White put a back door in the system at the time of the last security update. It looks like he did it on the day he resigned so he could steal our customer data once he'd left the business and sell it for profit – although it was only the data from the American company that was extracted."

"So, he was anti-American as well as anti-everyone else?" Stuart asked.

"It would appear so. It seems he wanted to destroy the American division before it got off the ground and the police have arrested him today. I'm sorry I've not been around but I've been up with Keith and Louisa putting a report together."

"Have they nabbed him?" Tom asked. "Did he 'come quietly' or did he run and force them to chase after him and shoot him?"

"I think you've spent too much time in America," Katrina replied. "The police are questioning him but it seems he was part of an online forum and met up with some bad people. From what little we've been told he wasn't happy that traditional British clothing was being sold overseas. He was against it when the idea was first suggested and, after being around such a diverse group of people in Atlanta, it triggered him and he snapped."

"That's terrible," said Bhavna. "I had always heard that he was a very unpleasant man but this is truly awful."

"You're right, Bhavna," Katrina continued. "The external security consultants have fixed the breach, removed the back door and secured our data. I understand that you and Stuart may have finished the reprogramming work over there?"

"Yes, we have. Everything is complete and all that is needed now is for Tom, Martin and Karen to test it."

"How long do you think that will take, Tom?"

"Probably the best part of a day."

"That's excellent news," said Katrina, although Tom didn't think it was excellent for him.

"Does that mean we get to come home early?" Martin asked.

"I have some good news for you all in that area. Tarquin and Louisa are so impressed with the way you've all worked together, put the hours in and resolved the issues quickly that they've given you all next week off as additional paid leave. I'd like to add my congratulations to you all as well; you've done an amazing job. Well done everyone!"

"Thanks, Katrina!" said Tom, closely followed by the other three. "When do we fly back?"

There was a slight pause at the other end of the line as Katrina connected the Bluetooth on her phone to her car so she could drive home safely while, for his part, Tom was quite disappointed that their company holiday was coming to a premature end.

"This is the part you might like," Katrina cut back in. "The cost of booking new flights for Saturday is about the same as the refund we'd get from the hotel for that week so you've got the choice of flying back on Saturday and having next week off at home or staying in Atlanta and having a free week there before coming home on your original flight next weekend. Just remember you won't be able to claim any expenses for meals or taxis for that week though."

"When do you need to know?" Tom asked.

"By 9 am UK time tomorrow, so we can re-book flights and cancel hotel rooms for those that want to come home."

"I will be coming home," said Bhavna.

"Me too," Stuart added.

"I'll be coming home as well," said Martin. "One of the boys isn't feeling too good according to Irma so she'll need the help."

"Are you all sure?" Katrina asked.

"Yes," said a chorus of three voices.

"I'll let you know later if that's okay?" said Tom.

"No problem, Tom. Just e-mail me later so I can tell Louisa and Debbie tomorrow morning."

They ended the call and went back into the main office. Tom went over to see Karen on the way back to his desk and updated her on the news. In return, she showed him an email she'd just received from Louisa advising that she would also be receiving paid leave for her part in resolving the crisis.

"Hell, I didn't do shit," Karen laughed. "I mean, you didn't do much, but I did even less. It was those three over there who did most of the work."

"Yes, but we supervised it," Tom said.

"You didn't supervise anything!" Karen replied, still laughing.

"I made sure nothing else went wrong."

"You broke our damned coffee machine on your first morning!"

"I fixed it again."

"No, you didn't. You watched Stuart fix it."

"But I told him to fix it and supervised him while he did it," said Tom, knowing this would be an argument he wasn't going to win.

"Well, whatever. But I still don't think you did enough to get yourself a free week off. What are you going to do when you get back home?"

"Er..." Tom hesitated, unsure if he was making the right choice. "I was thinking of staying here for the week."

"You bet your ass you're staying here," said Karen. "I'm sure as hell not going to put up with my dumbass sister and her stupid cats for a whole damned week. I need to get out of the house as much as possible so wherever I go, you're coming with me."

"Really?"

"Sure! If I go out alone, she'll want to come with me but if I take you along, she'll get the message and stay home."

"That sounds good," Tom said. "Shall we order some pizzas for lunch?"

"That's the most sensible thing you've said all week. In fact, that's the only sensible thing you've said all week," Karen said as her laugh erupted across the office.

***

While Tom and Karen were ordering pizzas, Detective Schrödinger was heading towards the crematorium.

His visit to Mary Normanson had convinced him that she would be strong enough to dispose of a corpse and may even be capable of murder if provoked sufficiently, but everything remained circumstantial at present. The vehicle, the proximity of her house to the park and her physical prowess all pointed towards her – or possibly a family member who had access to her car – but if her husband had been cremated several months ago, he still wasn't sure how she could have killed him last week.

Schrödinger reached the crematorium and called one of the uniformed officers on duty at the station. He may as well send him down to visit the pastoress in Riverdale while he was following his current line of enquiry. Satisfied that both angles were being covered, he stepped out of his car and headed towards the main building where a portly, middle-aged, bald man with a long, unkempt beard was painting the frame of the front door. The rain had stopped and he was painting at a speed that suggested he thought it was about to start again soon.

"Good afternoon, sir. How may we help you today?"

"Good afternoon. I'm Detective Schrödinger from Atlanta PD."

"Good to meet you, Detective. We haven't had anyone from the police around here since the snowstorm of 2014. An officer came to check we were okay but it was so icy he fell over more times than a one-legged man in a butt-kicking contest. He was madder than a wet hen when we started laughing at him."

"Would you happen to be the proprietor?"

"Yes sir, I would. I'm Dwayne P. Cleverley the sixth and I'm proud to be at your service."

"The sixth?"

Yes sir. This crematorium has been in my family for six generations. Well, not this exact one, you understand. When my great, great, great granddaddy first went into business in Tennessee in 1904, it was a lot more low-key than it is now."

"How so?"

"Well, truth be told, they just dug a big 'ole pit, threw people in it and set them on fire, even if they weren't always completely dead. Things have changed quite a bit since the old days, although the principle is still the same," Dwayne continued. "The business has been passed down from father to son or daughter ever since. Apart from Granddaddy Clyde of course."

"What happened to him?" Schrödinger asked instinctively but soon wished he hadn't.

"Well, the story differs depending on which member of the family you talk to but most folks around these parts say Clyde was murdered by someone else in the family and thrown in the furnace so the other party could take over the business, but of course, there's always an alternative version."

"What's the other version?"

"Clyde was one dumb son-of-a-gun who had always fancied himself as one of those inventor types," said Dwayne. "You could usually find him down in his barn

380

making stupid stuff and testing it out on himself. The family say that when his daddy died and he inherited the business, the first thing he did was test the furnace and it burned him to a crisp."

"Were the police involved?"

"Yes sir, they were, but they knew his cornbread wasn't fully done in the middle so they decided it was death by misadventure and the business passed down to my daddy."

Schrödinger grimaced and tried to get the conversation back on track but the old fool in front of him just carried on.

"Now, he was not a cheerful man, my father, but I remember on the day he took ownership he was as happy as a tornado in a trailer park. I took over the business two years ago when he retired. Anyhoo, Detective, I'm sure you didn't come here for the history of my family. What can I do for you?"

"I'm investigating a case and need to check one of your services from November last year."

"Sure, Detective. What is it you need?"

"I'm investigating a homicide, but the victim appears to have been cremated several months ago."

"Do you have a body?"

"Yes, we do."

"Would you like us to cremate it for you? If you've got it in the trunk of your car, we can do it right now. I'll just tell my assistant Erica to switch old Betsy on."

"No," Schrödinger replied. "Is it possible that your furnace could have been out of operation last November?"

"That's never happened yet, Detective," Dwayne said proudly.

"So the furnace works every time?"

"Yes siree, Bob. Old Betsy is the most reliable furnace in the whole state of Georgia. Every cremation we do is videotaped and the ashes of the deceased are given to the closest relative. We also have a mighty fine selection of high-quality urns at remarkably affordable prices. They make us a lot of money because folks don't usually want to take grandma home in a grocery bag."

"You have video footage of your services?"

"Yes, we make two copies from the CCTV feeds. One copy of the tape goes to the relatives – this is included in the price and is our unique selling point that helps us stand out from our competitors."

"That's good business sense," Schrödinger conceded involuntarily.

"Thank you, sir," said Dwayne. "We keep the other copy but only for three months because we recycle the tapes to help the environment. If it was November, it's likely to have been recorded over in February but we can go and take a look real quick if you'd like. If you'd care to follow me into the office, I'll show you our system – just be sure to watch the paintwork around this door."

The two men went inside, walked across a small entrance hall and through a battered door into a large, mahogany-panelled office which contained two huge wooden desks and a row of six assorted precarious-looking chairs. Death was a lucrative business but Mr Cleverley had not spent any money on his office or its furnishings. A young woman with long, light brown hair was sitting at a computer looking bored but perked up when the two men walked through the door.

"This is my assistant, Erica."

"Hello," said Erica, with all the enthusiasm of somebody who sat at a computer all day but would rather be out walking her dog.

"Good morning, miss," said Schrödinger.

"This is a proper, official, bona fide police detective, Erica. He's looking for details of one of the services we did back in November. Have you got the keys to the main cupboard?"

"They're here on my desk," said Erica and went back to looking at her computer screen.

"Thank you kindly, young lady," said Dwayne, picking up the keys.

"You're welcome," said Erica, who hadn't actually done anything at all.

"See here, Detective," said Dwayne as he gestured for Schrödinger to join him at a floor-to-ceiling cupboard he'd just opened that was full of boxes and files.

"Have you found something?"

"No sir, I have not. This shelf here has all the tapes on and they are numbered from one through ninety and from A through D. We do a maximum of four services each day. Today we are on day 43 so we'll be using tape 43A first, then 43B and so on. The tapes from November last year would have been used again in February."

Dwayne took out the VHS tape with 44A written on it and put it in what looked like a 30-year-old VCR and pressed play. He directed Schrödinger's gaze to a big TV on one of the walls and he could clearly see the date stamp from the camera was from the end of January. Dwayne was using a ridiculously simple system with very antiquated technology but it seemed to work, so Schrödinger couldn't fault it – although the video was not of the highest quality.

"Is this the same video that you would give to the relatives?"

"Yes sir. Usually, the person who organises and pays for the service."

"The picture is not of the very highest quality, is it?"

"No sir, but that's just how they like it. Most of the people we get in here are happy to have a record of them being here but they don't want anybody else to be able to identify them. With these videos, they can spot themselves because they remember where they sat, but nobody else can recognise them because the video is just too poor. It's a security measure."

"I see," said Schrödinger. Do you keep any other records?"

"We do, but this is privileged and personal information you understand. You would probably need to get some kind of court order to access it. I'm not trying to be difficult, Detective, but our clients pay for discretion. My lawyers would be right up my ass if they knew I gave client details away without the proper authorisation."

"I completely understand, Mr Cleverley."

"You see, Detective, we cater for the poorer and less noble elements of society and some of them pay cash because they don't have bank accounts. I don't mind telling you that back in the day some of my predecessors weren't too fussed about how the body came here or even how it went from being a live body to a dead one."

"I think I get what you're saying," Schrödinger said with a resigned sigh.

"My great granddaddy often got woken up in the middle of the night with an urgent cremation request because folks round here knew they could rely on him."

"To dispose of a dead body quickly?"

"Yes sir. I once heard that some of the bodies they brought in would still be warm. Many of them still had bullet holes with blood leaking out of them too."

Schrödinger stared at Dwayne P. Cleverley dumbfounded. The man was as dumb as a rock and had just admitted to a family history of body disposal for criminals. This was certainly something that somebody should look into, but at the moment he just wanted to solve his current case and go away for the weekend. He was beginning to see why some people poured themselves a large drink when they got home each night after work.

"These days everything's legit, Detective," Dwayne said with a broad smile. "We even pay some of our taxes."

"I'm glad to hear it," said Schrödinger. "I guess I'll need a warrant to see the records I need."

"I'm sorry I can't be of more help at the moment, Detective. There is a book of condolences you can look at though. It's not classified and most of my clients choose not to sign it, but you're welcome to have a look."

"Does it go back to November?" Schrödinger asked, not sure what it would tell him even if it did.

"Yes sir, it surely does," said Dwayne, reaching back into the cupboard and pulling out a large white box. "Here you go, Detective. This book covers October and the first week of November and this one covers the rest of November."

"Thanks," said Schrödinger, taking the first book and thumbing through its pages.

"Not everyone signs the book I'm afraid, but some do. We often get asked to send them copies of the completed pages as a souvenir so they can remember who was at the service and who wrote what about their loved ones. Given the type of people we get in here, sometimes the comments can be less than complimentary," said Dwayne, letting out a big, hearty laugh.

Schrödinger had stopped listening as he'd already started to search through the book of condolences to find the date he was looking for.

"In some cases, they're quite defamatory and the other family members get upset," Dwayne continued regardless.

"I bet," Schrödinger mumbled.

"It's not unknown for us to see almost the exact same set of mourners again within a couple of weeks because one of the original guests has taken exception to another's comment about their daddy or their uncle."

"I'm sure," said Schrödinger, distracted by what he was now reading.

He'd found the service for Walter Henry Normanson and he'd also found several messages of condolences, although only two of these were of interest to him:

"My darling Walter, I will miss you always. Rest in peace until we are together again. Your loving wife, Mary."

This confirmed that he was looking at the right service, but beneath this was another message that intrigued him:

"May you rest in peace, dear brother. I wasn't here for you much in life but I'm here for you today. Sleep well, Norman."

Detective Schrödinger read the messages once more. Walter apparently had a long-lost brother who'd attended his funeral in November, but how did he then find himself dead in April? As some of the fog had begun to clear from this mind, more fog had just rolled in.

"Do you mind if I make a copy of this page?"

"No problem," said Dwayne. "Let me do that for you."

Dwayne took the book over to a photocopier that looked as if it had been bought at around the same time as his VCR and took two copies.

"One for luck," he said, passing the two pieces of paper to Schrödinger.

"Thank you for your help today, Mr Cleverley."

"Anytime, Detective," Dwayne said as they headed to the door. "And remember, if you have any bodies you need to dispose of 'off the record' I'd be prepared to offer you a 5% police discount."

"Goodbye, Mr Cleverley. We have our own team that handles all of our unidentified victims."

"I know, but that's just the official ones. If you ever find yourself up a creek without a paddle because you've interrogated a suspect a bit too vigorously, we'll be here for you, come rain or shine."

"I'll bear it in mind," said Schrödinger as he walked quickly over to his car, got in and drove away as quickly as he could.

Chapter 32

Atlanta, USA

Schrödinger drove back to the police station armed with the most promising lead he'd yet had on this case. Assuming there were no complications from the visit to the other potential suspect, he could now apply for a warrant for the forensics team to search Mary Normanson's house for evidence that she'd killed her brother-in-law, Norman. His phone rang and he pressed the button automatically to take the call on his vehicle's speakerphone system.

"Hey, Detective, it's Officer Hampton. You asked me to check out a house in Riverdale for the Piedmont Park case."

"Good afternoon, officer. Do you have anything for me?"

"Unfortunately, no. I went to visit the property but it was unoccupied. I spoke to a neighbour and she told me that the owner – Pastoress June Lawrence – has been in hospital for a couple of weeks."

"What happened?" Schrödinger asked.

"The neighbour said the pastoress was doing some work on her roof and was at the top of a ladder when her two dogs got out of the back yard and ran round the front to see where she was. These are big dogs and the neighbour told me they ran around the corner and crashed straight into the ladder, knocking Miss Lawrence off."

"That must have been awful."

"She fell down 12 feet onto a concrete driveway and broke her hip."

"So where is Pastoress Lawrence now?"

"She's in a private hospital and her neighbour is looking after the dogs."

"Did you have a look around the property?"

"I did, Detective. The garage had a small window in it and I could see what looked like an old car under a tarpaulin. The car was up on bricks and the wheels were piled up in the corner of the garage. If I had to guess, I'd say it hadn't been driven for a long time; there was a lot of junk stored on and around it and the tarpaulin was covered in dust like it hadn't been moved in a while."

"Thank you, Officer Hampton. You'll send me a full report with the neighbour's name, won't you?"

"Of course, Detective. It'll be with you by the end of the day."

Schrödinger ended the call and pulled his car over in a safe place to review what he'd learned today. He always thought more clearly when he was sitting alone in his car without any distractions and he now felt as if he was on the cusp of solving this crime as he stared out at the rain that was now falling quite heavily. He considered the three core pillars of establishing guilt – means, motive and opportunity – and found he had two of them.

The depth, pattern and sheer number of wounds suggested a weak but repeated and passionate attack by somebody lacking in the strength needed to deliver powerful blows and would therefore be consistent with a woman of Mrs Normanson's age. Her wrestling experience would have given her the expertise necessary to manoeuvre a body around, despite being in her mid-70s, so Schrödinger considered that while Mary Normanson was not the most obvious of suspects, she would almost certainly have had the means to commit this particular crime.

The next issue was one of opportunity and Schrödinger was now certain that the victim was Mrs Normanson's late husband's long-lost brother who had come to Atlanta to attend his funeral. Given the physical likenesses between them and their similar age range, it was likely they were twins, or at least born within a year or two of one another. Schrödinger didn't like to guess but, if he had to, his money would be on them being twins.

The only hurdle that remained was a motive. Why would Mrs Normanson murder her late husband's brother? There didn't appear to be any foul play involved in her husband's death, although he would check that when he got back to his office. Perhaps the deceased had come to Atlanta to see his brother and there had been some bad blood between them?

If Schrödinger assumed he had come here to kill his brother (or if they had argued and it had escalated to the point where murder was the result), why would Mrs Normanson wait six months to take her revenge? The Italians had a saying that revenge was a dish best served cold but Mrs Normanson couldn't have predicted how long her late husband's brother would be staying in Atlanta. Also, she had a fierce temper and that type of person wasn't normally the cool, calculating type and would normally try to take the first opportunity that came their way.

It was far more likely that the deceased hadn't killed his brother, but Schrödinger couldn't think of a reason why Mrs Normanson would wait six months to kill him. Maybe he'd liked Atlanta so much that he'd decided to stay, had called round for dinner one day, complained about her cooking and she'd thrown a sandwich grill at him – after first hitting him on the head 20 times with a ladle.

Schrödinger let out a rare chuckle as he pictured the scene and then started his car to begin the drive back to the police station. He'd check the death certificate for Walter Normanson and apply for a warrant before going home; hopefully, they'd both come through tomorrow. He needed some light relief so he started to think about his upcoming weekend away with Wendy. Was he doing the right thing? Would things be any different this time? She was a lively and fun woman but, even though they'd only originally seen each other for a couple of months, she'd started to get on his nerves as time went on. Did opposites really attract or did they ultimately just lead to irreconcilable differences?

As he pulled into his designated parking space at Atlanta PD, Schrödinger thought about Mary Normanson and the happiness she'd shared over the years with her husband. He wondered if he would ever have that and if he did, who it would be with. Wendy had been fun for a while, but to be with her long-term would require him to show far more tolerance of her frivolous side than he had before. On the other hand, while she might be a total airhead, she had a kind heart and would never hurt anyone. She certainly wouldn't smash anyone's head in with a sandwich grill.

***

It was the end of the day at Classic Country Clothing (UK) Inc. and everyone was about to leave the office and head their separate ways. The UK team had decided to stay on a bit later to finish some critical updates so Tom and Karen could test them the next morning.

"Are you guys going to stay here and fix this shit for us tonight?" Karen asked as she was about to leave.

"Yes, if that's alright," said Tom. "It'll take a couple of hours and then we'll be done. Stuart and Bhavna will be doing most of the work."

"Now why doesn't that surprise me? You sure are great at avoiding work, aren't you?"

"He's the best," said Martin. "He's got awards for it at home."

"I bet he has," said Karen.

"To be fair, I have given them both the day off tomorrow as we won't need them for the testing part," said Tom.

"It will be nice to have a day off after the late evenings Stuart and I have had," said Bhavna.

"What will you two be doing?" Karen asked.

"We're going to the aquarium and the zoo," Stuart replied. "We would have done that last Sunday if it hadn't been for the food poisoning."

"Our flights are at lunchtime on Saturday so tomorrow will be our final day here; thank you for letting us have the time off."

"No worries at all. You both deserve it," said Tom as sincerely as he could, knowing that he'd asked them all to work late and sacrifice their evening so he and Martin didn't have to deal with Bhavna tomorrow.

"I'll see you guys in the morning then," said Karen, picking up her jacket as Delores did the same in the seat next to her. "Hey, Delores."

"Yes?"

"Can I ask you something about your jacket?"

"Sure Karen, it's mighty fine, ain't it?"

"No, it isn't. That is the ugliest jacket I have ever seen. Where did you get it from?"

"I got it from an online shopping website," said Delores, looking hurt. "It links buyers with suppliers in China to keep costs low and you can buy anything you want on there."

"Did you order that specific jacket?" Karen asked, not surprised that Delores had said it was cheap.

"Well, no, as a matter of fact, I didn't order this exact thing," Delores admitted.

"What exactly did you order?"

"I ordered a multi-coloured Jack-in-the-Box toy for my son for his birthday."

"And they sent you a jacket instead of a Jack-in-the-Box?"

"Yes."

"Do you even like the jacket?"

"No, but if it annoys you, I'm going to keep wearing it."

"Me and my big mouth," Karen said with a resigned sigh. "Have you used these people before?"

"A few times."

"Are they always that bad?"

"It can be a gamble," Delores admitted. "I once ordered some Coke socks for my brother as a joke gift for Christmas."

"Why the hell didn't you buy them downtown?"

"It was cheaper online. Also, he prefers Pepsi so I got them to send the parcel directly to him so he wouldn't know they were from me."

"Did he like them?"

"I don't know. I haven't seen him since he got arrested."

"He got arrested?!"

"There must have been a misunderstanding in China because they sent him some normal socks filled with cocaine. The package was stopped as it went through customs and the DEA went round and arrested him for buying drugs off of the internet."

"Didn't you step in to clear his name?"

"He's now doing 20 years in a federal prison," Delores said. "I'm worried that if I try to help, they might send me away too."

Karen stared at Delores but said nothing more. She made a mental note not to set up a 'Secret Santa' event next Christmas and then picked up her things and said goodnight to everyone. Going home to Wendy would be a breeze after this.

***

Detective Schrödinger had spent the remainder of his afternoon gathering information on Walter Normanson's death and trying to establish if he had a brother anywhere in any of the national databases. He'd also applied for a search warrant that covered Mary Normanson's house, garage, land and any motor vehicles in her possession and was wondering if tomorrow he'd be arresting his first septuagenarian.

Walter Normanson's death certificate recorded 'Congestive Heart Failure' with no other notes or observations so it appeared that his widow's statement had been true.

There was no luck in obtaining a birth certificate for either him or his brother, although this was unsurprising given his age and the lack of adequate records maintained during World War 2 when they were likely to have both been born.

With nothing more he could reasonably do tonight, Schrödinger made his way home and would call Wendy when he got in to confirm she was still available for their weekend away. He planned to drive her to Nashville so they could have a weekend of live music and dancing; that would certainly impress her, even though he knew she'd get so drunk he'd have to carry her back to the hotel each night.

Tom was busy sending emails to Katrina, Louisa and Keith in the UK to confirm he would be staying in Atlanta and updating them on the progress they'd all made. The others had sent him their reports already, so he combined them with his and was all set for the final testing tomorrow. He'd actually worked quite hard today and was both surprised and disappointed with himself.

Tomorrow would be another full day, but at least Miss Pedantic and Mr Beard wouldn't be with them – especially as he was sure Stuart's beard had grown since they'd been in Atlanta and now looked big enough to house a family of cats. Maybe Stuart could re-house Wendy's 'girls' and help Karen reclaim her house again.

The taxi arrived and took them back to their hotel. Tom and Martin went straight to the bar and ordered some fried chicken and two beers each while Stuart and Bhavna went back to their rooms, promising to join them after they'd showered.

"Do you think there's something going on between those two?" Martin asked as two servers brought over their cutlery and condiments – one of whom looked vaguely familiar.

"Good evening, y'all, my name is Annie and this is Becci. She's new and will be training with me tonight. She's going to be helping us out in the last few weeks before we close down. We're super lucky to have her with us, not only because she knows her shit but also because everyone else is leaving."

"Good evening," said Tom. "You look very familiar, Becci. I haven't seen many goth waitresses in Atlanta."

"Or anywhere," Martin added.

"Oh, hi," said Becci. "Will there just be the two of you this evening?"

"I think so. There are two upstairs who may join us later on but for the moment it's just us."

"That's good. I think I might be able to cope with two of you," Becci replied glumly as she and Annie moved on to serve another table.

"What did she mean by that?" Martin asked quietly.

"She was the one from the bar by the park. Every time she came over, we were laughing about something and she didn't join in. I thought the culture over here was

398

that the waitresses joined in as much as they could so they got a bigger tip. She didn't even smile, let alone laugh."

"She's a goth," said Martin.

"Fair point."

"Hey, guys!" said Stuart as he walked across the bar with Bhavna.

"That was a quick one," Tom said innocently.

"A quick what?" Bhavna asked. "How do you know what we were up to? Stuart, did you tell them?"

"I meant a quick shower. You said you were going for a shower."

"Yes, of course," said Bhavna, her face flushing. "Are we going to sit around and gossip all day or can we order some food?"

"We've just ordered but you might be able to add it onto the bill if you go to the bar."

"I will do that," Bhavna said and walked quickly over to the bar with her head down.

Stuart sat down, gave Tom and Martin a quick wink and then began telling them what he had accomplished that day. Everything had now been completed and just needed to be tested tomorrow and Stuart admitted that he couldn't wait to go home.

"What do you think of it here?" Tom asked him and Bhavna as she returned to the table and sat down next to Tom and opposite Stuart.

"We haven't seen much of the place to be fair. We got food poisoning and spent the whole day in bed on Sunday and haven't been far from the hotel or the office since then."

"Tomorrow will be good," Bhavna added. "I am excited to be able to visit the aquarium and the zoo. Maybe we can visit some other places if we have time."

"Well, I hope the food is okay tonight; you don't want to spend the whole day in bed together again tomorrow, do you?"

"Certainly not," said Bhavna.

"Stuart?" Tom asked.

"Sorry, I was just checking my phone. Did you say something about us spending the day in bed together again?"

Becci brought their food over and once again caught the tail end of a conversation she had no interest in hearing.

"Enjoy your meals. How long are you in Atlanta for?"

"Three of us are leaving on Saturday morning but Tom is staying for another week," said Bhavna, pointing at Tom.

"That's so great," said Becci. "Will you be staying at this hotel?"

"I think so," said Tom.

"And will you be seeing your American friends at all?"

"I hope so. I won't be working so we'll probably hang out together a fair bit."

"And will you be bringing them to this hotel?"

"Probably not. They all live in Midtown and Cumberland so we'll spend our time up there."

"Good," said Becci, smiling for the first time in a while. "Enjoy your food."

"I like her," said Tom. "She's different from most people here."

"You like everyone," Martin said. "Just don't let Karen hear you say that."

"What do you mean?"

"We all know about you and Karen. Glances here and there, always sitting next to one another, endless messages when you're not in the same room."

"We're just friends who have to work closely together," Tom replied sheepishly.

"It looks like you two are having a holiday romance," Bhavna suggested with a smirk.

"I don't think I'm the only one," Tom replied.

"I recommend that we all eat our food before it gets cold," said a red-faced Bhavna, looking down at her plate and starting to eat furiously.

The rest of the meal was eaten in relative silence. As soon as Bhavna finished, she made her excuses and went upstairs. Most business trips followed a familiar and predictable pattern; colleagues who don't know each other that well get thrown together for a few days, unfamiliarity turns to familiarity and friendships and bonds are often formed.

This works well on shorter trips, but for the longer ones, being in close proximity to people who aren't family or close friends soon begins to suffocate everyone and then arguments and disagreements rear their heads until everybody hates each other and wants to go home.

Tom and Martin had been lucky on this trip because they already had a lifelong friendship, but the strain was beginning to tell on Bhavna. Stuart was faring slightly better, although even he had lost some of his deadpan humour as the week had progressed. Either that or the sex with Bhavna wasn't that good.

Stuart signalled that he'd be heading upstairs for an early night as well – to obvious comments from Tom and Martin – and he soon left them to their evening in the bar.

"They're at it," said Martin.
"They're definitely at it," Tom concurred.

With that important point agreed upon, the two friends settled in with another round of beers and talked about work, old times and why Becci the goth waitress had only smiled when she thought they weren't going to be bothering her again. Although when Tom told her he might be bringing the others down to the hotel restaurant one evening, her face and tone had both gone back to their default settings of sourness and misery.

Chapter 33

Atlanta, USA

Breakfast on Friday morning was a more subdued affair than it had been most mornings. Stuart and Bhavna's secret romantic liaisons had been discovered – or at least guessed – and they were both quieter than usual (and less annoying in Bhavna's case). Martin was worried about one of his boys, while Tom was just keen to get the day over with as soon as possible and have a free week off in Atlanta. His mind had already left the project they were working on and he was now thinking about how he'd spend his time next week. He was particularly keen to learn if he really would be getting to see Karen as often as she'd hinted.

"We'd better make a move soon," said Martin, bringing Tom back from wherever his mind had gone off to.

"Okay, let's do it. You two have a great day off and we'll probably see you tonight."

"Thanks. We're off to the zoo first and then the aquarium," said Stuart.

"I would also like to visit the Botanical Gardens," Bhavna added.

"It looks like we're visiting the Botanical Gardens too," Stuart said with a sigh.

Tom and Martin left the breakfast table and went outside to call a taxi, leaving Stuart and Bhavna to finish their breakfast.

"I don't see it with those two," said Martin once they were safely outside the hotel. "He seems utterly miserable doing what she says all the time."

"Maybe he likes a dominant woman?"

"That might be it."

"Or maybe he's just practising his 'miserable face' for married life."

"It's not all bad," Martin said.

"Really?"

"At least I can have regular sex."

"When was the last time you actually had sex though – regular or otherwise?" Tom asked.

"Nine months before Ben was born," Martin said quietly, looking down at the floor.

***

Detective Schrödinger arrived at his office to find the search warrant for Mary Normanson's property had arrived, so he called together a small team of forensic officers, added two uniformed officers and set off along 10th Street to the southern end of Piedmont Park. Their convoy of three vehicles turned right halfway along that road and, after driving a short way down the next road, turned into the street where Mary Normanson lived.

After giving them all a quick recap of the case, Schrödinger led the team up the path that led to the house and knocked on Mary's front door.

"Good morning, Detective. How are you today? I see you've brought some friends. Won't you all come in?" Mary greeted them all, sharing a big smile that knocked Schrödinger off of his stride for a moment.

"Good morning, Mrs Normanson," he said. "I'm afraid I have a warrant here for a search of your property."

"Don't be afraid, Detective."

"Oh, right," said Schrödinger, beginning to wonder if this had all been a complete mistake.

"What can I do for you all? I'm afraid I don't have enough mugs to offer you all some tea."

"That's perfectly alright, Mrs Normanson. We're investigating the murder of a man who looked very similar to your late husband and have reason to believe that you may know something about it."

"Oh my!" said Mary. "Shall we go through and sit down? It's been quite chilly this morning so I've lit the fire. I do love a real fire for the cooler days, don't you, Detective?"

Schrödinger went into the sitting room and sat in a chair close to the window that overlooked the front garden. Mary sat opposite him while the three forensic investigators split up to search the kitchen, the garage and the upstairs of the house. The two uniformed officers stood by the sitting room door with their hands on their gun holsters in case this sweet, little old lady in her mid-70s tried anything.

"We are in the process of identifying the deceased but we believe him to be a man by the name of Norman Normanson, although he doesn't appear on any of our national databases. Have you heard of him?"

"Now that you mention it, Detective, yes I have. That would be Walter's twin brother. Did you know they hadn't seen one another for more than 70 years?"

"Please go on, Mrs Normanson," Schrödinger encouraged her.

"Walter told me that when he was very young, his parents separated and they each took one of the two boys. Walter stayed with their mother and grew up in Kentucky, while Norman was taken to Brazil with their father."

As the noise of the forensic officers doing their work came through the open sitting room door, Schrödinger couldn't help but wonder what he was doing here. Mrs Normanson was such a kind and unassuming woman that she couldn't possibly have killed her brother-in-law. Could she? Although the proximity of her house to Piedmont Park and the relationship connection between her and the deceased meant she was likely to be involved in some way, even if she was only on the periphery.

"You said they hadn't seen each other for 70 years. Are you saying that once the family separated, the two brothers didn't meet up again?"

"That's right, Detective. They sent the occasional letter and email to one another but Walter wouldn't fly anywhere and Norman always said he didn't have enough money to come here. He said he planned to visit us one day, but you know how these things are; we all plan to do things one day but never get round to doing them."

"Was Norman Normanson at your husband's funeral?"

"Oh no, Detective. I'm sure I would have recognised him if he'd been there."

Schrödinger paused; Mary Normanson had suddenly stopped being the kind, sweet old lady and had just lied to him. He took the photocopied sheet of the book of condolences out of his jacket pocket and showed it to her.

"This is a copy of the condolences book at the crematorium that you and Norman Normanson both signed. It looks like you were there together."

"Can I see that please, Detective? My eyesight isn't as good as it once was."

Schrödinger passed the sheet of paper to Mary; she took it from him, studied it for a couple of seconds and then threw it on the fire.

"Silly me," she said as one of the officers drew their weapon.

"Don't worry," said Schrödinger, calming the officer as he did so. "I have a second copy here."

Mary looked upset and her discomfort soon increased as the lead forensics investigator came in from the kitchen.

"Detective, we have blood splatters under the refrigerator and the oven. We also have blood in the trunk of the car in the garage and a selection of heavy kitchen utensils made from what seems to be the same metal as the fragments found in the victim's skull."

"Mrs Normanson," Schrödinger began. "I'm arresting you for the murder of Norman Normanson. Officer, please read Mrs Normanson her rights and take her into custody."

Schrödinger got up and walked towards the door while the two uniformed officers moved forward to arrest Mary. She started to get up from her chair but suddenly rolled across the floor and grabbed the poker on the other side of the fireplace. Before the officers could react, she was back on her feet and had swung the poker at them, narrowly missing their heads. She was ready for a second swing when Schrödinger raised his gun and pointed it straight at her.

"MRS NORMANSON!" he shouted as she turned to look at him. "Please do not make me discharge my weapon."

"He was a horrible man and fully deserved it!" Mary shouted. "How could twin brothers be so very different?"

"Would you like to confess?" Schrödinger asked, lowering his weapon but not yet putting it away.

"I'm sorry, Detective."

Mary put the poker on the chair and offered her wrists to the officers. She was soon in handcuffs and being escorted to the patrol car. Schrödinger watched from the front door as they walked down her front path. Before they reached the car, a neighbour appeared from the house next door.

"Hi, Mary! How's your Friday going?" she said cheerily, with a neighbourly wave.

"Hello, Dorothy," said Mary. "To be truthful, I've had better Fridays. Forgive me for not waving but I'm in handcuffs."

"Oh my! I'm so sorry to hear that. Why are you being arrested?"

"Well, my dear, you remember Norman who was staying here for a while?"

"The man who looked like your Walter?"

"Yes," said Mary. "He died quite suddenly and violently last week and the police think I killed him."

"Oh, my word! That's terrible! Why would they think you killed him?"

"Because I did. Have a nice day, Dorothy. I'll see you in 5 to 10 years."

The officers put Mary in the back of the patrol car and drove her to the station, leaving a shocked Dorothy standing with her mouth open. Schrödinger went back inside Mary's house and spoke to the forensic investigators again. The whole house was just as clean as it had been when he'd last visited, although the forensics officers were able to show him some small spots of blood underneath the major appliances that she'd missed when she'd scrubbed the kitchen floor after the murder

After finishing his discussion with the forensics team and instructing them to secure the property when they had finished, Schrödinger left the house and headed to the police station. He'd solved the crime and would hopefully get a full confession from Mary Normanson before he went away for his weekend with Wendy. It had been an unusual week so far, but a good one.

***

Tom and Karen were busy testing the reprogramming work that Stuart and Bhavna had done and Martin was making sure that everything was now correct from a data storage perspective. A lot less personal information would now be collected by the app and anything that was collected and stored would be encrypted so it could no longer be hacked into by a three-year child with a pretend smartphone.

"The fact that we got into this database so easily means that anyone else could have too," Martin said as he inspected the new, secure version they had implemented.

"I'm surprised nobody did," said Tom. "I think we just got lucky because the company isn't that well-known yet. We're probably still flying under the radar when it comes to brand awareness."

"Maybe if we let this leak, it would create more brand awareness," Martin suggested. "We'd be on the news."

"I don't think that's the type of publicity they want, but I will check with Louisa when I get back. If she says it's a terrible idea, I'll let her know it came from you."

"Thanks a lot. Are you definitely staying on?"

"Yes. It'll be nice to chill out here in the hot sun, eat some more fried chicken, try some Georgia peach cobbler, get some fresh country air and enjoy some of that Southern hospitality. I might even buy myself a checked shirt and a baseball cap."

"And wear it backwards?"

"Of course! I'll start a new trend when I get back to Brighton," Tom replied. "Have you finished what you need to do here?"

"Yes, you and Karen can finish the rest of the testing now."

"Okay; you may as well take the afternoon off rather than sit here."

"Thanks. I think I'll go to the College Football Hall of Fame. I'd like to find out why Americans love college football so much. Some games can attract 90,000 fans and it's basically just college students playing."

"That's more than any of our professional teams get," said Tom.

"I know," said Martin, wasting no time in packing up.

"I think Karen and the others will be coming out with us tonight. I'll let you know."

"See you later," said Martin as he made his way out of the offices of Classic Country Clothing (UK) Inc. for the final time.

***

Interview room number two was small, dark and cramped, but it was the only room available that afternoon so Schrödinger, a young female officer and Mary Normanson crammed into it and sat around a small table, their legs practically touching.

"Couldn't you find a smaller room for us, Detective?" Mary asked.

"It is a bit cosy, but it's all we have."

"I understand. Now what would you like to know?"

"You have the right to an attorney – would you like to call one?"

"Goodness no! They're such a waste of money. If I get a good one, I'll go free which, you know as well as I do, wouldn't really be fair. On the other hand, if I get a bad one, I'll be sent to prison where I'll have a bed, my own room and three meals each day. Which is exactly what will happen if I don't appoint one anyway, so please carry on."

"Thank you Mrs Normanson. I understand your logic and wish all of our suspects were as cooperative as you. As you know, we record all of these interviews using audio and video so why don't you start by telling us exactly what happened with Norman Normanson?"

"Certainly, Detective," said Mary and gave her statement:

"Walter and I were married for 52 blissful years and we were very happy. We had three beautiful children and our life was wonderful until he got Alzheimer's. He deteriorated over the time he had it and then the poor man had his second heart attack last October.

Walter had been in contact with his brother Norman on his computer so I sent him an email with the bad news. He surprised me by saying he would come to the funeral and he arrived in Atlanta two days before we put Walter into the furnace. The man at the crematorium was so very friendly, but I'm afraid he wasn't very bright. I hate to say it, but if he threw himself at the ground, I think he'd miss more times than he hit. Anyway, where was I? I get confused sometimes, Detective.

Oh yes! Norman had booked into a cheap hotel for five nights and I assumed he would then go back to Brazil, but he said he'd like to stay a bit longer before going back home. He told me he had a return ticket that allowed him to stay 30 days and because he was my dear late husband's brother, I invited him to stay with me. He stayed in the spare room you understand. I don't want you thinking

I'm a hussy, Detective. Maybe in my younger days before I met Walter you could certainly say I enjoyed myself, but certainly not now — although there was that one time with the judge when I was on jury duty, but that can be our little secret can't it?

I've lost track again, haven't I? Well, Norman moved in and at first it was fine. He reminded me so much of Walter that it was almost as if he had come back to me. It gets very lonely as a widow and I didn't have the heart to continue with my wrestling — especially not after that shameless harlot from Kirkwood took my title when I was unable to compete last year.

Anyhow, once Norman had settled in, I started to pretend he was Walter; it was so nice to see him sitting in his favourite chair again. It was the chair you sat in this morning, Detective — the one by the fireplace and the poker that I tried to kill your two officers with. Please tell them I'm deeply sorry for any inconvenience I may have caused them.

Now, Norman was very lazy and sat in that chair all day watching television just like Walter did, but he was also mean and expected me to do everything for him and would only leave his chair when he went for his daily walk around Piedmont Park. My Walter would always help around the house where he could — until he got Alzheimer's disease — but Norman just sat and watched television all day and night or went out to the park. It soon became infuriating and then he told me his flight ticket had expired so he'd have to stay for good.

Do you know what else he did Detective? Well, he didn't actually do it, but he certainly tried to. Yes, that! After a few weeks, he

414

started trying to get into my bed at night. Every single night, Detective. Not just once every six months like most normal people. And it wasn't very impressive at all. I've seen my fair share of those videos on the internet since my poor Walter passed away and I have to say that Norman would have needed a fluffer and a wooden splint.

Last Sunday evening, I was doing the dishes and he tried it on again. In the kitchen this time, Detective. Is a girl not safe anywhere in her own home? I was so mad that I grabbed the nearest implement I could find and stabbed him with it. Unfortunately, it was a ladle and it didn't make much of a hole in him, so I hit him over his tiny little head with it. He started to scream but I kept hitting him and managed to hold one of his arms behind his back so I could hit him again. I knew my wrestling experience would come in useful one day, Detective.

After what seemed like an awfully long time, he finally fell to the floor so I thought I would drive his body somewhere very far away and just leave it. I finished doing the dishes first because I don't like to go out and leave the house in a mess and then I went to move him. That was when he grabbed my ankle. A lot of men liked my ankles when I was a young woman, Detective and I was extremely popular at high school – although I think they would possibly use the word slutty nowadays. My dance card was always full and sometimes I would have multiple dance partners in the same evening.

Where was I, Detective? Was it the part where Norman was grabbing my ankle? Well, I have to tell you that it gave me such a start that I panicked and hit him with a sandwich grill. He made me buy it for him from one of those television shopping channels, but

I never used it myself so I didn't think it would matter if I broke it. The only time he went into the kitchen was to make himself a grilled sandwich so it came to symbolise everything I didn't like about the man.

I guess in the end it was quite fitting that I hit him with it — I certainly wouldn't have used my favourite teapot on him. When I hit him with the sandwich grill, he finally died, so it proved to be every bit as sturdy and well-constructed as the shopping channel had advertised. Do you think I should write them a product review, Detective? I know how much people rely on them before they buy things these days. I won't mention exactly what I used it for in case it starts a murder epidemic though.

I've gone off on a tangent again, haven't I? I'm so sorry, Detective. After I cleaned the kitchen, I loaded Norman into the trunk of my car and was going to drive him to a quarry, but the only one I know of is a long way out of town and by then it was getting dark. I don't like driving in the dark, Detective. If Norman had had the common courtesy to die more quickly, I could have got there and back before it got dark but he had to be his usual stubborn self so I took him to Piedmont Park. He always enjoyed it there — just like he enjoyed his sandwich grill — so I thought it was fitting to lay him to rest by the lake. Also, I wanted to get home to watch my favourite television show, so I couldn't go too far.

That's my statement, Detective. I hope I've covered everything, apart from nearly running down two young men in the park on the way home. My night vision is terrible and I didn't see them until I was nearly on top of them. Please apologise to them for me if they ever come forward. I'm so glad I didn't kill them and your two officers this morning or I'd be a serial killer. How many people do you need to kill to be classified as a serial killer Detective? Five would seem to be a reasonable number, but you may have other ideas and I would respect your professional view if you did."

Mary finished her statement and was shown to a holding cell while Schrödinger went to retrieve and view the video they'd taken of her confession. He couldn't help but feel sorry for her. She'd had a great life and a happy marriage until her husband had got Alzheimer's and began to decline. He then died and she'd allowed his brother to move in as a kind of replacement husband, although being subjected to unwanted attention in her own home wouldn't have been pleasant and she'd finally snapped and killed him.

Schrödinger could suddenly see the appeal of a loving partner to share his life with, especially his final years. Mary was such a sweet woman who was clearly lonely after her husband died and it made Schrödinger wonder if he could really live on his own for the rest of his life. Maybe Wendy wasn't such a bad choice after all. His taciturn personality probably annoyed her just as much as her vacuous one annoyed him.

He heard the door to the holding cells open and watched as Mary Normanson was escorted through. He could see certain judges on the circuit treating her with clemency and potentially letting her off, although she seemed to want to be sent away so she could enjoy the company of others – even if they were mostly hardened criminals. Maybe the best thing the courts could do would be to put her in a secure nursing home, although preferably one with no horny octogenarians in it. Or sandwich grills.

Chapter 34

Atlanta, USA

Tom and Karen had finished their day's testing and the job was now complete. The Classic Country Clothing (UK) Inc. smartphone app now only collected data on its customers that was reasonable and appropriate to tailor product offers more accurately. It was also stored more securely so no third parties could access it.

Tom had received an email from Katrina confirming that Racist Roy and his equally unpleasant bunch of associates were in custody and he now had a week off in Atlanta. Life suddenly appeared perfect and, while he wasn't sure what he'd be doing each day, Karen had offered to show him around the city and the surrounding areas. As he closed his laptop for the last time in Atlanta, he couldn't help but feel pleased with his week's work.

Not only had he been carefully selected to take a task force of highly-trained professionals to Atlanta to resolve a serious computer problem, but he'd also managed it without doing a great deal of work himself. He'd also made some interesting new friends and been a crucial witness to a grisly murder that — while it may not have shocked the city of Atlanta to its very core — had at least been featured on the nightly news, just after a story about a man with a dancing pet raccoon.

"Hey, Tom!" Karen called out as she approached his desk. "Instead of you getting a taxi back to the hotel, why don't you come back with me and we'll go down later with Wendy?"

"That sounds good. I'm not sure where all the others are at the moment so I'll message them."

"There's a new restaurant and bar opened close to the Skyview so we could try that. They specialise in fried chicken and it's meant to be awesome."

"I'm in. I'll let the others know."

"Okay, come on. Let's get out of here," said Karen as they walked towards the door.

Tom got in Karen's car and started to message Martin and the others to let them know the plan for the evening. He was immediately startled by the speed at which she drove out of the car park towards the main road and decided the messages could wait until she slowed down, although when that would be wasn't yet clear. Karen turned onto the I-75 and it seemed as if she was trying to push her accelerator pedal through the floor of her car.

"Are you trying to kill me?" Tom asked half-jokingly but with a small amount of terror.

"I'm just driving us home," Karen said, smiling as she glanced across at him.

"It does look a bit like you're trying to kill me though."

"Could you prove that in a court of law?"

"No."

"Then everything's good."

"I was hoping for more of a denial than that. I don't feel very reassured."

"Friday nights can be busy up here so we've got to get ahead of the traffic."

"You just want to get me back to your house, don't you?" Tom said with a cheeky grin.

"Oh, I bet you wish that were true," Karen replied, with her booming laugh echoing around the car as she squeezed it between two large trucks.

Tom held onto his laptop and closed his eyes as she weaved through the traffic. Overtaking cars on both sides had always seemed like a good idea to him, but seeing it in practice was like being in a giant slalom race with other vehicles that were ten times bigger than the one he was in. As Karen moved expertly (or luckily) through the traffic, Tom wasn't quite as keen on the idea now and was relieved when they finally reached their exit and found themselves on quieter roads. Karen's speed didn't reduce significantly on the smaller roads, but at least there were now fewer vehicles to crash into.

A few minutes later, they turned into a quiet suburban street and Karen pulled the car to the side of the road and stopped. They both got out and headed towards her front door as a familiar figure opened it for them.

"Hi, sis! Have you brought your boyfriend back?!"

"Do you see the shit I have to put up with?" Karen said to Tom as they both greeted Wendy.

"The others have all been doing different things today so Karen suggested I come up here and then we can all go downtown together later."

"That'll be great! I've had a call from Pete. He wants to meet us later on because he's solved the case of the body in the park. He's so clever!"

"That's not being clever, dumbass. That's just doing his damned job," said Karen. "Maybe you should try getting a job – now *that* would be clever."

"I'm thinking of auditioning for one of those reality TV shows; you know the ones where they put a bunch of different people together and see how well they get on. They're making a new one here called 'Zombie Farm' and they need 12 people to live on a farm that's threatened by zombies. Each week one of them gets voted off the show and the winner gets a million dollars."

"Do the losers get thrown to the zombies?" Tom asked.

"They haven't said. I'm not sure I'd like that – especially if they used real zombies. It would be okay if they were actors though."

"You'll have to excuse Wendy; there's a tree growing in my backyard that's got more sense than her."

"I love trees!" said Wendy. "Apart from the green parts."

"When we were kids, she climbed up the stupid tree, fell out of it, banged her head on every branch on the way down and then climbed back up it just so she could fall out of it again. Just agree with her and your life will be a whole lot simpler."

"Don't be mean, sis. I helped solve a murder."

"How exactly did you help?"

"I told Pete to keep going when he was about to give up. I was the fire beneath his wings."

"I bet he appreciated you burning his wings," Karen said. "Now why don't you get your ass ready and both of you start messaging people to meet at the Skyview at seven o'clock while I take a shower."

***

Martin stood alone with his camera in Centennial Park taking pictures of the fountains, the Ferris wheel and the College Football Hall of Fame that he'd visited earlier. He'd explored the American obsession with college football and read up on the rivalries between different schools, but was still not entirely sure he understood why three times as many people would watch a college game than would watch his favourite Premier League football team. Even the professional NFL games didn't draw the same crowds as some of the college games.

As he continued his early evening walk around downtown Atlanta, he received a message from Tom suggesting they met at the Ferris wheel at 7 pm. He messaged back to tell him he'd be there but had just met Stuart and Bhavna who were going into the aquarium and wouldn't make it. He knew Tom would be happy and now they thought the other two were getting together late at night, he saw them both in a whole new light.

Martin continued taking pictures for a while and then went over to the Ferris wheel to wait for the others. He bought himself a bottle of water from the kiosk and sat at one of the tables to think about everything that had happened to them this week. He'd enjoyed his time in Atlanta but would be happy to get back to Irma and the boys. He was a family man at heart and, while there were a few disadvantages, he was more than content with his life.

"Hey, Martin!" Dave shouted as he and Sadie approached the table he was sitting at.

"Hi, guys. How are you doing?"

"We're good thanks," Sadie replied. "This is your last night, then?"

"Yeah, three of us are going home tomorrow. Tom's staying for another week though."

"I wonder why," said Sadie, grinning and squeezing Dave's arm.

"He probably wants to bone Karen," said Dave, laughing and making a fist-pumping gesture.

"Well, duh!" said Sadie. "I think we all know that."

"So why…" Dave began but was interrupted by the arrival of Tom, Karen and Wendy.

"Hi, y'all," said Karen. "I'm glad you could all make it. There's a great new place around the corner that supposedly does the best fried chicken in Atlanta. Shall we get going?"

The group made their way to the restaurant and were shown to a table in the corner and handed menus, while the waiter proudly pointed out their vegan selection.

"That's very kind of you," said Wendy. "I'm a vegan but my girls love chicken," said Wendy.

"We would certainly be happy to serve them if they came in."

"You wouldn't want to serve these 'girls' because they're her damned cats – and even then, one of them is a boy," Karen told the waiter.

"Can I get you some drinks?" the waiter asked Tom and Martin, who seemed to be marginally more sensible than the others.

"Just a round of beers please," said Tom.

"Coming right up sir," said the waiter, thinking he'd probably need to focus on this customer all night if he wanted to get any sense from this table.

"Pete said he'll be coming in later to tell us about the case. He's solved it and they have a little old lady in custody," Wendy told them once the waiter had left.

"That can't be right?!" said Dave. "How did she kill a tall man and drag him to the park?"

"Pete said she was a wrestling champion," said Wendy. "She murdered him with a sandwich grill and drove his body to the park because it was too far to drive him somewhere more remote."

"If she hadn't chosen the park, we wouldn't have found the body and I wouldn't have seen Pete again," Wendy said with a broad smile. "Everybody wins!"

"Apart from the man with the tiny, little bashed-in head," Dave added.

"I guess so," said Wendy. "But he was dead anyway so he probably doesn't mind that his murder brought Pete and I back together."

The waiter returned to the table with their drinks and began to wonder what was wrong with these people. He'd just taken a second job at a bar near Piedmont Park because a waitress had quit unexpectedly after having had to deal with some weird customers. Surely not? He placed their beers on the table and returned to the bar as quickly as he could, passing a stern-looking man who appeared to be heading towards that table. Hopefully, he was a mafia hitman who was about to assassinate them all.

"Pete!" cried an excited voice from behind him as he picked up the next round of drinks to take to an adjacent table. It didn't sound like the stern-looking man was a mafia hitman if they were on first name terms with him. That was a pity.

"Good evening, everyone," said Detective Schrödinger as he pulled up a spare chair and joined their table.

"Good evening, Detective," said Karen. "Are you here to update us on the case? I hear you've solved it; Wendy is very impressed."

"Thank you, Wendy," Schrödinger said with a slight smile.

"You're the best, Pete!"

"Let me begin by saying thank you to you all for discovering the body. I'm sure it would have been found eventually, but time is always of the essence in these cases. Luckily the perpetrator wasn't a flight risk and lived close to the park but, in many cases, they can be out of the country before we even know a crime has been committed."

"I told you we helped them solve it," Wendy said, looking at her sister indignantly.

"It appears that the victim was called Norman Henry Normanson but we haven't yet been able to confirm this. Unfortunately, I can't share too many more details with you because the case has to go to trial, but the accused is a woman in her 70s who was allegedly being sexually harassed by Mr Normanson. He proved to be her late husband's twin brother."

"Wow! You wouldn't have thought he would still have it in him at his age," said Tom.

"He came to Atlanta for the funeral of his brother and persuaded his widowed sister-in-law to let him move in with her. There was no record of him in the system because he'd been living in Brazil since he was a young

427

boy. We're still working to corroborate the details of the confession we received from our suspect."

"Do you have a birth certificate or any childhood pictures?" Dave asked.

"Unfortunately, not. It looks like he was born during World War Two and records were pretty sketchy back then."

"There are a lot of pictures of me in the system," said Dave.

"I'm sure there are," Schrödinger said with a sigh.

"I even saw one of those e-fit pictures they made of me once. Sometimes when I get drunk and the cops arrive I manage to get away, so the bartenders have to describe me to the police sketch artist."

"What was the picture like?" Sadie asked. "Did it capture your awesome rugged jawline and your manly good looks?"

"Not really. They took a composite from different bartenders and I looked like an escapee from the CDC research and testing lab."

Schrödinger stood up and said goodnight to the group, telling Wendy he'd pick her up tomorrow morning at ten o'clock for their weekend away; he also shared with her that they'd be going to Nashville. She got up and hugged him – partly out of excitement and partly to embarrass him – and then watched him leave the restaurant shaking his head.

"Pete's going on a communication skills course next week," Wendy said as she sat back down at the table. "I think it will be really good for him – and also for me. But mainly for me."

"Does he still talk in grunts and words of one syllable?" Karen asked.

"Yes, although I get around that by talking more so it works out."

"I've got to go on a course at work in a couple of weeks. It's called 'Respecting your Colleagues' or something like that," said Tom.

"Is that the whole company or just you?" Karen asked. "I haven't heard about it."

"It's just me, a bunch of losers from the Sales department and a couple of obnoxious idiots from Accounting."

"I'm surprised they don't make you stay in there permanently," Karen laughed. "You don't like anyone there!"

"I told you not to tell anyone," Tom said. "Anyway, I like Martin; Katrina is alright too."

"I'm sure you'll come out of it a better human being," said Karen.

"He won't," said Martin. "This is the third one he's been on since I started. He comes out thinking that everyone else in the company is even more stupid than they were before he went in."

"That's true," said Tom, drowned out by the mocking laughter coming at him from the rest of the table.

***

On the northern edge of Centennial Park, Stuart and Bhavna were leaving the aquarium and heading back towards the part of downtown where both the hotel and the restaurant where their colleagues were spending the evening with their four American friends. The zoo, the Botanical Gardens and the aquarium had all been fun, but their day hadn't ended yet.

"Should we go and call in on Tom and the others?" Stuart asked.

"I would prefer not to," said Bhavna. "He is just about acceptable in small doses but I think I may have overdosed this week."

"I know what you mean. I keep catching him looking at my beard; I think he might have a weird fetish for men with beards."

"You do not need to add the gender, Stuart. Women do not have beards."

"My grandmother did," Stuart replied.

The rest of the journey passed in silence and when they got back to the hotel, Bhavna told Stuart she'd be going upstairs for an early night, so he went into the bar for a drink and some food. As he waited for his order to arrive, his eyes tried to focus on the TV but his mind kept wandering to the events of the last week.

Tom and Martin's selfishness in wanting to spend time with Karen and her friends had worked to his advantage and what had begun as a long flight with an annoying colleague had turned into a weird relationship. As they were recovering from their food poisoning, they had bonded and subsequently shared some surprisingly good evenings together. He wasn't sure what would happen when they got back home, but at the moment things were going well.

A few minutes after finishing his meal, a message came through from Bhavna with just one word – 'Upstairs' – so he hastily finished his beer and went up to her room. Somewhere, under several acres of beard, was a smile as wide as the Chattahoochee River.

Chapter 35

Atlanta, USA

All across the city of Atlanta and the state of Georgia, people were waking up to a hot and humid Saturday morning. In a small house with three bedrooms, two argumentative sisters and four cats, coffee was brewing against the background of the younger woman hurriedly packing her bags.

"Pete will be here soon! It's your fault I'm not ready!" Wendy complained.

"How on this big green Earth is that my fault?"

"You shouldn't have let me drink so much last night."

"Do you remember dancing on the coffee table?" Karen asked.

"Yes, I remember that."

"Do you remember falling off?"

"No, but I do have a bruise on my arm. Maybe that's where it came from."

"Well, you landed partly on your head. I was hoping it might have knocked some sense into you but it looks like you're still a dumbass," said Karen, pouring them both some coffee.

"My head hurts too. I thought that was just the alcohol."

"Drink this and maybe you'll feel better."

"Thanks, sis!" said Wendy, taking the coffee and hoping it would help sober her up before Schrödinger arrived.

As she sat and sipped the hot black liquid, Wendy's phone buzzed with three messages so she looked down, expecting them to be from Schrödinger. They weren't, so she read them aloud to Karen:

"Hi, Wendy! Dave and I got arrested last night on the way back from the bar. It was our first arrest together and it was so romantic! We walked home and I saw some of my old friends sitting in the parking lot of a strip club so I went to say 'hi' and offered to bring them some comfort behind a dumpster. Just as soon as I'd got started, the police arrived and we all got arrested! 1/3"

"Dave was very gentlemanly and tried to attack the officers, but he was so drunk he managed to punch the dumpster instead of the cops! It was a hoot! We got put in the same patrol car and he got taken to the hospital to look at his hand – he's broken a small bone but he'll be okay. 2/3"

"We've just been let out and are going for some coffee. That was the only downside to the whole night – the coffee in this station isn't good. Have a great weekend away with the Detective! I did mention his name while Dave was fighting with the officers but it didn't help. Love you all! 3/3"

"The only downside was bad coffee?!" Karen asked when Wendy had finished reading Sadie's messages.

"She always says that some police stations have better coffee than others. It's a shame they got taken to one of the bad ones."

"How about they don't try to smash shit up and then they won't get arrested and can drink coffee at home like normal people?"

"You're so boring, sis! Let them have their fun," said Wendy.

"Says the woman just about to go away with the most boring man in Georgia."

"He's very talkative when he's working. It's just when he's off duty he's a bit quiet. Maybe we'll need to solve another murder together while we're away to liven him up."

"When will you two lovebirds be back?" Karen asked.

"Monday night, I think. Pete needs to be back at work on Tuesday to finish his report on the case of the old lady and that man with the small head."

"So I get three days of peace? Hallelujah!" said Karen, looking up at the ceiling.

"Yes, you do. I know it'll be quiet, but you'll have the girls here to keep you company."

"Ain't that just peachy," Karen said with a sigh as the doorbell rang and Wendy rushed to answer it.

"Hi, Pete!" she shouted before she'd even opened the door.

"Good morning."

"Good morning, Detective. Can I offer you some coffee?"

"Thanks, but we need to get going as soon as possible. It's a four-hour drive."

"Can't we take a patrol car and put your lights on all the way?!" Wendy asked, ramming the last few things into her bag.

"No," said Schrödinger.

"When are you going on that communications course, Detective?"

"On Wednesday," Schrödinger replied.

"Pete is great at work but he struggles a bit in real life."

"I do sometimes," Schrödinger admitted. "Are you ready?"

"I sure am!" said Wendy, going over to give Karen a hug. "You'll look after the girls for me won't you sis?"

"We will," Karen replied absent-mindedly.

"Thanks," said Wendy, but then paused. "What do you mean 'we'?"

"Stop asking so many stupid questions and go!" said Karen. "If you accidentally leave her in Nashville, I promise I won't file a missing person's report. We'll just immediately consider it a cold case," she added with her booming laugh.

"I'll bring Wendy home safely, Karen. Have a good weekend."

"Bye, sis!" said Wendy, giving Karen another hug. "Bye, girls!"

Karen closed the front door on the chaos that was Wendy. Hopefully, they'd keep driving and just elope and get married so some sanity would be restored to Karen's world again – although she wouldn't wish that on Detective Schrödinger. He was doing her a huge favour just taking Wendy off her hands for the weekend and for that, he would always be her favourite police officer.

Looking around her house now that Wendy was gone, it did seem suddenly quiet. The cats needed to be fed, so she planned to do that first and then tidy the house before getting ready to go out. This week had been interesting; it had probably been the most random week of her entire life, but it had also been fun. The nights out with the UK team had been great, although if she'd designed this week for herself, she probably wouldn't have included finding a dead body in the park.

As Karen fed Wendy's cats, she thought that Norman Henry Normanson may have planned the week differently too.

***

In downtown Atlanta, Tom had woken up, showered and was now ready for the first day of his free holiday in Atlanta. He went along the hotel corridor and knocked on Martin's door. After a few seconds, Martin answered and they went down to the next floor to find Stuart and Bhavna. They knocked on both doors but there was no reply from either occupant.

"Surely they haven't got food poisoning again?" said Tom. "I mean, you could understand it once, but it would be a bit careless of them to get it twice."

"I'm not sure they'd have any choice, to be fair," Martin offered.

"Stop being so sensible," said Tom. "I like it better when you're dopey."

"It won't be a good flight if they have," said Martin. "I hope I'm not sitting next to them."

"That's very public-spirited of you."

"I'm just saying."

"Let's go down for breakfast and catch up with them later," said Tom, turning away from Bhavna's door, unaware of Stuart standing on the other side of it waiting for them to leave so he could go back to his room undetected.

"What are you going to do while you're here?" Martin asked as they reached the stairs and a half-naked Stuart quietly slipped out of Bhavna's room and across the corridor into his own.

"I don't know yet. I'll probably just hang out with the others. Karen was talking about going to Stone Mountain one day for hiking. They've got a cable car ride there too."

"But you don't like heights," Martin reminded him.

"I'll close my eyes," Tom replied.

"But you don't like the dark either."

"I might have to give it a miss then."

Tom and Martin went into the restaurant and were greeted by a young goth waitress who asked them if they would be ordering from the menu or going to the week-end buffet. To Becci's relief, they both selected the buffet so she showed them to a table and left them to it. As she walked away, she noticed that they seemed to be talking about normal things; maybe they just turned weird in the evenings.

"Are you looking forward to getting back with Irma and the boys?" Tom asked Martin when they returned to the table with their food.

"Yes and no. It's been great over here with no responsibilities each evening but I'm not sure I could do it long-term. I like being married and being a family man."

"I can understand that," said Tom. "It's all very well being single and independent but sometimes it must be nice to come home to a loving family."

"I wouldn't go that far, but it's nice to be part of something."

"I think I'd like half a wife," said Tom as Becci came over to refill their coffee.

"Which half? The top half would be good because you'd have someone to talk to," Martin said, nodding thoughtfully.

"I'd get the boobs as well," Tom added as Becci stared at him and overfilled his coffee cup.

"Well, obviously."

"I meant having a part-time wife. Maybe one week on and one week off."

"I think that's called having your cake and eating it," said Becci, unable to resist the urge to put these fools straight.

"You're right," Tom agreed. "But if you brought me some cake now, I'd eat it."

"Do you want some cake?" Becci asked.

"Not really. But if I had it, I'd eat it," said Tom. "There's no point in having cake and not eating it."

"I'd like some cake if you have any," said Martin.

"Just don't eat it when it arrives," said Tom, earning a death stare from Becci.

"When are you leaving?" Becci asked them both.

"I'm going today but he'll be here for another week, won't you?" said Martin, then looking at Tom.

"Er….yeah," said Tom, looking down at his over-flowing coffee cup.

"Lucky me," said Becci as she walked away in despair, just as Stuart and Bhavna joined them.

"Morning," said Tom. "We're almost finished here."

"No worries, we'll see you when we check out," said Stuart as he and Bhavna went and sat at a clean table.

"I'm still convinced there's something going on between those two," Martin said to Tom as they left the restaurant.

"There definitely is. Did you see Stuart sneak out of Bhavna's room this morning as we turned to go down the stairs?"

"No?!" Martin gasped.

"Yes. He must have crept out just after we knocked on her door because I saw him carrying his clothes across the hallway out of the corner of my eye."

"Are you sure it was Stuart?"

"That beard is difficult to miss," said Tom.

"True," said Martin.

***

The clock on the wall behind the hotel reception desk struck eleven as Stuart and Martin were checking out. The lift doors opened behind them and Bhavna came out with her case and walked over to join them.

"Have you ordered the taxi as I told you to, Stuart?" she said as she gave her key to the young man behind the desk.

"Yes," said Stuart. "It'll be here in ten minutes."

"Thank you. I find life is much easier when people do what you ask."

"I'm beginning to realise that," said Stuart.

"Hello, mate," Martin exclaimed as the doors of the other lift opened and he saw Tom come out and approach the reception desk. "Why have you got your case with you?"

"Are you checking out?" Stuart asked.

"Yes, I am," Tom said sheepishly.

"I thought you weren't coming back with us today," said Bhavna, confused for once.

"Hi, y'all! It's a hot day out there! I hope you have a good flight!" came a booming American voice as Karen

440

walked through the lobby and stood next to Tom. "You'd better not be as annoying as my dumbass sister or you can stay your ass here," she added as her laugh erupted across the lobby.

"Are you…?"

"Yes, he is. He's offered to keep me company while Wendy is away with Detective Schrödinger."

"I'm a gentleman like that," Tom grinned.

"I hope you're good with cats...Wendy left four of them for me to look after."

"I'll try my best," said Tom, knowing he wouldn't actually try at all.

"I'm sure we all know what your best looks like and it ain't at all good," said Karen, laughing again as the taxi pulled up and the others began to gather their bags.

"Have a safe flight," Tom said to them all as they said their goodbyes. "I'll see you all next Monday."

"That's if I haven't killed you first," said Karen, squeezing Tom's hand as they stood and watched Martin, Stuart and Bhavna leave the hotel and begin their journey back to the UK.

Chapter 36

Atlanta, USA

As Tom and Karen left the hotel and the taxi took the rest of the UK team to the airport, Wendy and Schrödinger had reached the halfway point in their journey to Nashville and were passing through Chattanooga. Across Atlanta, Sadie and Dave had found an independent coffee shop opposite the police station they'd just been released from which served the quality of coffee their refined palates desired and Mary Normanson was looking forward to spending what was left of the rest of her life in prison.

She was hoping to make some new friends there and possibly join a gang. That would be exciting! She started to imagine fashioning shivs out of bars of soap, trading narcotics with the other elderly criminals and digging an escape tunnel with her bare hands while the guards weren't looking. Life was certainly looking interesting at the moment.

The loss of her dear Walter – first to Alzheimer's and then to death – had shown her how lonely life could be on her own and Norman hadn't proved to be much of a replacement for his brother, despite looking the part. He was far too physically minded and, at her age, she didn't appreciate being constantly mauled. She'd enjoyed it

when she was younger and had garnered quite the reputation among the young men in Atlanta and most of the
surrounding towns, but not now. She was glad she'd finally got to meet Walter's brother – but was equally glad
she'd killed him.

Mary lay down on the bed in her cell at the police
station, closed her eyes and reminisced about her life in
Georgia. She could see Walter's smiling face in her mind
– or was it Norman's? It must have been Walter's because
Norman had only smiled when she'd made him food. She
thought about all the things she'd done down by the
banks of the Chattahoochee River as a young woman and
then she looked back at meeting Walter for the first time.
She remembered how they'd begun courting, his pro-
posal and their subsequent wedding that had upset most
of the young men in Atlanta.

Mary's thoughts moved forward to them having three
wonderful children together and the things they had done
as a family before reminiscing on her two wrestling careers and all of the trophies she'd won.

Mary decided that – on balance – she'd lived a good
life. There was one small blemish with that judge when
she was on jury duty and she hadn't paid a speeding ticket
in 1978 but, aside from that, she'd been a good person –
if you didn't count the murder.

She suddenly felt extremely tired – it must have been
all the excitement this week. She let herself drift slowly

off to sleep and felt content and blessed as her eyes closed.

In her mind, she was now back down on the banks of the Chattahoochee River; the sun was shining and the birds were singing on a beautiful spring morning. Her beloved Walter was walking towards her and reached out to take her hands. Mary had missed Walter terribly since he'd developed Alzheimer's, but here he was once more – smiling, happy and with all of his faculties fully restored. She walked towards him, they embraced tenderly and Mary left the physical world behind her and joined Walter for eternity.

Chapter 37

Atlanta, USA

Karen drove Tom out of the city and told him of all the things they would be doing in the coming days. While she loved her sister dearly, she couldn't face spending all day and all evening with her once Schrödinger brought her back from Nashville so she was planning to go hiking and visit the various attractions in the city that locals rarely go to. This would limit the time they would have in the house listening to Wendy's latest fads and phobias and would also let her appreciate her city from a different perspective.

"We'll go to Stone Mountain tomorrow – it's far too hot today – then I'll take you to the Atlanta Botanical Gardens, the Atlanta History Center, the Martin Luther King Center and the zoo if you like that type of thing?"

"It all sounds cool," said Tom. "I'm just happy to be able to stay here while the others go back."

"A couple of them are weird, aren't they?"

"Stuart and Bhavna?"

"Yeah."

"There's something going on between those two. As we came down this morning, I saw Stuart sneak out of Bhavna's room carrying most of his clothes."

"Oh, man! That's awesome. They seemed so much up their own butts I didn't think they'd have time for anything else."

445

"Well, they had time for each other last night."

"Good for them. That woman really needed to get laid," Karen replied as she left the I-85 that went through the city and joined the I-75 heading north.

"Your driving hasn't improved much since yesterday," Tom observed.

"Are you sure you don't want to walk?"

"I could get a taxi."

"Good luck with that. Did you know I once tried out for a rideshare company?"

"Which one?" Tom asked.

"Both of the major ones and an unlicensed one that was run by an ex-con from his garage."

"What happened?"

"I got rejected for being 'overly aggressive' behind the wheel," Karen said indignantly. "Can you imagine that?! And think very carefully before you answer."

"Well, in that case….I'm shocked," Tom said diplomatically.

"You ain't shocked at all! I wasn't expecting to get the major ones but I thought that a creepy guy running a shady business and not paying any taxes wouldn't have had such high standards."

"Us creepy guys can have high standards too."

"Well, don't be expecting too much this week," said Karen as she turned into her street and pulled up outside her house.

"I'm sure spending the week with you will be awesome."

"You might wish you were back at that shitty hotel by Monday," Karen warned him as they got out of the car. "Do you want some coffee?"

"Yes please," said Tom as he took his case out of the car and followed Karen to her front door.

"The mailman's been," Karen said, taking a large envelope from her mailbox. "I sent off some DNA to get myself tested and find out what my roots are."

"I love these mailboxes you have at the end of your path. We can't have those in the UK."

"Why not?" Karen asked.

"People would steal each other's mail."

"We don't have that problem here. I'd be more worried about drunk drivers."

"Why?" Tom asked, struggling to see the connection.

"If you forget to get your mail until the evening there's a chance a drunk driver might come down the street and run you down. It happened to Dave. He was telling Wendy about it last night."

"That's awesome!" said Tom. "Dave's a legend."

"He's pretty cool for a redneck," Karen admitted. "Only Dave could get hit by a car checking his mail."

"I wonder if I could be part redneck. I might do one of those DNA tests too when I get home."

"Don't waste your money," said Karen. "It'll just tell you that you're a dick and we already know that."

"That's not fair," said Tom, watching Karen walk away from him and go into the kitchen.

"It doesn't matter if it's fair or not if it's true," she shouted from the kitchen.

"You might be right."

Tom sat down on the sofa and looked around the room while he waited for Karen to return with the coffee she'd promised. Yesterday's visit hadn't allowed him much time to check the place out but it was undoubtedly Karen's house – chaotic, busy and loud. The decor was vibrant and colourful like its owner and he was glad to be out of the hotel.

He'd complained so much about the hotel on Friday afternoon while he and Karen were doing their final system testing in the office that she'd offered to let him stay with her this week. She'd also told him that she knew that was exactly what he was angling for.

Karen returned with the coffee, sat down next to Tom, picked up the envelope with her DNA test results in and opened it.

"What does it say?" Tom asked.

"It's got this pie chart here, look," said Karen, showing Tom the contents of the pack.

"It says I'm 50% African – well, duh! – 35% Native American, 10% Italian and 5% Chinese. How the hell am I part Chinese?!"

"Do you like Chinese food?" Tom asked, rather unhelpfully.

"Hell yeah, but it shouldn't affect my DNA."

"I wouldn't have thought so, otherwise your DNA would change every time you ate chow mein."

"Maybe if I ate more pizza I'd become more Italian?" Karen asked.

"It would be interesting to find out," Tom agreed, laughing along with her.

"I never knew I had all these different nationalities inside me."

"Have you got any English in you?"

"Not according to this."

"Do you want some?"

Karen paused and looked up at Tom.

"Is that the best you've got?" she asked, staring straight through him and out of the back of his head.

"Yes," said Tom meekly, looking at Karen's changing expression as she suddenly burst out laughing.

"You are so gonna regret that! Get your ass upstairs!"

Tom ran up the stairs as the events of the last few days flashed through his mind; it had been a good week so far but was about to get even better. As Karen pushed him onto her bed, he couldn't help thinking that – all things considered – the month of April had been far kinder to him than it had been to Norman Henry Normanson.

Epilogue – Two Months Later

Brighton, UK

It was a warm and sunny Monday morning and Tom had been back in his familiar routine for several weeks. The week he'd spent in Atlanta with Karen had been every bit as good as he'd hoped and they'd had a great time together. He came back to the UK and was given the promotion Katrina had hinted at and even HR seemed pleased to see him.

Tom parked his car on the driveway he rented in Brighton city centre and began his regular walk down the hill towards the clock tower in the centre of town. He then turned left into North Street and ultimately took a right turn into Ship Street. As he walked past the old post office and headed towards the head office of Classic Country Clothing Ltd., he turned to the person walking alongside him and couldn't help but smile.

"Are you nervous?"

"Hell no! Why would I be nervous?" his companion asked as they walked through the main door.

"It's your first day at HQ."

"If you think I'm worried about some hoity-toity Brits looking down on me for drinking my tea the wrong way then you're an even bigger dumbass than my sister. Hell, you'd be dumber than her four cats, too."

Karen's laugh filled the foyer as they approached the reception desk for Tom to sign her in.

"Hi, Bert," Tom greeted the receptionist as they approached the desk. "This is Karen from our Atlanta office. She's over here for a couple of weeks of IT training."

"Hello Mister Tom, sir," said Bert. "Very good, sir. Would you mind signing in please, Miss?"

"No problem," said Karen. "Good morning to you, Bert. Y'all have a great day now."

"Thank you, Miss," said Bert. "Although there's only one of me here."

"Don't worry Bert, it's a saying from the American South," Tom clarified.

"Okay Mister Tom," Bert said and then turned to Karen. "Well, Miss, I'll be fixing to get you an ID badge today from that office over yonder and if the creek don't rise, you'll have that doohickey by lunchtime and be happier than a dead pig in the sunshine."

"Woah, Bert! You're my man!" said Karen, offering him an enthusiastic high-five.

Unfortunately, Bert wasn't quite ready so she accidentally slapped him in the face, but he took it in his stride.

"Are you okay, Bert?" Tom asked, trying not to laugh too much.

"Yes, thank you, Mister Tom."

"Where did you get all those phrases from?" Karen asked.

"My wife LeeAnn is from Louisiana. We met at Live Aid in 1985 and it was love at first sight," Bert said proudly. "We got married the very next month and she's been with me ever since. I'm retiring in a few months and she wants to move back home."

"Are you looking forward to that?" Tom asked.

"Not really. I'd rather stay here where we have friends and family but she wants to move back to Baton Rouge."

"What will you do?" Karen asked.

"We've decided to compromise," Bert said with a weak smile. "So we're moving to Baton Rouge."

***

Katrina and the other members of Tom's old team had settled into their desks as Tom and Karen walked into the office. After his promotion, Tom was now at Katrina's level and had his own team who sat behind her, although they were only trusting him with one person at the moment. Hopefully, he would soon have an empire of underlings to do his bidding and he could take over the world – or at least take more time off while they did all the work.

"Hey, y'all! I'm Karen. It's great to meet you."

"It's lovely to meet you too!" said Katrina, extending her hand. "This is Sue and that's Colin."

"It's great to meet you guys!" said Karen.

"Hi, Karen! It's good to see you again," said Martin, turning round from his new desk on Tom's team. "How are the others?"

"Well, my dumbass sister Wendy is thinking of moving in with Schrödinger this week so hopefully she'll be taking her damned cats with her and I'll get my house back soon."

"What about Sadie and Dave?"

"They're still living together in Dave's parents' basement. Neither of them got arrested last week so I think they're balancing each other out. Either that or they're planning a heist."

"Dave was cool," said Tom.

"Yeah, well he had an accident at his new job a couple of weeks back so now he's started a personal injury lawsuit. He should find out if he's won in the next few weeks."

"What happened?"

"He got a job at Atlanta Zoo and some of the animals attacked him," Karen explained.

"But he had a phobia of animals, didn't he?" Martin asked.

"He sure did, so they gave him a job in the gift shop."

"That seems safe enough," said Tom. "How did he injure himself?"

"The maintenance men were fixing some fences outside and a few of the flamingos got out and made their way towards the gift shop. Dave saw them coming through the door, panicked and fell into a display of cuddly giraffes. He's suing them for mental trauma."

"The cuddly giraffes?"

"The zoo."

"Will he win?"

"I don't know," said Karen. "But if he does, you might want to prepare yourselves for him and Sadie to come over here because he really wants to see England."

"What exactly do they want you to do over here?" asked Sue, bringing the subject back to work.

"Well after the problems we had with the database back in April, the company said it would be more cost-effective to transfer the knowledge you've got here to me so you don't have to come over and help us wipe our own butts if it ever happens again."

"That sounds like we won't get to go to Atlanta again," said Martin.

"You told us you didn't like the hotel anyway," said Sue.

"No, it wasn't very nice," said Martin.

"And you broke your camera when that old lady nearly hit you with her car," said Colin.

"Well, yeah, that wasn't very good either."

"And you didn't want to be away from Irma and the boys," Tom added.

"I suppose not," Martin said with a sigh before turning back to Karen. "Have they given you a better hotel here than the one they gave us in Atlanta?"

"It depends on what you mean by the word 'hotel'" said Karen, glancing at Tom.

"You're staying with Tom, aren't you?" Martin asked.

"We all know how the company likes to save money so it was the right thing to do," Tom said modestly. "Also, I've got plenty of room."

"You live in a one-bedroomed house."

"I know," said Tom.

"Well, I think it's very generous of Tom to give up his bed for Karen," said Colin. "I've slept on my sofa a few times and it's not very comfortable," he added as the rest of the team looked at him and burst into laughter.

"Shall we go and make some coffee?" Tom suggested.

"Please," said Karen.

As the two of them walked towards the kitchen, out of the corner of his eye Tom could see Sue, Colin and Katrina each passing some money over to Martin. Finally, something had gone right for the dopey bastard – although it had taken a lot of messages to convince Martin to select the right option on the sweepstake of where Karen would be staying.

At the end of the day, Tom didn't care about the rest of them; everything he wanted was standing next to him in the kitchen trying to operate the coffee machine.

"Are you going to help me work this thing or do you just want to stand there and look at my butt all day?"

"Can't I do both?"

"Just make the damned coffee," said Karen, smiling at him with real warmth.

"Yes, ma'am!" said Tom with a grin.

A few minutes later, Tom escorted Karen to the HR department to introduce her to Louisa and Debbie. As he left her on the top floor and returned to his own department, he paused for a few seconds and said a silent thanks to Racist Roy and Johnny Pervert for making all of this possible.

THE END

Printed in Great Britain
by Amazon

22860177R00260